Winter Iris

Winter Iris

Book Two

J.L. Robison

This is a work of fiction. Names, characters, places, and incidents either are the product of the author's imagination or are used fictitiously. Any resemblance to actual persons, living or dead, events, or locales is entirely coincidental.

For information, contact J.L. Robison at joanlrobison@yahoo.com or https://linktr.ee/j.l.robison

First edition
ISBN 978-1-7358382-5-0

Edelweiss Saga

Edelweiss

Winter Iris

The White Orchid

Beneath the Cornflowers

Don't ever mistake my silence for ignorance, my calmness for acceptance, or my kindness for weakness.

— Carson Kolhoff

I would like to dedicate this book to all those who helped me with editing, was patient as I spent countless hours writing it, and who took the time to read it after. Thank you!

Chapter One

✠

February 23rd, 1941
Beelitz, Germany

It was another frigid February morning. God, how she hated these long winters. Forget walks in the park and budding flowers. It was thick coats, scarves and gloves, and lungs that burned from the bitterly cold air.

Eva tucked her head lower in her coat to shield herself from the rain and quickened her pace. The water on the sidewalk splashed inside her shoes, soaking into her wool socks. The pavement was hardly visible beneath her feet, but she could feel its solid surface.

Looking down the Nach Fichtenwalde Street, Eva focused on the Beelitz Heilstätten hospital a few blocks away, hastening towards it.

Eva held the umbrella low, attempting to keep the rain off her freshly curled hair. However feeble the attempt might be.

Once in the lobby, she shook the water from the umbrella and stuck it under her arm. As she made her way across the foyer towards the stairs, the water squished in her shoes. She would have to dry them for the third day in a row.

She climbed the stone steps to the second floor and went to the small room that was the nurse's lounge. It was still early, and she was the only nurse on the morning shift that had arrived. Small lockers were given to the nurses, and that is where Eva kept her purse, coat, and umbrella. The soaked shoes clung to her feet, then a sucking sound came when she pulled them off. Pushing a towel inside, she tried to soak up as much water as she could, then tied the shoestrings together and set the them on the small table. Reaching inside her locker, she took out another pair of shoes and sat down to put them on. She always kept a second pair at the hospital for days like today. The ones she took off needed to dry, so she sat them near the furnace, hoping they would be by the end of her shift.

The room was empty and quiet, but the faint, lingering perfume of nurses hung in the air. While tying the laces, she focused on the stain on the wall, the stark differences between Berlin and Paris dampening her mood like the rain outside. It did not have the romantic atmosphere Paris did, with lovers holding hands and freely kissing in the streets. People who have never been there wondered what it was about the French capital, more than any other city in the world, that made people go weak at the knees. Her time there convinced her that it was a reputation well deserved. Berlin was missing the charm and wonder, the exquisite food, and French sophistication, but during the day, there was a hustle to it that Paris lacked. Everyone had somewhere to be, and they always needed to be early. There was a sense of purpose in the city, which was a representation of Germany itself. That was one of the many differences between the people of France and the people of Germany. But to her, there would never be a city like Paris, and if you were lucky enough to go there, it would always stay with you. Strangely enough, though, her fondest memory of Paris is because of a German. And even though she romanticizes it, Paris still has the same pitfalls as any other city.

Eva pushed back against the invading memories. She did not want to think of Paris or him because both made her nostalgic with the aching, craving inside for the two things that were unattainable to her. So much that she loved had been left behind in France, and whenever the memory of it would enter her thoughts, it always pricked at her heart, slowly becoming a hot iron poking deeper into her until she felt emotionally raw. She constantly tried to push those two thoughts away.

She had been in Berlin since November of last year, and America was not yet at war with Germany. The fact that she had come here before Germany declared war on the U.S. alleviated some of her worries. The time she had spent in Germany helped improve her German, and she hoped that her accent would eventually get better too. It also allowed her to adapt to the culture and become established in the small German underground. The resistance here was not as effective or feared as it was in France, but it was still a thorn in the German's side, and that was good enough for her. Thanks to her eleventh-grade history teacher and his constant daily info dump, she knew of the small German resistance. Now that she was alone and no longer had Gerhardt's help, the knowledge she had brought from the future was useful.

The man from the resistance in Paris left her wondering what happened. She didn't see him again after that day, and he never sought her out either. What transpired before their meeting that led to him never showing for their meeting at the café still wasn't clear.

After fleeing the farm in August of 1940, Eva went back to the Red Cross in Paris and found the nun who had offered her a position in Berlin. Because she was left with virtually no other choice, accepting the job was inevitable as she didn't know what else to do. Having lost everything and everyone, the loneliness and uncertainty morphed into fear and panic. Life had taken an unexpected turn that left her broken, a shell of the person who used to enjoy picking flowers on lazy summer days and appreciated the quiet country life on a farm. Hungry, homeless, afraid, and probably being hunted by the Gestapo in France, it was the only thing she could think of to keep herself off the streets and out of a prison camp.

In a dark corner deep inside was the hope that she would see Gerhardt here in Berlin, but so far, that had not happened. Sometimes, on her day off, she would sit outside the Reichstag building, the most likely place he worked, hoping to catch a glimpse of him. None of the people coming and going were ever Gerhardt, leaving her to think she had guessed wrong. She could always ask someone who worked there about him, and they would probably know, but mustering the courage was hard. Simply thinking about how they parted ways and how she had treated him that last night they were together made her cringe. The pain her words must have caused him always resurfaced with the memory of that night, and the look on his face spoke volumes. He probably didn't want to be found by her and had no intentions of looking for her either. It was possible he died in the war or was transferred again somewhere else. If he didn't want to see her, she could hardly blame him. Why would he after the way she treated him? There were strong doubts that their paths would ever cross again, and she tried not to think about it or feel sad about that realization. The more important thing was to focus on living and getting through this war one day at a time. She constantly told herself affirmations that Jon was still trying to get her out of mainland Europe, but since being in Germany, there was no word from him either. Coming here made it even harder for Jon to get to her, but how hard was still unclear.

Working at the hospital as a Red Cross nurse kept her busy and helped stave off unwanted thoughts. There was more than one hole in her heart to fill, and the painful memories slowed the healing. Most nights, dreams of Sabina, Gerhardt, and sometimes Fabien played like an old reel in her mind, forcing her to relive what happened. They haunted her, so taking on more night shifts at the hospital helped control the thoughts that ran through her head. The one downside to working at the hospital was that every time she went to work, she feared the worst, that one day Gerhardt would be there. It was almost a daily thing to check the new patients to make sure he wasn't among them, and she often checked the morgue as well.

It was infuriating that she still thought of him so much because being with him was the last thing she needed while living in France, and it was still true now. Sleeping with him had been a mistake, one that she hoped to not make again if put in the same situation. There was a constant battle against the internal voice that said she wasn't strong enough to say no to him, survive this war, or make it another day without her family. Every time she was feeling down, the lies overpowered the truth, muddling reality with fear.

So many bad things had happened, and the war was still young. Some days, she was barely holding on, but the nights were always the worst. The dreams felt so real that it was difficult to distinguish them from the present, and every night, the pain cycled again, and she woke in a cold sweat, leaving the sheets damp and her body shivering under the blankets. Then came the morning, and she would feel stronger again. The nights were tough because so many of them she lay awake staring into the darkness, feeling that life was cruel. Most of the hurtful things could not be remedied, but when it came to him, it could be. Constantly, she wished for him to walk into the hospital and say that he needed her and could not live without her. But crying herself to sleep was tiring.

"Eva, you are here early," a voice said, interrupting her solitude.

Eva looked up into Liesel Schäfer's warm, brown eyes. Liesel had been the one who helped her learn the ropes of the hospital the first few days and was now a friend. Eva, Liesel, and another nurse named Heidi Krüger had become friends in the past few months. Eva already knew Liesel when Heidi came to work at the hospital. They started eating lunch together and eventually going to clubs at night to unwind after long days at the hospital, and soon it became a routine any Friday night they didn't work. After a few months, Eva suggested that the three of them move in together to save money, so they got an apartment in Potsdam, between Beelitz and Berlin. It was close to Berlin, where the entertainment was, and the hospital in Beelitz, where they worked, so Potsdam seemed like the obvious choice.

"There was no reason to sit at home listening to the rain, so I came in early and started the prep work." The thick coat hardly fit inside the small locker, preventing the door from closing every time Eva tried. She punched the balled fabric in an attempt to make it stay.

Liesel watched Eva frustratingly push the coat to the back of the locker and then slam the door. "A shipment is scheduled to come in today," Liesel said.

Eva let out a breath and turned to Liesel, placing her hands on her hips. "Really, I am surprised one is coming, even though it's overdue. Do you know what it will be?"

"No. It's supposed to be here this evening, so we will see."

Supplies were in short stock at the hospitals in the cities because most were sent to the front to the field hospitals. When the time comes that the Germans begin losing the war and the fighting gets closer to Berlin, the decision to send most of the medicine and supplies away will only serve to hurt them. Eva did not want to be here when that happened but felt for the doctors and nurses who would have to care for the wounded men coming in by the hundreds, not to mention the women and children from the city. It would be overwhelming and daunting, and so many would die. Helping the wounded while the city was continuously being bombed and soldiers pouring in from the east and west was not something she was willing to do. Although the thought of leaving when the city and the German people were in need and at their most vulnerable weighed heavily on her, it was hard to keep away the crushing guilt, knowing something they didn't and having the opportunity to leave before the real danger came. It was almost cruel.

"Is Heidi working today?" Eva asked.

"No, but she will meet us at the vagabond tonight."

"Oh, not the suggestion of that club again." Eva's face contorted in exasperation.

"Remember, we agreed we would go to a nicer, upscale one in the city center this time. You always say no when we ask, and I get it. Really, I do. You don't like soldiers, but please, this one time. The food and drinks are much better there, not to mention the entertainment."

Eva gave her a sideways glance. "We have been over this."

"I know you don't like them, but Heidi and I do. Can you please sit and drink while we mingle, then?"

A while back, Eva had agreed to go to the nicer club before finding out it was a spot German soldiers frequented. "If I go tonight, will you not ask me to go again?"

"I swear, I won't ask you anymore."

"Alright, but you have to let Heidi know."

"I will go to the apartment and tell her when I take my lunch," Liesel happily agreed.

Eva changed into her nurse's uniform and walked with Liesel to the patient ward, already dreading agreeing to go to the new club.

The first thing she did was scan the hospital list, but no new patients had come in during the night, so she looked at the ones that had arrived the night before. Gerhardt's name wasn't on the list, but she decided to check each bed anyway to make sure.

"Why do you hate soldiers?" Liesel asked, following Eva from bed to bed as they made their rounds. "I know you are American, but that doesn't strike me as the reason."

Eva had not told Heidi or Liesel why she would not interact with German soldiers, especially the officers. There was only one German officer Eva didn't mind being around, and that was Klaus Möller, the doctor she worked closest with at the hospital. He was a kind person who was similar to her father in disposition. Klaus had no children but had looked out for her since she arrived in Berlin, kind of like a daughter. Being a doctor, he held the rank of captain but did not act as the other officers or seem like he was in the German military, not to her. Klaus was gentle and caring, and she was sure there wasn't a mean bone in his body. He was stern only if the situation required, like when in the operating room, because he had to be. There was no room for mistakes. Once, Eva witnessed a new nurse pause when asked for a scalpel and then drop it on the floor while handing it to him. He yelled at her to get out and told the other nurse at the table to take over. He was not trying to be mean, but the man's life on the table depended on their skill, ability, and accuracy. After surgery, he found the nurse waiting in the hall and explained that he was not mad at her, but in the operating room, you have to think on your feet. She was never used in the operating room again, and after the incident, the head nurse told the girl she would change bandages and empty bedpans from now on.

Dr. Möller cared about each patient. It was in his nature to be that way, the need to help others. Being a doctor suited his personality well.

Eva carefully cleaned the wound, trying to not pull the thick hair on the patient's leg that was stuck in the scab. This kind of thing usually didn't bother her, but today, the hair stuck to the blood, and the mangled flesh around the wound made her stomach churn.

"Let's just say that nothing good has ever come from knowing them. The only memories I have of German soldiers are of pain and misery." That wasn't exactly the truth, but it was the only answer she would give Liesel now.

"Why is that?"

"I don't know how I would even explain it to you."

"Were you in love with one? Is that it?"

Eva paused, wiping the wound. "Why would you say that?"

"Because what else would it be. You don't want to talk about it, and you refuse to go anywhere because you might have to interact with them outside of the hospital. I wish a soldier would show me attention, even once."

"It's not what you think."

"So, tell me then."

"There was a misunderstanding. I got brought in for questioning, and the officer in charge was not very nice. He threatened to torture me until I admitted to something I didn't do."

"Oh my God, I didn't know. Eva, I'm sorry. If I had known it was something like that, I never would have asked. He didn't actually hurt you, did he?"

"No, something came up, and he never got the chance to, but he told me he would be back."

"And this was in France?"

"Yes, but that doesn't mean he isn't in Germany." Eva decided against mentioning Gerhardt. It was still too painful to talk about.

Liesel put her hand on Eva's shoulder. "Don't worry; he won't be there tonight. He is probably still in France or maybe even dead. If we are lucky, that is what he is."

Eva smiled at the last comment. "I know. Let's see to the

rest of the patients," she said, wanting to end the conversation.

Eva wrapped the wound, then went to the next bed and unhung the clipboard from the end. This soldier was one of the new patients that had come in the night before. He had a fractured leg, which was fixed at a field hospital before being sent here. He was given pain medicine at three this morning and would need his second dose at seven. Eva went to the next new patient, then another, and another, until she had read the charts for all of them. Satisfied that none were Gerhardt, she returned to the end of the line of beds carrying a tray of clean bandages, alcohol, and scissors. She laid it on the table next to him and pulled the blanket back over his legs, then inspected his bandage before cutting through it with the scissors. She laid the scissors back on the tray and gently pulled the bandage away from his wound, revealing a swollen and purple lower leg with stitches from the ankle to the knee. Taking the chart from the end of the bed again, she read it more closely this time. This patient had been near artillery fire, and some shrapnel had gone in his leg, shattering the bone. The tibia tore the skin, allowing the muscle and fat to poke out through the flesh.

"He had been in North Africa like most of the wounded that has come in over the last few days."

Dr. Möller's kind voice filled her ears. He was standing close behind her in his white lab coat. Eva turned to him, then looked back at the patient. "It's awful. No one should have to suffer like this, none of them. I mean, the men and boys from both sides."

"This is war. Someone always has to pay the price." He came to stand beside her and looked down at the boy. "I know it's tragic, but this is what happens. There has been a lot of suffering, and there will continue to be suffering, but hopefully, something good will come from all of it."

"Somehow, I doubt that." It was difficult to keep the resentment from her voice.

"I know it's hard to see any of this as positive, but I like to think it will come later." He squatted down beside her. "I saw you with the new patients last week. You did well. You were calm while handling them, and you knew what to do and where to send them. Good job. I'm proud of you. I think you are a natural at this, and you work well under pressure. That is exactly what we need here."

"Thank you. But all the nurses do well."

"They do, though not at everything quite the way you do. I know that Oberschwester Wagner is cautious and can't understand why we allow you to work in the hospital at all. She is distrusting of your reasons for helping Germans because you are American. There is a lack of respect for the work you do because she can only see your nationality."

"I don't pay her any mind. I actually understand why she feels that way."

His lips pulled into a crooked half-smile. "Well, the way you put up with the treatment here is remarkable. I would not want to be a nurse working under her."

"It's not always easy, I'll admit. It still upsets her when I talk to you. She says that doctors and nurses should not fraternize, that their work is meant to be kept separate, and that we should only speak to the doctors when given instructions or when asked a question."

"Does she? I did not know that. She will have to be upset then, I suppose. She is an unhappy woman who thinks everyone else should be as unhappy as her."

Eva laughed at his assessment of Frau Wagner. "That she is."

"I will let you get back to your patient." He patted her on the knee before standing.

"I was going to ask," Eva spoke before Klaus walked away. "Will he ever walk again?" She focused on the boy in front of her.

"As of now, it is uncertain. When the swelling goes down, we will take some X-rays of his leg, then we will have a better idea."

The doubt that the boy would walk again showed on his face before he turned to leave. Taking a cotton ball from the tray, she soaked it in alcohol, and patted it on the stitches. He made a groaning noise and opened his eyes.

"I'm sorry. I know that hurts. I will be as gentle as possible. And as soon as I'm done, I will give you some more pain medicine." It was sad to see someone as young as him and know that they might lose their leg.

"How is my leg? Is it really bad?" His voice was strained and rough from a dry throat.

The desire to tell him no and that it would be fine almost slipped out, but she held back, not wanting to lie. "I don't know, but we will do everything we can for you."

A tear escaped his left eye. "I don't want to lose my leg.

I will need it when the war is over. I have to help my mom and dad on the farm. They will need me."

"No one said anything about losing your leg. There is no need to worry about that now," she assured him. "The bones in your leg are still broken, but we will get an X-ray and put it back together for you as soon as the swelling is down." She wrapped his leg in a new bandage and tied it. "You will be alright. I'll be back soon with your medicine." She pulled the blanket over him and went to find Liesel, who was at the other end of the long room, helping another patient.

"I feel so bad for them," Eva said, her eyes roaming over the beds as she came to stand next to her. "I hate this war. I hate everything about it. German, French, British, Russian, it doesn't matter. They are all human and are being slaughtered like cattle."

"Shhhh, if they hear you talk that way, they could arrest you. Remember, some of these men are officers, and even the enlisted men might not hesitate to snitch on you. Make sure a comment like that doesn't fall upon the wrong ears."

"I know. But it makes me sad and angry to see them like this. There are some days I'm not even sure I can deal with it anymore. If I continue pushing it to the back of my mind, one of these times, I'm going to snap."

"We all feel that way. Dealing with it is all you can do. It's all any of us can do."

"I know." She was right, but it wasn't something that was easy to do. "Why don't you take your lunch first today and tell Heidi about the club? And I will take mine when you return."

"Alright. Are you sure you are OK?" Liesel's concern emanated from her.

"I'm fine." Eva crossed the room to the nurse's lounge to get some morphine from the cabinet. When she pulled the morphine box from the shelf, the vials slid to the front. Morphinc was not the only thing that they were low on; some of the other medicine spots were empty, and most of the others were only partly filled. They needed to get some in the shipment because this was the last box.

She went back to the bed and set the needle on the table, then pulled the blanket back. "I'm going to give you a shot in the leg for the pain. You will only feel a pinch."

"Alright." He focused on the needle in her hand with uncertain eyes.

"It might make you tired, but that is good because you need to rest."

"Can I ask your name?"

"Sure… my name is Eva." She wondered if he was talking to distract himself. "What is your name?"

"Otto. Otto Bern." His eyes flicked from her face to the needle.

"Otto, that is a nice name. Where are you from, Otto?"

"I'm from Bremen. It's in the north, near the sea. We have a farm close to town. Do you know Bremen?" He was now focusing on the line of beds behind her.

"I must admit that I don't, but I know where the North Sea is, so I have some idea of its location." She poked the needle in his thigh and pushed the top down until the syringe was empty.

He flinched. "I feel a little sick. Do you have something in case I throw up?"

"Of course, I'll grab it for you."

Laying the needle in the disinfecting tray filled with alcohol, she went to get a bowl. She brought one back and sat it on the floor next to him.

"Here is a bowl for you. If you need anything else, ask any of the nurses." The pen scratched the paper as she wrote the time, date, medicine, and amount given on his chart, then hung it back on the end of his bed and turned to leave.

"Fräulein, where are you from?"

She turned back around, resting her hands on the metal footboard, gazing down at his young, cherub-like face. "I am from America."

"I knew you sounded different. How are you here? I mean, why are you here?"

"Well, that is a long story. Maybe some other time."

"Tomorrow?"

"Maybe. Get some sleep."

She left his bed and went to the nurses' quarters to look for Liesel, but she was not there. Liesel was still gone, and Eva's stomach hurt from hunger. All the patients had been attended to, so there was time to eat lunch. She pulled the brown paper bag from her locker, then walked the long corridor to the stairs, climbing each step with some effort to Dr. Möller's office and knocked. It was only midday, but her energy was waning.

"Come in."

She opened the door and held up the lunch bag. "Have

you eaten yet?"

"No, but now is a good time to stop, I guess." He laid his pencil down on the desk and leaned back in his chair, linking his fingers behind his hand.

She walked in and closed the door, placing` the bag on his desk, then sat in the empty chair without waiting to be asked to do so.

"So, what are you going to do this weekend? I saw you are off?"

"I don't even know. Sleep and clean my apartment, probably."

"That doesn't sound like much fun." He unlinked his fingers, then reached for the bag and unrolled the top.

"I'm going to a club with Liesel and Heidi tonight. I will have some fun then."

"That sounds more exciting. Going to go meet young soldiers, huh?"

"Me, no! Heidi and Liesel are. I'm only going because they wouldn't leave me alone about it. And you, what will you do this weekend?"

"Work," he admitted with a half-smile while taking the food from the bag, rustling the crinkly paper as he reached inside. "That's all I do."

"You need to have some fun and relax, too."

"I do sometimes, but this is what makes me the happiest, helping these men." He lifted his chin to the door, indicating to the patients below them.

"Now you are making me feel bad for going to the club and not staying to help."

"No, you should not feel bad. You are young, and things are different for you. You need to get out and mingle with people, and hopefully, someday, you will meet a nice young man, marry, and have babies."

She huffed. "Have babies? I'm not even sure I want to get married, much less have babies or even a baby."

"Sure, you do. You don't want to be like me. Old, single, and childless. I should have grandchildren by now sitting on my knees as I tell them stories."

"So, you regret never getting married and having children?"

"I do at times. I chose my path a long time ago, a career over a family, only later realizing I could have had both. That choice for me, though, has passed. What I'm saying is don't follow in my footsteps."

"I think someday I will get married and maybe have children too, but during a war is not an ideal time to start a family."

"Well, now definitely is not ideal, but then again, when is?"

"Actually… I'm not sure I want to be with a man not from my country. I think it would be hard. I mean, what country would the children be born in, and where would we live? It is too confusing. I think I will wait to make those kinds of decisions until I get home. It will make life simpler."

"I understand. If you were to fall in love with a German man, it could turn out badly in the end."

That sounded like something Adele would have told her.

"Can I ask why you think that? Not that I disagree with you. It's only that I want to know your reason."

"As you said, it would make things too complicated. Our countries are not at war, but they are not allies either. I believe a German and an American would have different ideas about how to raise a child. The different cultures would certainly influence ideas of the world and everything in it. Plus, German men run a high risk of dying or being captured, which would always be present in your mind. I am not a woman, but I think it would be hard to be married to a soldier with the constant worrying. I wouldn't want to do it."

"I agree, and those are some of the reasons I will wait until I return home before even thinking about marriage."

"Is this all you brought to eat?" He held up the small bowl of soup, ending their conversation.

"Yes, why?"

"It's not enough. Here." He put an apple and a piece of bread in front of her.

"No, I don't want to take your food."

"I always bring a little extra."

"Do you?"

"Yes, in case someone else needs it."

"But I don't need it."

"Eva, look how skinny you are. I have never seen you eat more than a snack-size lunch, and some days, you don't eat lunch at all."

"I do. You usually aren't there when I eat."

"You can't lie to me, Eva. Your body tells on you."

"Fine, I will take the apple and bread today."

“I need to do my rounds, but you can stay here and finish your lunch if you want.” He poked the last of his sandwich in his mouth.

“Thanks for the food.”

“It is no problem.” He squeezed her shoulder as he walked past.

Eva quickly downed the bread and apple. She could not remember the last time she had a lunch this big. Nurses didn’t earn much, and food was scarce, especially for someone in her pay bracket. You had to be a soldier or wealthy to buy many things these days, even if it was from the black market.

When Eva returned to the nurses’ lounge to put the soup bowl away, Liesel was standing in front of the open locker, putting on her apron.

“You already had lunch?”

“I did. I ate with Dr. Möller.”

“See, all the officers are not bad.”

“He is not like the others, and you know that. I don’t count him as an officer, plus he is too old for me to even think of him in that way. Did you tell Heidi?” She opened the locker door and set the bowl on the top shelf.

“I did. She will meet us there at six.”

“Are we really going to stay out past curfew again? We can’t keep doing this. Eventually, we are going to get caught.”

“This time, we will be with officers. No one will bother us.”

“You instill me with so much confidence.”

Liesel threw her hat in Eva's direction. "No sarcasm."

Eva threw it back at her, laughing, but in all actuality, she worried about tonight. There was no way of knowing who they would see tonight, and if they got caught breaking curfew, it would be worse for her than Liesel or Heidi.

Chapter Two

✠

February 23rd, 1941

Eva drank her schnapps alone at the table while watching from across the room as Liesel and Heidi danced and laughed with some soldiers. They seemed so relaxed and carefree. Both were having a good time, and she was happy for them.

Looking down at the drink in her hand, she twirled the cup, sloshing the liquid around. The atmosphere here differed quite a bit from the clubs they usually frequented. Here, they covered the tables in white cloths and tea light candles. It was a stark contrast to the bare, chipped, stained wood tables that were at some of the other clubs they visited. The room was dim, and the walls were covered in a deep red wallpaper with black lotus flowers printed across them that reminded her of an oriental establishment. The club was not as busy as some of the others, and more than half of the soldiers here were officers. It was definitely more upscale.

Heidi came back to the table with a lower-ranking officer in tow. "Eva, come dance with us, please?"

"No, I'm fine. You guys have fun, though. I'm going to stay here and finish my drink."

"We are having fun, but we would have more fun if you were out there with us. You look so miserable sitting here all alone."

"I'm not miserable, I promise you. Besides, who would I even dance with?"

Heidi looked at the man she brought to the table. "Fredrick, don't you have a friend that Eva can dance with?"

"I do. I'll go get him."

"No, please. I don't want to dance with anyone." Eva waved her hands back and forth.

Heidi nodded to him, and he turned, cutting through the crowd, going to a lone man standing near the wall. They exchanged a few words, then the two of them walked back to the table.

"Heidi, why did you do that?" Eva didn't hide her frustration.

"Because you look sad sitting over here by yourself?"

"But that is what I want. I want to sit here, have my drink, and be left alone. I only came for you and Liesel."

"This is Karl," the man with Heidi said once he and the other man reached the table.

"It's nice to meet you, Karl," she said, barely looking at him.

He took her hand and kissed it. "It is my pleasure. And what is your name?"

This was out of her comfort zone. "Eva."

He sat in the chair beside her. "Do you come to the club often?"

She gave Heidi an annoyed glance, then looked at him. "Not this club. This is my first time here."

"I'll let you two get to know one another. We are going back to the dance floor. Have fun," Heidi said, smiling.

"Wait, you aren't going to stay?" Eva asked, a little panicked.

"No, I'll leave you guys alone to talk." Heidi winked at her, then took Fredrick's hand, leading him towards the dance floor. Eva shot her a glance of frustration.

"So, you came here with your friends?"

Eva wanted to be alone, so any question he asked was intrusive. "I did. I told them I would come, but this will be the only time."

"Why is that?"

"Because I don't really like it here." She gestured towards the dance floor with the swoop of her hand. "There are too many people." That was a straight-up lie because it was not crowded, but there was no way she was going to tell him the real reason. He would be upset if he knew the truth, that she did not like German soldiers.

He scanned the room and then rested his eyes on her. "We can go talk outside?"

"Honestly, I would rather sit here alone."

"You don't want me here?"

She felt bad at the thought of making him leave, but if he stayed, she would have to talk. Both made her uncomfortable, but she chose the lesser of the two. "No, you can stay. So, are you stationed here in Berlin?" she asked to break any awkward silence.

"I am. And do you live here?"

"I live in Potsdam with the girls I came with."

"And what do you do in Potsdam?"

"I don't work in Potsdam. I work at a hospital in Beelitz, but I live in Potsdam."

"A nurse, that is an honorable trade. I don't know if I could work in a hospital with all those wounded men. The screaming, the blood, and the smell. It's not for me."

"Yet you are in the military and see violence all the time."

"Actually, I don't. I work at a desk in an office. I joined early so I could have an office job because I didn't want to fight. I know that sounds like I'm a coward."

To Eva, he was an unusual German. Most seemed to glorify fighting and war. But to be honest, he did not look like the fighting type. He was tall, skinny, and very young. His appearance was Aryan, with blond hair, blue eyes, and fair skin that was blemished with red patches. "No, I don't think you are a coward. But why do you not want to fight?" She was honestly curious about his reasons.

"It's alright if you think me a coward. I didn't want to kill anyone, but also, I didn't want to die alone on some far-off battlefield."

"Really, I don't think you are a coward. That makes

perfect sense to me. I would feel the same way if I were in your situation."

"Do most of the men that come to the hospital survive?"

"Ummm, I would say most of them. Although a lot leave less of a person than when they got there, and some arrive already less than whole."

"That is terrible. I am now even happier with the position I have."

She folded the corners of the napkin under her glass. "So, do you work in the Reichstag?"

"I do."

He said what she was hoping he would. If he worked at the Reichstag, that meant he might know Gerhardt. She was grappling with whether or not she should ask him. Maybe she would fish around for the information instead of coming out and directly asking.

"Do you know a lot of the people that work there?"

"I know some, mostly the ones in my department."

"Really, and what department do you work in?" She took a sip of her drink, watching his expression change.

"I'm not sure I can tell you that."

"Right, of course. So, have any of the people you work with seen battle?"

"Yes, a lot of them, actually."

He would not tell her what department he worked for, so maybe now it was time to ask. "Do you by any chance know Hauptmann Gerhardt von Schulz?"

He looked like he was thinking about her question when suddenly he stood up from the table and snapped to attention, clicking his heels together. "SS Obersturmbannführer Bauer."

He was looking past her, and hearing those words roll off his tongue made her breath hitch in her throat.

"Lieutenant, why don't you join the people you came here with."

"Yes Obersturmbannführer. It was nice talking with you, Eva," he told her, then turned and disappeared into the crowd.

Eva sat still in her chair, fear threatening to consume her. Bauer walked around to the chair Karl had been in and sat down, placing his officer hat on the table in front of him.

"Miss Abrams, I must say I am surprised to see you, and here in Berlin, of all places. When I noticed you from across the room, I questioned my own eyes. What I can't figure out is why you are here. Maybe it's because you are a spy, or it could be you are simply stupid. What are you doing here?" He looked right at her with his penetrating hazel eyes, intensely focusing on her.

"What?" she asked, almost in a whisper.

"You seem uneasy, Miss Abrams. Is it because you fled France as we were rounding up the Dubois? You knew we were taking in everyone who lived there, but you were nowhere to be found when we went to the farm. How is it you knew to leave right before we arrived? The only way you could have known is if someone warned you. Now, I don't pretend to be ignorant of who it was, but I'm sure when he helped you, he never imagined you would ever come here amongst the very people who were looking for you."

"I was at Madame Blanc's when all of that happened. I knew nothing of it except what I heard." The pit of her stomach twisted into knots for the lie, saying she knew nothing of the Schullers and trying to make him believe it was all Fabien. But they were dead, and the truth would not benefit her or the lie wrong them. It would only serve to hurt her in the end.

"Are you trying to convince me that you lived with a family who had been hiding Jews, and you knew nothing of it? I find that hard to believe."

"I did not ask them about their business, and they were obviously good at hiding them."

"Why did you leave La Chapelle?"

"Because I knew soon, I would no longer have a place to stay."

"Madame Blanc would have happily let you live with her."

"There was nothing left for me there, so I went to Paris." Eva did not look at him. She was afraid she could not handle the pressure of his scrutinizing gaze and falter under its weight.

"That doesn't explain why you are here."

"I came for work." She focused on the flickering flames of the tealight candle, using it to keep her focused and calm.

"Work? And what kind of work did you come here to do?"

"I went to Paris to work for the Red Cross, but they told me after I got there that the Red Cross in Berlin had more need of my help than the one in Paris. So, I came here. I had to find a way to support myself, and if that meant coming to Berlin, then that was what I was going to do. I can't go home, you have seen to that. So, I have to make my way where I can."

"Indeed. So, you are a nurse for the Red Cross here in Berlin?"

"Yes."

"I am appalled that they would let you treat German soldiers. They deserve better than you. They should have proud, loyal German women taking care of them. Nurses who understand why they sacrificed so much."

"You don't think I care about my patients because they are German? I care about all of them. I only see people, not Germans."

"It's a disgrace," he said, leaning down so he could look at her face better. "You know I am going to have to take you in for questioning."

Her eyes widened as his words were internally digested. This could not be happening again. "For what? I have done nothing wrong!" When she thought about her response, it was calm in her mind, but once the words were spoken it didn't come out that way. They was high pitched and frantic.

"Oh, but you have. I warned you this would happen. If you play with fire, you eventually get burned." He stood, retrieving his hat from the table but didn't put it on. "Come with me, Miss Abrams."

She looked across the room at Heidi and Liesel. She could not leave them like this. "You haven't told me what

I've done."

He took hold of her arm, pulling her to her feet. The heels of her shoes caught on the carpet, almost twisting her ankle. "Let's go."

She grabbed her purse from the back of the chair before he pulled her away. Bauer led her to the front of the club, where his orderly was waiting for him. When the orderly saw her and Bauer, he opened the front door for them and then followed them out to a car parked near the front. He opened the back door, and Bauer waited for her to get in. Once she was in the car he got in the back with her. She scooted to the end of the seat away from him and leaned against the door on the other side. Was this ever going to end? She felt like she was stuck on a merry-go-round with Bauer.

The tears spilled over even though she tried to blink them away and ran down her cheeks. For the first time, she didn't care if he saw or heard the quiet sobbing.

"You can't keep doing this to me. I have done nothing wrong." The quiver in her voice was audible. "Do you hate me so much that you are going to keep tormenting me?"

"Don't play innocent with me. You are as guilty as sin, and you and I both know it. I will do this to you as many times as it takes to get the truth."

The car moved slowly down the street, the city lights reflecting off the wet road in a blur. The buildings passed by, but she hardly noticed them, nor did she notice the smell of the rain, or Bauer's cologne that lingered in the car. The only thing she could focus on was the hopelessness that was eating her up inside. This man would be the end of her. He would not stop until she was in a camp or dead, and the truth of it was, which one would be worse was unclear.

The car pulled to the curb, and Bauer opened the door and stepped out without waiting for his orderly.

"Get out," he ordered in his usual stern voice.

She slid across the seat and stepped out, then Bauer slammed the door. He grasped her upper arm again with a firm hand as if he thought she would try to run.

Lifting her head, realizing where they were as the Reichstag towered over her. Above the main entryway of the building, hanging over the steps, was a large red flag with a black swastika. The mere sight of it made her blood run cold. To her, it was the symbol of true evil.

He led her up the steps and through the doors into the main lobby of the building, then down a long corridor. He stopped outside a brown wooden door on the left and opened it, pushing her inside. He followed her in, shutting the door and flipping on a light.

"Sit down."

It was hard to tell how big the room was because the only light came from a hanging lamp over the middle of a metal table, illuminating its surface while leaving the rest of the room in darkness. On each side of the table were two metal chairs and nothing else. He pushed her down in one chair, then pulled the other from the table, its feet scraping loudly on the floor. The unpleasant memory of the last time this happened forced its way into her thoughts, and she wondered if it would be the same or worse.

Bauer leaned back in the chair. "Start from the beginning of that day."

"Which day?"

In a measured motion, he moved forward. "Do not play dumb with me. I will not hesitate to throw you in a cell."

Did he mean the day the German soldiers were killed at the farm? she wondered. "I was at Madame Blanc's. I arrived there the day before everything happened. On the day of the raid, I went for a walk, swam in a nearby pond, then came back, ate dinner, and went to bed. I was told of it the next morning. That is when I left for Paris."

"But you went back to the farm between the time the soldiers were killed, and you left for Paris because all of your belongings were gone from your room."

Crap! she thought. That had slipped her mind. "Yes, I got my things and left. I did not want to stay there any longer than I had to."

"You had to know we would want to talk with you?"

"At that moment, it had not crossed my mind. I was more concerned with collecting my things and getting out of there."

"Tell me about the Jews that he was hiding?"

"I told you already. I did not know about them."

"But you did. Did he bring them there, or did you?"

She was growing more flustered by the minute; he was going to keep asking until the answer was what he wanted.

"He must have." Her voice was weak and the normal cadence off. She fidgeted with a folded piece of fabric from her dress.

"You know, if I chose, I could report that Hauptmann von Schulz helped you escape, even though he knew you were implicit in harboring Jews. If I did that, they would send him from Berlin, and that is only after they punished him for his disobedience. I have half a mind of arresting him anyway."

She grabbed his hand that was resting on the table. "Nooo, please, you can't say anything! Please, don't arrest him. I will tell you what you want to know. Don't say anything, I beg you!" The words came rapidly and slurred together. "It was my fault. He did it for me. Punish me, but not him!"

He pulled his hand away and said in an apathetic, deepened voice. "Then tell me, and no more of your duplicitous behavior."

She couldn't stop the newly surfaced tears from spilling over. They felt hot on her cheeks. "I knew Fabien was hiding the Jews, but I did not want to get him into trouble. I knew it would put him and his daughters in danger, so I kept quiet about it." She hoped he would believe the story if part of it was true. "Gerhardt didn't know Fabien was hiding Jews until the day before everything happened. I never told him, and he only saw one of them for the first time the day before. The Jewish man showed himself to Gerhardt. He only learned he was a Jew when the soldiers went to the farm."

"Yes, I remember the report he filed about a suspicious man working on the farm. But after he discovered Fabien was hiding Jews, he helped you escape?"

Peering into the steely eyes that stared back, obsidian in

the darkened room, the only sound was the wild beating of her heart. "You won't get him in trouble?"

He stood up and paced beside the table. "Let's move on to another question. You have answered enough regarding that for now. Are you a spy, Miss Abrams?"

"I swear I am not a spy. I left because I didn't know what to do."

"And I have told you before that I don't believe that."

"I promise you, I—"

With a sudden movement, her head was being pushed down on the table, held there by the back of her neck. His hand was hot on her skin and large enough for his fingers and thumb to reach around to part of the front, near her throat.

"A man is sitting in a cell tonight that I finished interrogating this afternoon. He is missing some teeth and will never use his fingers again. He can't see because his eyes are swollen shut from the beating he received. I am telling you this because it is nothing compared to what I will do to you if you don't start talking. Who are you spying for?" he said in an ominous voice into her ear, his face so close to hers that she could feel his breath on her cheek, the air from his nostrils blowing strands of her hair.

Eva could barely talk through the tears and hyperventilating sobs. She tried to steady her breathing and calm the panic, but it paralyzed her in the chair. The menacing look on his face kept her frozen in that position. The fear of what he would do, of what he was capable of, crept in like an angry beast holding her captive.

"I can't hear you." His words were low and firm.

She tried to respond a second time, but her breath was trapped in her lungs, and the sound of her heart pounding was deafening in her ears. She wanted to scream, but she couldn't get it out, and no one would come to save her even if she did. The thought of trying to run flashed through her mind, fear and desperation fueling her thoughts, but his grip on her neck was like a vice. Besides, she would never make it out of the building, probably not even out of the room.

He let go of her and straightened, readjusting his jacket. "You will be here again, that you can be sure of. My orderly will take you back to the club." He walked towards the door and opened it, then turned to look at her. "I always punish those who are treacherous." He stepped into the hall, his glossy boots clicking on the tile, then closed the door. A deadly silence hung in the air.

She bitterly wept, and the feeling of dread crept up from the pit of her stomach. *Oh God, what have I done?* Had she sealed her and Gerhardt's fate? Had she sentenced him to a hard life or death?

She was still leaning over the table and could not control her hands as they trembled to an odd rhythm against the cold metal surface.

The door opened, and Bauer's orderly stood in the doorway. "It's time to go, Fräulein."

She stood, dizzy and lightheaded, her legs shaky, and followed him into the hall, through the elegant lobby of the Reichstag, and back to the car. They did not cross Bauer's path on the way out, and she was relieved.

The orderly dutifully opened the door for her, and she got into the back seat. Then he closed it and went around to the front. The car pulled away, and the lights of the Reichstag reflected in the rearview mirror before disappearing entirely as the car turned a corner.

Eva quietly cried in the backseat. The overwhelming feeling of guilt that Gerhardt might be punished was smothering her. She had been doing alright, keeping her head above water and feeling stronger by the day, but Bauer was like an atomic bomb that had been dropped on her world.

As the car pulled in front of the club, she opened the door and hopped out before it came to a complete stop and ran inside. She searched the crowd for Heidi and Liesel and spotted them standing in the far-right corner, scanning the room. She knew they were looking for her, too. Quickly, she made her way towards them, and when they saw her, they moved from the wall and came to meet her as she crossed the dance floor.

"Eva, where did you go?" Liesel asked before noticing she had been crying. "What happened? Did he try something? If he did, I'm going to—."

Eva shook her head. "No," she said through the tears. "Nothing like that."

Heidi put her arm around Eva's shoulder. "Come and sit down." She led Eva to the nearest table and sat her on a chair.

"Eva, what happened?" Liesel asked, sitting next to her.

"Do you remember why I didn't want to come here?"

"Because you don't like soldiers?"

"True, but the main reason was that I didn't want to run into a certain person, remember?"

"Yes, I remember."

"Well, I ran into him. He was here tonight, at the club. Of course, the night I finally chose to come with you guys, he was here, and now I will pay the price for it."

"Wait, that officer was here?"

"Yes, and he took me to the Reichstag for interrogation. He knows things about me that could get me into serious trouble and about a person who I care deeply for. I think he is going to do something terrible to them and to me."

Liesel cupped her hand over her mouth. "Eva, I am so sorry. I truly didn't think you would see him here. I mean, what are the chances of that happening?"

Eva stood. "I can't stay any longer. I have to get out of here." She hurried toward the doors as Heidi and Liesel followed close behind.

"Eva, we can't walk home. It's past curfew," Heidi called.

"I don't care, and it doesn't matter now. I'm going to prison anyway, I'm sure."

Liesel grabbed her arm and pulled her around to face her. "What are you talking about?"

"I will explain, but not here."

"We need to get a ride," Heidi insisted. "I can ask Fredrick. I'm sure he will take us home."

"No. I don't want to ride in a car with one of them."

"What other choice do we have?" Heidi intreated.

"There has to be another way."

"There isn't," Liesel agreed.

She was too tired to fight with them. "Fine, I simply want to go home. Ask him, and let's get out of here." She hated the thought of riding in a car with another German soldier.

Heidi hurried back into the main part of the club. "Eva, what do you mean you might go to prison? You are worrying me."

"I don't want to talk about it here. I'll tell you back at the apartment."

Heidi reappeared with the same man she had been with earlier. "Fredrick said he would be happy to give us a ride."

"Thank you," Liesel said to him.

"I am happy to help three pretty ladies in need."

"I think I might vomit," Eva whispered in Liesel's ear.

"We won't be with him long."

They followed him outside to a black car, and Eva got into the back with Liesel as Heidi slid into the front with him.

"Karl said he didn't get to visit with you long, that a Lieutenant Colonel who wanted to talk with you interrupted shortly after... Do you two know each other?" Fredrick asked.

"Unfortunately, yes."

"Why unfortunate?"

"Because he is an asshole. No, that's too good for him. He is the devil."

Liesel squeezed Eva's hand to silence her.

"Hmm… that is a strong opinion. Why do you think that? I don't know SS Obersturmbannführer Bauer personally, but I've heard he is as loyal as they come. He is as devoted to the German cause as anyone could be. What has he done that is so bad?"

"It doesn't matter. Besides, I think that you and I would differ on what constitutes bad."

He looked at her in the rearview mirror and squinted, a crease forming between his brows. Eva looked down at her lap, not wanting to talk with him anymore. At this point, she was convinced that most German soldiers were the same, so what was the point in trying to reason with any of them.

He parked in front of the apartment and let them out. "Will I see you again?" he asked Heidi.

Smiling, she said, "You know where I live," then closed the door and waved as the car pulled away.

The night air was chilly, and the tip of Eva's nose and fingers were stinging. "I'm going in now." The first thing she did once inside was turn on the light and then drop her purse on the floor. She pulled her coat off, hung it on the wooden coat rack, and unbuckled her shoes, kicking them in the corner before plopping onto the couch. Heidi and Liesel joined her on the sofa.

"Tell us what happened?" Liesel asked.

She took a deep breath and let it out. "I'm going to have to go way back. This started long before tonight." She, of course, would have to leave a lot out. It was unsafe to let them know more than they needed to. She didn't think that they would betray her, but if they were interrogated, they might tell out of fear. Besides, you can't say what you don't know.

"When I was in France, I lived with a family on their farm. I stayed with them for a long time and became extremely fond of them. But they were not the only ones I became fond of. Over time, I became acquainted with a German officer. As much as I hated to admit it, he was kind to me and always treated me with respect. Later it progressed from acquaintance to friendship and then to something else. We grew close, and that summer, I realized I loved him. He had told me he cared for me before I realized what my feelings were for him. I didn't want to love him, and I didn't want him to love me either, in the beginning, but by the time I was ready to accept it and allow myself to truly explore those emotions, I realized that they were already there. We later became intimate, and things were amazing, but that changed after the first time we… well, you know."

She looked at Heidi and Liesel to make sure they were following. They gave her a look of understanding, and she continued.

"The family I lived with was hiding a Jewish family, and I found out. I did not want them to get into trouble because I cared about them, so I chose to not say anything. One day, when Gerhardt, that is the man I loved," she added for clarification, "was walking me home, he encountered one of the Jews the family was hiding. Gerhardt was suspicious of the man, so he reported him, which I didn't know at the time. The officer who took me tonight had come to the farm a few days before and found a letter from a co-worker in England.

I used to work there before I came to France. He thought I was a spy, so he arrested me and was going to torture a confession out of me. Something happened, and he never got to finish what he started, but he told me he would be back for me, which, of course, he has. The morning after Gerhardt and I were intimate, I woke to find him gone. I didn't realize until later that he had left early so he could go to the farm with soldiers. Many people died that day, including most of the family I lived with. They shot Fabien and the Jewish man in the square that evening, and the next morning I fled with the help of Gerhardt."

Heidi's face was fixed in an expression of shock, and Liesel's face was pensive. They exchanged a quick glance before one of them spoke.

"I didn't know you had gone through that, Eva. I am sorry." Liesel placed a hand on Eva's knee.

"SS Obersturmbannführer Bauer, the man who arrested me, told me tonight that if I did not admit I knew about the Jewish family, he would report Gerhardt for helping me escape. So, of course, I told him I knew, but he said he was still tempted to have Gerhardt arrested anyway, even after I confessed. I think he will come for me again soon. I am so worried he will report Gerhardt. He is evil and vindictive."

The tears came again, blurring her vision. Her nose was stuffy, and the pressure in her head was all in the front, pushing against her forehead and eyes.

"I don't know how to get out of this, and I can't wait around for him to come for me."

Heidi stroked her hair. "We will help you figure this out,

don't worry."

"How?" She wiped her nose with the back of her hand. "You guys can't stop him if he comes to arrest me, and if you try, he will only arrest you, too."

"Why don't we all get some sleep and figure something out tomorrow. We are too tired to come up with anything useful tonight," Liesel said.

"I am exhausted," Eva admitted. "I will go to bed." She got up from the couch and went to her room. You guys can use the bathroom if you want. I'll shower in the morning."

"I think it will work itself out in the end."

Heidi's words were meant to be comforting but fell short. "I don't know that it will," Eva said honestly. "Goodnight." After closing the bedroom door, she pushed the straps of her dress from her shoulders, letting it fall around her feet; then, she rolled her stockings down and tossed them next to the dress. Lifting the blankets, she crawled into bed and wrapped the covers around her neck and closed her eyes. She felt unusually cold, and her head pounded from the alcohol and all the crying she had done. Squeezing her eyes shut even tighter, she tried not to think about anything. Asking the resistance for advice tomorrow would be the best choice. Maybe they would have an idea about what should be done.

Chapter Three

✠

February 24th, 1941

"So, he knows what you did in France and thinks you are a spy?" he asked, combing his fingers through his straight, sandy blond hair.

"Yes, there is no denying it anymore. I believe he knows all of it." Helmut Mayer was the leader of the small Berlin underground.

"We need to rethink what we have you do from now on. He likely has someone watching you."

"Are you sure it's safe letting her continue at all?" Lina Schubert was the other female resistance fighter helping the German underground.

"There should still be things she can do to help. I don't think they suspect her of working with the resistance or taking medicine from the hospital. Eva can continue doing that. There is something else she can help with, too. She is more familiar with the German high command than we are. She will come with us and point out the highest-ranking officers and the officer who is giving her trouble, that is, if he is among them. We have recently gotten some information from the inside that there is to be a meeting of the SS command along with officers of the Kriegsmarine, Wehrmacht, and Luftwaffe in four weeks. And when they are all in the same place, we can take as many of those bastards out as we can."

"You want me to be there when you do this?" That information horrified her.

"Yes, it would be helpful if you could point out the most important ones if you recognize any."

"What makes you think I will know any of them? I'm not friends with the Germans. Besides, what if I work that day?"

"You will have to find a way to get off. I know you aren't friends with them, but you have to see them from time to time."

"Do you even know the exact day this is happening?" All of this made Eva uncomfortable.

"We do. It is exactly four weeks from today. On Monday, March 24th," Helmut said.

"I could ask for that day off, but it might look suspicious if I request to take off the same day an attack occurs on the German command. It would be more believable if I pretended to be sick the day before so I could take the next day off too."

"If you think that will work. So, between now and then, keep your head low and don't take any more supplies from the hospital. As I said, he might be having you watched."

"Who gave you this information from the inside?" she asked.

"The fewer people who know their identity, the better. It keeps them safe, and it keeps you safe."

"I understand. I was simply curious." It was natural to wonder who they were getting their information from, but Eva doubted she would know them even if he said their name.

"Is it true that you used to be friends with a German officer in France?" Frank Klein, one of the original organizers of the Berlin resistance, asked from the corner of the room, leaning against the wall. He had been quiet until now.

She gaped at him in surprise. How on earth could he have known something that was never made privy to him or any of the other members of the resistance? "Where did you hear that?"

"From the person on the inside who gave us the other information. Everyone who is part of the resistance must be checked to make sure they are who they say they are and not actually working with the Germans."

"You think I am helping the Germans because I used to be friends with one?" The faces around the room focused on her.

"But you were, you could say, friendly with him?" Frank asked.

"Sure, we were cordial with one another."

"I don't mean that kind of friendly. They think that the two of you were involved."

"I don't know why that would matter, even if I were how it is anyone's business."

The room fell silent. "It matters a lot," Lina said.

"And how would you know?" Eva demanded accusingly.

"Because I have been in love before, you would do almost anything for that person."

"I'm not in love with him." Her protest flew in the face of truth.

"So, you were using him for your own gains?"

"I didn't say that."

"Then what are you saying?"

"No, Lina, what are you saying? If you are trying to get me to admit that I love a German and am helping them, it will never happen. I am not loyal to them, and I am not a traitor. Perhaps you should take a good look at yourself or anyone else in this room if you want to point fingers. You are all German. You all have more cause to be loyal to the Nazis than I do."

"How dare you!" she sneered, taking a step towards Eva.

"I'm only asking you the same thing you are asking me. You don't like it when it's turned around on you, so maybe you should stop making accusations directed at me."

Helmut stepped in between them, putting his arms out. "Alright, enough. Why don't we all calm down. Lina, we are not saying she is a traitor. It is wise to ask those questions because she had close contact in the past with a German officer. Both of you go home and cool off. We are all on the same side here." Lina's apparent disdain was palpable in the atmosphere.

Lina huffed and turned away from Eva, roughly pulling her coat off the rack, almost knocking it over. She opened the door to the cellar and slammed it hard behind her.

"Don't worry about her. You simply hit a nerve." Helmut was calmer now.

"So, this person who gives you information from the inside has given you information on all of us, or only me?"

"All of us. It's not personal, Eva."

She sat down in the nearest chair and put her hands on her knees. "Do you think they would torment me all the time if I was working with them? I nearly escaped torture when I was brought in by them for the second time last night."

"I will admit, it looks like they think you are a threat, but that could be nothing more than a cover, not that I'm saying it is. I believe they suspect you of more than you are saying, but they don't have enough on you yet to put you in jail or keep you. That is why I said keep your head low for now."

"I'm sure they have more on me than we think."

"Then why have they not thrown you in jail yet?"

"I don't know. That is the one thing I am still trying to figure out. You are probably right, and they are having me followed, hoping I will slip up and lead them to something or someone."

"You are certain someone did not follow you here now?"

"Yes. I went in the front door four buildings down and out the back into the alley, then came in through the back door. There was no one in the alley. I checked."

"Good. However, we will have to limit our meetings until the attack. I will contact everyone through a secret code. None of us can risk being followed or captured, especially now that the attack is so close. We need to make sure this happens with no hiccups. Each one of us has a job to do, and we must play our parts. The week leading up to the attack, we will have one last meeting to make sure all of us are clear about the mission."

"Besides pointing out the Germans, what else will I be doing?"

"You will drive the car I will be in, but we will go into more details at the next meeting. It's better if you don't know too much right now in case the worst happens."

"I should let you know that I don't know how to drive." In truth, she could drive, but not a standard transmission. "When fleeing France, I left in a truck, but I was barely off the farm when I had to abandon it. I never could get it to shift into second gear, and the first time I had to stop, I killed the engine. I started it again, but I couldn't seem to make it move. I would try and take off, but the truck would jerk and stall. I killed the engine over and over. I realized I had to give up and walk.

"You never learned to drive?"

"No."

"Well, this changes things." He placed one hand on his hip and rubbed the hairs on his chin. "I will drive then, and you will shoot from the window."

"I have never fired a gun either."

"You will manage." He leaned in close to Eva. "I need you to help; you have to fire the gun. If you do nothing, the others will start suspecting you of being disingenuous, and not only Lina."

"This was so much worse than only being the driver. "I can, and I will. Promise." For now, lying was all she could do.

He got his coat from the rack. "I know you will. I'll see you all in three weeks."

"See you then."

Everyone left, and Eva was now alone in the cellar. She looked at the map of Berlin hanging on the wall next to a wooden shelf. It had red Xs that marked different locations around the city that were of interest to the resistance. Sitting on the shelf was a typewriter, a small printing press, a stack of paper, some ink jars, a radio, and a pair of headphones with a telegraph sounder.

Did they really not trust her, or were they simply being cautious? It was like being caught between two angry lions that were circling, and she did not know which one, but one of them would eventually kill her. She couldn't run; all she could do was wait to see which one attacked first. She thought now she knew how a gazelle felt. And the gun, could she pull the trigger? She thought about that for a second. She didn't have to shoot anyone. Yes, that is what she would do. She would fire the gun, but she wouldn't shoot at anyone.

She got off the chair and took her coat from the hook, opened the door, and turned the light out. She glanced back into the dark room and focused on the pictures of German officers that hung on the wall across from the map. Beside the pictures were a few guns leaning against the wall in the corner, and she wondered how much good they were doing. From what she remembered from her history classes in school, the German resistance did not accomplish as much as, say, the French or Dutch underground. And how did she feel about taking part in killing someone? More than someone, she would participate in what would be a mass killing. The thought gave her goosebumps, and a knot formed in the pit of her stomach, twisting, making her nauseous. She was not entirely sure she could go through with it, but there was no backing out now. They would almost certainly think she was working with the Germans if she did. She wished she had more time and a chance to think things over, but that was not an option.

Eva closed the door and walked up the stairs that led to the upper level, then stepped into the alley and went back the way she came. She pulled the coat tight around her chest to keep warm against the frigid February wind, then walked along the Spree River. If they did not live so far from downtown Berlin, she would walk home, but it would make for a miserable hour in this cold.

She waited for the trolley to Potsdam with the other people huddled together. It was so hard to keep warm; she could only imagine what it must be like for the soldiers who had to be out in this daily. The winter here was far worse than she remembered the winter in France ever being.

Four soldiers stepped in front of her to wait for the trolley. They were having a conversation she could not make out, so she focused on their breaths as they conversed. Then the thought of last night with Bauer flooded her thoughts, and it was like she was back there, in that room with him. She forced that thought away, but it only went to Gerhardt. Was Gerhardt here in Berlin? The way Bauer spoke made it seem like maybe he was, but of course, Bauer would not tell her that. She looked to her left at the dome of the Reichstag building that could be seen from blocks away, towering over most of the other buildings. She could not sit back while Gerhardt was punished because of her. At the very least, she could warn him of what might be coming. Turning away from the crowd of people, she walked past the soldiers, squinting her eyes as the wind blew snow in her face and her shoes crunched on the ice.

Men in uniforms were coming and going as she made her way up the stone steps to the building, and she eyed all of them. All at once, the feelings from last night came over her; the scared, helpless feeling she had while being pinned to the table by Bauer halted her in her tracks. The fear of entering Nazi headquarters was one of the reasons she had never looked for Gerhardt sooner.

She took a deep breath and held it in, trying to calm herself. If she did not go in now, she might never find the courage to ever return. Gerhardt needed her, so she had to do this for him.

Releasing her breath, it came out in front of her like steam, and she took the first step and then the second.

Once inside, she ascended the same flight of stairs that Bauer had taken her up last night, but instead of taking the second flight of stairs to the left, she went to the large mahogany desk that sat at the top. Behind it was a long hall that extended to the back of the building. It had doors on both sides, and she wondered what was behind them.

A young woman in a blue dress and blond curls piled on top of her head sat behind the desk.

“Excuse me, who would I go to if I were looking for a specific officer?”

She lifted her head to Eva. “What department does he work in?”

“That is the thing. I’m not sure. I can give you his name.”

“Alright, what is his name?”

“Gerhardt von Schulz, does that name sound familiar?”

“Yes, I know who he is. He works in the Abwehr department, and civilians cannot go up there.”

“Is there a way I can get a message to him?”

“You can leave a message with me, and I will see that he gets it.”

“You can go into that department?” Eva didn’t think the receptionist would be allowed in either.

"No, he passes this way each day on his way in and out. If you prefer, I could give it to one of the secretaries in that department?"

"I don't know which would be the best way to get it to him."

"Things can get hectic up there, so it might take longer if I send it up. Because it is not urgent or a military document, it will go to the bottom of the stack. I can give it to him today when he leaves if you would like."

"When does he usually leave?"

"It really depends on the day. He sometimes stays late. Don't worry. I'll get it to him." She gave Eva an encouraging smile.

"Thank you. Do you have a pen and paper I could use?"

The receptionist laid a pen and piece of paper in front of her. Eva decided it was best not to put any information on the note that she did not want to be read by the secretary or anyone else, so all she wrote was to meet her at her apartment when he was off, then she put the address and her name. She folded the note and handed it along with the pen back to the woman. The receptionist smiled at Eva and took it from her.

"Thank you again," Eva told her. The woman was more helpful than she had imagined she would be and nicer. She knew now that it was silly to be afraid and that she should have gone in sooner. She could have found Gerhardt months ago, although it was still unclear if he wanted to see her.

"No problem. I'll keep it here and pass it along when he leaves."

Eva smiled, then turned and walked back down the steps. Though it was not as bad as she had imagined it would be, she did not want to stay any longer than necessary. Bauer had taken her here, which meant there was a chance that he, too, worked at the Reichstag or possibly came here often.

She walked back to the same stop she had been at and got behind a group of people. She wasn't there long when the tram came down the street. It came to this stop every twenty minutes, so the wait was never very long. Although if you had to wait the full twenty minutes in the cold, it felt much longer.

The tram stopped, and everyone piled on, but there was only standing room left by the time Eva was inside. The tram moved, and she wrapped her fingers around one of the metal poles to steady herself. As they got closer to Potsdam, the people slowly thinned, so she took one of the newly empty seats. She had her head leaning against the wall, her breath fogging up the window. Reaching with her index finger, she wiped a line through it, internally battling feelings she wished would go away or, at the very least, ignore. It reminded her of the cold nights when she would drive home from Provo, Utah. It seemed so long ago now, and she wished more than anything to be back there; it was so lonely here. But she had to accept this was her life now, living amongst the enemies while the devil was after her, closing in with each day.

The sun had long set by the time it was her stop, and she was the only person left on the tram. Stepping off, she wrapped her coat tighter to prepare for the six blocks to the apartment. When she reached the building, she could barely feel her hands and feet. She hurried up the stairs to the second floor and tried the knob, but it was still locked. Heidi and Liesel must still be at work. They both had the evening shift tonight but should have been home at six. She took the key out of her purse and stuck it in the lock, then pushed the door open to the chilly, dark apartment. She stepped inside, flipped on the light, and shut the door. She went to the heater and turned up. They didn't keep the heat turned high in the apartment while they were gone to save money.

She sat on the couch and folded her hands in her lap, nervous that Gerhardt wouldn't come. How should she act if he did? It was hard to know what his opinion of her was now.

Sitting around, waiting for him to come, was pointless, and it made her more anxious by the minute. Tea sounded good, so she got off the couch and went to the kitchen, putting the kettle on. She tapped her fingers on the countertop and waited for the water to boil. When the kettle whistled, she jumped, instantly feeling silly. She turned the burner off and poured the water into her cup, steam billowing from it. She placed the kettle back on the stove, then carried the cup to the living room, and peered out the window as she took a cautious sip of the hot liquid. The street was empty; it looked as it always did this time of night. The secretary said he usually worked late, so she tried not to worry too much.

She set the cup on the small coffee table after finishing her tea, then lay on the couch, covering up with the blanket they kept draped over the back.

The front door opened, and Liesel and Heidi's voices echoed through the apartment, jolting her awake.

"Sorry, Eva. We didn't know you were sleeping, or we would have been quieter," Heidi said when she saw her on the couch.

Eva sat up and looked at them, the memory of waiting for Gerhardt slowly came back. She gasped and looked at her watch; it was a quarter past nine. She threw the blanket off and stood up. "Oh my gosh, I slept for over three hours."

"OK… why are you acting like that is a bad thing?" Liesel asked.

"I…" She trailed off. She was not ready to tell them about Gerhardt possibly meeting her here tonight. "It's only that I can't believe I slept so long."

"Well, you must have been tired. Besides, it's always nice to curl up in a warm blanket when it's cold. I would have taken a nap, too, if I had been home," Heidi said.

Eva sat back down on the couch and tried to process what happened. Did Gerhardt come by while she was sleeping, and she didn't hear him, or did he not come by at all? If he did not come by, was it because he didn't get the message, or did he decide he did not want to see her? The likely answer worried her because it was probably the latter.

"Are you alright, Eva?" Liesel asked.

"Yes, I'm fine. I'm still trying to wake up." He probably wasn't coming, but she did not want to give up yet. "I think I'm going to go to bed." Eva went to her room and closed the door for some privacy, then walked to the window to watch for Gerhardt. She pulled the curtain aside and peered out, not changing into her pajamas in case he came. There was a knock on the bedroom door. She moved away from the window and sat on the bed. "Come in."

The door cracked open, and Liesel peeked her head in. "Eva, you are acting strange. Are you sure you are alright?"

The truth was, she didn't know if she was OK. Not knowing if he was coming or her own feelings about it made her anxious.

Liesel, noticing her silence, came into the room and closed the door, then sat beside her on the bed. "Is it that officer again? Has he done something else?"

"No, it's not him. Do you remember the officer I told you I knew in France?"

"Yes."

"Well, he works here in Berlin at the Reichstag. I have suspected for a long time now but never went to find out until today. I felt like I should warn him about the threat the other officer made. I think I owe him that."

"You met with him today?"

"No, I left a note with a secretary there, and she said she would give it to him. I am not allowed in the department he works in. I told him in the note to meet me here at the apartment after he got off work, but he hasn't come."

"Do you think maybe the secretary never gave it to him?"

"No, I think she did. He probably doesn't want to see me. The last time we spoke, I said some very mean things to him. I think he no longer wants anything to do with me. If I were in his shoes, I would probably feel the same way, although I was justified in some of the things I said. He was part of the reason some people very dear to me lost their lives."

Liesel put a hand on Eva's knee. "Are you sure that you want to see him again?"

"I am. I can't let this be it for us. As crazy as it sounds, despite what he did, I still love him. I have to warn him, but how will I do that if he won't see me?"

"Keep trying. He can only avoid you for so long."

"The problem is, if that officer does what he has threatened, I don't know how much time I have left to be a free woman. He will come for us. It is only a matter of time before we are both behind bars or up against an execution wall." The only reason Eva could speak of this so easily was that it did not feel real to her. Lately, all she felt was numb inside. It was like her mind flipped a switch to protect her from all the things that were happening, but she knew behind the wall of self-preservation was a mountain of turmoil, chaos, and confusion.

Liesel leaned over and wrapped her arms around Eva's shoulders. She could not understand what Eva was going through because she had never been in her shoes, but Eva appreciated the emotional support. Liesel held her in a compassionate embrace of friendship but said nothing. She let go and looked Eva in the eyes as they glistened with fresh tears.

"Eva, don't lose hope. He will find you."

Eva forced a smile, then shook her head. "I don't think so."

"You don't know that. Why don't you get some sleep and try again. The second time might be different."

Chapter Four

✠

February 26th, 1941

Blood sprayed from the open artery of the man's leg onto Eva's white apron when she moved it to the side. Placing her hands over the gash, she pressed firmly against the wound. "Where is Dr. Gaebel?" she called to the other nurse.

"I don't know. I haven't seen him today."

"Where are all the other doctors?" It was odd to not have one roaming the hospital.

"Dr. Helsing and Dr. Koch are in surgery."

"And Dr. Möller?"

"I think he is doing rounds."

"Go get him now. If this man doesn't get into surgery soon, he will die."

Brigitta ran into the hospital while Eva kept her hands

firmly on the man's leg.

That morning, before the sun was up, British RAF bombers flew an early morning bombing raid. By the afternoon, the hospital had been swamped with the wounded, from the elderly to little children. Usually, the ambulances would pull in front of the hospital and unload the patients as the nurses and doctors waited outside to evaluate them. They would check to see which ones were critical, but today, they were short three doctors who were in Austria for a medical conference, so choosing the patients that would be treated first fell mainly upon the nurses. The man that Eva was holding her hands to was a high-ranking German officer, an older man, probably in his mid-fifties. Scratches were bleeding through the dirt and soot that covered his face; it was even in his nose and ears.

Brigitta returned with Dr. Möller, who came to stand next to Eva. "Move your hands so I can see the wound."

Eva lifted her hands from the man's leg, and blood rushed out of the wound and dripped onto the ground. He surveyed the opening. "We need to get him in the operating room now." He took hold of the handles at one end of the stretcher and waited for Eva to do the same. She tore a piece of material off the man's shirt and tied it around the wound to slow the blood flow, then they lifted the stretcher.

"Brigitta, get Frau Wagner. We will need her in the operating room, and after you find her scrub in, I will need all of you," Dr. Möller instructed.

Brigitta disappeared down the hall, and then Eva and Dr. Möller carried the stretcher in the opposite direction. They set it on an empty table, and Eva grabbed the man's feet as Dr. Möller wrapped his arms around the man's chest, and they lifted him onto a surgical table. Dr. Möller put on his surgical gown and then went to the sink to prepare for surgery. He was getting ready to put on his gloves when Brigitta and Frau Wagner came into the operating room.

"Let me help you with those," Frau Wagner told him.

"Brigitta," Dr. Möller called. "Take over for Eva so she can scrub in for surgery."

"Yes, doctor." She came around the table and waited for Eva to move her hands. Eva lifted them, and then Brigitta pressed hers on the leg.

Her hands were sticky, covered with thick, already drying blood. Eva went to the sink and washed it from her hands, the red water swirling down the drain. This was a site she saw almost every day. She dried her hands and then put on a surgical gown. While tying, Dr. Möller went to the table and looked at the patient, and Frau Wagner gathered the tools they would need. Pulling on a pair of gloves, Eva came to stand beside Dr. Möller.

"We can't wait any longer. We have to start now," he said.

Frau Wagner pushed the small table with the tools over to the bedside. "I will go get ready." She hurried over to the sink.

"I'm going to clamp off the artery to slow the bleeding while I sew it back together. We are going to have to work fast if we want to save the leg, so you need to be ready to do exactly what I tell you when I say it. Can you do that, or do you want Frau Wagner to step in?"

There was a fleeting moment of doubt that she could not do it, that maybe she would not be fast enough, but deep down, she knew she could. "Yes, I can do it."

He nodded. "Give me the Hämostyptikum then." Eva handed him the hemostat. "Alright, Brigitta, move your hands and step away."

Brigitta lifted her hands and took a step back from the table.

He untied the piece of shirt, and blood squirted from the leg, running onto the table. Eva cut the pant leg away with scissors, and Dr. Möller pulled the wound apart and found the side of the artery closest to the heart and clamped it. Immediately, the blood flow slowed. "Give me the eye needle with the suture." Eva handed him the already threaded needle.

Frau Wagner came to stand at the left side of Dr. Möller and assist if needed.

"Give me the needle holder," he instructed.

Eva handed him the needle holder, which looked like small pliers. He took them from her and clamped them on the needle. "Clamp the wound open."

Eva put the clamp on the skin and gently tugged the wound apart, holding it open; then, he began sewing the two ends of the artery together. He worked as quickly as he could without making a mistake; it was a delicate balance between saving the leg while at the same time not getting sloppy. Time was of the essence.

He tied the thread off and clipped it. "Hand me another

needle."

She took the needle from his hand and then gave him a freshly threaded one. "Take the clamps off."

Eva removed the clamps, and he pulled the skin together. "Hold it here."

She pinched the skin where he had placed it, and he sewed it together, again tying it off.

"Good, I think we finished in time to save the leg, but I won't know for sure yet. We should have a better idea in a few days." He pulled off his gloves and threw them in the trash. "Clean the leg up and bandage it," he instructed, looking at Frau Wagner.

"Yes, Doctor. Brigitta, bring me some warm water and gauze."

The gloves made a smacking sound when Eva pulled them off. She threw them in the trash and followed Dr. Möller out of the operating room.

"You did very well in there, as I knew you would."

"Thank you. It might not have looked like it, but I was nervous. I didn't know if we could save his life, much less his leg," she admitted.

"I wasn't sure either. Although you were nervous, you still performed well. I'm going to have you help more in the operating room."

"Frau Wagner won't like that."

"Well, it's a good thing I don't need her permission then." He shot her a smile.

"You are right. You don't need it."

"Why don't you take a quick break, and we can do the

rounds together," he said.

"Sitting down sounds really good right now after standing all night."

"I'm sure. Go sit for a few minutes, then meet me in the east ward."

"Alright."

She followed the long corridor to the nurse's station as she took off her blood-stained apron. There was a sense of relief that they saved the man's life because she knew that bleeding to death was a likely outcome. She tossed the apron in the bin for dirty work clothes and sat at the little table in the center of the room. She sighed, then folded her arms on the table and laid her head on them, thoughts going to Gerhardt and last night. Why did he not come? It was easy to pretend that he never got the message instead of it being him not wanting to see her. She didn't know what to do now. If he truly had no desire to see her or have anything to do with her anymore, then it made staying in Germany pointless, but she didn't know where else she would go. Jon still had not found a way for her to get home. Being in Germany was going to get harder for her very soon. Some days, every German reminded her of him, and she lived in a land surrounded by them. She would have to find a way to endure it for now. There weren't a lot of choices left.

She leaned back in the chair and glanced at the clock on the wall; it was almost time to head back to the patient ward. Standing from the chair, she went to the cabinet and took out a clean apron. She pulled the door open as Heidi was coming in.

"Eva, where have you been?"

"Assisting Dr. Möller with a surgery. He says that he is going to have me help with more from now on."

"That is great, but Frau Wagner will not like it, though. She believes it is she who should choose the nurses who assist with the surgeries. After all, they are her nurses," Heidi said in a mocking tone.

Eva smiled. "That is what she thinks. She hates to admit that the doctors can overrule her. If she had her way, she would be running the whole hospital."

"I don't doubt that. So where are you going now?"

"I'm going to the patient ward to meet Dr. Möller."

"To check on the patients?"

"Yes. I think he wants to check on the one who recently came out of surgery."

"Which one is that?"

"Do you remember the man that came in with a severed artery in his right leg?"

"The officer, right?"

"Yes. We managed to save his life, and we think the leg, too."

"It would be a miracle if you did. Was Frau Wagner helping assist with the surgery?"

Eva couldn't help the smile that cracked at the corner of her mouth. "No, she watched me assist, then was told to dress the wound."

"No… really?" Heidi's mouth opened wide when she said no.

"Yup," Eva said, her smile growing.

“She is probably so mad right now.”

“Frau Wagner hasn’t said anything to me, at least not yet.”

“Well, I will be surprised if she doesn’t,” Heidi postulated, pulling her apron over her head.

Eva looked at her watch. “I really have to go. Dr. Möller is waiting for me.”

“Alright. Good job impressing the doctors.”

“Not all the doctors,” Eva corrected. “Only one.”

“Dr. Koch doesn’t count. He is an ass,” Heidi blurted.

“Yes, he is. I’ll see you at home in a few hours.”

“Alright. Remember, we are doing something to take your mind off things.”

“I haven’t forgotten,” Eva called behind as she headed towards the patient ward. Heidi and Liesel knew she was hurting because Gerhardt never showed, and like her, they were worried about what would come of the situation with Bauer. But she couldn’t sit at home, scared of what might happen, so she continued to go to work.

She entered through the double doors to the patient ward and found Dr. Möller standing by the bedside of the man they had recently finished surgery on. “How is he doing?” she asked.

“He seems to be stable. He should be awake by tomorrow, and we can see how he is feeling. You are working tomorrow, aren’t you?”

“I am.”

“Good. I won’t be in until later in the day. I have some things in the morning that I must attend to. Make sure you check on him first before any of the other patients. The officers always take precedence over the enlisted men."

She stared down at the patient, then brought her gaze to Dr. Möller, shocked by what he was telling her to do.

He noticed the look on her face. "I know it sounds awful, but that is how it needs to be. In war, officers are worth three enlisted men, if not more, depending on their rank and experience. If you want to win a war, it is imperative to keep as many of your officers as you can alive, especially the seasoned ones."

"Yes, but their lives aren't worth more than the enlisted men."

"No, they are not, but the role they play is. Without good leaders, the military would be in chaos, and we would have no hope of winning the war."

"I guess if you look at it like that, it makes sense," she agreed, though it was sad.

"I know you don't want to show one patient preference over another, but sometimes we have to," he added.

"I'll check on him first when I get here tomorrow, promise."

He smiled warmly at her. "Thank you, Eva. You are a good girl." He patted her on the back. "Let's finish up, and then you can go home."

She nodded, then walked with him along the beds as they checked the patients and updated the charts.

"This is the last patient. I'll take care of it. You go."

"Are you sure? I don't mind staying a few more minutes."

"I've got it."

She handed him the chart. "Have a good night then, Doctor."

"Eva, you know to call me Klaus."

"I do. Only it's strange calling you by your first name. It seems disrespectful."

"It is not disrespectful because we are friends, and I told you to call me by my first name. You can call me Doctor whenever we are with the other doctors or nurses, but call me Klaus when no one else is with us."

"Alright, Klaus."

A smile broke at the corner of his mouth. "That's better."

"I'll see you tomorrow."

"I should be here no later than two."

"Do you want me to report to your office when you get in?"

"No, why don't you meet me at Oberst Heinrich Schmitt's bed, and we can check his leg together. I know you will have already seen him when I come in, but I still need to look at the stitches and make sure his vitals are stable."

"I will meet you at his bed tomorrow, then."

Eva went back to the nurse's lounge, removed her apron and hat, and stuffed them in her locker. It had been a long day, and she was ready to leave. Heidi and Liesel had already gone home and were waiting for her. They didn't say what they had planned, but she could really use a distraction right now. She slipped on her coat, then pulled on the worn leather gloves and wrapped the thick knitted scarf around her neck, ready to leave when Frau Wagner came into the nurse's lounge.

"Fräulein Abrams, follow me to my office, please."

Eva suspected this had something to do with what happened in the operating room. Frau Wagner probably wanted to talk in her office instead of the nurse's lounge because it was more private, and it made her feel in control and powerful sitting behind the big desk while the person on the other side sat in a small, low-to-the-floor chair. It made her seem more intimidating, and Frau Wagner liked that.

Eva followed her down the familiar, off-white, high-ceilinged corridor to her office on the main floor. They entered the office, then Frau Wagner closed the door and took her chair behind the desk.

"Have a seat." She pointed to the chair across from her.

Eva sat down, crossed her legs, and folded her hands over her knees. The idea was to control her body language and prepare for what she knew was coming.

"Fräulein Abrams, are you the head nurse, or am I?"

"You are, Frau Wagner."

"Then why were you the one who assisted the doctor with the surgery today?"

"Because he asked me to."

"That is no excuse, Fräulein Abrams. You know I assist the doctors with all the complicated surgeries, especially on any high-profile patients."

"What was I supposed to do when he asked me?" She already knew what the answer was going to be.

"You are to tell them no, that I am the one who assists first. I don't know what you have going on with Dr. Möller, but it needs to stop. If you think he is your way of climbing to the top, know that you are wrong. You will only succeed in ruining any chance you have of remaining at this hospital."

"Frau Wagner, I can promise you that nothing is going on between Dr. Möller and me. He thinks I am an excellent nurse; that is all. And I don't want your job. I'm simply doing what I'm told."

"Then do what you are told now, and don't let this happen again. I am your boss, not the doctors. You do what I tell you because my word will always be the final one."

How did she respond to this? Dr. Möller would ask her to assist as the primary nurse again, and how could she tell him no? But if she said yes, Frau Wagner would make sure that she never worked at the hospital again. The only thing to do was talk to Dr. Möller about it. She was confident he would have a solution to the problem.

"What do you think Dr. Möller will say if I start telling him no? He will wonder about the sudden change in my willingness to help."

"I will have a word with him and make certain that he knows he has overstepped the bounds of what is professional."

Eva would not tell Frau Wagner not to speak to him because it would backfire. Dr. Möller wouldn't let Frau Wagner tell him what to do, nor would he stop asking her to help. He did not take kindly to being bossed around, especially by a nurse. It was likely that he would start asking her to assist even more now because he knew that Frau Wagner didn't want her to. The downside to him continuing to ask was that her relationship with Frau Wagner would become even more strained than it already was.

"If that is what you think is best," Eva said.

"It is what's best. I see that you were getting ready to go home, so I will let you be on your way."

Eva stood up from her chair, thinking that she had handled the situation well. All the times Bauer had interrogated her made her tougher, thick-skinned, so to speak, or she liked to think.

"Eva," Frau Wagner said as she put her gloved hand on the doorknob.

Eva turned and looked back into the room. "Yes?"

"I know you are good at what you do, and someday maybe you will be a head nurse, but now is not that time. You are young and less experienced than me, and that is why I am the head nurse and help with certain operations and not you."

"I understand, although I can't help but feel you are trying to hold me back. Your attitude towards me is never welcoming, but I'm not sure why."

"It's not that I don't like you. It's that the things which are still beyond your skills are exactly what I find you doing, even though you are not ready for them. You think you know more than you actually do. You walk around here high and mighty like you are better than all the other nurses, but you are not."

"I don't think I am better, but I am more experienced than you give credit for."

"Shut the door on your way out," she said, picking up a pen from her desk and looking away from Eva, clearly not wanting to hear more from her.

Eva walked out of the office and closed the door. This was going to be a long battle, and Frau Wagner was never going to give an inch or let her have the credit she was due.

She pushed open the front door of the hospital, and a gust of cold wind hit her in the face. Tears welled in her eyes. She tugged the scarf up over her mouth and nose and put her hands in the coat's pockets. She carefully went down the slick steps, passing some nurses coming up, then cut through the hospital grounds, heading towards the street to shorten the walking time to the trolley stop.

While walking through the hospital grounds, she noticed two men in suits and overcoats standing near the trees that lined the walkway; they were looking in her direction. When she was halfway to the street, they moved away from the trees and headed across the lawn towards the road, trailing behind. She kept a steady pace but continually looked over her shoulder. Once the ground changed from the crunchy grass to solid pavement, she picked up her pace. The two men strode a steady thirty feet behind, and every time she quickened her steps, they did the same. She was walking as fast as she could now without sprinting. What if they were Gestapo? They often wore suits and trench coats and not uniforms to blend in and look like civilians.

She cast another nervous glance over her shoulder, but

they had not lost an inch. Their pace kept up with hers. Bauer was SS, but she wasn't sure which kind. There were several branches of the SS, and because Bauer had brought her in every time she had been arrested, he was most likely in the Gestapo and sent these men after her. He had always been present when she was brought in before, but maybe he decided to send someone else this time. It made sense that he would use others to do his dirty work.

Her heart pounded in quick thuds against her ribs, and the urge to run was intensifying. The adrenaline raced through her body, and the cold air burned her lungs and nose, making her eyes water. The trolley stop was straight ahead, and she wondered if she should keep walking, but there were a lot of people waiting. Maybe it would be better to get in the middle of the crowd. Perhaps then the men wouldn't try to take her.

Eva increased her speed to a jog, hoping not to slip on the ice, but the shoes were hardly getting traction. Turning to look back one more time, her eyes locked on the men. They were still walking at their fast pace behind her. She broke into a full-on run, and when reaching the crowd, she pushed her way to the middle, some of the people glaring as she squeezed past them.

She peered in between two of the people waiting for the trolley and watched as the two men following her went past, only glancing in her direction briefly before they walked by, continuing down the snowy sidewalk and turning a corner.

Thinking she was being followed had triggered the primal fight or flight. The massive flood of adrenaline that shot through her like a drug warmed her body as the rush of blood to every part of her increased like someone had set a match beneath her center, igniting a slow, steady burn deep in the pit of her stomach. Her pulse came in hot waves as her heart pounded in her ears with each breath.

She scanned the sidewalk at the corner of the building where the men had turned, but they weren't coming back for her. Realizing that she might have overreacted and maybe they weren't following her, sparked doubt about her sanity. Bauer had driven her to have this paranoid, anxious mindset. He had sown the unwanted fear of men in suits, men in uniforms, or any man that was German.

The crowd probably thought she was crazy, and it was possible they were right. She almost didn't want to wait for the trolley anymore, but it was so cold she didn't want to walk home. Going to the back of the crowd, she waited there until the tram came, then got on last, still watching out of the corner of her eye for the two men, finding it difficult to override the internal sense that there was danger. She was sure Bauer would come for her again one day, but the next time might be her last.

She stepped off the tram and hurried the few blocks to the apartment, her shoes sloshing in the partly thawed snow. The adrenaline was at a normal level now and she no longer felt hot. The whole ordeal left her body weak and shaky, allowing the cold to penetrate deeper. All she wanted was to take a hot shower and crawl into bed, but she had promised to go out tonight. Heidi and Liesel were probably wondering what was keeping her.

Heidi and Liesel were sitting at the kitchen table having a cup of tea when she walked into the apartment.

"Eva, where were you?" Liesel asked.

"I got held up. Frau Wagner wanted to talk to me in her office. It upset her that I assisted Dr. Möller in surgery today. She feels like I am overstepping my bounds, as well as him, and that I want her job."

"I knew this would happen when you told me you helped with that surgery today," Heidi said.

"I know, but what am I going to do? Tell Dr. Möller no next time he asks me to help?"

"Maybe that is what you will have to do," Liesel advised.

Eva tossed her coat, gloves, and scarf on the couch and sat down. "No. She is going to talk with Dr. Möller, and he will more than likely tell her to stay out of it, that he can choose his nurses."

"And how will you know if that is the way it goes?" Liesel sounded doubtful.

"Well, if he stops letting me assist him, then I will ask him about it."

Heidi took a sip of her tea, setting the cup back on the saucer with a clink. "You know she is jealous of you, right?"

"I'm not sure that's it. What do I have for her to be jealous of?"

"You are a fantastic nurse. Why do you think she suspects you want her job?"

"She is not jealous of me. It's because she is an angry person. Enough talk about Frau Wagner." Eva wanted to leave the drama at the hospital and not bring it home. "What are we doing tonight?"

"I thought we could go to the movies," Heidi said.

Eva hadn't been to the movies since being in this time. The thought of going to an old-fashioned movie theater and watching a black-and-white film seemed fun. It had never crossed her mind to go to one before.

"That sounds amazing. I would love that."

"We know you need a break, something to get your mind off of what has been going on," Liesel said.

"I do." The incident today with the men trickled back, giving her goosebumps.

"We better go if we are to catch the five-thirty showing," Liesel said, standing to put her cup in the sink.

"What movie are we watching?" Eva asked.

"It's a surprise."

Eva sighed. "Fair enough." Standing, she took the coat and scarf from the couch, put them on, then stuck the gloves in her pocket. It really didn't matter what they watched. Any movie would help distract her. "I'm ready."

They took the tram to Berlin because it had the best cinemas. There was a tram stop only a block from the cinema, and Eva was happy they didn't have to walk in the cold for very long. When they arrived at the ticket booth, Eva read the names of the movies that were showing. There were only three films playing. Wunschkonzert, Jud Süß, and Der Ewige Jude.

"I hope we are not watching Jud Süß or Der Ewige Jude," Eva said.

“No, I don’t want to see those, and we knew you didn’t either,” Liesel assured her.

Heidi said, “We were thinking about watching Wunschkonzert.”

“What is it about?”

“It’s a love story about this soldier who falls in love with a girl, and they plan to get married, but before they can, he has to leave suddenly on a secret mission. She doesn’t hear from him for years, and in that time, a childhood friend of hers asks for her hand in marriage, but then he goes off to war too. She later goes looking for her first love and finds him. They write letters for a while before he goes on another mission, as does the second man. Then they both go missing.”

“Heidi, I think you told me everything but the ending.”

“Sorry, I tend to give too much away.”

“It’s alright, let’s go watch,” Eva told Heidi, then walked up to the ticket window.

“We are getting your ticket, Eva,” Liesel informed her.

“I can buy my ticket.”

“No, we are taking you out for a fun evening, so we will pay.”

Liesel pulled some money from her purse and slid it on the counter through the hole in the glass to the man on the other side. “Three tickets, please.”

He tore three tickets off the roll and slid them back to her with the change. “Enjoy the show. I hear it’s a good one.”

“Thank you. I’m sure we will.”

“Liesel, you didn’t have to pay for all three of us.”

“I didn’t. Heidi already gave me the money for her ticket.”

Eva looked at Heidi, who gave her a smile. They went inside and found seats as the movie was starting. Half of the people in the theater were soldiers, which made her uncomfortable. She realized Liesel had chosen the seats that were the farthest from them and was thankful.

The room darkened, and music played overhead. Then, the screen lit up in black and white as names were displayed across it. She had forgotten that old movies always gave the credits first.

It was strange to watch a film in German. Her German was good, but she still had difficulty understanding some parts. Surprisingly, she understood most of the movie and enjoyed the story. Even though there was underlying German propaganda in the plot, but she would be shocked if there wasn’t.

After the last scene, the ending credits traveled up the screen, then the lights in the room brightened.

“Did you like it?” Heidi asked.

“I did, although some of it was a little difficult for me to understand.”

“You didn’t understand the plot?”

“No, Heidi, she meant she couldn’t understand everything they were saying,” Liesel was more clipped than she should have been.

“Ohhh, sorry,” Heidi apologized.

“It’s that some of the dialogue was a little hard to follow.

But I understood the movie, and I liked it. It was sad that she didn't get to be with her first love, though."

"It was, but it's only a movie," Liesel said to her.

The movie hit closer to home than Eva would have liked. "I know. We better go home before it gets too late."

Heidi looked at her watch. "Oh, I was hoping we could eat out, but the movie lasted longer than I had expected."

"We can have leftover soup," Eva reminded her.

"We had that last night and the night before when we made it."

"Don't worry, tomorrow we will make another dinner we can eat for days," Liesel said, smiling at Heidi.

"If you are trying to make me feel better, you're not," Heidi glowered.

"I'm not trying to make you feel better. It's called sarcasm. This is wartime, Heidi, and we don't have the luxury of eating out every time we get tired of eating leftovers."

"I agree with Heidi that it gets tiring, but it is necessary, so you are both right." Eva didn't want them to antagonize each other.

Sometimes, Heidi and Liesel's personalities could not be more different. Heidi was what you could call ditzy but optimistic, while Liesel was highly logical and a realist. Eva viewed herself as being somewhere between the two of them.

"Well, let's go home and eat those leftovers," Eva said, linking her arm through Heidi's.

They got on the tram for the long ride back to Potsdam,

and Eva sat in between Liesel and Heidi.

"Do you think that officer will bother you again?" Liesel asked.

"Yes, I do."

"Why?"

"That man doesn't give up easily. And because he is so full of hate and malice. He resents me, and there is an undeniable animosity between us."

"People like that hate everyone. His heart is probably black from having no soul, and I doubt he is capable of feeling any normal human emotions, like sympathy or compassion. There is a reason they put men like that in those kinds of positions," Liesel told her.

"Well, it obviously doesn't bother him to do abhorrent things," Eva said, remembering everything he had done to her.

"He will give up because you have done nothing wrong," Heidi said.

The truth was that Eva had and was currently doing things that made her guilty, and in the eyes of the Germans, were grounds for arrest and execution.

"It doesn't matter if I'm guilty or not, Heidi. All they have to do is think I am and want me out of the way bad enough."

"Maybe you should leave Germany." Liesel's face was serious.

"And go where? I can't go home, and if I stay in Europe, they will most likely find me again."

Liesel and Heidi were quiet, only occasionally looking at

Eva. How did they respond when it was their people doing it to her?

Chapter Five

✠

February 27th, 1941

Eva checked on the officer whose surgery she assisted with, as Dr. Möller instructed. He had not yet woken up, so she continued with her usual rounds.

Three new nurses had arrived that morning, and Eva was told to take them with her while doing the rounds and show them how things were done. She wondered if Frau Wagner had done that to keep her out of the operating room.

"Do we have to check the patient's pulse every time?" asked Christa König, the youngest of the three nurses.

"Yes, every time. It is to ensure that they are still stable and nothing has changed."

"Isn't it exciting getting to work with all these men every day?"

Eva looked up from the chart, hardly believing she had said that. "No, Nurse Roth, it is not. It is not exciting working with men who are in pain and dying, watching them cry and scream out in agony as they drown in their own blood. And the ones with less severe conditions are focused on getting better so they can get back to fighting this war. And you, as a nurse, should only be concerned with making certain they get the care they need so they can get better, not flirting with them or anything other than your duties. You are not here to find a husband or boyfriend." Eva quickly looked back down at the clipboard. She had not expected to go off on the new nurse like that. She was on edge as of late, and everything bothered her more than usual.

"Don't you think it would boost their morale to see the nurses more and have them flirt with them? Some of these men have not seen a woman in weeks, or even months," Karin Roth said.

Eva looked up at her. "Maybe, but I think it would do more harm than good. And if I were you, I wouldn't say things like that around Frau Wagner. I'm sure she has told you they strictly prohibit the nurses from fraternizing with the doctors or patients."

The girl looked down, almost seeming a little embarrassed. "She did."

"Then I would listen if you want to stay here." Eva checked her watch. It was ten till two. "I have a patient who needs my attention. Continue changing the bedpans, then bring the patients their food. The laundry needs to be washed as well. You can start on it after the food has been passed out. You should report to Frau Wagner when you are finished."

"Yes, Nurse Abrams," they said in unison, then disappeared into the room with patients.

Eva went to Oberst Heinrich Schmitt's bed, took the clipboard from the end, and sat on the edge of the mattress. She was checking his pulse when he opened his eyes; they were red-rimmed and bloodshot. He looked around the room, then focused his gaze on her.

"Where am I?"

"You are at the Beelitz Heilstätten hospital."

He scanned the room again, then set his eyes back on her. "The last thing I remember is being in Schönefeld, coming into Berlin for a meeting. Then there was an explosion, and I don't remember anything after that."

"There was another raid. A bomb must have hit near your car."

He creased his forehead, pulling his thick brows together. "You are not German?"

"No… I'm American." She wondered if that was going to be an issue for him.

"An American here in Germany, that is unusual," he said, then started coughing.

Eva put her stethoscope on his chest and listened for any unusual sounds in his lungs. "I suppose it is. I have not met another American since being here." She put the stethoscope back around her neck.

He cleared his throat and swallowed hard. "And I doubt you will." Pulling in a deep breath, he held it, then blew it out through his pursed lips.

"Is your leg hurting?"

“It hurts like the devil.”

She looked at his chart. “You are ready for some more morphine. Let me go get it.” She stood up from his bed and went to the large medicine cabinet in the patient ward, took out a vial of morphine, then returned to his bed and sat back down. She pulled the blanket back. “I'm going to stick it in your leg.” There was no response from him, so she poked the needle in his upper thigh, but he didn't flinch. “In a few seconds, the pain should be gone,” she told him.

“I can already feel it lessening.”

“Good.” She looked at her watch. “The doctor will be here in a few minutes to look at your leg.”

“So, will it need to be amputated?”

“I don't believe so. We worked hard yesterday to save it. It's good I saw you when I did, or we might not have been so lucky.”

“You are the one who alerted the doctor?”

“Yes, I knew you had a severed artery and quickly sent for him. You didn't have a lot of time. We had to get you in right then.”

“Well, I am grateful to you, then. Thank you for your fast thinking. I would like to repay you for what you have done for me.”

She shook her head. “You don't have to. It was my job.”

“But I do. A ball is being held on Saturday, March 29th, at the Hotel Adlon at six o'clock. When you get to the entrance, tell them I am expecting you, and they will let you in. I would be delighted to have you as my guest.”

“And what about the doctor who did the operation on

your leg? Is he invited too?"

"Of course. When he comes to check on me, I will extend an invitation to him as well."

Dr. Möller would most likely not go to a ball, but it was unfair that she was getting all the praise for saving his life. It also made her feel a little strange that he was inviting her to a formal ball. The ball was the same week as the attack on the German high command.

"How are you feeling today, Oberst Heinrich Schmitt?" Dr. Möller said as he came up behind Eva.

She quickly stood up from the bed. "Doctor, I have already checked his vitals and given him morphine."

"Good. Let's have a look at that leg," Dr. Möller said, pulling the blanket back. "Hand me the scissors."

Eva passed them to him, and he gently cut the gauze away from the wound, pulling it out from under the leg, and handed it to Eva along with the scissors. He leaned closer to inspect the stitches. "It does not seem to be infected, and there is minimal bleeding." He looked to Eva. "Put a clean bandage on, and we can check it again tomorrow."

"Alright." She took a roll of gauze, a towel, and a bottle of alcohol from the rolling cart.

"Your leg is doing better than I had expected, but how are you feeling?" he asked, looking at the colonel.

"As long as I'm on the morphine, I feel alright."

"Any nausea at all."

"A little."

"It's probably from the morphine. I can give you something for it?"

"Yes. Thank you."

"I will have the nurse bring it to you."

"Are you the doctor who performed the operation?"

"I am."

"The nurse here told me she is the one who found me, and I have thanked her for her part in saving my life. I would now like to offer my gratitude to you as well for saving my life."

"You are welcome, but there is no need to thank me."

"I have invited this young lady to the ball we are having in March. You, too, are invited."

"Thank you for the offer, but I am needed here, so I will have to respectfully decline."

"I understand. You do our soldiers a great service. If you change your mind, the offer stands."

"I'll keep that in mind."

He patted Eva on the arm. "I'll leave you to it."

"Oh, can I talk to you after I finish here?" she asked.

"Sure, come up to my office when you are done." He turned and left the room.

Eva wet the cotton with alcohol and dabbed it on the wound, then wrapped the bandage around his leg.

"I know the doctor might not make it, but I hope to see you there," he told her.

"I will try to come." Eva honestly didn't know if she could make it, not with the attack happening that same week. Did she even want to go?

She pulled the blanket back over him. "I'll come by later when it's time for another dose of morphine." She hung the clipboard back on the end of the bed, then climbed the stairs to Dr. Möller's office. She knocked on the door, then opened it and peeked in.

"Come in, Eva," he said, looking up from the papers on his desk. She stepped in and closed the door, then sat in the chair at his desk. "What did you want to talk about?"

She took in a deep breath and slowly released it. "I wanted to let you know that Frau Wagner asked to see me yesterday and told me you and I overstepped our bounds in the operating room and that I am not to assist as the leading nurse anymore. She is planning on talking with you today about it."

"Well, I can't say I'm surprised, but I don't believe that conversation will go the way she thinks it will."

"Please don't fight with her about it. She will take it out on me because she can't take it out on you."

"If she comes after you again when I ask you to assist, come straight to me."

"She basically threatened to fire me if I accepted the next time you asked me to help."

"Eva, let me worry about Frau Wagner. When she and I are done talking, she might be cross with you, but she won't do anything. I can assure you when we are done, she won't threaten you again."

Eva forced a smile. She appreciated his help and wanted him to know it, though everything about the situation was unpleasant. He was going to deal with it, but she hated having someone else take care of her problems for her. This situation, however, she was not in a position to fix. He had the power to deal with it, and she didn't. “Thank you. I would not have said anything, but I knew it wouldn’t get better, only worse if I didn't do something.”

“You were right, too. Don't worry about her. She is a good nurse but can be set in her ways.”

“I think she believes I am trying to replace her.”

“I know she does, and I will also set her straight on that. No one is taking her place, and I should reassure her of that.”

“You should. She is irreplaceable. On a different topic, why don't you come to the ball with me? I don't want to go by myself. It will feel strange, and frankly, the thought makes me a little uncomfortable.”

The corner of his mouth pulled up, and his warm eyes beamed at her. “I will think about it, but the truth is, I'm not good at that kind of thing. And I am needed here.”

“You are going to let me go to a ball with all of those German officers alone? I will have no idea what to do or how to act around them.”

“You would dance, I hope.”

“With whom? If you come, we can both stand in a corner as we drink, and no one will ask me to dance.”

He pursed his lips. “Would it really be so bad if someone asked you to dance?”

“I don't think I'm ready for that, even if it’s only dancing.”

“Let me think about it. We still have a while. If there aren't too many patients that day, I will go. But if I am needed here, you will be going alone and will have to fight the men off with that sharp tongue of yours.”

She raised an eyebrow. “I will be nice. I won't leave them with a bitter heart of rejection. I'll let them down easy.”

He chuckled. “I know you will.”

She stood. “I'm going to check on the other patients, and then I'll take my lunch.”

“Alright. I already ate lunch and have some paperwork to do, so I will be up here for a while if you need me.”

“I'll see you on the floor then.” She walked to the door.

“Eva…”

She paused in the doorway and turned back to him. “Yes.”

“Remember what I said. Don't worry about Frau Wagner. Focus on your work, and you’ll be fine.”

She gave a faint smile. “I'll try not to.”

As Eva descended the stairs, she could see the three new nurses standing around a patient's bed. One laughed, but Eva could not see their faces or the face of the patient, only their backs.

“What is going on?” Eva asked as she approached them from behind.

They turned to look at her. “We were talking with a patient,” said Christa.

“Frau Wagner will be upset if she sees you spending too much time with any of the male patients.”

“We were getting ready to leave.”

“This is the last time I'm going to warn you. If you keep doing this and are caught, that's on you,” she told them.

They exchanged glances and, one by one, went their separate ways. She could not believe they were being so foolish, but then again, who was she to criticize? She was doing far stupider things than those three nurses were and lying about them.

She stopped at the young soldier's bed with the broken leg she had helped four days ago. She read his chart, then pulled the blanket back. She took the scissors and cut the bandage off. The swelling had gone down considerably. It was time to take an X-ray of it. She went to the side of his bed. “Peter, I'm going to take an X-ray of your leg.”

He opened his veiny red eyelids and looked up at her. “What?” His voice was faint.

“I said it's time to take you to get an X-ray. I'm going to help you into a wheelchair so that I can take you to another room. You should not feel much pain because of the morphine.”

“Alright. So, the doctor will know soon if he can save my leg?”

“Hopefully, yes.”

She took a wheelchair from the corner of the room and parked it next to his bed, pushing down the brakes on each wheel. She wrapped her arm around his upper ribcage under his arms and helped him from the bed and into the wheelchair. He grunted as she sat him down.

“Did that hurt?”

“It's not hurting now that I'm sitting.”

“It won't take long.” When they got to the room, she took the X-rays quickly, then brought him back to his bed and helped him into it. “I'll take these to the doctor, and he will come and talk with you about what is going to happen.”

“What do you think will happen?”

“I wish I knew. I'll be back soon.” She patted him lightly on the shoulder. “Try not to worry.” She left with the X-rays, then went upstairs to Dr. Möller's office and knocked on the door.

“Come in.”

Eva stepped into his office, shutting the door behind her. “I took the X-rays of the patient with the broken leg.” She laid them on his desk.

Dr. Möller took them, holding each one up to the light as he looked them over. He drew in a deep breath and sighed, laying them back on his desk. “I'm afraid I don't have good news.”

“He asked what was going to happen. I told him I didn't know. We didn't know yet. We only suspected, so I didn't want to take away any hope he has.”

“You were right to tell him that.” He took the X-rays from his desk and stood from his chair. “Well, let's give this young man an answer, but before we do, I want to look at them a little closer.”

She followed him back to the room where she took the X-rays. He hung them over the white glass and turned on the light that illuminated it from behind. She did not need to be a doctor to see the extent of the damage that had been done to the bone.

“That is what I thought. There is no way I can save his leg. We are going to have to amputate.”

Eva felt a twinge of sadness. Breaking it to him was going to be hard. “When will you do the surgery?”

“Today.”

Should we tell him now or wait until right before the operation?”

“I think it would be best to prepare him for it now.”

They left the X-ray room together, and she followed him to the patient ward. She watched as Dr. Möller broke the bad news to the young man, and as he cried, he reminded her of a child. He was innocent to her, and she truly felt bad for him. It was hard to imagine this boy with a gun killing people and playing at war. Despite what she thought, his innocence was probably all but gone now. She suspected he was no longer the same bright-eyed boy he was when he left home in his freshly pressed uniform, hugging his parents and thinking how proud he would make them. The idea of war and actually being in one were two very different things.

As Eva took hold of the end of the bed to help Dr. Möller push it to the operating room, the ground beneath her feet shook, and a loud explosion caused plaster to fall from the ceiling, landing at her feet, narrowly missing her. The air was thick with dust, and she could no longer see Dr. Möller at the other end of the bed.

Eva coughed several times. “Dr. Möller,” she called through the cloud, panicked, fearful that something had happened to him.

“I'm alright. We need to get this bed to the operating room. I will find an orderly to lead the way with a flashlight. Stay here.”

“Alright.” Eva could not see him leave, but she could hear his boots on the tile floor. It didn't take long for him to return with an orderly. The light beam shone through the haze that was beginning to settle.

“Ok, let's get this bed moving,” Dr. Möller called from the other end.

Eva took hold of the bed again and pushed as he pulled. “That bomb hit close. I think it damaged part of the hospital. It's odd that they are bombing during the day.”

“It is, but I think they are growing desperate. Let's hope only a few people were hurt. It will be hard now operating without the normal lights, especially in these conditions,” he said.

“But we shouldn't put it off. He won't make it if we wait too much longer.”

“I know. That is why we are going to do it now rather than wait.”

They pushed the bed into the operating room; all the while, Eva wondered if it was even going to be possible to perform the operation in the poor lighting and with a dust cloud around them. This would test her skills, patience, and her nerves in a way they had never been tried before. As they prepared for surgery, the bombing continued, shaking the hospital. It was going to be a long day.

Chapter Six

✠

Sunday, March 23rd, 1941

Although the air was still cool, the sun warmed her face. She welcomed the weather of spring as it finally melted the snow that had lingered through the month of February and the first week of March. While walking the streets of Berlin, her mind wondered again to Gerhardt and the fact that she still had not heard a word from him. It had been a month now since she dropped off the letter. She had even gone by the Reichstag and asked the receptionist if she had given him the note, and she assured her that she had. To her, it was clear that Gerhardt didn't want to see her, and God knew he had good reasons not to. She was more alone now than ever, and the increased bombings on Berlin were wreaking havoc on her nerves. She was a mess lately, and Liesel and Heidi noticed. It was difficult to keep it hidden completely.

The first bombing she was in had been the one at the hospital almost a month ago. She was lucky the plaster that fell from the ceiling hadn't hit her. It missed her by only inches. The surgery was challenging because as they operated, the bombings continued. The hospital had lost power, forcing them to finish the operation with only the light of flashlights. Despite the blast and the shaking, the surgery went well, and the boy was now back home with his family. She personally saw him off when he left and wished him well but knew he had an arduous journey ahead of him.

She continued turning down different streets to make it harder for her to be followed and easier to notice if someone was. If another person were to turn on more than two of the same streets, she would go in the opposite direction. She could not risk leading someone to their meeting place. It did not appear that she was being followed, so she continued zigzagging through the streets and alleyways until reaching the shopping plaza where they usually met. She went into the same store she always did and out the back to the alley. She turned left, walked past the first three stores, then entered through the back door of the store they always met in and down to the basement. When she opened the door to the tiny room, the only people there were Helmut and Lina. The others hadn't arrived yet.

"Eva, glad to see you. We are still waiting on Derek, Thomas, and Frank, who should be here shortly," Helmut said.

Lina said nothing but looked at her in askance. Eva did

not meet her gaze. Instead, she chose to look at the floor. Finally, she went to a chair in the corner of the room and sat down, but they didn't have to wait long when the door opened, and Derek entered the room.

"Where are the others?"

"Thomas and Frank should be here soon. Eva only showed up a few minutes ago, too."

Derek took off his hat and gloves and sat at the desk with the radio.

Eva looked down at her trembling hands and hoped no one else noticed them. She crossed her arms to stop her hands from shaking, or at least hide them. Her anxiety was through the roof. The bombing at the hospital had been the preverbal straw that broke the camel's back, and ever since then, she could not stop her hands from shaking anytime she was in an uncomfortable situation. She would take medicine to help calm her nerves, but the only ones available in the 1940s were in the opioid family and were highly addictive, and she knew from the experience of taking opium when her wrist was broken that it made her sick to her stomach.

It took Thomas and Frank longer to show up than Derek, but after what seemed like ages, they both came through the door.

"What kept you?" Helmut asked as they removed their coats.

"For a while, we thought someone might be following us, so we detoured westward until we lost them, then rounded back," Thomas said, glancing at Frank, then back to Helmut.

"You were being followed?" Helmut's face was tense.

"We are not sure, but we think we could have been, so we took precautions."

"And you are sure they did not follow you here?"

"We are sure," Frank assured him. "There was no one behind us the last eight blocks."

"Alright. Let's get this meeting underway. The longer we stay here, the more dangerous it is. This all needs to be coordinated exactly. It is imperative that everything goes as planned. We cannot afford any mistakes. If even one of us messes up, we will all go down. Remember, a single mistake could cost one or all of us our lives tomorrow or down the road. Eva, you will ride with me and shoot from the passenger window. We will sit and wait one block from the building while Frank and Lina plant the bombs. When those go off, and everyone is panicking, Thomas and Derek will lay down fire during the confusion. Frank and Lina will have already started heading away on foot, and our job is to pick Thomas and Derek up. When they see the car moving down the street, they will walk in our direction, and once they are in, we'll do a drive-by and shoot from the windows. Aside from laying down cover fire, your job is to identify as many of them as you can, especially the one who is on to you."

"I understand." Everyone's gaze in the room was on her now.

"Are you sure she is up for it?" Lina questioned.

"Lina, we all know our parts and will do them well. We can't have any of us doubting one another, especially now," Helmut said.

Lina was leaning against the wall with her arms crossed over her chest. She glared at Eva. "We'll see."

"We know the meeting starts at noon and ends at three. It's when they are all coming out that we will attack. Eva, did you cover for tomorrow?"

"I did. I switched shifts with my roommate. It actually worked out well. Her mom was wounded in the bombing two days ago and is at a different hospital than the one we work at. I told her I would cover her night shift so she could spend the evening with her mom."

"Perfect. What time do you have to be there?"

"Four. I should have enough time to get there. I will already have my uniform on under my coat."

Derek looked at his watch. "We have been here for over twenty minutes now. If we all know our parts, we should leave."

"You are right. Eva, Thomas, Derek, you three will meet me here tomorrow at two. Lina and Frank will already be there planting the bombs when we arrive."

"Where will they plant the bomb?" Eva asked.

"In trash cans on the sidewalk," Frank said.

"What about any civilians who might pass by? Won't they get hurt too?" she asked.

"That is a possibility," Frank admitted.

"It's the risk we have to take if we want this to work," Lina said.

Eva looked at Derek, hoping he would disagree with Lina.

"We will try to detonate it when there are no innocents

around if that is possible," he said to her.

"We can't worry about the few pedestrians who might get caught up in the explosion. We need this to happen," Helmut said. "This is more important than any of us or them."

"I know. But I wanted to make sure we are at least trying to keep the innocent out of this."

"You are such a sentimental fool," Lina snapped. "You are too soft for this. I don't know why you are even here."

"Why? Because I actually care about someone other than myself?"

Lina's mouth dropped and she unfolded her arms. "Are you really going to trust this bitch tomorrow?" Her gaze bore into Helmut.

"Whatever issue you two have with one another, you better square it away right now. No more of this shit. And yes, Lina, she is coming tomorrow. Now, let's all go home and get some rest." He looked at Eva and Lina, daring them to say something else.

"I could do with some rest," Eva said. "I will be here tomorrow." She stood from her chair, not wanting to be in the same room as Lina any longer. She walked to the door without looking at Lina and went up the stairs to the alley. She took in a deep breath when she stepped into the cool afternoon air. She didn't know why, but it was so easy for Lina to get under her skin. It seemed like Lina wanted to hate her. In the beginning, she tried to be nice to Lina even when she was impertinent, but when she realized Lina didn't want her kindness and would not reciprocate it, she stopped trying.

Eva did not feel like being home alone. Heidi was working, and Liesel was visiting her mom in the hospital. She decided it would be best if she went to the hospital to show her support to Liesel, who probably could use an emotional crutch now.

On the way to the hospital, she could not shake the feeling of what was going to take place. The image of all those people dying and their blood would be on her hands after tomorrow. To make matters worse, she left the meeting feeling that it lacked solidarity. The thought that innocent people could get caught up in it and die made her feel sick. Even the idea of killing the German officers caused a strange feeling in the pit of her stomach. They couldn't all be bad, but how could you tell the difference between them? She thought of Klaus and how awful she would feel if something ever happened to him.

She tried to push the thoughts from her mind and the uneasiness from deep in her gut, but they were replaced with thoughts of Gerhardt. If she let her guard down even a little, he would sneak in.

When she entered the lobby of the hospital, she asked for Schäfer at the front desk, and the woman directed her to the second floor. Eva found room two hundred and knocked on the doorframe. Liesel looked up from her mom's bedside. Her face was ashen, and her eyes sunken and shallow, as if she had not slept in days. The salt streaks from her tears were still on her cheeks.

"Liesel, I am so sorry." Eva came to the bedside and

embraced her. "How is she?"

"Not well. They don't expect her to make it through the night."

Eva let go and looked down at her tear-stained face. "What can I do?" The pitiful look on Liesel's face made her want to cry, too. She could already feel a tightening in her chest.

"Nothing, there is nothing you can do," she said through tears.

"Liesel…" Eva sat on the bed next to her and put an arm around her slender shoulders, then laid her cheek on top of Liesel's head as she held her close.

Liesel squeezed her fingers around Eva's forearm as she cried. "I can't lose her, Eva. She is all I have left." Liesel was an only child, and her father had died from tuberculosis when she was seventeen.

"Liesel, you are not alone. You have Heidi and me. We are here for you. You have always been there for me, and I will not abandon you.

Liesel leaned up and forced a smile. "I know, Eva." She looked down at her mom. "She has been all I've had for so long until you and Heidi."

"You will never be alone, Liesel. Heidi and I might not always be with you physically, but we will always be here." She put her hand on Liesel's chest, covering her heart. "And you will find a good man that will give you support, and he will show you love like no other. And when you have a family of your own, you will feel whole again. You will always love your mother, but you will no longer feel empty."

Liesel, for the first time, gave her a genuine smile through the tears. "I know what you are saying is true, but right now, it doesn't feel that way."

"I understand. Look, I will stay here with you all night if that is what you need, and as soon as Heidi is off work, she will be here too."

Liesel squeezed her hand. "You don't have to do that."

"Yes, I do. I know they will give you a couple of days off from the hospital. They will understand."

"I don't want to take time off. It will be another reminder that I'm mourning."

"But you have to mourn, Liesel."

"I will when I'm ready, but I don't want to be told when that is. I want it to be a time I choose, where I can mourn her in my own way and not feel that I am letting other people down because I can't cope."

"No one would think that."

"Whether or not they say it to me, it would be the truth."

"I understand why you feel that way. If you are like me when you are broken, you don't want to show it for fear of bringing others down with you."

Liesel met her gaze, and there was an unspoken understanding. A knock sounded from the doorway, and Eva and Liesel looked up. "Can I come in?" Heidi asked.

"Of course, you can," Liesel told her.

"I didn't know if I was interrupting something."

"You are not interrupting. I am glad you are here."

Heidi briskly walked to Liesel and wrapped her arms around her. "I can't believe this is happening. Why won't they stop? They are only killing innocent women and children when they bomb our cities."

"The Germans are doing the same to England right now. I think the point of the bombings is to cripple the country and break the will of the people," Eva told her.

"Well, they are succeeding," Heidi said.

"They haven't broken me, Heidi." Liesel's voice was full of iron willpower.

A tear escaped Heidi's eye. "But… your mother?" Heidi peered down at the dying woman.

"They may have taken my mother from me, but they cannot take my conviction." Liesel looked at Eva. "I don't mean that directed at you, Eva. It's not your country bombing mine."

"Not now, but if that time comes, you know they will side with England," Eva told her.

"I know, but I can't hold what your country does against you."

"I feel the same," Eva told her.

Liesel glanced at the clock on the wall. "It is getting late. You guys should go home and get some rest."

"I can stay with you."

"No, Eva, go home. I need to stay with her until she passes, but there is no need for the two of you to be sleep-deprived as well."

Eva would insist on staying if she didn't need to be alert tomorrow. She got up from the bed. "Alright, but if you need anything, you have to promise that you will call."

"I promise."

Eva gave her one last hug before turning and leaving the room. She needed a second to compose herself before Heidi came out; she didn't want to be seen as the weakest one. Leaning against the wall, she wiped the tears from her eyes and waited for Heidi.

"I feel so bad," Heidi said as they walked to the stairs. "It could be any one of us next time. I almost want to leave the city and move to the country. At least they won't be bombing there."

"I have thought that many times, but the truth is I would feel useless in the country. I want to help people, and I can do that best here," Eva said.

"That is one reason I haven't left. And because of you and Liesel, of course."

Eva took her arm. "I know that, Heidi. You have been a good friend to me."

"On my first day at the hospital, I felt so out of place. I didn't really know what was going on, but you and Liesel helped me and showed genuine kindness, unlike most of the other nurses. They seemed indifferent to my struggles, and they showed no interest in helping me learn or adapt. They were quick to point out my mistakes without giving any assistance or advice."

Eva met her gaze. "War is a rough time. It's hard to be compassionate among so much death and suffering. You become numb to the things going on around you and focus on self-preservation because if you don't look out for yourself, who will."

"But you are always so kind to everyone. You show so

much compassion. I see you with the patients. How do you do it?"

"I don't know, maybe because I believe there is still good in the world. It's so inhospitable, and a little compassion goes a long way. Most of those men don't want to be here, and they deserve kindness, even if they are on the other side of what I believe."

"I don't think I could look at it the way you do." Her face was solemn.

"You don't have to. If Germany were bombing America, I would have a harder time not hating the men that come into the hospital, knowing that they were killing my countrymen."

"So, you don't hate any of them?"

"I didn't say that." Heidi gave her a questioning look but didn't press the question.

They took the tram to the apartment, and as soon as they were back, Eva took a hot bath and went straight to her room. It was a rough day, and she needed to be alone; she wanted to prepare herself emotionally and mentally for tomorrow the best she could. She pulled the blankets back to crawl into bed when she caught sight of the music box Gerhardt gave her on top of the dresser, next to Sabina's teddy bear. She went over to it and stroked the music box with a finger, then picked it up and cranked the little golden knob on the bottom before setting it back down. It came to life, and the wheel turned, playing the German lullaby. It was the first time she had played it since she left France, and the sound was sweet as it filled her ears. She lifted the teddy bear from her dresser and hugged it to her chest as the music played, her eyes filling with tears. She lay on the bed holding the bear while the tune echoed in her room. It reminded her of him and the meadow by the pond. That time felt so long ago and very different from now. The war had seemed a million miles away when she was there, and being alone with him felt wonderful, adding to the calm peace.

The wheel played its last note and stopped. She could not bear to hear it again, so she let it sit open on the dresser. She pulled the string of the green lamp on her bedside table, then covered up, still holding onto the bear, and pulled the blankets over her head. She wanted to feel in that moment like she could hide from the world. She closed her eyes and let sleep take her.

Anti-aircraft guns and sirens echoing through the city jolted Eva awake. She sat up in bed, still dazed from the deep sleep it pulled her out of. She threw the blankets off and hopped out of bed, going to the window and pulling one curtain aside. The bombs lit up the night, and the strafing of the guns crisscrossed the sky. It looked like fireworks going off all over the city, except this was louder. Every time a bomb exploded, the floor would shake under her feet. She went to the living room to watch from the bigger window and noticed Heidi standing in front of it, peering out.

"I can't believe this is happening again. Stop bombing us, you bastards," she screamed at the glass, then took a step back, away from the window.

Eva came to her side and placed an arm around her

shoulders. “They are not bombing Potsdam. We will be fine. Those bombs are being dropped on Berlin. I feel sorry for the doctors and nurses in the hospitals there, though. They are going to be swamped for days. I don’t know where they are going to put everyone. They are already filled to the max,” Eva said, peering out at the destruction that was taking place before her.

“At the other hospitals around town, and probably ours too,” Heidi’s low voice broke her focus.

“You are probably right, Heidi. We should try to get a little more sleep before the sun comes up, and we have to deal with this mess.” She gestured towards the window.

“Do you care if I sleep with you?” Heidi asked.

Heidi somehow seemed more frail than usual. “No, I don’t care. It will be a little cramped, though, in my small bed.”

“I don’t mind.” She glanced back to the window. “The bombs make me uneasy.”

“Come on,” Eva nodded towards her room. Heidi followed, and they both crawled into the twin bed. It was comforting for Eva as well. Not being alone helped her fall asleep faster than she would have alone.

Monday, March 24th, 1941

Heidi leaned partway on her back, waking Eva. She opened her eyes, squinting against the light that was coming through the window. She had forgotten to close the curtain after opening it to look at the bombing. The light of a new day swallowed up the darkness of the night before. She rolled her head on the pillow towards Heidi, who was still fast asleep. She turned back to the side table and read the clock. It was barely past eight-thirty, and she knew she could not go back to sleep. She eased the covers off, hoping to not wake Heidi, and tiptoed to the living room, closing the bedroom door behind her. She put the kettle on to boil some water for tea because coffee was hard to get, then sat at the kitchen table to wait. The bombings last night, Liesel's suffering, and what was to take place today filled her mind. The panic rose in her chest, so she timed her breathing and rubbed her thumbs on her temples. It wasn't working, so she released the air she was holding. Tears flooded her eyes, so she drew in a sharp breath and squeezed them shut, putting her hand over her mouth as she cried. At first, the breaths were ragged sounding, but then they came slower as she tried to bring herself out of the anxiety attack with calculated breathing. Losing control was not really an option, and she could fight it if she tried hard enough.

The kettle whistled, so she stood and got a cup from the cupboard, turned off the burner, and poured the hot water into her cup. She took it back to the table and sat down. Serious doubt was creeping in about her ability to follow through with what they expected of her. After today, she would, in part, be responsible for the death of many people.

She could not sit at the apartment and wait until it was two o'clock. She went back to the bedroom and picked her uniform off the floor, taking it into the bathroom to change.

Heidi was still asleep, and she didn't want to wake her, so she left a note on the end of the bed saying there were some things she needed to do before going to work. She put on her coat and hat at the door, then got her purse and slipped out into the hall. She had no idea what she would do, but she had to get out of the apartment.

For a while, she walked the busy streets of Berlin, happy to be ignored, but finally opted for a bench in a park across from the Reichstag. She wanted to go inside and ask for Gerhardt again but knew it would be the same as last time. A military car pulled in front of the building, and three officers got out and went inside. She focused on their faces and wondered if they were going to be at the attack. Would they die today because of her? Would they be among the unlucky ones who lost their lives? She would never forget their faces now, and the guilt was consuming her. The doubt that she could keep doing this after today was suffocating. Stealing medicine was one thing, but this was something entirely different. She was worried that Oberst Heinrich Schmitt would be there. Ever since she met him in the hospital and saved his life, they had become well acquainted. He had been released barely a week now, and she had seen to it that Doctor Möller wrote in his release forms that he had to rest at home for the first couple of weeks. When he was in the hospital, she would sit and talk with him and tell him about home, and he would tell her stories of the war and his family. After they released him, they went to lunch a couple of times, and there was still the ball on Saturday. However it might not happen now after the attack. She would be surprised if it did. He had given her an official invitation so there wouldn't be trouble getting in, but she still wasn't sure she would go, even if it still took place.

She got off the bench and walked the streets of the shopping district, admiring the fancy dresses and hats on display in the windows that she could not afford. Her stomach growled, and she was reminded that she hadn't eaten breakfast. She stopped in a café and ordered a small plate of eggs, sliced cheese, cold-cut meat, and a real cup of coffee. The cup of tea she had that morning, combined with the adrenaline, was making her hands shake, though the tea she had at the apartment was not enough caffeine to keep her awake.

The waitress set the plate in front of her and a small tea-sized cup on a saucer with black coffee beside it. Eva thanked her, picked up the small cup, and inhaled deeply. It was the most amazing thing she had smelled. She sipped the hot liquid and closed her eyes. It was robust and delightful.

After eating, she stayed at the café for a while before heading to the meeting location. It was still early, and she was tired of walking around. She checked her watch; it was almost eleven, and there were still three hours before the attack. It would take at least twenty minutes to get to the building, and then she could sleep for a bit on the loveseat in the room.

She left the café and went straight to the meeting place. Then she hurried down the steps to the basement room and turned on the light. She took off her coat and laid down on the loveseat, then covered up with it and closed her eyes.

The exhaustion was numbing, and she hoped that the coffee would kick in soon. Her day was only getting started, and she still had the night shift at the hospital. Focusing on the silence in the room, she tried not to think of what was going to happen in only a few hours.

There were shuffling steps on the floor, then a hand pressed on her shoulder and gently shook her. "Eva, wake up. Eva…."

Her eyes slowly opened, and she looked at the person hovering over her. It took a second for her to register who it was. Helmut looked down at her with his hand still resting on her arm.

"What time is it?" she asked.

"It's almost two, and everyone else will be here soon."

"How long have you been here?"

"Not long, maybe ten minutes," he said.

She sat up, then wished she hadn't as every heartbeat thumped in her temples from the raging headache that came on while sleeping."

"Are you feeling alright?" Concern was etched in his voice.

"My head is hurting, but I'm fine other than that."

"Is it going to hinder you?"

"No, I have some medicine in my purse I can take." Reaching into her bag, she retrieved the little brown medicine bottle she had taken from the hospital. She tipped it, poured two white pills into her hand, and washed them down with some water from the sink.

The door opened, and shoes clicked on the steps above. Then Lina and Frank's voices echoed in the room. Eva didn't even turn to look at them. She would only be greeted with a look of disdain from Lina anyway. She went back to the loveseat and sat down, draping the coat over her legs. Thomas and Derek walked through the door right after Lina and Frank and came to sit next to her on the loveseat.

"Good, we are all here. Lina, Frank, get what you need and head out now. We will be there at 2:45 to drop Thomas and Derek off, and then we will wait a few blocks away on the same street. Everyone knows their parts, so let's get it done."

Lina and Frank collected the stuff they needed and divided it into two bags, each of them carrying one. They left, and Eva listened to their footsteps on the stairs, happy Lina was gone. Thomas and Frank got pistols and machine guns, loaded the clips with ammo, then grabbed extra rounds and put them in their pockets. Helmut took two of the guns from the wooden box and loaded them, then put extra ammo in his pockets. He handed Frank and Thomas their masks, then threw one on Eva's lap and held out a pistol to her. She slowly took it from his hands, surprised by how heavy it was. This was the first time she had ever held a gun, and it was scary. He then took a handful of ammo and held it out to her as well. She pinched the bullets in his palm and put them in her coat pocket. She laid the gun in her lap and looked at it, apprehension filling her.

"As far as we know, nothing has changed. The meeting should be taking place now and is scheduled to be over by three."

"All we can do now is pray," Derek said.

Eva tore her eyes away from the gun and focused on the mask, the perspiration forming on her forehead, yet she was cold, chilled to the bone. Both symptoms stemmed from the same thing, fear and anxiety.

Helmut looked at his watch. "It's time to go. I parked the car in the alley so no one should see us."

Eva stood as a dizzy spell hit her like an ocean billow, so she put a hand on the table, afraid her knees would buckle. Clamping her fingers tightly around the edge for support, she squeezed her eyes shut and took long breaths through her nose. When the feeling subsided, she straightened and put her coat on, then pushed the mask down into its deep pocket. No one said anything to her, so she assumed they hadn't noticed.

Eva followed them to the car and got into the passenger seat. Helmut slid in next to her, and Thomas and Derek climbed in the back, laying the guns in their laps.

"Button up your coat," Helmut told her. "You don't want anyone to see your uniform."

She buttoned the coat, then he started the engine, put the car in gear, and squeezed the steering wheel with both hands as the car lurched forward.

"Why are you holding the gun by the window? Put it in your lap." Helmut's words were rushed.

"I…" she said, stopping herself before giving away that she was scared out of her mind. Not only was she terrified that they would be captured or killed during the attack, but also because she was to help deliver death to others.

The car pulled out onto the main street and picked up speed as Helmut drove in the direction they were to drop Derek and Thomas off. When he stopped the car, Derek and Thomas hopped out, hiding the guns under their trench coats, then walked several yards apart in case one of them was caught. Helmut pulled away from the curb, and when they arrived at the spot where they were supposed to wait, he turned off the engine.

"Alright, Lina and Frank should have their bombs in place now. As soon as we hear the shooting, we'll put on our masks and drive towards it."

She nodded but could not speak without her voice trembling. Trying to control her breathing, she took shallow breaths and focused on the building a few blocks away. Seeing Gerhardt come out kept playing over in her mind. What would she do if she saw him leaving the building? She couldn't save him. She would be an enemy of both sides if she tried. There was no way of knowing if Gerhardt would be there, so she suppressed the thought. He might not be high-ranking enough, she hoped. Checking her watch to see how much time was left, she sighed with relief that it was seven minutes until three, and the Germans would come out soon.

What seemed like the longest seven minutes of her life were finally over, and it was now three, so she fixed her eyes on the doors of the building to wait. At almost thirteen minutes past, the front doors opened, and German officers started trickling out, but something in the distance caught in her peripheral. Tearing her gaze away from the doors, to her horror, was a woman pushing a baby stroller heading right in the direction of the crowd of German officers.

“Helmut, look.” She pointed to the women.

“Shit!” He scanned their surroundings as he tapped his fingers on the steering wheel. “There is nothing we can do, Eva. If one of us were to warn her, it would jeopardize the entire operation.”

“So, we are going to blow up a baby?” she asked, horrified.

“We all knew this could happen.”

“Not a baby. I was thinking adults.”

“Children had not crossed my mind either, but it changes nothing.”

“Helmut…?”

“Eva, you will stay in this car,” he growled in a hushed voice.

Right as he finished saying it, several loud explosions shook the car, and a plume of black smoke billowed in the air, followed by gunfire. He started the car. “Eva, put your mask on,” he demanded.

She took the mask from her pocket and pulled it over her head. Helmut drove down the street slowly towards where the commotion was, all the while, Eva was searching for the woman and her baby, but she could not make out any single person in the chaos and smoke. Thomas and Derek were shooting from across the street, but when they saw the car, they stopped and hurried down the road towards it in a sprint.

Helmut slowed but did not stop as Thomas and Derek hopped into the back. Derek and Thomas rolled down their windows, stuck the barrels of their guns out, and laid down fire as the car drove past the fleeing Germans. They were scattered on the lawn and up and down the sidewalk, and those who were not injured as severely returned fire, putting holes in the side of the car. A bullet hit the windshield, shattering it, and Eva screamed. Never had she thought about bullets hitting the car, even though it was probable.

Helmut pushed on the gas, and the car accelerated, speeding past the commotion, bullets hitting the back as they drove by. Eva stuck the gun out the window, her hands shaking uncontrollably, the gun rattling on the door, but she pulled the trigger anyway, not firing at any of the people. Her hands were shaking so badly she couldn't hit them even if she tried. Plus, she had never shot a gun before and had no practice with aiming and hitting a target.

"Get down," Helmut yelled. They lay low in their seats as Helmut drove, trying not to wreck.

In the rearview mirror, Eva noticed a car right behind them. "Helmut, we are being followed," she yelled over the wind blowing into the car from the missing windshield.

"We can't go back to the meeting place. I'll keep driving. We have to lose them." Helmut looked in the backseat at Thomas and Derek, and they both nodded in understanding. Each of the men stuck the barrel of their gun out a window and shot at the car behind them. Helmut turned down one street after another, hoping to lose them. On one turn, he clipped another vehicle, knocking its mirror off and breaking the left headlight. Her whole body was numb except for the pins and needles that pricked all over her. The only thing registering was the shock and adrenaline. Strangely, at this moment, she thought of the pins and needle feeling she had when she was with Gerhardt. What she felt with him was anticipation and excitement. This was fear. The adrenaline now was preparing her for survival, not for the throes of passion.

There was a loud crash behind them so Eva looked over the top of her seat. The car that had been following them crashed into a parked car. Steam was rising from under the hood. She turned back in her seat and squinted against the wind.

"We got the bastards. I shot the driver right in the head," Derek shouted, pleased.

"I'm going to slow down now so we won't draw as much attention. And everyone needs to take off their masks."

Eva reached up with one hand and pulled off the mask, throwing it on the floor at her feet. "We need to ditch the car and walk the rest of the way. It's too easy to spot with the broken windows and bullet holes." He slowed but continued to turn down different streets, so they would be harder to be follow.

She hadn't noticed her body's physical reaction to all the adrenaline until now. Her hands were cold and clammy on the gun in her lap, still shaking, and he breathing was low and deep. Her grip on the gun was so tight that her knuckles were white. "Was the woman and her baby among the casualties?" she asked to anyone that would answer.

"I don't know. I didn't see them when we drove by," Helmut told her.

"They couldn't have made it; the woman was right by the trash can when the bomb detonated." Thomas's voice sounded apologetic.

"You saw her?" Eva asked.

"I did."

She swallowed hard. "And did the bomb take out many of the Germans?"

"Quite a few, and they were falling like flies under our gunfire. I don't know how many of them suffered fatal shots, but we should know in a few days," Derek informed her.

She was now officially the murderer of a baby, an innocent woman, and all of those men. She felt sick to her stomach. She needed to get out of this car.

Helmut pulled to the curb beside a building that had been damaged in a raid and turned the engine off. "We need to throw the masks and rifles into the river. It's too risky to take them with us.

But hang onto the pistols, those we can hide."

They got out of the car, and Helmut, Thomas, and Derek tossed their guns into the river and their masks. Eva handed her gun to Helmut and picked up a brick, wrapping her mask around it before throwing it into the river.

"We shouldn't walk together in case one of us is seen or is being followed," Helmut added.

"I have to go to work soon?" Eva told him.

"That's right, go to the hospital then. Each of us will leave here in a different direction. It is no longer safe to meet in the basement after today. We will need to find a new place. When I have found another location, I will inform everyone. I don't know in what way I will contact everyone yet, but be patient and wait to hear from me. It shouldn't take more than a few days."

When the men had walked away, Eva doubled over and vomited, stabilizing herself with a hand on the wall. After emptying the contents of her stomach, she dry heaved a couple of times, then straightened and wiped her mouth on the back of her hand. Kneeling, she dipped her hands into the river to clean the vomit from them, then wiped the splatter from her shoes. She stood and shook the water from her hands, then walked towards the tram that would take her to Potsdam.

Chapter Seven

✠

Monday, March 24th, 1941

When Eva arrived at the hospital, it was utter chaos. Ambulances were lined along the front as doctors and nurses frantically scrambled to check the patients as they came in. She knew immediately what the cause was. These patients were from the attack. The hospitals in Berlin were already full, and the staff was stretched thin, so the wounded had to come here.

Gerhardt, she thought. She ran towards the ambulances, starting with the first one she came to.

"Eva, when did you get here?" Heidi asked. She was standing at the back of the ambulance Eva stopped at.

"A few minutes ago. What happened?" She feigned ignorance.

"There was an attack on the German high command today."

"Are you serious?"

"Yes. I can't believe it. Who would be stupid enough to do something like this? I hope they catch them."

Eva looked away, afraid the lie would show on her face. "Me too. I'm going to check the other ambulances."

She made her way down the line, checking each wounded man on the stretchers and in the ambulances. Six of them were dead, but neither Gerhardt nor Oberst Heinrich Schmitt were among them. Feeling assured that Gerhardt wasn't with the wounded or dead, she began checking the patient's conditions and instructing the orderlies on which ones should be brought inside. If she thought they had a chance to live, the orderlies would take them inside the hospital. She would mark an M on the ones she determined could not be saved or had a slim chance and would leave them outside. The wounded that were in the best condition also got left outside but would be brought in by the hospital staff later.

"Eva," Ingrid, one of the new nurses, called from a few stretchers away.

"What?" Eva said as she wrote an M on a man's forehead.

"I have a patient here, and I don't know if I should send him inside or mark him. I can't tell."

Eva took off her purse and coat and tossed them on the curb so she didn't get blood on them, then walked towards Ingrid. "Let me see." She came to stand next to her, peering down at the man. As soon as she saw his face, her body tensed. A wounded and bloodied Bauer was lying on the stretcher in front of her.

"Eva, what is it? Do you know him?"

She cleared her throat. "No… no, I don't."

"Why did you react that way?"

"I don't know, the shock of seeing him, I guess."

"Should I mark him?"

Eva met his glossy eyes, and in them was death. He was fading. His life was now in her hands. She could choose to try and save him or leave him to die here on the stretcher. If she decided not to save him, it would make her life easier, but the real question was, should she let him die. The blood on her hands and the deaths she was responsible for were mounting.

He coughed, snapping her back to reality. Blood splattered all over his military jacket and on her white apron. He coughed again, and the blood dribbled onto his chin and ran out of his mouth over his cheek, dripping onto the stretcher.

"Eva, you have to tell me now. What do I do?"

"Let me look at his wounds." She unbuttoned his jacket, then pulled apart his shirt, ripping off the buttons. Lifting his undershirt exposed the wounds on his abdomen. There was a cut on his neck that had been wrapped with gauze, which was now soaked in blood. His upper left arm sleeve was also saturated in blood, indicating that it, too, had been wounded. There was a bullet hole in his left shoulder, and on the right side of his stomach was a piece of metal protruding from it, shrapnel from the explosion, she guessed. There were also minor scratches all over the right side of his face and a bullet hole on the inside of his left thigh. She honestly wasn't sure if they could save him. He had already lost a lot of blood. "Write an M on his…." she trailed off when he turned his head with some effort to look at her, their eyes meeting as he held her gaze, then his eyelids closed. Eva drew in a deep breath and held it.

"Is he dead?" Ingrid asked, leaning over him slightly.

Eva reached for his wrist and checked his pulse. She could barely feel a heartbeat; it was so weak. The memory of the woman and her baby and all the bodies she saw on the ground haunted her. That image would be burned in her brain for the rest of her life. A tear slipped from her eye and fell to the ground, but Ingrid hadn't noticed. She was aware of the guilt and anxiety mixed with a tinge of dread creeping in. What she and the others had done was a false moral equivalence. How could she justify her actions because of theirs?

"Take him inside and find Dr. Möller. Tell him this man is critical and needs to be operated on now." Her voice was forceful, matching the urgency of the situation.

"But, I thought you said to put an M on him?"

"I know what I said. Now take him inside and find Dr. Möller," Eva yelled at her in a harsher tone than she had intended.

"I don't think he is going to survive," Ingrid insisted.

"Ingrid," Eva said in frustration, "just do it. And tell Dr. Möller I will be right there to help assist with the surgery. I need to hurry and check the rest of the patients."

Ingrid gave her a strange look, then found another nurse

to help her carry his gurney to the front of the ambulances where Dr. Möller was.

Eva ran along the line of patients that had arrived while she was checking Bauer, only looking at their faces to see if Gerhardt or Oberst Heinrich Schmitt was among them. She didn't see them with the rest of the wounded, but it didn't mean that someone had not already brought them inside or that they hadn't arrived yet. Eva grabbed her coat and purse off the curb and ran inside, checking every operating room to find Dr. Möller and to look at the patients who were already on the operation tables. She found Dr. Möller three rooms down, preparing for surgery, but she ran past to check the other rooms. None of the people in the other operating rooms were Gerhardt or Heinrich Schmitt, so she returned to the one with Dr. Möller and Bauer.

Frau Wagner, Ingrid, and Dr. Möller were already there around the table Bauer was lying on.

"Eva, I don't know if he will survive. You should have left him outside. We have too many wounded, and we need to focus on the ones that can be saved," he said.

"She insisted I take him in and find you," Ingrid told him before Eva had a chance to respond.

"Do you know him?" he asked.

"No, I don't know him." She didn't sound very convincing to herself but hoped she did to him, at least.

"Scrub up."

Eva scrubbed in, then went to the table. Frau Wagner was at Bauer's head, controlling the amount of ether he was given, and Ingrid was standing across the table from Dr.

Möller. Eva came and stood beside Dr. Möller and looked down at Bauer's limp body covered in blood. It was a gruesome sight.

"Give me the scissors, Ingrid, and give Eva a pair, too," he told her. Ingrid handed them both a pair of scissors. "We need to cut his clothes off. You start with his pants, and I will work on his jacket and shirt."

She looked at his bare feet, only now noticing that his boots and socks had already been removed, so she undid the suspenders from his pants and started cutting up the left leg. When the tip of the scissors cut through the last bit of thick fabric of his pant waist, she stopped and moved it away so they could see the wounds. She paused and looked at Dr. Möller. "Do I have to cut these too?" she asked, referring to his underwear.

"Yes, at least away from the leg on this side."

Eva clipped through the blood-stained white undergarment up the left leg and through the elastic around his waist. Carefully, she pulled it away from his leg, trying to leave the rest of him covered the best she could. She moved Bauer's leg, looked at the bullet hole, then stuck her hand under his leg to feel for an exit wound and found one.

"The bullet went all the way through."

"That's a good thing," Dr. Möller told her.

Eva went to the other side of the table and cut the right pant leg, then pulled his pants out from underneath him, tossing them on the floor, out of the way. Dr. Möller had already cut the jacket away and was now working on the shirt. He had Ingrid begin applying pressure on his shoulder while he cut the shirt to try and stop the bleeding. Eva got a better look at the shrapnel in his side. It was larger than she had noticed the first time, and it was deep in him. When it was time to remove the shrapnel, it would not take them long to learn if he was going to survive. There was a real possibility that he would bleed to death on the table seconds after removing it, or he would go into shock.

Dr. Möller pulled the tattered shirt away, then cut through his undershirt and pulled it off. "We are going to remove the shrapnel first, and if he survives that, then we will take care of the bullets in the shoulder and leg and the wound on his neck. Eva, get ready."

She got some gauze and a threaded needle from the table and waited. He took hold of the piece of metal and slowly pulled it out. Blood started pouring from around the shrapnel before it was even out. When it came free, a large amount of blood flowed from the wound. "Give me the gauze," he said. She put it in his outstretched hand, and he poked it in the wound to soak up some of the blood so he could see it better. He turned the overhead light so he could see better, then pulled the gauze out and peered inside the wound. "His appendix is ruptured. It is going to need to be removed. Give me a scalpel."

She passed the scalpel, and he started cutting; after a few minutes, he pulled out a small, pink, narrow, finger-shaped pouch from Bauer's stomach. She had never seen an appendix before.

He put it on the metal tray beside him. "Needle." She placed it in his hand and got a second one ready for when it was time to close the wound in his side. He sewed the intestine, then paused. "Eva, dab it with gauze. I can't see a damn thing." She wiped the blood away, then quickly stuck the gauze inside the hole and pulled it out before laying it on the tray. Blood had run off the table onto the floor, making a puddle that she tried not to stand in, not wanting to get it on her shoes or slide in the slick liquid. She glanced at Bauer's face; it was pale, and his skin was cool and clammy to the touch. His breathing was rapid and labored, and every time he let out a breath, there was a gargling sound.

"What is his pulse?" she asked Ingrid.

Ingrid put the end of the stethoscope to his chest. "It's about thirty-eight beats a minute."

Eva looked at Dr. Möller. They both knew that if he lost any more blood, he would go into shock and die.

"Cut the thread," Dr. Möller said. Eva cut it and then held out the other needle for him. He took it from her and poked it through the flesh, closing the hole. "Alright, let's move to the shoulder."

She followed him to the other side of the table and watched as he inspected the gunshot wound. "This one did not go through. Give me the forceps." Eva handed him the forceps, and he stuck them down deep in the bullet hole. "Got it." He pulled out the forceps with the mangled piece of lead pinched at the tip. "It hit a rib in his back, which is most likely cracked, but that is the least of our concerns right now." He removed the gauze from Bauer's neck to reveal a graze from a bullet. "Ingrid, get this bandaged up while Eva and I work on the leg, and bandage the shoulder too"

"Yes, doctor."

Eva followed him back to the other side of the table, and he squinted through his glasses at the leg wound. "It appears to have been a clean shot. He is lucky. A few centimeters to the right would have gone through an artery or shattered his femur and a few centimeters to the left, and he would never father children. I need this gone," he said, pushing Bauer's underwear from the wound, exposing all of him. "Cut the other leg hole and get it out of the way."

When he did that, she glanced away, then turned her head back, trying to avoid looking at specific parts of him. She took the scissors and cut the other leg to his underwear, then pulled them from under him and tossed them on the floor by his bloodied pants.

"Let's sew this side first, and then we are going to have to roll him over. Give me another needle." Eva passed the needle, and he sewed the hole on top of his thigh. "Alright, let's roll him on his side." Frau Wagner kept the cup over his mouth as they rolled him onto his right side. Eva held him so he didn't roll off the table or onto his back again while Dr. Möller stitched up the hole in the back of his leg. "That should do it. I honestly can't believe he is still alive."

Eva looked around at all the blood on the floor and the amount covering his naked body. There was so much.

Dr. Möller pulled off his gloves. "Ingrid, put bandages on those wounds, start a blood transfusion, and get him cleaned up and into some clothes."

"Yes, doctor."

"Eva, come with me. I'm going to need you on the next

operation."

"Alright. Let me put on a new surgical gown."

"As soon as you are done, come and find me."

"I will."

"Frau Wagner, I will need you too."

"Right away, doctor." She pulled her gloves off and walked past Eva, eyeing her with suspicion.

Eva removed her gown and threw it in the dirty bin. "Ingrid, go get the clothes the patient will need. They are in the cupboard in the hall."

"Sure." She pulled off her gloves and left the room.

Once Eva was alone in the room with Bauer, she finally allowed herself to look at him. She pulled a sheet over him and then leaned down close to his ear. "You owe me for this. If it weren't for me, you would be dead now, still outside on a stretcher with the others, but I chose to save your life. Maybe it was out of guilt, I don't know, but the reasons don't matter. You are alive now because of me." Footsteps echoed in the hall, so Eva quickly straightened and walked to the cabinet with the surgical gowns. Ingrid entered the room as Eva pulled out a fresh one.

"I have the clothes."

"Do you need any help cleaning him? If you do, I can send another nurse in?" Eva asked.

"I think I can manage."

"Alright. You did well today."

"Thank you."

Eva turned to leave the room when Ingrid spoke. "I know that you are acquainted with him somehow." Eva stopped in her tracks but kept her back to Ingrid. "What I can't figure out is why, at first, you told me to put an M on him, then changed your mind. Is it that you hate him, and that's why you originally wanted to leave him out there, or is it that you care for him, which is why you sent him in, even in his condition?"

Eva turned back to look at her. "It is neither. It's that I wasn't sure he would survive, the same as you. I had to decide quickly, so I chose to send him in. I'm a nurse. It's my job to save people, and that is what I did out there."

"But your reaction when you first saw him says more than what you are telling me."

"I don't have time for this. Ingrid, Dr. Möller, is waiting for me. Whatever you saw or think you saw doesn't matter. I need to go." She walked out of the room, the whole situation with Bauer leaving, her unsettled. And Ingrid, she could not have her asking questions because nothing she could say about the situation was good. If she said she wanted to leave him outside because she hated him, that could get her into trouble, and if she said she helped him because deep down she felt guilty that she was partially responsible for why he was there in the first place, that would be even worse.

She checked each operating room until she found the one Dr. Möller was in. She put on her gown and went to the sink to wash her hands.

"I expected you here sooner."

"Sorry, I was helping Ingrid with something."

"Next time you are needed in surgery and she asks for help, tell her to find someone else."

"I will." She pulled on her gloves and met him at the table. The man lying on the table had a piece of his hand missing and was blinded in the left eye. The guilt she was trying to pull herself out of sucked her under like quicksand in a matter of seconds. Seeing Bauer's body mangled was one thing, but this man did nothing to her. Not a single part of her felt good about what transpired, and the remorse and culpability wracked her with shame. She had sinned and wondered if she was going to spend the rest of her life in penance or hell. She wasn't catholic but felt like she needed to go to a priest and ask for absolution and a way to atone.

By the end of the surgery, she felt queasy and needed to sit down. She lowered herself onto the hall floor and leaned against the wall. The operations were all done, and eight were dead, two in critical condition, and another four wounded.

"Eva…?"

She raised her eyes to Heidi's face hovering over her.

"I'm tired, Heidi. It has been a long five hours. I haven't sat down, gone to the bathroom, or eaten the whole time I've been here."

"Why don't you go to the bathroom and eat now?"

"I'm going to. I will need to ask Frau Wagner if I can take my break first."

"I saw her in Ward C not more than a minute ago. Why don't you go ask her?"

"I thought I could change something, Heidi. I believed I could make a difference, but I know now it can't be changed."

Heidi pulled her brows together. “What can’t?”

“The past.”

“Eva, what are you talking about?”

She rubbed her forehead. “Nothing, I’m only rambling.” She got to her feet. “I’m going to go talk to Frau Wagner now.”

Heidi touched her arm, studying her face. “Are you alright?”

“I think the exhaustion is getting to me.”

“Go rest.”

Eva forced a smile and walked away. She found Frau Wagner in the operating room, laying out freshly cleaned tools. “Is it alright if I take a break now?”

“Yes. Go eat something and rest for a bit.”

“Thank you.”

Eva first went to the patient's ward to check that Gerhardt wasn’t there one more time. Quickly, she made her way up and down each row of beds, but she didn’t see him. Before leaving the room, she stopped at the end of Bauer’s bed. He looked like he was on death’s doorstep. His complexion was still pale and ashy, and around his eyes, the skin had turned to a bluish-purple hue. There was an IV line running down a pole attached to his arm. She took the clipboard off the end of his bed and skimmed over it. His pulse was still low, but finally in the forties. Right now, he was stable, and his temperature remained normal. He had not yet woken up from the anesthetics, but they had given him morphine. His breathing continued to be labored, and she wondered how long that would last. She hung the clipboard back on the end of the bed and looked around to ensure no one was watching her. It was nighttime, and the lights were out in the room so the patients could sleep.

She looked back at him, lying still on the bed, feeling conflicted as the two opposing emotions struggled to dominate. Part of her wanted to smother him with the pillow he slept on, and another part of her wanted to tell him that she was sorry, but she didn't know which feeling was stronger. She couldn't look at his bruised, disfigured body any longer, so she left the patient's quarters and went to the nurse's lounge. She had brought no food with her but was still going to rest for a while.

She lay on a cot and was glad no one else was there. A growl came from her stomach, and she contemplated seeing if Dr. Möller had any extra food that he would share with her but decided against it. The faces of the patients from the attack played in her mind, their wounds and the sound of their agony. *I am such an awful person*, she thought. Tears escaped her eyes and ran down her cheeks onto the pillow. *What will the resistance do when I tell them I can't help in that capacity anymore*? she wondered. She wanted to go home to her time so badly. The feeling was suffocating. *Why can't Jon find a way to bring me back? Why is it taking so long?* She got off the bed and found a pen and paper, then sat at the small table in the nurse's quarters and began writing.

Jon,

I haven't heard from you in a long time now. I really need to get out of here, and I don't understand why it is taking you so long. You don't know what it is like to be stuck here; it is so much worse than when I was in France. At this point, I am willing to do almost anything to go home. If it means risking my life to do so, then that is what I will do because, to be honest, that is what I am doing every day that I am here. If you can't find a way, then I will have to find my own. Please write to me as soon as possible and tell me if you have learned anything. I need to leave this place before I am no longer myself. Every day I feel like I lose a little piece of who I am.

Eva

She folded the letter and put it in her pocket so she could mail it in the morning, then went to find Dr. Möller and see if he was going to have dinner soon. First, she checked the operating rooms, but he wasn't in any of them, so she went to his office. Light was coming from under the door when she reached the top of the stairs. She knocked lightly and heard his voice on the other side.

"Come in."

When she stepped into his office, he looked up from the charts on his desk, staring at her, his glasses low on his nose as he latently rubbed his fingers on the top of his balding head.

"May I sit?" she asked in a quiet, tired voice.

"Of course."

She took the chair across from him. "Have you had dinner?" she asked.

"No, not yet. How about you?"

"No, it actually slipped my mind to bring food."

He reached under his desk, pulled out a brown paper bag, and set it on the table in front of her. "Have part of mine."

"Don't you need it?"

His kind eyes met hers. "You can save me some."

She opened it, peering inside. It contained two apples, a sandwich, and a jar of soup. "Do you have any bowls and an extra spoon?"

"No, but you can use mine."

"You don't know what I have. I could give you something." She chuckled.

"I'll take my chances."

She shot him a smile and opened the jar. "Do you want me to heat it?"

"That would be better than eating it cold."

"I'll heat it on the stove in the nurse's station." She took the soup downstairs, but when she turned the corner, someone called her name, and she halted.

"Eva." Ingrid came jogging down the hall towards her. "I was looking for you. That patient woke up."

Eva tensed but tried to conceal it quickly. "Did he?"

"Yes. But he kept saying, 'Where is she?'"

"And you think he meant me?"

"Well… who else would he be talking about?"

"Oh, I don't know, maybe a girlfriend. I'm sure he knows plenty of women. He was probably talking about one of them." She was already on edge, short-tempered, and didn't need this right now. She was tired, hungry, and confused about the events of the day.

"It didn't seem that way to me. It was like he was upset."

"I'm on my way to heat some soup. I would really like to eat my dinner while I still have time."

"Please come and check. He was fitful, and I'm not sure if I should give him some morphine early. His chart said he had some recently, but I wondered if we should up the dose."

"Ingrid, I'm not a doctor. That's the kind of question you should ask one of them, or at the very least, Frau Wagner."

Ingrid didn't move or speak. She didn't seem to accept Eva's answer. "I am not partial to this patient above any of the others. I don't know him. You should not be coming to me about him. The only time you should ask me is if you can't find one of the doctors or it's a situation like yesterday where you truly needed help."

"But I do. I don't know if I need to give him more morphine."

"You were looking for me, Ingrid. I'm on break now, so you will have to find someone else to help you."

"Please, if you check on him now, I promise I won't single you out anymore."

Eva grunted. "Fine, let me put this on the stove first." Ingrid followed her to the nurse's station as she dropped off the soup; then, they went to the patient ward together. They stopped at Bauer's bed, but he was lying still, and his eyes were closed.

"I thought you said he was awake?" Eva looked at Ingrid, her annoyance spiking again.

"He was, I promise."

"Well, he isn't now, so I am no longer needed."

Eva started walking back to the hall. "Wait, his breathing is still labored. Should we do something about that?"

Eva came back to the bed and gave Ingrid a vexed look. "Let me see your stethoscope." Ingrid took the stethoscope from around her neck and handed it to her. Eva sat on the side of the bed, put the earpieces in, and stuck the diaphragm down his shirt, holding it to his chest. She then moved it to his side and, after a few seconds, moved it to the other side of his chest and listened. She furrowed her brows and put it back on his left side, then removed the diaphragm from his shirt and pulled it out of her ears, handing the stethoscope back to Ingrid. Leaning over him, she put her head close to his mouth and listened to his breathing for a minute without the stethoscope.

"Well…?" Ingrid asked.

"There is definitely something wrong with his breathing. When I listen on his left side, I hear a gargle."

"So, I was right. There is something wrong."

"Perhaps." She unbuttoned his shirt to check his chest. There was the bandage where they had removed the shrapnel, but another dressing was also on the left side. "Who put this here?"

"I did."

"I don't recall there being a wound there."

"While I was cleaning and bandaging his other wounds, I saw a cut there, so I put a bandage on it too. The blood had made it hard to see. I only noticed it after I cleaned him up."

Eva pulled the bandage off to look at the wound. "I need light. Bring me a flashlight." Ingrid went to the cupboard in the room and retrieved a flashlight, then hurried back. Eva took it from her and clicked it on. She pressed the wound, and when she looked at her finger, there was blood. She leaned in close, and blood was slowly coming oozing from it. She turned to Ingrid. "This is a minor wound, so it should not still be bleeding. Give me some forceps." Ingrid disappeared again, then returned after a minute with the forceps and handed them to her. "Hold the light, please." Ingrid took the light and held it over the wound so she could see. Eva stuck the nose of the forceps down the small hole until they hit something. "There is something in there. It is small. That must be how we missed it."

"Do you think something punctured his lung?"

"I believe so, yes. I'll go tell Dr. Möller. You will assist him in surgery so I can eat. And I want you to tell him you found it."

"But I didn't. You did."

"You knew something was wrong, which is why you went to find me."

"But I would not have thought to check that small of a wound."

"Doesn't matter. I'm going to go get him now." Eva left the patient ward and went back upstairs to Dr. Möller's office. This time, she didn't knock but walked in. He looked up from a piece of paper he was holding.

"Where is the soup?"

"I haven't warmed it yet. On my way to the nurse's station, I ran into Ingrid, who said the patient who had a gunshot wound to the thigh and shrapnel in the stomach woke up and seemed in distress and that he had labored breathing. His breathing was labored when he came in, but he should not still be breathing that way. There is liquid in his left lung."

"Liquid in his lung? How do you know this?"

"I could hear it, so I checked his chest for wounds and found a small hole over his left lung that was still bleeding. I stuck some forceps in the hole and found a piece of shrapnel. I believe it has punctured the lung."

"That was good thinking on your part. Let's get that out of him." He laid the paper on the desk and stood.

"I told Ingrid that she should help because she is the one who figured it out. Plus, I really need to eat."

"Are you sure?"

"Yes, let her help. I'll be making rounds with the other patients. That's where you can find me when you are done."

"Very well."

She followed him out of his office but went to the nurse's lounge and heated the soup, bringing it back to his office. She ate half of the soup and one apple, leaving the rest of the food for Dr. Möller. She returned to the patient ward and checked the other patients from the attack. They were all stable, and most were sleeping soundly, which was a good thing.

“Nurse, could I have some water?” the patient with the missing eye asked.

“Of course. Let me grab you some.” She went to the kitchen, filled a water glass, and brought it back. “Here, let me help you.” She held the cup in one hand and the back of his head with her other.

He drank the water, then laid back down, and she set the cup next to his bed. “I will leave this here in case you need more.”

“Thank you.”

The sound of a bed being rolled on the stone floor echoed through the room. Ingrid was pushing Bauer back into the ward. Eva walked to the end and waited in the spot where Bauer’s bed would go. “How did it go?”

“It went well. There was a long but thin piece of metal in his lung, which was causing blood to seep inside. The doctor said it should heal now, but he will need oxygen for a few days.”

“Aren’t you supposed to be going home soon?” Eva asked.

“I was due to leave half an hour ago.”

“Why don’t you go find Frau Wagner? I can take care of the rest.”

“Are you sure?”

“I’m fine. Go home.”

“Thanks, Eva.” She hurried out of the patient ward.

Eva got the oxygen tank and turned it on, placing the mask over his mouth and nose and putting the strap around his head. She checked his chart to make sure there wasn’t anything else he needed before she left. His chart was up to date, so she went to find Dr. Möller.

"Ingrid said the surgery went well." Dr. Möller was writing on a patient's chart as she approached.

"It did. I had not noticed that small hole before. There was so much blood on him when he came in and scratches on his body that I completely missed it. It was hectic, and I didn't have time to check every inch of each patient."

"I missed it too. It was the most chaotic day I have ever had. Ingrid said she found it when she was cleaning him and thought it was only a small cut, so she put a bandage on it."

"Well, you both did well tonight."

"Thank you, although it was mostly her."

He shot her a disbelieving look. "No, it was both of you." He looked around the room and then back to her. "You can go home now."

"My shift doesn't end for another two hours."

"That's fine. It is slow now, and I'm sure you are exhausted."

"I am. It has felt like an endless day. I think I will take you up on that offer."

"You seemed distant today. Is there something you want to tell me?"

"No, it's only that it was shocking to see all of those officers coming in like that. They looked like the men that come from the front lines."

"Someone was very brave and also incredibly foolish. They will eventually get caught, and when they are, that will be the end for them."

Eva swallowed hard. "You are right; they were very foolish." Her eyes stared past him, distant in thought. "I'm going to go now."

"Have a good night, Eva."

"You too, and please don't work all night. You also need to get some sleep."

"I'll probably sleep here."

She gave him a disapproving look. "Before I leave, you never gave me an answer about the ball this Saturday, that is if there is even still going to be one."

"How about I tell you later this week when we know if it's even happening?"

"Alright, but you are coming if I don't hear from you by Friday."

"I will make sure and give you an answer by then."

She cracked a smile. "See you tomorrow night." She got her purse, put her coat on, and was heading to the exit when the sign to the morgue caught her attention. She stopped and looked around, but no one else was in sight. The hall was dark and quiet, so she turned and walked in that direction instead of leaving. She went through the swinging double doors and flipped the switch. The lights flickered as they came on. Tables with bodies were lined in neat rows, all covered with white sheets. At first, she felt numb from the shock of it, but then she softly started to cry, still standing by the doors, looking at all of them.

She walked to the first table, hesitated, and then lifted the sheet from his face. There was a bullet hole in the side of his head, dried blood on his cheek, and matted in his hair.

She pulled the sheet farther down, and there were three more bullet holes in his chest. "I am so sorry. I didn't know you or what sort of life you lived or what kind of person you were, but I doubt you deserved this." She moved the sheet all the way down to his feet, but there were no signs of damage to the body from the explosion. The bullets alone had killed him. She pulled the sheet back over him and moved on to the next body. By the time she got to the fourth, she was sobbing uncontrollably, and the sight of them unnerved her, so she backed away from the table. She could not look at the others. The men's faces would haunt her dreams.

She turned and ran from the room, the door hitting the wall as it swung open. She didn't even bother to turn out the light. She went down the hall that led to the front door and kept running. Pushing it open, she hurried down the steps and stopped when her feet hit the grass. Sucking in a deep breath and forcefully blowing it out, she watched the cloud of air in front of her. She leaned over and put her hands on her knees, breathing heavily. The next few days were going to be difficult.

Chapter Eight

Saturday, March 29th, 1941

Eva could not believe they were still going to have the ball. Oberst Heinrich Schmitt had come by the hospital the day before to inquire if she was going to come. It surprised her how happy she was to see him alive. He had not been among the dead or wounded, but she still had her doubts that he was alright like she still had her doubts now about Gerhardt. She told him she would go to the ball and tried to appear excited, but inside, she still had her reservations. Could she bring herself to eat with the Germans and dance with them at an event that was meant to be celebratory when she helped kill many of them only days before? But she wasn't going to say no to Heinrich Schmitt. Her hope was that Dr. Möller would go, but that was probably hoping for a miracle.

"Eva," Frau Wagner called from two beds down.

Eva looked up from the patient she was helping to eat. “Yes.”

“When you are done there, the patients on this side of the ward need to be bathed.”

Eva was taken a little by surprise. “The duty roster for the day said nurse Roth and König were doing the bathing.”

“I changed it. You are doing it today.”

“By myself?” She didn’t why Frau Wagner was having her bathe all the patients on that side of the room alone, but she had her suspicions.

“Yes, you are obviously capable of doing a great many things by yourself. Why should you need help with this?”

“There are eleven patients on this side of the room. It will take the better part of the day to do it by myself,” Eva pointed out.

“You should get to it then.” Frau Wagner stuck her clipboard under her arm and walked out of the patient ward without looking at Eva.

Frau Wagner had to be trying to punish her somehow, for what this time she didn’t know. She gathered a tub of water, a washcloth, and a stack of clean PJs and towels, then started with the patient at the beginning of the row, working her way down to the end. Without the usual assistance, rolling the patients who couldn’t move on their own onto their side was harder than expected, and she had to rely on any help the patient could give, and dressing them was even worse. If she were going to finish in time to make it to the ball, she would have to skip lunch. It was a lot easier to clean the patients who were not conscious; it was a little uncomfortable for her, and she knew it must be for some of them, too, which made it even worse for her. But if they were unaware that she was bathing and changing them, it made it better.

When she got to Bauer's bed, she stopped. He had finally woken up but had been in and out of consciousness over the last five days because of his severe condition and the high doses of medication he was on. She didn't want him to wake up when she was near him, much less while she was bathing and changing him. He appeared to be sleeping, but moving him could easily wake him. She was almost tempted to skip him and move on to the next patient, but Frau Wagner would probably notice.

Going to the side of his bed, she looked at him and waved one hand in front of his face, but he didn't move. *Maybe he is in a deep sleep?* she thought. She picked up the washcloth and wrung it out, then gently wiped his face and neck, barely applying pressure so she wouldn't wake him. She moved the blanket back and pushed up the sleeves of his shirt, then wiped his arms, unbuttoned the top, and rubbed the cloth over his chest, careful to avoid the bandages. She cleaned his feet up to his knees, and that was where she was going to stop. No one would know. She took hold of his PJ bottoms and pulled them off, then put one foot at a time in the legs of the clean pair and pulled them up to his hips. Though doing so was difficult. She had to roll him a little to one side, then the other, in order to get them up all the way. She straightened, panting from the exertion. He was heavier than she had expected.

“Aren’t two of you usually doing that?” the patient on the bed next to Bauer’s asked.

“Usually, yes, but today, it is only me.”

“You didn’t bathe all of him like you did the others.”

She put her hands on her hips, still breathing heavily, and looked at him. “Don’t worry about the other patients. I’ll help you bathe and change when I’m done with him.” The patient next to Bauer had only a slight wound on his arm that he had gotten from the bombing, but he was not a soldier.

She pulled one of Bauer's arms out of the shirt, then the other. Once again, she had to roll him over on his side, push the shirt under him, then go to the other side and roll him over, pulling the shirt out from underneath him. She checked his bandages to make sure they didn’t need to be changed before she finished putting on his top. They would need to be changed soon, but for right now, they would keep. She put his right arm in the sleeve of the clean shirt and rolled him on his side again, poked the shirt underneath his back, then went to the other side and rolled him over and pulled the sleeve out from underneath him. She picked up his arm to put it into the sleeve when he opened his eyes and turned his head towards her. She gasped, letting go of his arm, and it fell back onto the bed with a light thud. He squinted his eyes at her. First, there was a look of confusion, then it faded, and anger was etched on his face.

“You…” His voice was low and scratchy, almost like a growl.

She looked around the room, but for what reason, she wasn’t sure. She hoped that someone else was standing close and they were who he was talking to.

"You were outside," he said.

"I'm sorry?"

"I remember. I was lying on a stretcher, and you were standing over me with another nurse."

"Yes, I was here when they brought you in."

"You told her to take me inside. Why was it you that gave that command and not a doctor?"

"All the doctors were busy. The other nurse wanted to put an M on your forehead to separate you from the patients with a better chance of survival but asked what she should do, so I took a chance and had you brought in."

"That was not your decision to make."

"You bastard, you act like you are mad that I saved your life instead of letting you die on that stretcher. In all right, I should have left you lying there. Heaven knows you didn't deserve my compassion." She couldn't believe it upset him that she had saved his life. The anger inside was mounting to a new high, but she couldn't let the feelings erupt in front of him.

"You are right." He reached over, took ahold of the other sleeve, and tried to put his arm in. She watched him struggle as his range of motion was limited because of his wounds. After his third attempt to put his shirt on, she took a step closer and took hold of his hand to help guide his arm, but he jerked it away.

"No," he said sternly, fire in his eyes and venom in his voice.

"You need help," she insisted.

"Not yours." He looked away from her and continued grappling with his shirt.

"Fine, go ahead and struggle. Do it yourself then." She turned to the other patient. "Let's get you cleaned up and changed."

The man looked at Bauer and then back at her. "What did you do to him?" he whispered.

"I saved his life," she said. "That's what."

"Looks like there is more to it than that. Why would any man be upset that a pretty nurse saved his life?"

"He is mad that this nurse saved his life, and he is not like other men. No more talking, please. I have a lot of other patients I still need to attend to."

"You must have done something to make him mad."

"I have not, and I don't want to talk about this with you." She could feel Bauer's eyes on her back. "You are all done." She picked up the PJs, put them in the dirty clothes bin, and then moved on to the next patient, happy to be farther away from Bauer. One of the other nurses would attend to him from now on. She wouldn't continue doing it.

When she was done with all the patients, she left the room without looking in his direction and breathed a sigh of relief. She liked it better when he was sleeping because she knew it would be unpleasant once he woke up. When she went to the nurse's lounge, Heidi and Liesel were already there changing.

"Eva, you look tired," Heidi said.

"You have no idea, and tonight is the ball. I don't know where I'm going to find the energy for that."

"I forgot all about the ball. Are you still going?" Liesel asked.

"Yes, I told Oberst Heinrich Schmitt that I would. He said he would pick me up at the apartment at six."

"Do you need someone to do your hair?" Heidi asked.

Eva smiled. "That would be nice, Heidi. Thank you."

"Well, I think you are going to need some warming up before you go to a dance," Liesel told her, taking a record from her locker. She put it on the player and turned the crank. Swing music filled the room, echoing off the walls, crackling as records always did.

"Liesel, you are a rebel. I didn't know you had forbidden music."

"Oh, I'm full of surprises," she said, smiling at her reckless decision.

"I believe that."

Heidi poured them each a glass of schnapps and held her glass high in the air. "May Eva be free of that awful man and fall in the arms of the most handsome man at the ball."

Eva smiled. "I am not a princess, and I doubt that will happen."

"Either way, you are going to have a hell of a good time," Heidi remarked.

They threw their drinks back, and Eva coughed. Her eyes watered, and her nose burned. "That is stronger than I had expected."

"Good." Liesel filled their glasses again, and they threw them back like before. Liesel led Eva to the middle of the room and they placed a hand on each other's shoulders, swaying to the music as Heidi danced by herself.

Dr. Koch came into the nurse's station and closed the door loudly behind him. "What on God's green earth is going on here? You know that music has been banned." He lifted the needle from the record, and the music stopped. "Are you guys crazy? What if someone else heard that?"

"We were only having a bit of fun," Heidi protested.

"Until the wrong person catches you, then it's no longer fun and games. Don't play that again in the hospital, and you really shouldn't play it anywhere." He turned and left the nurse's station.

"Well, he killed the mood," Heidi grumbled.

"Maybe he is right," Liesel said. "If we were to get caught, it would be bad, especially for Eva."

"You are probably right. Well, when you go to the ball, dance until your feet hurt. Do it for us," Heidi told her.

"I doubt I will be dancing at all, Heidi."

"Why would you not dance?"

"I won't even know anyone there except for the colonel. Who would I dance with?"

"A tall, handsome stranger," Heidi mused in a daydream.

"Heidi, sometimes I think men are all that goes through that head of yours."

"Can you blame me? I need to do something to keep my mind off the war, and besides, look around you. We are surrounded by men."

"I have, trust me."

"Should we have one more schnapp before we leave?" Liesel asked.

Eva knew she shouldn't, but she wanted to be more relaxed at the ball. "Alright, one more," she said against her better judgment.

Liesel poured some into each of their glasses, and again, Eva coughed and patted her chest as she swallowed the liquid.

"You are in Germany now. You have to learn to drink German alcohol," Liesel told her.

"I think you are right because it burns going down. Is it always like that?"

"No, when you get used to it, the burning goes away."

Eva set her glass on the table. "I was going to ask if either of you have seen Ingrid? I need to talk to her about something."

"The new nurse?" Liesel asked.

"Yes."

"The last time I saw her, she was doing laundry. Is everything OK?"

"It is. I need to tell her what I have done and what still needs to be done before I leave." She couldn't tell them the real reason she needed to talk to Ingrid.

"I'm going to find her, then head home. I will see you guys there." Eva headed to the laundry room to look for Ingrid. Karin and Ingrid were folding sheets when she walked in. "Ingrid, can I talk to you out in the hall for a second?"

"Sure." She handed the sheet to Karin and followed Eva into the hall.

"Ingrid, from now on, you will do everything with the

patient you asked me to help you with."

"I don't understand."

"I mean, anytime I am supposed to help with him, you will do it instead of me."

"Why?" Ingrid sounded suspicious.

"Because he doesn't like me, and he is making my job hard."

"Why would he not like you? He doesn't even know you, or does he?"

"He doesn't like me because I'm American. He only wants German nurses attending to him."

"Really? He said that?"

"In so many words, yes."

"I will help him, but only if you tell me the truth."

"I just did."

"No, you are telling me partial truths. When he called out saying where is she, I knew it was you he was talking about, and your reaction when you saw him, and now this."

Eva looked up and down the hall before turning back to Ingrid. "Fine. I know him, and we have hated each other from the very beginning. The main reason he doesn't like me is because I'm American. I don't know what his other reasons are, and that is the truth."

"And that is all of it?"

"It is. I did not get the chance to finish checking on him when he told me he didn't want my help, so I would appreciate it if you would finish up with him. I will be in the nurse's lounge changing, and you can meet me there when you are finished and tell me how it went."

"I guess." She turned and headed to the patient ward, looking back once at Eva.

Eva went back to the nurse's lounge and changed out of her uniform. She checked the clock, and it was four-forty; she was cutting it close.

Ten minutes later, Ingrid came through the door and sat at the table across from her. Eva gave her a questioning look.

"I took care of it, gave him his medicine, and changed his bandages. He watched me like a hawk the whole time. It was making me nervous."

Eva huffed. "He is like that. He is an awful man. I don't think he has an ounce of kindness in him. I'm sure his heart is black because he lacks a soul."

"Wow, you do really dislike him."

"Did he say anything to you?"

"No, but he watched me with those scrutinizing hawk eyes."

"I'm sure it will get better. At least he doesn't hate you."

"Hopefully."

Eva patted her hand and then stood. "I will see you tomorrow. My shift starts at one."

"I work the morning shift, but I'll be here until four."

"I'll see you then." Eva put on her coat and hat, then pulled on her gloves and walked to the tram stop. She hurried home because she didn't want to make Colonel Schmitt wait. She walked in the door, then shrugged off her coat and tossed her hat and gloves on the floor. "Liesel, Heidi?" she called.

"We are in here," Heidi called from her room. She

followed the voice and pushed her bedroom door open. Heidi was rubbing the wrinkles out of a dress on the bed, and Liesel was sitting on the edge looking through her makeup.

"What are you guys doing?"

"We decided to help," Liesel told her.

"Thank you, but you didn't need to do that."

"Yes, we did, or you would be late to the ball."

Eva sighed, "You are right. I would be."

"Sit on the bed, and I will do your hair while Liesel does your makeup," Heidi said.

"I can do my makeup while you do my hair. I don't need Liesel to do that for me."

"I don't mind. It will give me something to take my mind off things."

"Your mother?" Eva asked.

"It's hard not to think of her. I miss her a lot."

Eva took her hand. "I am sorry, Liesel."

"It's fine, Eva. I'm dealing with it."

"Are you? Liesel, you can talk about it. I have found that it helps when grieving. I know what it's like when you can't talk about the things that are weighing on you. Eventually, it will become too much to bear, keeping it to yourself all the time." Eva knew all too well the pain of keeping so much bottled up inside, but she also knew that Germans rarely enjoyed talking about their feelings.

"I will talk when I am ready," Liesel said.

"It got so gloomy in here, guys. Come on," Heidi said. "Let's think of the exciting ball Eva is going to. Plus, if we don't get started now, she will be late."

"Let me put the dress on first. That way, I don't mess up my hair or makeup while changing."

"Alright, hurry," Heidi said.

Eva took the dress off the hanger and went into the bathroom. It was a sleek silver dress covered with sparkles and an open back. The dress belonged to Liesel, who was roughly the same size as her. Liesel had several fancy dresses, and Eva didn't have one. The dress that Gerhardt bought her in France was still with him. She had forgotten to get it, and then everything happened. She slipped the dress over her head and came out of the bathroom. "How do I look?"

"Beautiful," Heidi said.

"I think it looks better on you than me," Liesel mused.

"I don't believe that."

"You should. Every man there will be falling all over you."

She shook her head, knowing they were only trying to make her feel better. "Do you have any shoes that go with it?"

"I do." Liesel disappeared for a few minutes, then returned with a pair of shoes that matched the dress. "I think they might be a little big for you, but they should stay on."

"It's alright. I can poke something in the toes to make them tighter if I need to." Eva sat on the bed, and Heidi rolled her hair in curls and then pinned them on top of her head, leaving a ringlet hanging on each side of her face. Liesel applied mascara, blush, and some red lipstick as Heidi did her hair. When they were finished, Heidi and Liesel took a step back and inspected their work.

"It's a masterpiece. She is a vision," Heidi said, smiling at her as if she was Michelangelo, who had just finished carving David.

"We did good," Liesel agreed, her arms crossed and her head tilted.

Eva smiled. "You guys are so overdramatic." She put the shoes on and stood up. "He will be here any minute."

Liesel went to the window and peered out. "I think he is already here. There is a fancy car out front with flags on the hood."

Eva hurried to the window and peered down at the car. "Yes, I believe that is him." She got her purse off the bed.

"You can't go in that ragged coat you wear to work," Heidi said. She left the room and quickly returned with a fur coat and a pair of silk gloves.

"What… no. That is too much."

"It is not. You have to look like you belong there. Hurry, put them on." She handed them to Eva, then sprayed her with some perfume.

"Heidi…" Eva said, waving her hands in front of her face to dilute the overpowering smell.

"Sorry, last thing."

"Here," Liesel said, holding the red lipstick tube out to her, "you might need this."

"I won't be kissing anyone if that is what you are suggesting."

She gave Eva a wry smile. "I suggested nothing."

Eva took it from her hand when there was a knock at the

door. She put the lipstick in her purse and shrugged into the coat.

"The gloves too, Eva, the gloves," Heidi said hurriedly.

Eva slipped her hands in and felt the smoothness of the silk. It was a pleasant feeling. "I'll see you guys tonight, don't wait up. I don't know when I will be home."

"We won't, but we want to hear all about it tomorrow," Heidi informed her.

"You will."

"You better go." Liesel took her arm, ushering her out of the bedroom.

Eva went to the door and opened it, and standing in the hall was Oberst Heinrich Schmitt's driver. "I am here to escort you to the car, Fräulein Abrams."

She looked back at Liesel and Heidi, then stepped into the hall and followed him outside to the car. He opened the back door for her, and she slid in.

Oberst Heinrich Schmitt was sitting in the back. "You look beautiful. This is a big change to the nurse's uniform you were wearing when we first met, and I mean no offense."

"None taken."

The driver got into the front seat, and the car pulled away from the curb and headed through town.

"This ball is not only for the enjoyment of the officers. It also serves as a reminder of the camaraderie of the Axis countries," Heinrich told her.

"So, this ball will have Italians and Russians as well?"

"It will. It is following a meeting that took place this

morning among the three countries."

"I had wondered why there was still going to be a ball after the attack Monday. That explains it."

He pushed the bridge of his glasses up on his nose with his index finger, and rubbed his right hand up and down his leg. "We had considered canceling it after the attack but then realized we needed something like this now more than ever. We have to show that something like this won't break us. We are a strong people and have been through more."

"It's terrible what happened," she said, not looking at him.

"It is. We lost a lot of good men and excellent officers. Unfortunately, there were some civilian casualties as well."

"I heard about that. Their deaths were sad and unnecessary."

"The people who did this will be captured and made examples of."

Her heart beat faster in her chest at his words. She couldn't stop thinking about the attack and all the wounded that showed up at the hospital, and being in the car with him now made her feel like the word guilty was written on her face.

"Did you know any of the victims?" she asked.

"I knew all of them, but not on a personal level. I was friends with a few, but all of them were good men."

She looked at him in astonishment. How could he say that about Bauer? She was sure that he had no moral compass or conscience at all. He lacked common decency as well as other normal human emotions, like compassion, empathy, or any higher-level feelings, for that matter.

"And you can say this about them with certainty that they are all good men?"

"I can." He turned in the seat and looked squarely at her. "Why?"

"I… what I mean is, how do you know that if you don't know all of them on a personal level?"

"Well, I know of each of them professionally and have dealt with them on a personal level. I have also spoken with men who have worked with each of them. I know they were all loyal, patriotic soldiers who did their jobs well."

"Yes, but that doesn't make them good people."

"Miss Abrams, are you trying to say that you know one or more of them to not be a good person?"

"No, not exactly. I was simply wondering how you knew that if you didn't know all of them personally. Did any of your friends survive?"

"One, but the other two died."

"Who is the survivor?"

"His name is Sebastian Graf."

"I remember him. He is doing well. His condition was better than all the other survivors when they arrived."

"That is what I was told. And how are the two in critical condition doing?"

She clenched her jaw. "They will survive. I can assure you of that." After her encounter with Bauer earlier today, she was already regretting saving his life.

"That is good. Germany will need them."

The car turned down a road lined on both sides with

Nazi flags and headed towards a massive white building with a large Nazi flag hanging on the front. She was going into the lion's den and of her own free will. Why did she choose this?

The car pulled in front of the building, then the driver got out and opened Heinrich's door. He stepped out, and she scooted over to his side, and he took her hand, helping her from the car. Then, the driver returned to the front and drove away. Heinrich held his arm out for her, so she linked hers through his, and they ascended the stairs. A man in a tuxedo was at each door to open it for them as they approached. When they were inside, another man in a tuxedo took their coats and directed them to the flight of stairs. Heinrich led her up the steps and down a hall to a closed set of double doors, which was opened for them by yet another doorman. They entered a large, opulent ballroom with a massive crystal chandelier hanging in the middle of the high ceiling. The room had tall windows spaced about every foot and a half all the way around, and the white plaster walls were covered in ornate carvings plated in gold. Around the edge of the long room, near the walls, were tables and waiters serving food. She had never been anywhere like it.

"Why don't we get a table and some food," he said, leaning in close so she could hear him.

"That would be nice. I didn't have time for lunch today, so I'm pretty hungry."

"Perfect." He led her to a table in the far corner of the room and pulled a chair out for her. He pushed it in as she sat, then took the chair across the table from her. When the waiter came by, they had the choice of fish or chicken, so she chose the fish. She couldn't remember the last time she ate it.

The waiter disappeared into the crowd, and Heinrich turned towards her. "Are you good at dancing?"

"I'm alright. What about you?"

"I'm fair."

Eva looked around the room, hoping that Dr. Möller had come, even though she doubted he would. It was hard to get him away from the hospital. The waiter returned with their food and sat the steaming plates in front of them. She looked down at the fish with a side of steamed mixed vegetables and wondered how she kept finding herself in situations where she got such fine food when so many others were starving.

"Is there something wrong with your food?"

She looked up. "No, I was merely trying to remember the last time I had fish."

He smiled. "You should eat it before it gets cold. Besides, the dancing will start soon."

She picked up her fork and knife and took a bite. The buttery lemon taste of the fish made her mouth water. It was one of the best meals she had eaten in a long time.

"Eva."

She looked up as Dr. Möller was approaching the table. She laid her fork next to the plate and stood to greet him, and he leaned in, kissing her on the cheek.

"Klaus, I am so glad you came. I honestly didn't think you would."

Heinrich also stood and shook his hand. "It is good to

see you again. Please," he gestured to an empty chair, "have a seat."

Klaus pulled out the chair next to Eva and sat down. "It was hard to get away from the hospital. For a while, I didn't think I was going to make it."

"We need to get you a plate of food," Eva said.

"Yes, an enjoyable meal will be a welcome change from what I usually eat. What are you having?" he asked, peering at her plate.

"I decided on the fish."

"Sounds delicious. I'll have that too." He waved to the waiter and asked for a plate of fish and a beer.

Heinrich looked at Eva. "I can't believe that we forgot about the alcohol. Would you like some?"

"I would. What are my options?" she asked the waiter.

"We have wine, beer, champagne, whisky, gin, schnapps—"

She held her hand up to stop him. "I'll have a glass of champagne."

He looked at Heinrich. "And you, sir?"

"I'll have a beer."

"I will be right back with your drinks." He turned and left their table.

"I was talking to Eva about the patients that came in on Monday from the attack. She says that the survivors are doing well," Heinrich said to Klaus.

"As well as can be expected. There was a complication with one of them a few hours ago, which is why I was late getting here."

Eva gave him a questioning look. "Which one?"

"The first patient you assisted me with, the one with a piece of metal puncturing his lung."

She had a spike of adrenaline. Was Bauer truly dying? Maybe he would, and most of her troubles would be over. It could undo the mistake she had made in saving him. She felt a little guilty for thinking that, but it was the truth. Part of her wished she had made a different decision that day.

"What was wrong with him?" Eva asked, trying not to sound too interested but only curious.

"He started having trouble breathing, and somehow, he had torn the stitches in his stomach. I honestly cannot think of how he could have done that unless he got out of bed or moved around."

Or twisted around to try and put his own shirt on, she thought. "I can't imagine how he could have done that," she said and put another fork full of fish in her mouth.

"Well, we got him re-stitched and upped his oxygen. We gave him a high dose of morphine, and he was sleeping when I left. Ingrid said she would keep an extra close eye on him tonight."

Eva smiled to herself. Ingrid was doing as she had asked.

The waiter came back with their drinks and Klaus' plate of food. Eva continued eating while she listened to Heinrich and Klaus talk about the war. As she listened, it was apparent that they both thought Germany was in the right and was justified in starting the war, as Bauer and Gerhardt did. The more time she spent with them, the more it convinced her they did not know about all the atrocities against the Jews. They had to know of them being rounded up and deported, but she doubted they knew about all of the mass killings, especially Klaus.

"What do you think of the fish?" she asked Klaus.

"It is very good. I need to strive for meals like this more often."

"I know. My dinners are usually lacking too."

"What is wrong with your usual dinners?"

"It's that we don't always bring the best food to the hospital, and half of the time, we don't eat dinner anyway, so it really doesn't matter, I guess."

"I see."

A man stood in the middle of the room and whistled until the people at the tables were quiet, then he announced that the dancing would begin in ten minutes.

They looked at one another. "Are you guys going to dance?" she asked.

"I suppose if you are my dance partner, I will dance to one song," Klaus said.

"I would love to."

"And one with me as well," Heinrich added.

"I'll give each of you at least one dance."

Once the music began playing behind them, people started crowding in the center of the room. Klaus stood up and held out his hand to her. "Shall we?"

Eva put her hand in his. "Yes."

He led her to the floor, then placed his hand on the middle of her upper back, and led.

"You are a fine dancer, Klaus. You should do it more

often."

He chuckled. "With whom?"

"Exactly. You need a woman in your life."

"I don't have time for a relationship. You know that."

"That's only because you don't make time."

"Don't worry about me, Eva. You should focus on securing your own future."

"I think about it, but now isn't the time, and we weren't talking about me."

"I think you use that as an excuse because you are afraid."

"Afraid? Afraid of what?" she asked.

"I don't know, you tell me?"

"I'm not afraid. It's that I want it to be with the right person. And remember what I said, during a war is not the time for that."

"There is some logic in that. However, it could very well be the happiness you need in this dark time."

"I'm happy–enough."

Klaus raised his eyebrows, his eyes locked on hers, challenging her words.

The song ended, and he led her back to the table. Heinrich stood up, took her hand, and led her back to the dance floor for the next song. He was not a bad dancer either, but it felt different dancing with him because he was closer to her height than Klaus, who was tall.

"You seem very fond of him."

She looked over to the table where Klaus was sitting. "I am. He is like a father to me. One of the kindest people I have known."

"It is good that you have the opportunity to work with a person of his character and integrity."

"I consider myself very lucky."

"I was planning on checking on the wounded men tomorrow. I thought it would lift their spirits to know that we have not forgotten about them," he said.

"I'm sure they would appreciate that."

"I almost forgot. If you want, I can introduce you to our guest here at the ball?"

"Oh, sure. Would they even want to meet me?"

"I'm sure they will be happy to make your acquaintance."

When the song was over, she followed him back to the table. "Do you want to meet them now or wait until you have rested for a minute?"

"Let's wait."

"Alright."

They both sat back at the table with Klaus. "Will you be at the hospital tomorrow?" Klaus asked her.

"Yes, I work the night shift."

"Frau Wagner had made a comment when I re-stitched the patient today that you had not done your job and bathed him," Klaus told her.

"Why would she say that?"

"Something about he didn't look or smell clean."

"Well, I will make sure to do it better next time."

"Can I have this dance?" A voice said from behind.

The deep, smooth sound flooded her ears, and

goosebumps spread over her body. She would know that voice anywhere. She almost didn't have the courage to turn around. The doubt came out of nowhere. Could she look at his face again or into those deep blue eyes? It didn't matter, she knew she had to. Turning in her chair, she peered up at Gerhardt standing over her, in a pressed uniform, with his shiny blond hair combed to one side. The dim lights in the room glowed on his face, and the corner of his mouth pulled up into a smile. Her mouth, however, was slightly agape from shock at the sight of him, and looking up into those bright blue eyes felt like coming home.

He held his hand out to her, and she didn't hesitate. Reaching up, she put hers in his. He closed his hand around her fingers and pulled her from the chair, leading her to the dance floor. He faced her, then their fingers interlocked as he placed his other hand firmly on her lower back. Their eyes met, and the gaze lasted for a second, then he glided them across the dance floor.

Chapter Nine

✠

At first, she didn't speak but simply looked at him, watching his eyes move over her face as he took it in. She was at a loss for words, all this time not seeing him or even so much as a message, and now they were dancing.

"Why are you here?" she asked.

"This is an officers' ball. I should be the one asking you that question."

She felt a tinge of embarrassment. "What I mean is, why did you ask me to dance? I left a letter for you at the Reichstag some time ago that you never responded to, even though you knew I was in Berlin. You left me here all alone in this city, surrounded by the enemy. It was a cruel thing you did. I asked you to come and see me, but you didn't. I mean, I get that you are upset with me, which you have every right to be."

"Eva, I am not mad at you. I knew you were hurting. I probably would have said something like that, too. I didn't come to meet you because I thought it would be dangerous and too much for you to bear. When I got your letter, it shocked me that you were in Berlin. Of all the places you could have gone, why did you come here?"

"Because I was left with only one option. You told me to leave France, and I could not return to England or go home. Coming here to work with the Red Cross was the only option left open to me."

"Germany? No, I don't believe that is true." His eyes bore into hers.

"They told me in France that this is where I was needed, so I came."

He shook his head. "You never should have come here, Eva?"

"I was scared, Gerhardt. I had recently lost the only people I knew, and then you came to my room telling me I was going to be arrested and that I needed to leave. I thought maybe they would not think to look for me living among them, right under their noses."

"SS Obersturmbannfürer Bauer is here, Eva."

"I know he is."

He furrowed his brows. "You know? How?"

"He has already brought me in for questioning. He knows you helped me escape, Gerhardt."

"I don't know how he could not. It was obvious. You have to leave Berlin."

"And go where?"

"It doesn't matter, anywhere. Go to Sweden or Spain. They are neutral countries."

"And how would I get there? I would need a pass, and I have no chance of getting one. They are not going to give me one."

"I will see what I can do," he said.

"No, you can't do any more for me. Gerhardt, Bauer said he is going to report you for helping me. Don't dig yourself in deeper."

"I'm actually surprised he hasn't done it already."

"You knew he might?"

"I suspected, yes."

"He won't for a while. He was a victim of the attack on the German High command. He almost died and is still in critical condition at the hospital," she informed him.

"At the hospital, the one you work at?"

"Yes, I assisted with his surgery." She didn't want to tell him it was her who saved him or that she was to blame for him being there.

The song ended, and some couples left the dance floor as others came on when the new song started. He didn't let go of her. "Dance with me again?"

"Of course." He twirled her once and moved them to the middle of the floor, then her hips swayed with his. He was an excellent dancer and held onto her firmly but gently as their bodies moved in sync.

"Until I got that letter, I thought you had found a way home and were safely back in America, away from all of this. That is what I had hoped happened."

"When I got to Berlin, the first thing I wanted to do was look for you, but then I thought maybe you wouldn't want to see me, so I didn't try to find you for a long time. I don't know the reason, but one day, when I was waiting for the tram, I decided I was going to let you know I was here. I'm not sure what made that day different from all the others. A moment of weakness, I guess."

"I wish you had let me know sooner." His face grew serious. "Eva, I have to tell you something. So much time had gone by, and I had not heard from you, and like I said, I assumed you had made it home. I was certain that day I watched you drive away that it would be the last time I would ever see you."

She let go of his hand and pulled from his grip, taking a step back, letting her own hands fall at her sides. She already knew what he was going to say.

He looked down into her hazel eyes. "When I returned home to Berlin, it was clear my dad still expected me to get married. The man Emma had been seeing while I was away wasn't nice to her, so she left him. Our parents still wanted us to get married, and I already knew her, so we talked about it and decided it made sense for us to get back together. We were a couple again a month after I returned home."

The pain in her heart was searing like a hot iron poking deep in her chest as it tightened, restricting her breathing, and she wondered if she could manage to stay standing or if someone was going to have to pick her off the floor. Her happiness, her world, had been shattered for the second time by the same man.

He took a step towards her, but she moved back again. "Eva, I did not think I would ever have to tell you about her because I didn't think I would ever see you again. I will always be yours, and in my heart, you will always be mine, but we cannot be together now. This war makes it impossible, and it would only get harder for us. Through all of this, it has been you and me, and in the end, it will be you and me again. Only it can't right now, not like this. Please try and understand."

Tears rolled down her cheeks. Who was going to save her from being broken this time? Who was going to help her pick up the pieces? "I don't quite know what to say or how I'm supposed to be feeling right now. I didn't want this to end."

"There is no end to my love for you, Eva."

"I don't understand you. You made me love you, and then you stomp on my heart." She walked off the dance floor back to the table, and he followed her. When she got close to the table, Klaus stood, watching the two of them closely, keeping his eyes fixed on Gerhardt.

"What is going on here?" he asked, noticing her distress.

"It's nothing to worry about. He was just leaving," she said, glaring up at Gerhardt.

Heinrich stood from his chair, too. "Explain yourself, captain. Have you done something to the lady?"

"No, sir."

"Then why is she crying?"

"It's a personal matter that I wish to discuss with her if that's alright?"

"No, it's not alright! Please leave," she said, stepping back to stand next to Klaus.

"Eva?" he pleaded.

"Go!" she yelled, louder than she had intended.

"You heard her," Heinrich said.

They briefly made eye contact before he turned and disappeared into the crowd. Heinrich and Klaus both sat back down after Eva took her seat.

"Eva, what happened?" Klaus asked.

"Really, it's nothing." She looked at the table, smoothing the cloth in front of her, not looking at him.

"It doesn't look like nothing."

"Nothing I want to talk about, then."

"Do you want to leave?" Heinrich asked.

"No. How about you introduce me to your guest." She really wanted to leave, but she couldn't allow Gerhardt to have this kind of control over her, not anymore. From now on, she needed to harden her heart and adjust to this new reality, but she was afraid she would always live in the shadow of his memory. Again, she found her heart and mind were at odds, and like before, she wanted so badly to hate him, but at her core, she loved him. This was the second time he had hurt her, and she needed to try harder to keep her heart guarded when it came to him.

Heinrich glanced around the room. "It looks like some of them went home, but I still see a few near the back wall I can introduce you to. Follow me."

She stood and walked with him to the back of the room towards two men in the corner holding beers as they talked. One of them was very short, shorter than her, and had shiny black hair and a thin mustache. The other man was tall with light brown hair, blue eyes, and broad shoulders, wearing a Russian uniform.

"Eva, this is Lorenzo Ricci. Lorenzo, this is Eva Abrams," he said, speaking to the short man.

He took her hand and kissed it. "Nice to meet you," he said in Broken German with an Italian accent.

"And this is Sergei Ostrovsky."

The Russian also took her hand and barely touched his lips to the back of it. "It is a pleasure," he said in German. His was better than the other man's.

"Eva here is an American," Heinrich told them.

"An American. What brings you here?" Sergei asked.

"Well, that is a very long story. How much time do you have?" She could use a distraction right now, and running through the last few years would do exactly that.

"I have the rest of the evening."

"Then have a drink with me, and I will tell you all about it."

"I never say no to a drink."

He followed her back to the table along with Heinrich and pulled up an extra chair. He waved the server over to their table and ordered them all a round of schnapps.

One hour and six schnapps later, Eva had covered her life in Utah and her journey to England, France, and Germany. She told of how she broke her arm and couldn't leave France before the Germans invaded. She talked about wanting to help in some capacity, so she joined the Red Cross and came to Germany. She was now feeling tipsy and light-headed from the six schnapps.

Heinrich observed Eva's decreasing mobility and how she struggled to speak normally. "It is getting late. I should take you home now."

"No," she said and took a sip from the seventh glass of schnapps she had recently ordered.

"You can't go home by yourself like this."

She waved her hand at him. "I'm fine… goo." Her speech was slurred.

"I can take her. I was planning on being here a while longer anyway," Sergei told him.

Klaus looked at Eva. "I can stay and take you home if you like?"

"No, you have patients that will need you tomorrow, so you should go."

"If you are alright staying?"

Heinrich stood, then took her hand. "I will be by in a few days to check on the patients." He then planted a kiss.

She gave him a smile, then he released her hand and left the table.

When Klaus stood to leave, she grabbed his hand. "Be careful with Bauer. He might arrest you, too." She pointed her finger up at him with an unsteady hand.

"Who?"

"The hateful one. He would rather hurt himself than accept my help. He is so arrogant and prideful."

"Eva, what are you talking about?"

She started laughing. "He has even you fooled." She dropped his hand to the table.

Klaus turned to Sergei. "Take care of her. Make sure that

she gets home safely, and it should be sooner rather than later. I will find out if something happens, and you know what I mean."

"I will make sure she gets home safe. And I promise nothing will happen to her."

"Yes, you will," Klaus said and gave him one more, don't disappoint me look, then left the table.

"Who is this man that you speak of?" Sergei asked once Klaus was gone.

She chuckled as she finished her schnapps. "He is a patient at the hospital and an ass."

"Well, either way, it sounds like you don't like him."

"You have no idea." Her expression changed to one of solemn. "You know, once he held me down to a table and told me he would do worse to me than break my fingers and knock out my teeth."

"This man at the hospital did that to you?"

She hiccupped. "He did."

"Why would he do that?"

"Because he is a psychopath, you can't reason with people like him. They can't be trusted."

"They who?"

"The Germans. I don't want to talk about him or this anymore. Let's talk about something else."

He eyed her strangely. "What would you like to talk about?"

"How about Russia? Tell me about your home." She leaned forward and put her chin in her unsteady hands.

"Alright. I grew up in the small town of Chelyabinsk

near Kazakhstan, but I now live in Smolensk. It's a town west of Moscow, close to the Belarus border."

"I know where it is."

"You do? I did not know that you were familiar with Russian geography outside of Moscow and Saint Petersburg. Have you been to Russia before?"

"No."

"Would you like to go?"

She lifted her head from her hands. "To Russia?"

"Of course. We have a lot of gatherings there like this one. You should come. I think you will find Russian hospitality to your liking more than that of the Germans. They are not the most outgoing people, and they don't know how to have a good time like the Russians."

"I don't know–it's not the best time to be going to Russia."

"Why would it not be?"

The room seemed to be spinning, and the taste in her mouth was of schnapps mixed with vomit. "Because of the invasion."

His amusement at her drunkenness faded. "What invasion?"

She quickly stood up. "I feel like I'm going to puke." She cupped her hand to her mouth and ran out of the ballroom to the women's bathroom. She went into a stall and dropped to her knees, leaning over the toilet, and threw up the schnapps along with the remains of her dinner. She flushed it, then slid to the floor, leaning back on the stall wall, her breaths coming hard and ragged. Her skin was damp, and some of her hair was matted to her wet forehead. She got some toilet paper and wiped her mouth, then hung onto the toilet to stand. It took enormous effort to stand and stay upright, so she put a hand on the wall to steady herself. She needed to lie down and was more than ready to go home. She rinsed her mouth in the sink, then returned to the ballroom.

Sergei was still at the table, waiting for her. He stood when he saw her. "Are you well? Do you need anything?"

"A cup of water would be nice."

"I'll get it for you. Sit down." He left for a minute, then returned with a cup of water and set it in front of her. "Drink."

She emptied the glass and set it back on the table. "I would like to go home now."

"Of course. Honestly, I'm surprised you can still stand. You were really putting them down. I've never seen a woman drink like that."

She stood up without looking at him. "I'm ready." She hoped all the alcohol would make her forget about Gerhardt and escape reality, even if only for tonight, but he was still there. She couldn't turn down the voices in her head. They were loud, and the image of Gerhardt kept running through her mind, spinning like they were still on the dance floor.

Sergei took her arm, picked her purse up from the table, and guided her to the front door. He got their coats and helped her into hers, then put his own on. "The car will be out front waiting," he said.

She nodded her head. The exhaustion came on so fast.

All she wanted was sleep.

She followed him to a black car parked out front, and he opened the back door for her, helping her in. She laid her head on the cold window, realizing how bad it was hurting. She could feel each heartbeat in her temples. She was barely aware of the drive to the apartment except for when the car would hit a rough patch of road, causing her head to lightly bump against the window.

She woke from someone gently shaking her arm. "Eva, we are here." Sergei's low voice helped finish waking her.

She sat up in her seat, trying to make sense of what was happening. She looked around the car, resting her gaze on Sergei. "Where is here?"

"Your apartment."

"How, I didn't tell you where I lived?"

"I looked at the ID in your purse while you were sleeping."

"You dug in my purse?"

"To see where you live. I didn't want to wake you, plus I wasn't sure if I could, anyway."

"Right."

"Let me help you." He got out of the car and went to her side, opening the door for her again. He took her hand, keeping hold of it until she was out, then grabbed her purse. "Do you need help inside?"

"I can manage." She took a step forward, but it felt like she was on a treadmill. She threw her hands out, trying to catch her balance, when Sergei grabbed hold of her arm.

"Maybe I should help you inside to make sure you don't

fall down the stairs."

"Maybe you are right."

He held onto her arm all the way to her front door. She opened her purse and rummaged around for the keys.

"Let me." He took her purse, found the keys, and then unlocked the door. He dropped the purse on the floor next to the door and helped her inside. He pulled her coat from her shoulders and hung it on the wooden coat rack. "Which room is yours?"

"The one in the back corner, there," she pointed toward her door.

He helped her to her room, sat her on the bed, and then pulled off her shoes. She fell back on the bed, so he picked up her legs, turning her so all of her was on the bed. "I will leave you now."

"Uh-huh," she said, not even opening her eyes.

Sunday, March 30th, 1941.

"Eva… Eva."

She opened her eyes to Liesel's face hovering above hers. "Why are you laying on top of your blankets still wearing your dress? What time did you come in last night?"

She sat up and put a hand on her forehead. "I don't remember. Actually, I don't really remember coming home or how I got in my bed."

"Someone must have brought you home."

"I think this Russian I was having drinks with is the one

that took me home."

"Maybe he left you this," Heidi said, picking up a folded piece of paper from her nightstand that read "Eva" on the outside and nothing else. Eva didn't even realize that Heidi had been in her room, too.

She took the piece of paper and unfolded it. "Yes, I was right. It was him who brought me home."

"It says more than that," Heidi said.

"It does. He is reminding me of the invitation from last night."

"What invitation?"

"To visit Russia."

"He wants you to go to Russia? Do you even know him?"

"Not really. I had met him last night, but I think I'm going to go." She tossed the note on the bed beside her.

"Are you serious?"

"I am. I need a break from Berlin."

"Then why don't you go to the country?" Liesel asked.

"Because Russia sounds more entertaining, and I need a distraction right now."

"I know it has been crazy at the hospital, but—"

"No, you don't understand. Gerhardt was at the dance last night and told me he was getting married."

"Ohhh… Eva, I am so sorry."

"It's fine. I simply need to forget about him. Somewhere inside, I knew this would happen, and I was stupid for ignoring the feeling."

"How could you have known?" Heidi asked.

"But I did. I even told him in France that we couldn't be together, but then I saw a spark of hope and thought that maybe we could, only I was being naïve. That is exactly what he told me last night, that we could not be together. It felt like he was tearing out my heart. That ounce of hope I had been holding onto was gone in an instant. I tried to drink until I couldn't remember who he was or feel the pain of it anymore. That is why I don't remember coming home. I was so drunk that I even puked at the ball."

"You should not have done that over a man. He isn't worth it," Liesel said.

"But I wanted the pain to stop."

"I know. Maybe it would be good if you went to Russia for a few days after all. Did he say in the letter when to come and for how long?"

"He did. There is a ball there next Saturday. I will leave on Friday and come home on Monday if I can get it off."

"Honestly, do you really think this is a good idea? Russians are strange people," Heidi said.

"Not any stranger than we are, Heidi. Did you guys get home now?" She asked, realizing they were wearing their uniforms.

"We did. It was a long shift."

"I'm going to get in the shower. I smell of alcohol and vomit."

"Yes, you do," Liesel agreed. "We are going to go lie down. Do you need anything before we do?"

"Not unless you can make my head and heart stop hurting."

"I would if I could."

"You guys go lay down. I'm going to go for a walk after I shower and try to shake this hangover."

Liesel took her hand and squeezed it. "It will get better."

"I know it will, with time."

Eva showered and ate something to settle her stomach and give her a little energy. She checked the medicine cabinet and took something for her head. The apartment was quiet, so she figured Liesel and Heidi were already asleep. She picked her purse up off the floor, not remembering how it got there, and stuck the note inside, then put on her coat and scarf. She closed the door softly behind her and descended the steps. She followed the address on the note that Sergei had left on her nightstand. He told her that he would go back to Russia on Friday and to come by the hotel where he was staying and let him know her decision.

He said he was staying at the Hotel Kaiserhof on Reichskanzlerplatz. She could see the building not far ahead on the right side of the street. It was a simple, square five-story building made of white stone, but still a pretty building nevertheless.

She crossed the street and entered the lobby, going straight to the front desk. A short man with dark hair, a mustache, and little round glasses looked up at her when she rested her hands on the desk. "Hi, can you tell me what room Sergei Ostrovsky is staying in?"

"Is he expecting you?"

"He is. He asked me to meet him here."

"He is staying in room five-eleven, but he is not here

right now."

"Oh, do you know what time he will be back?"

He looked over his glasses. "I don't. Keeping track of the times the guests come and go is not my job."

He seemed annoyed that she asked. "I'll come back later then." She would have to find something to do while she waited. Once back outside, she found a bench and sat down. She wasn't going to stay on the bench all day, but she needed to think about what she was going to do for the next few hours. Her head was feeling better, thanks to the medicine. She looked up and down the street, watching people walk by and the cars pass on the road. She wondered if she should try to leave Berlin as Gerhardt suggested. She thought of the letter she had sent Jon a while back and wondered when she would hear from him again. She knew it always took a long time for correspondence to travel between England and mainland Europe. That mail had to be directed to a neutral country first.

To her right was the steeple of a church towering over the top of a building a few blocks away. She stood from the bench and walked in that direction. She wasn't entirely sure why, but she had the desire to sit in a church, to be in its quiet, comforting space.

She paused on the sidewalk across from the church and read the golden sign next to the door. It surprised her a little that it was a Roman Catholic church. She crossed the street and ascended the steps, pulling open one of the heavy brown doors as it creaked against the strain. She pushed open the second set of smaller doors and entered the main chapel. She found a pew near the front and sat down on the hard, polished wood, admiring the beautiful architecture of the building, from the high ceiling to the pillars and down to the white marble flooring. She marveled at the enormous Gothic structure and loved the atmosphere. She was the only person sitting in the chapel, which made her happy. She stood and went to light a candle; she had never believed in things like this, but now it seemed like the right action. She couldn't think anything of better. She dropped a coin in the box and picked up a small white candle, lighting it from one of the already burning ones. She set it in the candle holder and prayed about everything that seemed wrong in her life.

When she was finished, she got off her knees and stared into the flame, not knowing if her prayers would change anything. The stress was a little less, but the sadness remained the same, eating her up from the inside.

"Is there something I can do for you?" A voice echoed from behind.

She turned, and a priest was standing a few feet away in his long black robes. "I came in to sit for a while."

"And has that helped?"

"Some."

"But not what you were hoping for?"

"I don't know what I was hoping for, a miracle, maybe."

"Well, those can happen, but you have to give it time. I'm guessing you need proof of one, though?"

"I guess…."

"I understand. We all struggle with faith, but I don't think that is why you are here."

She looked back at the burning candles. “No.”

“Do you want to talk about it?”

“I do, but I don’t know if I can.”

“How about I go in the confessional booth, and you on the other side and tell me whatever you want, or we can sit there in silence if that makes you more comfortable?”

She nodded and followed him to the confessional booth at the back of the chapel and stepped into the side opposite him, closing the door. She sat down and pulled the divider back, revealing a screen. “I have never given a confession before,” she admitted.

“That’s alright, you can simply talk. I knew right away that you weren’t Catholic. This isn’t really a confession anyway. It’s you talking and me listening.”

“The thing is, I don’t even know where to start.”

“How about you start by telling me why you are here.”

“Alright, I can do that, but if I am going to talk about why I am here, I have to go back in time a little.”

“That is fine.”

“As you can probably tell, I’m not German.”

“I can.”

“Before the war came to France, I was there helping people fleeing occupied countries. I was supposed to return to England before any danger of an invasion was imminent, but I broke my wrist and was stuck there. I stayed with a family, who I became very close to, and was still living with them when the Germans invaded. During my time there, I also became friends with one of the German officers occupying the town, and with time, it became more than only a friendship. I found out he was engaged, but we didn't take our relationship any farther until he broke off the engagement. I guess their relationship wasn't that good when I met him, which is why he ended it. Sometime later, some soldiers came to the farm where I lived, and an accident happened. One of them shot and killed a little girl who was like a sister to me. The man that I loved is the one who sent the soldiers to the farm, but if I had never befriended him, that would not have happened." Tears rolled off her cheeks and fell onto her lap.

"Do you believe some things happen for a reason and others have no purpose?" he asked her.

"I don't know, I guess."

"That might have been one of those things that happened without reason."

"But it's not. Everything that led up to that was because of me, everything. We make choices, and life makes us pay for them."

"If that is the case, I will ask you another question. Do you believe that everyone is worthy of forgiveness?"

"Maybe not everyone."

"Yes, everyone, that is why Jesus died on the cross. If he didn't die for everyone, then who did he die for?"

"I suppose you are right."

"So, in that case, you, too, can be forgiven. But from what I understand, you did nothing wrong. What happened was not intentional on anyone's part. I think the only one who needs to forgive you is you. You need to stop blaming yourself for this. You didn't know this would happen, but this isn't the only thing bothering you, is it?"

"No, it is not. After all of that, I left France and came to Germany to work for the Red Cross. I was hoping to see this German again, who I knew was here. I saw him for the first time yesterday, and he told me he was back with his fiancé, although in France, he told me he loved me and wanted us to be together. I don't even know what to make of that. If he was really in love with me, why would he get back with his fiancé?"

"Did he not tell you why when you saw him?"

"He thought I had found a way back to England because he had not seen or heard from me in so long. He said he was sure he would never see me again."

"If he told you he loved you, I'm sure he meant it. He probably really thought he would not see you again and didn't want to be lonely, so he returned to what he was familiar with."

"But what do I do? Do I fight for him or let him go?"

"I think if you two are supposed to be together, he will see that and come back to you, and if not, then I would leave it alone."

"When I saw him yesterday, he told me he still loved me, but he was going to marry her, anyway."

"And again, I believe he was telling you the truth."

"But then, why would he still go through with marrying her? I don't understand."

"Because you have to take other things into account besides only your love for a person. I know love can be all-consuming, which is why we need to think with our heads, too, and not solely our hearts. He is most likely trying to think with his head right now and not his heart. But, sometimes, the combination of these two things makes our emotions and our decision-making inseparable."

"So, he is doing this because it is the logical thing to do?" she asked.

"In a way. I don't know him. I only know the little you have told me. But yes, I would say that is what he is trying to do. If someone has had a big impact on our lives and our experiences, and when you combine that with love, what we might feel for them is a mix of emotion and reason, and that influences our behavior. Unfortunately, we make most decisions based on a subconscious yet emotional impulse, and I think that is because they are always intertwined. He seems to have a firm resolve, though."

"Sometimes I wonder why we love at all. Why do we have to feel its sting? Then, you look at this war and realize that pain is all around us. It is a broken and cold world that we live in."

"Because if we didn't have love, we wouldn't be whole, and if there wasn't love, the world would be so much worse than it is now."

"Yes, but love is painful and opens us up to a world of problems we didn't have before we had it."

"This is true, but if you could, would you go back and never fall in love with him, never meet him?"

She thought about what he said and knew she could never go back to not knowing he existed. "No."

"That is what I'm saying. Even if it hurts, it was worth

it. Sometimes, the loving thing to do is to leave, even if it hurts the other person because staying would hurt them even more. I obviously don't know all the details about your relationship, but from what you have told me, I believe he is doing what he feels is the right thing for both of you, even if you disagree with his decision."

"But I don't want to wait around to see if he comes back to me."

"And you shouldn't. You now have to make decisions as if he never came into your life."

"You are right, but it's so hard. Even knowing I should try to do what is best for me."

"Time can do a lot."

"Can I ask you something else?"

"That is why I am here."

"Do you think someone can be forgiven for anything, even if they did something really terrible?"

"I do, but I think the time spent repenting and the effort put into it must equal the sin. And they truly need to be sorrowful and want to be forgiven with all of their heart."

"How can someone make amends if they did something truly awful to many people and want to make it right, but they don't want those people to know they were the one who did the thing to them?"

"Oh, now that is an interesting question. Did they hurt these people in some way?"

"You could say that."

"Then maybe they should right the wrong they did to these people in whatever way they can and ask for forgiveness, if not from the people, then from God."

"You must know that one of these people is a terrible person who also hurts others."

"Then that is between them and God, but it is still up to the person who hurt them to do what they can to make it right."

"And you think that person deserves that?"

"They do, and the same forgiveness as everyone else."

"And what would this person need to do to make it up to them?"

"Whatever it takes."

"And what if that person rejects their efforts to amend?"

"They need to keep trying, and eventually, they will have done all they can, and whether the other person accepts it or not is up to them. What they do is independent of the other person's willingness to repent."

"Sometimes it is hard to feel you can come back from something and be forgiven." She didn't know if she could ever forgive herself for hurting those people. Even Bauer.

"I believe we judge ourselves more harshly than anyone else. The grace of God is gentle and forgiving, even if we feel like we don't deserve it."

"Thank you, Father." Eva stood and opened the door, stepping out of the small booth. He came out of the other side. I appreciate you listening to me."

"That is what I am here for. If you want to talk again or feel the need for a quiet place to sit, you are always welcome."

"Thank you." She turned and walked through the chapel,

her footsteps echoing through the building. She stepped outside and turned back towards the hotel, the cool breeze nipping her face. She felt better and worse at the same time, only she didn't understand how that worked. But finally, there was a sense of where she thought her life would go from here. Gerhardt was going to get married, and they would never be together. That was something she had to accept. She also needed to muster a lot of humility and swallow her pride if she was going to make it up to the people in the hospital for what she had done to them.

Chapter Ten

✠

Monday, March 31st, 1941

It was relatively slow at the hospital, which was strange but nice. It allowed Eva to clean the nurse's quarters, mop the floors, and help bring the patients their food before it was time for them to be washed and helped into fresh clothes. She would have to deal with the patients from the attack and dreaded the thought. How could she make it up to them without asking for their forgiveness? The only thing she could think of was to give them the best care she could and be as kind and accommodating as possible. The one person she had doubts about was Bauer. She wasn't sure she could bring herself to grovel at his feet. He probably wouldn't welcome it anyway, or her help, like before. Maybe it would be fine if she only tended to the others for her penance and left him be, but would that truly make her feel better? She felt ashamed for what she did to him and the others, and yet she couldn't help but feel that Bauer deserved what he got. Maybe letting him die instead of saving him would have been a just reward for the things he had done and for the people he had hurt. A thought popped into her head. Maybe her saving his life was enough. Perhaps no more was needed for forgiveness on his behalf but required for the others. She hoped that was true, and even if it wasn't, she was going to treat him as if it was.

She passed out trays of food and helped those in critical condition eat. The man who was blinded in one eye also had a badly wounded hand, so it was difficult for him to feed himself. He gave her a faint smile as she held the spoon to his mouth. A knot formed in her stomach; he was being nice to her, the person who did this to him, but he didn't know. She smiled back and dipped another spoonful of porridge from the bowl.

"How are you feeling?"

"It hurts when the medicine wears off, and I feel dizzy when I'm on it."

"I'm sorry. In a few weeks, it should be better. Hopefully, you won't need the strong medicine longer than that. Your wounds seem to be healing nicely."

"I think most of that is because of the good care I get here."

"The nurses and doctors are all very good at what they do, and they care, which makes a big difference. I will be back to bathe you, then some orderlies will come to help you into a different bed so we can change the sheets on the one you are in now."

"Another thing that helps is that the nurses here are so pretty."

She smiled. "Most of them are, yes." She stood and carried the tray to the food cart and slid it on the bottom with the other trays of empty dishes, then picked up another tray of porridge. She walked to Bauer's bed and set the tray on the table next to him. He had his eyes closed, and she wondered if he was asleep or merely resting his eyes. She looked around the room for Ingrid, wondering if she should let her help him eat. Ingrid had agreed to help him from now on, but she couldn't find her anywhere, so she turned back to Bauer. She looked at the food next to his bed, and the thought of putting a large amount of pain meds in it popped into her head. She glanced away. *Why did I think that? What is wrong with me?* After a thought like that, it was clear she should get Ingrid to help him. She wasn't sure she could trust herself around him.

She left his bed to find Ingrid and ran into Frau Wagner, who was coming in. "Eva, where are you going?"

She paused. "I… was going to find Ingrid?"

"Why do you want to know where Ingrid is?"

"She was going to help me with something?"

"It's a slow day. I don't think you need her help with anything. Besides, she is busy doing something else now.

"I'll catch her later then." Eva turned and went back to Bauer's bed.

"Eva," Frau Wagner called after her.

She turned back, and Frau Wagner was holding out a piece of paper. "A man came in a little while ago and asked me to give this to you." Eva took a few steps and took the paper from her. "Don't let this become a habit. We are a hospital, not a mail service," she said with her usual sternness.

"It won't," Eva assured her.

When Frau Wagner left the room, Eva sat on the end of Bauer's bed and unfolded the note.

The winter iris blooms not only in Düsseldorf in November, but it will also take center stage amid the change from winter to spring in March as it grows to be tall and exotic. They can best be seen from the Schildhorn at Grunewald as the sun sets.

She folded the paper and stuck it in the pocket of her apron. She understood it to mean that Helmut wanted to meet her before the sun was down, but she wasn't sure where the location was that he mentioned. Irises grew around the city, but maybe there were fields of them at Grunewald. Her shift ended a few hours before sunset, and she hoped she could find the place and get there and home before curfew.

She put her hand on Bauer's shoulder and lightly gave him a shake. He opened his eyes, but it took a few seconds for them to focus on her, and then he blinked a couple of times. "What do you want?"

"What do I want? I don't want anything from you, but I

have to help you with your food because it's my job."

"There are other nurses."

"Right now, there isn't, so you are stuck with me. And if you act like you did the last time I tried to help you, I swear to God I will slap you."

He seemed surprised by her comment and the forcefulness of her voice. "You presume that you have power over me because of my current physical state." His glare was intense.

"I presume nothing, and I do. Your life is in my hands now."

"And that is a truly unsettling thought."

"If I wanted you dead, I would not have saved your life in the first place, and I could easily kill you in your sleep, so obviously, I don't want you dead." That was a lie because, most of the time, she did want him dead.

"You know I can't figure you out because if I were in your shoes, I would want me dead. I think you do, and yet you pretend you don't. It's true, you saved my life, which I still haven't figured out why, but I will."

"I told you why."

"You gave a reason, but not the real one."

"You don't have to believe me. Look, you need to eat because I have other things to do. Patients need to be bathed, and bed sheets need changing."

"Give me the bowl," he said, holding out his hand.

"No."

"No?" he asked, surprised by her response.

"You will let me do my job. Your left side is injured

more than your right side, and I know you are left-handed."

"How did you know I was left-handed?"

"Because in France, you held your fork with your right hand but drank your tea and did everything else with your left."

"I wasn't aware you paid that close of attention to me."

"You are not the only one who observes the people around you." She took a spoonful of porridge and held it up to his mouth. "Eat it." He opened his mouth, and she stuck the spoon in. Then he closed it, and she pulled it out harder than she had intended. She repeated the process gentler this time until the porridge was gone. He watched her every movement the whole time, scrutinizing her as he did. She swore the resentment he had towards her was tangible. Knowing that he was the vulnerable one now relying on her for the smallest of things, like eating, must infuriate him.

She put the bowl on the tray. "I'll be back shortly to bathe you and change you into a clean pair of PJs.

"You are the one that is going to do it?"

"Yes, I assisted with your surgery, and we had to remove your clothes. I was also the one who changed you the first time while you were still unconscious." She could see the anger on his face, but he said nothing. She only hoped that her decision to save him didn't come back to haunt her later. It was so hard trying to be nice to him, especially when she was forced into a position where she had to interact with him in a caring capacity.

She put the tray on the food cart and pushed it to the kitchen, where she left it to be dealt with later. She went to the nurse's quarters and sat down, completely drained. The door opened, and she looked up as Ingrid walked in.

"I was looking for you. Were you not helping with the patients today?" Eva asked.

"No, Frau Wagner had me cleaning the operating rooms because this is the first time in a long time that none of them were being used."

"I suppose that is a good thing."

"Why were you looking for me?"

"Because I wanted you to take care of Bauer. He still needs to be bathed and changed into a clean pair of PJs. Would you mind doing it?"

"I would, only I'm getting ready to go home. Is it really that bad having to be around him?"

"Yes. He told me today that he thinks I want him dead."

"What? Why on earth would he think that?"

"Because he hates me and thinks I hate him, which isn't too far from the truth, actually."

"Whatever has happened between the two of you, is there no reconciling it?"

Eva laughed cynically. "I think that ship has sailed. It might be possible on my part, but he has no interest in reconciliation. His personality fits his job, a cold and callous person who lacks empathy and compassion for anyone. That is the kind of people they look for to work in the Gestapo."

"He does seem that way from the little time I have spent with him."

"Well, I will get a break from him soon. I'm going on a trip for a few days. It will be nice to get out of here for a while."

"Where are you going?"

"Russia."

"Russia, why?"

"Because someone invited me."

"Who?"

"Someone I met while I was at the ball. I think they are excited to show off their country to someone who has never been there."

"Wow, I have never been to Russia. That sounds exciting."

"I think it will be an interesting experience. I guess I better finish up so I can leave on time. I'll see you later," Eva said, getting up from her chair.

"I really am sorry," Ingrid told her.

"It's alright, don't worry about it. At least right now, I have the upper hand. He is in no condition to fight with me."

"Not yet."

"I know. He is probably biding his time. I've got to get back." Eva went to find Frau Wagner and let her know she would be gone over the weekend. She also had to tell Dr. Möller that she was leaving.

She stood in the doorway of Frau Wagner's office and knocked on the doorframe. "Come in," Frau Wagner said, seated at her desk. Eva walked in, closing the door behind her. She took the seat across from her. "What can I do for you, Eva?

"I wanted to let you know I will not be in Berlin this weekend. I'm leaving on Friday and will be back on

Monday."

She narrowed her eyes. "I did not give you the approval to leave. Where is it you are going?"

"A Russian officer has invited me to visit him in his country."

"Why would he invite you to Russia?"

"I don't know his exact reason. Maybe because I told him I have never been to Russia, and he wanted me to see it."

"Many here have never been to Russia, but no one invited us."

"I don't know what you are implying, but I assure you he did it only to be nice."

"I'm not sure we can spare you."

"It has been very slow lately," Eva quickly said to counter Frau Wagner's reason for not wanting her to leave.

"True, it has. I suppose I will let you go, but I'm going to need you to make up for it later. There will come a time when I really need a nurse to step up, and I expect that nurse to be you."

Eva did not know what she meant by that. Step up to what she wondered? Whatever that situation might be, she thought she could probably handle it, and it might never come, so agreeing to it did not seem unreasonable.

"I can do that."

"Alright, make sure you are here for the night shift on Monday. Early!" she stressed.

"Of course. Thank you."

"Be sure you get all your stuff done before you leave."

"I will." Frau Wagner was a stern woman who rarely gave praises or accepted them from others. She never complimented someone when they did a job well but was always quick to scrutinize when someone made a mistake.

Eva stood from the chair and left Frau Wagner's office, pleased that it went as well as it had. She was going to finish up with the patients, and then let Dr. Möller know about her leaving. She went back into the patient's ward and gathered the things she would need to wash and change the four patients she was assigned. Liesel was also helping with the washing and changing of the patients today, and she was going to ask Liesel if she would switch one of her patients with Bauer.

She brought the wash pan and clean PJs to the other patient who was in critical condition and figured she would start with him. She looked around the room for Liesel and found her at the other end, helping a patient into his PJ shirt. She walked along the beds towards her. "Liesel," she called.

Liesel looked up from the patient. "Hi."

"I have a favor to ask."

"What's that?"

"I wanted to know if you would switch a patient with me?"

"You want to switch a patient? Why?"

"Because he wants a German nurse."

"Seriously?"

"Yes."

"That seems silly. He needs to not be so picky. We all have a job to do."

Eva sighed. She wasn't going to tell her the real reason for asking. "It will make my life easier if you would switch. He really is insistent."

Liesel stood and put her hands on her hips. "Which patient is it?"

"He is over there." Eva pointed to the other end of the room. Liesel followed Eva, and they stopped before they were in earshot of Bauer. "It's that one," she said, pointing to him.

Liesel walked towards him. "What are you doing?" Eva called after her.

"I'm going to have a talk with him."

"Liesel, no!" She hurried after her. "Liesel… wait."

Liesel didn't stop until she got to his bed. "I heard you wanted a German nurse."

"I don't recall saying that."

"Well, Nurse Abrams here says that you did, and I believe her. I don't know what rank you are or what you do, but here in the hospital, the doctors and nurses are the ones in charge. We all have our jobs to do, and we all do them well. So, Nurse Abrams here is going to help you, and you will not bitch about it."

Eva hid her face in her hands. She couldn't believe Liesel had done that. She made an unpleasant situation worse.

Liesel turned and gave her an I've got your back look before returning to her own patients. Eva watched her walk away, then turned and looked at Bauer, and for the first time, he did not appear angry, confused more than anything.

"If I were a betting man, I would say you told her I did not want your help because you didn't want to be the one to tend to me."

"Yes, I asked her to switch patients with me. I thought that would be best for the both of us."

"I don't like being helped by you any more than you like helping me, but for today, it looks like there is nothing we can do."

"I guess not. I have another patient I need to tend to first, then I will be back to help you." She turned and walked away without waiting for a response.

She returned to Bauer's bed after she was done with the other patient, poured some water into a wash pan, then picked up the bedpan, and held it up. "Do you have to go to the bathroom?"

"I do, yes."

"Alright. I won't look, but I need you to lift your bottom after I pull your PJs down. Then I will slide the pan under you."

"I know how this works," he said, looking at her like she was dumb.

She narrowed her eyes at him, then reached under the blankets and tugged his PJs down. She lifted the blanket slightly, sticking the pan under him as he lifted his hips and held the blanket for him. This felt so awkward compared to the other patients she usually did it for.

Once the pan was under him, she turned her back and waited. "You can take it now," he said a few seconds later.

She pulled it out from underneath him, carried it to the

bathroom, poured the yellow liquid into the toilet, and then set it with the other bedpans that needed cleaning. She washed her hands, then returned to his bed, retrieved the washcloth, and looked at him. There were no emotions that could be read on his face, but she saw something in his eyes.

"I know it takes great patience in learning to depend on others, and that's not always easy, but I think all of us, at some point in our lives, find ourselves here in a situation where we have to rely on someone else."

"Some more than others."

"Sure, but we are all weak at times or simply find ourselves in a precarious situation. All I'm saying is that it's OK to need someone's help once in a while. It doesn't make you weak."

"That depends on who you ask."

This was going nowhere, and, of course, he was never going to agree with her; they thought nothing alike. "I will be off soon, so we need to hurry this up. I have to get you changed and into clean bandages." She pulled the blanket down to his waist and unbuttoned his PJ top. "You are going to have to sit up." She put her hands on his shoulders and helped him into a sitting position. He made a grunt as he sat up, and the pain registered on his face. She pulled his arms out of the sleeves and laid the top on the bed. She took the rag from the pan and wrung it out, then wiped the warm cloth over his skin. For the first time, she noticed he had a few moles and freckles on his back.

The silence was deafening, and the situation couldn't be more awkward. She needed something to make the most of this less-than-pleasant situation they both found themselves in.

"Where did you learn to speak English?" she asked in German.

He turned his head to look at her. An odd look was on his face. "In school," he said in a dry tone.

She repositioned herself on the bed so she could wash his chest. She tried not to pull at the hair on it as she rubbed. "In college or public school?"

"At a university."

"Why English?"

"Why not English? It was a language I didn't already know."

"And you speak French as well."

"Yes, and Spanish."

"You speak four languages?" This surprised her. She really wanted to see him as an idiot.

"That shouldn't seem like that many to you, Miss Abrams. You speak three."

"I can, yes. Why did you decide to learn Spanish?"

"I like Spain. I go there whenever I get the chance."

"That is a good reason to learn Spanish, I guess," she said as she wiped at his stomach above the gauze. She was surprised by the muscles under his skin that defined his abs. She tried to ignore any features of his body.

"I find it strange for an American to speak a language other than their own. How do you know so many?"

"Well, my grandmother is French, and I took German when I was in school."

"Well, you truly are unique amongst your people."

"In France, you had told me you were stationed in Poland; do you speak any Polish?"

"I picked some up while I was there, enough to get by, but I would not say that I can speak it."

"You must have an aptitude for languages."

"I do, among other things. I don't believe in laziness. Dedication and hard work should be applied to all things. When you have that mentality, you can accomplish almost anything, which is why I know so many languages."

"It is good to work hard. It is one thing that will take you far in this life," she agreed.

"True, Miss Abrams, because no one is going to do it for you."

She wasn't sure what he meant by that, but knowing him, she understood it had some hidden meaning. Did he mean that no one was going to do anything for her? "I'm going to replace your bandages now. Then I will clean the lower half."

He nodded. She unraveled the gauze from around his stomach, then removed the square piece covering the wound. She cleaned it, placed a freshly cut piece of gauze over it, then took a fresh roll of gauze and re-wrapped it around his stomach. She then changed the bandage on his arm and shoulder and helped him into his PJ top. "I'm going to have you lie back down now." She held onto him as he lay back on the bed, then buttoned his shirt.

"Why did you choose German in school?" he asked.

"Because I could already speak French, and I don't like

Spanish and have no interest in Mandarin so that left German."

"No other explanation is needed, I suppose."

"I know that relying on someone to help you like this is intrusive. When I'm done washing your hair and shaving you, I can have one of the male orderlies clean and change the rest of you if that would make you feel more comfortable?"

"I don't give a shit. Now finish."

Eva was surprised by his sudden change of attitude. "Alright. I'm going to have you hold your head off the bed." She helped him scoot to the edge and put her hand under his head for support. She slid the bucket under him with her foot, then picked up the pitcher from the cart and poured some of the warm water over his hair. She put the pitcher back on the cart, picked up a bar of soap, and rubbed it in circular motions over his head until she had a lather. She rubbed his head with the tips of her fingers and massaged the soap into his scalp, then poured the rest of the water over his head, rinsing it, then took the other pitcher and poured it over his head to make sure all the soap was out. She took the towel from her lap, dried his hair, then helped him straighten back up. She picked up the shaving cream, dipped the brush in it, and rubbed it over his two-day facial hair. In the 1940s, they only used straight razors and safety razors. Both, in her opinion, were tricky to use. She took the razor and held it near his neck.

"I'm going to shave your neck first, so I need you to stay very still." He didn't speak but looked into her eyes. She took that as her cue to go ahead. She put the blade to his neck and went up in long strokes, careful not to cut him. She had to take extra caution when she got to his Adam's apple. It was so hard shaving men. She didn't know how they could do this every day. To her, it was harder than helping them bathe. She was always afraid she would slip up and cut one of them.

She was relieved when his neck was finished, and she moved on to his cheeks. After he was shaved, she wiped the rest of the cream off with the towel and inspected his face to make sure she didn't miss a spot, then returned the blade to the cart.

"I will make this as quick as I can."

She reached under the blankets and pushed his PJ bottoms down to his ankles, pulled them off, and then his underwear. She moved the blanket from his legs, then took the towel from the tub, wrung it out, and started at his feet, moving up. She dipped the rag in the water one more time before she washed the rest of him.

"Can you roll slightly to your left side?" He paused for a few seconds before rolling onto his side so she could get underneath him. She wiped the back of his legs and his butt. She was happy she could not see his face while doing it.

"Roll on your back again," she instructed.

He rolled onto his back, and she made sure to not look at his face as she mentally prepared to clean the front of him. When she reached under the blanket with the cloth, she was shocked by what she found. It was not what she had expected. Instead of his penis being in its normal state, it was erect. She had it happen a few times with some of the other patients, but she never expected it from him. For some reason, the thought that he could even do that never registered in her mind. She understood that it was an involuntary reaction for men in situations like this most of the time, but this happening to him had her more than a little embarrassed.

Before Eva started bathing there, she chanced a glance at him. To her horror, he made eye contact with her when she looked up, and for the first time, she thought she could see something in those well-concealed eyes of his.

"Miss Abrams, I believe you are blushing." A smile slowly formed when he caught sight of her flushed cheeks.

She looked at the floor, even more embarrassed now than before. She honestly didn't know if she could finish bathing him. "I… umm, I'm sorry. It's that I'm not used to this happening."

"I know this happens to the other patients too, Miss Abrams. This can't be the first time you've encountered this."

"No, it's not."

"Then why the embarrassment? Imagine being me."

"I can still get a male orderly for you."

"Do you honestly think this is the first time a woman has touched me there?"

Oh God, he was making this so much worse. "I don't know. I try not to think about you at all, so the thought of you being intimate with someone has never entered my mind."

"Sure, it has."

Her head shot up. "What!"

"Tell me, Miss Abrams, when you look at me, do I register to you as someone who would be a virgin?"

"I don't…" She trailed off.

"No, it is a simple yes or no question."

"Fine. No."

"Good. So, there is no reason to be worried about my innocence or shyness. Seriously, your embarrassment is making me embarrassed for you."

She cleared her throat and lifted the blanket, looking in the opposite direction as she cleaned him. She had no idea what face he was making now, nor did she care; she wanted to hurry and get this disaster over with. She tried not to think about the fact that there was only a thin piece of cloth between his penis, testicles, and her hand.

She cleaned that part of him as fast as she could, then moved her hand from underneath the blanket and put the cloth back in the pan. "OK, let's get you dressed and a fresh bandage on your leg." She moved the blankets back, uncovering his feet and legs as far up as his knees. She slipped the underwear over each foot, pulled them up to his knees, put the PJ bottoms on, pulled them up to his knees, and then covered his feet back up with the blanket. She moved the blanket away from his thigh and replaced the bandage on his leg.

"Lift your bottom, and I will slide the underwear and pants up all the way." He once again lifted his hips, and she pulled the underwear up first, attempting not to brush her hand against his penis as she tried to figure out how it was supposed to go in the underwear the way it was. Usually, the men were flaccid when she did this. Once she felt like she got it in, she then pulled up the PJ bottoms.

"After I take your vitals, I will be done. Hopefully, you can shower soon, then you will no longer need someone's help." She picked the bucket off the floor and sat it on the cart.

"Eva." She heard her name echo in the room.

Colonel Oberst Heinrich Schmitt was walking towards her. She looked at her watch; it was almost six, so she only had a little over an hour and a half to meet up with Helmut because the sun would set soon. *Crap.* She thought. *Did he really have to come now?*

"Oberst Schmitt, how are you? I didn't expect to see you today."

He came and stood next to her at Bauer's bedside. "I was a little worried about you after the ball. What happened? Did that guy do something to you?"

"No, it was a misunderstanding, that's all."

"I take it you got home alright then?"

"I did."

"I'm glad to hear it. It looks like you were tending to this gentleman."

"I was. I have to check his vitals, then I can take you around to meet the patients."

"How about we start with him?"

"Sure... he was injured in the attack. He was shot twice, once in his leg and the other in the shoulder. He also had shrapnel in his neck, arm, and stomach, which resulted in the removal of his appendix. We also found a tiny piece of shrapnel that had punctured his lung."

"I'm surprised you could save him."

"To be honest, I am too."

He walked over to Bauer and took his hand, giving it a shake. "You must be a hell of a fighter. What is your name, soldier?"

"SS Sturmbannführer Bauer, sir."

"I have heard of you. They assigned you as the Gestapo officer to oversee France."

"I was, I am, sir."

"Don't worry about catching the people who did this to you. We will find them."

"Oh yes, we will," he said slowly and deliberately as he looked at Eva. "I have no doubt."

She had to look away. His words and tone terrified her. The panic was building inside of her.

"It appears the nurses are doing a fine job taking care of you."

"They do as well as is expected of them, most of them."

He loved to beat people down. There was no way anyone could ever do anything good enough for him. She could not stand this man. "Why don't I show you the rest of the patients? I can take his vitals later," she said, wanting to get away from Bauer.

"Of course, I am taking up your time. Let's go see the other patients." He did the Sieg Heil salute to Bauer, who did it back with his right arm.

She walked away from Bauer's bed briskly, and Oberst Schmitt followed. "You treat these patients well. I remember the care you gave me when I was here. An American woman being so tender with German soldiers was unexpected. I've been watching you for the last few minutes as you helped that officer. You do it with such dedication and consideration. You truly care for them, and that is what makes you such a wonderful nurse."

"I believe life is a precious thing, and not only the life of my countrymen."

"I see why you work as a nurse." She gave him a warm smile that did not reach her eyes but did not want to speak further on the matter.

As he met with the rest of the patients, she continued checking her watch. She was cutting it close, too close. She walked him back towards Bauer's bed. "Can you show yourself out? I still need to take his vitals?"

"Sure. I'll come and check on you again sometime soon."

Again, she smiled. "I would love that." When he was gone, she turned to Bauer. "I'm going to check your vitals. It will only take a minute."

"I'm not going anywhere."

She took his wrist and looked at her watch as she counted his heartbeats. She wrote it on the clipboard, then stuck a thermometer in his mouth. When she checked it, she noticed that his temperature was a few degrees high. She frowned, then checked his blood pressure, which was still a little on the low side. That was to be expected because he had been in a bed for a while now and wasn't keeping his body active, but she wasn't sure about his temperature. Neither his body nor the antibiotics were fighting the infection as well as they should be. She sat on the side of the bed and pulled the blanket back, lifting his shirt. She lightly pushed on and around his wound, and he flinched.

"Does this hurt?"

"Of course, it hurts. You're pushing on it."

She really wanted to slap him. "I mean, is the pain severe? Is it getting worse?"

"No." His voice was flat, and his no lacked truth.

"You are lying. I saw your face." She pulled his shirt back down. "I can't help you if you won't let me." She then pulled his pants down on his left side and removed the bandage, checking the wound on his leg. It seemed to be healing as it should. She put the bandage back and checked his shoulder wound, and it, too, appeared to be normal. She pulled the bandage off his neck and looked at it, but it was like the others.

"I'm going to speak with the doctor about this later." She looked at her watch, and it was already six-fifty. She gave him his morphine shot along with his antibiotics, then wrote about the fever on the clipboard along with the medicines he was given and hung it on the end of the bed. She took the blanket and covered him up. He watched her do this, but his gaze wasn't angry or annoyed. It almost seemed appreciative.

"You seem like you are in a hurry."

"I am. It's time for me to go home."

She would have to hurry if she was to make it in time now. There was no way of knowing how long Helmut would wait.

Chapter Eleven

✠

Monday, March 31st, 1941

Eva walked briskly through the heavily wooded grounds of the hospital and kept checking the time. It was likely she would not make it before the sun was down and curfew started, and that worried her. She was almost to the road when someone grabbed her arm and pulled her behind a cluster of trees. She gasped and jerked her arm free as the person's grip was not tight and wheeled around to face who had done it. She found herself looking into Gerhardt's deep blue eyes.

"What are you doing?" she snapped.

"You left the dance without giving me a chance to fully explain myself."

"I heard all I need to know."

"I see you are off work; can I walk you home and explain?"

"I am not going home. I have somewhere to be, and you are not coming."

"Eva, I am sorry for what happened and how you found out about it. I know this isn't fair or what you expected, but please let me make it right somehow."

"You can't make it right." She looked at the waning sun. "I have to go now." She pushed past him.

"Eva, don't do this. We can't leave it this way."

She called back over her shoulder. "You are the one who made it this way, so you are going to have to learn to live with it." She might learn to forgive him later, but right now, it was still too fresh in her mind, and she was hurting.

She got on the tram and hoped that Gerhardt hadn't followed her. She asked the driver what Schildhorn was, and he told her Schildhorn was a peninsula in the forest Grunewald. When the tram arrived at the stop near the woods, she asked the driver if he could show her where the peninsula was located in the park. He pointed in the direction and told her it would take about twenty or thirty minutes to walk there.

She thanked him and got off the tram, following his directions, and walked a little over twenty minutes before coming to a small peninsula in the lake. This had to be the spot Helmut was talking about in the note. She looked around, hoping to see him, but no one was there but her. She did a three-sixty while holding her hand above her eyes to block the evening sun and squinted into the distance. What if she missed him, or something had happened, and he wasn't coming? She sat in the grass to wait, to make sure he wasn't going to come before she decided to leave.

After a few minutes, she spotted a man approaching her from the west, out of a grove of trees. She would wait and see if this was him, but if it wasn't, she was going to leave. She couldn't stay any longer because the sun was almost down.

She was relieved when he was closer, and she could see it was Helmut. She got off the grass and walked towards him.

"I am sorry I kept you waiting. Some soldiers seemed interested in me while I was coming here, so I had to lose them."

"Why were they interested in you?"

"I don't know. Most of us have been lying low these last few weeks, but we need to have another meeting to decide the next course of action."

"Have you talked with the others?"

"I have. You were the last one that I needed to see. The meeting will be in three days, on Thursday. Eight in the morning at the abandoned mill in Bornstedt. Do you know where that is?"

"I do. It is north of Potsdam. It shouldn't take me long to get there from where I live."

"Good. We should go. It's getting late, and we don't want to be seen together."

"You are right." Eva watched as he disappeared back into the trees and then left. She waited for the next tram to come and thought of what her role with the resistance would be now. She was no longer emotionally capable of doing something like they did, not again. But, if she could not help them in the capacity they wanted, then what good would she be to them. The thought was there that maybe she should leave the resistance while she still could. Besides, she needed to focus on getting home and staying away from dangerous activities that could get her killed or arrested. There was a pang of guilt because she saved Bauer, and the others, for that matter. They had recently tried to kill them, and here she was, saving them. It seemed counterintuitive. Her heart had decided the course of action instead of logic because logically, she should have let them die. It made their efforts less effective and put her more at risk. If Bauer didn't hate her before, he definitely would after this if he ever found out. In truth, he should have died, and the more she thought about it, the more she couldn't believe he hadn't. Deep down, she knew it was inevitable that she would have to pay in some way for it later, either for trying to kill him or for saving him. If the others found out that she went out of her way to help one of the wounded, they would feel betrayed.

The headlight of the tram came down the road and reflected on her. The sun had already set, and she would get home past curfew. She had to be sneaky so they wouldn't catch her out on the streets.

When the tram arrived at the stop near the apartment, she turned to the window. There wasn't a single person on the streets. It looked like a ghost town. She stepped off the tram and searched for any patrols but didn't see any, so she walked at a brisk pace towards her apartment. She turned the corner onto her street but stopped when she caught sight of Gerhardt leaning against the outside of her apartment building, smoking a cigarette. What the hell was he doing here? She mustered her courage and walked toward him. When she was close, he looked up and moved away from the wall.

"You are out past curfew," he said.

"Yes, I know."

"Why?"

"The tram was running late." *Couldn't I come up with a better lie than that?* she thought.

"This late? You expect me to believe that you are home at this hour because of a late tram?"

"I took the last one, and it was late. That's not my fault. Why are you here, Gerhardt?"

"Because we need to talk about this."

She looked at the flower in his hand. "I have nothing to say to you. You already explained yourself very well at the ball."

"I don't think you understand." She sidestepped him and walked to the front door of the apartment complex. "Eva, come to France with me?"

Her hand paused on the door handle. She wasn't sure she had heard him right. She let go of the handle and turned to him. "What did you say?"

"I will be going to France again soon, and I want you to come with me."

"Are you crazy? You want me to go back to France, and with you? You are the one who told me I was not safe there.

Besides, you are engaged now."

"I will have a few days of leave, and I know you would like to see Madame Blanc and Adele again."

"And how could I possibly go back to France? It is probably still not safe for me there, even now?"

"Bauer is in the hospital, and the soldiers that were stationed there have long been gone. No one will know who you are. You will be safe for a short while. We won't be there for very long."

"And what about the little thing of you being engaged?"

"It's nothing more than a trip to see old friends and a familiar place to give us the chance to reconcile what took place between us. We can't pretend it didn't happen."

"You mean the reckless choice we made that led to heartache?" She gestured to the flower in his hand. "I'm sorry, but flowers will not make things better. Besides, I can't go. Not only do I have my work, but I am leaving for Russia on Friday."

"Russia?"

"Yes, I have been invited."

"You shouldn't go to Russia."

"Why? Because Germany is going to invade it?"

His face paled. "What did you say?"

She glared at him. "Nothing."

"I don't know where you got that idea, but I wouldn't repeat it to anyone else if I were you. What made you say it?"

"If not for that reason, why else would you tell me not to go to Russia?"

"It is not like the other countries you have been to. It is not a good idea for you to go."

"You still haven't told me why."

"That's all I'm going to say about it, but I don't think you should go. I would like an answer from you about France."

"I told you. The answer is I can't go with you."

"What if I left after you got back? Would you consider it then?"

"I don't even know if I will consider it at all. I need time to process what you have asked. I need to think about what that means for me, for you…"

"I would like for us to come back from France both feeling content with whatever our lives will be moving forward. The way we departed the last two times we were together left unresolved feelings and unwanted tension between us. At least it did for me."

"I don't know, Gerhardt. Ask me again when I get back."

"I will let you go to bed now. When you return, you know where to find me," he said.

"I do." She opened the door and made sure to close it behind her, glad that it separated her from Gerhardt. She leaned against it, trying to figure out what had happened. He told her that they would not be together at the dance, but now he wanted her to go to France with him. Perhaps it was so he could end what they had on a high note and feel a little less guilty about the pain he caused her because he was the one who ended it.

She lay in bed but couldn't sleep. His offer to go to France kept her awake. It confused her because she didn't truly know his reasons for asking, but her own feelings confused her more than he did. She felt happy that he had asked her, yet it made her want to cry. It made her angry with him and, at the same time, it made her feel special that he loved her like no one else, yet she couldn't help but feel that he was using her. Being a part of this love affair wasn't easy. It felt like she was on a lifeboat in the middle of a hurricane in the dead of night. No direction, no control, just the blind force of the storm. That is what their love was. She was going to need some advice on what to do, and the only person that would be objective was the priest. She had time to see him before work on Wednesday, so she would go then.

Wednesday, April 2nd, 1941

"Do you work today?" Eva asked Heidi while they ate breakfast. The table they were seated at barely fit in their small kitchen.

"I have the night shift. You and Liesel both work the day shift today, right?"

"We do. Tomorrow though, I have the night shift again," Eva told her.

"So, you are still going to Russia, then?" Heidi asked.

"I am. I'm actually looking forward to it. It is something

I never thought I would do."

"I think it sounds exciting, despite what Liesel thinks."

"I know she worries, and I can understand her concerns. They are not completely misplaced."

"Liesel is always that way, but I think she has gotten worse now that her mother passed," Heidi said, a pang of sadness in her voice.

Eva looked around the room to see if Liesel was in earshot. She wasn't, so Eva spoke. "She is grieving. We don't know how we would act if it were our mothers who died."

"We all grieve in different ways. I do understand that."

Liesel walked into the kitchen. "Should we go together today?" she asked Eva.

Eva looked at her watch. She still had almost an hour before her shift started. "There is somewhere I want to go before work. You go ahead without me."

"Alright, if you're sure."

Eva stood from the table and put her plate in the sink. "I'll see you at work," she told Liesel.

Eva took the tram and rode it until it reached the stop near the church. She made it a point to remember what part of town it was in, so if she wanted to come back or felt like she needed to, she could. The stop was a block from the church, so it took less time to get there than it had the first time.

She walked through the large mahogany doors, then through the interior doors, and the smell of burning candle wax flooded her nostrils. She scanned the chapel for the priest, but he was not there. Only a few people were in the pews. Some of them had their heads bowed in prayer, others were staring at the cross with Jesus near the front of the church behind the pulpit.

She went to the confessional booth and sat down. “Father, are you in there?” she whispered. There was no answer on the other side, so she stepped out, wondering what to do next. There was a corridor to the right of the stage leading to the back of the church, so she followed it, hoping to find his office. On both sides of the hall were a lot of doors, all unmarked. She walked until she got to the last door. Above it was a golden plate that read, ‘Father Becker.’ She knocked on the door, hoping he was in his office. On the other side of the door, heavy footsteps thudded dully on a carpeted floor. The door opened and Father Becker stood in the doorway.

“You’re back,” he said. “I knew I would see you here again.” He gave her a warm smile.

“How did you know you would see me again?” She wondered why he was so certain of it.

“Because the story you started last time isn’t done being told.” She gave him a confused look, so he clarified; “It hasn’t all unfolded yet. When you left my church last time, you were unsure about many things.”

“Right,” she said. He spoke the truth because there was a lot that was up in the air. “That is why I am here now. Some new things have developed since the last time, and I wanted to know what I should do.”

“I can’t tell you what to do. I can only tell you what your

options are and maybe help you understand the situation better. Then only you can choose the path."

"I guess that is what I meant. I think I need someone to help point me in the right direction."

"That I will help you with if I can. Do you want to talk in my office or go back to the confessional booth?"

"I think I would rather do it in the confessional booth. For some reason, things are easier to talk about when you can't see the other person's face."

"I understand that."

She followed him to the chapel and got into the confession booth. She slid the little door open that covered the screen.

"So, what has changed?" he asked.

"Last time I was here, you told me to let the man I love go because he is engaged to another woman, and if we were meant to be together, he would come back to me. Well, he has, in a way. He came to the hospital and wanted to talk, but I told him we had nothing to talk about. Then he was at my apartment waiting for me when I got home last night. He wants us to go to France together. I should have told him to leave again because I was aware of where the conversation would lead. I knew it would be more than him apologizing for breaking my heart, but I let him stay and talk, and now I find myself faced with a hard choice."

"Is it hard?"

"What do you mean?"

"What I'm asking is, should you tell him no, or do you really feel like something good will come from this trip?"

"He said he wanted to make it right by me and that he hoped we would both feel content with our lives and choices when we returned home."

"And you believe him? You think that is all he wants?"

"Yes, I do. He made it pretty clear at the dance that we would never be together."

"Do you believe that you would feel better and be ready to truly let him go if you went on this trip, or do you feel like it would complicate things further?"

"I'm not sure. That is why I came to you."

"As I said before, I can't tell you what to do. All I can do is help you come to the right decision. To point you in the direction that will lead you to the choices you know or feel are right but are having trouble finding. If you think in the end it would be best to go, then go, and if you don't, then don't."

"I don't think I can decide that right now."

"Then I would suggest that you pay close attention to how the thought of going or not going makes you feel over the next few days. I believe that will give you the answer you are looking for."

"Thank you."

"I am always here. You are welcome anytime."

"There is a chance that I will be back."

"I'm hoping you do."

Eva stepped out of the booth, as did the priest. "I don't believe I ever caught your name," he said.

"Eva."

He took her hand in both of his and held it tight, looking

into her eyes. “There is something different about you, but I can’t quite figure out what.”

His comment alarmed her. There was no way he could know she was from the future, could he? Maybe he sensed that she had a secret. “Different, how?” she asked.

“I’m not sure. But you seem different from anyone I have ever met.”

“Maybe it’s because I’m a foreigner.”

“No, I don’t believe that is it.”

Eva looked at the doors. “I better go, or I will be late for work.”

He let go of her hand. “I look forward to our next talk.”

She smiled at him, then left the church. She stepped into the bright sun that was finally peeking through the broken clouds. It was still cool, but the sun was shining, so it was a nice day. She caught the tram to the hospital and took her time walking across the grounds, trying to soak up as much of the sun’s rays as she could.

“Eva.”

From behind, someone called her name, and she halted. The butterflies twisted in her stomach at the sound of that smooth voice. It always had that effect on her. She turned and looked at him, trying not to smile.

“I have been waiting for you. They told me you had the morning shift.”

“How long have you been here?”

“An hour.”

“Why are you out here in the cold? Why didn’t you wait inside?”

“Because I wanted to talk to you before you started your shift, and I didn’t want to miss you.”

“Are you here for an answer?”

“I was hoping you had one for me. Am I right in hoping?”

“It so happens that I have decided.” She could see his jaw tense in anticipation of her answer. “I will go with you… but only after I have returned from Russia.”

His face relaxed some. “I am happy that you decided to come.”

“I will let you know if I am glad when we return.”

“Fair enough. I understand your skepticism.”

“I have to go.” She turned and walked away. When she went into the nurse’s quarters, Liesel was already there, changing into her uniform.

“Where did you go this morning?” she asked.

“A church.”

“A church.” Her tone came across as disapproving. “Why?”

“Because I needed to unburden myself and get some guidance.”

Liesel stopped mid-changing. “What?”

Eva focused on Liesel. “Why are you looking at me like that?”

“Eva, I’m afraid to ask.”

“Why are you acting like I did some deplorable thing? I know you don’t like religion, but some of us need it once in a while.”

“It’s not that you went to a church. It’s why did you feel

like you needed to."

"Because Gerhardt has asked me to go to France with him."

"He did what… you are not going, are you? Please tell me you are not?"

"I am. He said that he wants it to be a way to reconcile the unresolved feelings between us."

"If that is what he wanted, wouldn't he simply say it to you here? Why does he have to do it in France?"

"Because the time we had together was there. It's hard to explain."

"You don't need to explain that part. I get that you two had a connection there, but won't it make it harder if the two of you go back to the place you had the connection?"

"The priest told me that I needed to give him up and that I needed to work out my feelings. He thinks this trip could help both of us do that, to let go."

"And you believe that?"

"It will either make it better or worse, but I won't know which one if I don't go. I can't keep feeling like this, Liesel. It's miserable. I need to get him out of my head, and hopefully my heart."

"I know. Go… if you think that will help. Though I would hate to see you come back feeling worse than you did before you went. When are you going?"

"I'm not sure. It will be sometime after I return from Russia."

"You're still doing that too, huh?"

"I am. Whether I go to France or not, I still need to get

away and clear my head."

"Oh shit, we are late," Liesel said. She threw her clothes in her locker and left the room. Eva hurried and finished putting on her cap, then headed to the patient quarters. As she entered through the doors, she caught sight of Frau Wagner checking the patients. "Dammit," she said under her breath. Eva inhaled deep and walked in her direction but was intercepted by Ingrid.

"Are you going to help with the surgeries today?" Ingrid asked.

"What surgeries?"

"Several new patients came in today. They are in the back by the loading dock, waiting to be sorted. There wasn't enough room in the lobby for them."

"Um, I'm not sure if I'm helping with surgeries today. It really depends on whether or not Frau Wagner or Dr. Möller want me in there."

"Maybe you won't be helping with the surgeries then."

Eva took hold of Ingrid's arm as she started to walk away. "Ingrid, who is that woman over there?" Eva asked about the older woman sitting on the edge of Bauer's bed. The woman had silver-gray hair in a neat bun on top of her head. She wore an off-white dress that looked like silk, even though it was hard to come by now. The woman was a little on the heavy side but far from being fat.

Ingrid looked over in their direction. "That is his mother. She arrived a little while ago."

"I have never seen her here before."

"She has been here several times, actually."

"How come I have never seen her?" Eva asked, a little confused.

"She usually comes in the morning, and you typically work the evening shift. I think that is why you have never seen her."

"You are probably right. I'm going to find out what they need me to do."

"I'll see you later," Ingrid told her.

"Alright." Eva smoothed her apron and walked towards Frau Wagner, trying to keep her gaze forward and not look in the direction of Bauer or his mother.

"Nurse?"

Eva stopped when the older woman's voice called to her. She mentally prepared herself, then turned to the woman sitting on Bauer's bed.

"Yes, ma'am."

"He is cold and needs another blanket."

Eva raised her brows. "He feels cold?" She came over to his bed and put her hand on his forehead."

He pushed it away. "I am not cold; my mother is mistaken," he said, turning his gaze to the older woman.

"There is no need to treat her that way. I called her over here," she told him. "You had mentioned to me that they kept the hospital cool. I would have brought a blanket from home if I had thought of it." She looked at her son, her eyes squinted.

"I was only making an observation," he said.

"It's fine. I can bring another blanket."

"Thank you," his mom said, giving her a genuine smile.

Eva walked away, thinking about what a strange encounter that was. His mother seemed nice enough, so how was it she had a son like him? Did she even know how her son really was? Maybe she didn't, and that is why she loved him, or perhaps she did know but still loved him anyway. Eva didn't understand a mother's love because she wasn't one, but to love a person like him, even if you were his mother, still puzzled her.

"Eva, where have you been? You were supposed to be here twenty minutes ago." Frau Wagner berated.

"Sorry, it won't happen again."

"Make sure it doesn't. Dr. Möller needs someone to help sort the patients at the loading dock. I have paperwork that needs to be done and some letters to write, so I need you to go."

"Of course, let me bring a blanket to one of the patients, then I will meet him out there." Frau Wagner glared at her and then walked past without saying another word.

Eva went to the closet in the patient quarters, pulled out an extra wool blanket, and carried it back to Bauer's bed. She unfolded it and draped it overtop his other one. The whole time, his eyes bore into her, making her feel uncomfortable.

"There, that should help." She started to walk away when his mother spoke to her again.

"When do you give him his next dose of pain medicine?" she asked.

"Let me see." She took the clipboard from the end of his bed and read over it. "It looks like he will be ready for his next dose in about an hour. Is he in pain?"

"If he is, he doesn't tell me," his mother said, turning to look at him with a disapproving look.

It seemed that he was as stubborn towards his own mother as he was with her. "I will come back when it is time for his medicine, but right now, I have somewhere else I need to be."

"I understand. Thank you for helping save his life."

Eva had started to leave but stopped when she said that. "You are welcome, but it is a team effort. Every doctor and nurse that helped him that day is responsible for saving his life. But it is the doctor who truly saved him."

"Mother, she needs to go," Bauer said. "And as she said, it was the doctor who ultimately saved me."

Eva was a little insulted that he agreed with her, but she probably would be equally upset if he didn't agree with her. She glowered at him before she turned and walked away. She found Dr. Möller at the loading dock, checking the patients with another nurse.

"Eva, there you are. I need you to check the patients on the other side. If they don't look like they will live, leave them and go to the next one. Only tell me of the ones that look like they will survive. The others can wait."

She gaped at him, surprised, even though she knew his orders shouldn't.

"We can't save all of them," he said, noticing the look on her face. "We don't have the manpower, beds, or medicine."

She knew he was right, but it pained her every time she

had to leave one on a gurney to die. She went to the first patient at the end of the line. When she looked at him, she immediately knew he would not make it through the day. Most of his right leg was gone, and he was bleeding severely from his chest. A field hospital had been evacuated, and they sent the patients to Berlin in the same condition they were in when the field hospital received them. She was getting ready to go to the next patient when the man took her hand.

"Nurse, please, can I have some medicine?"

"I will see what I can do." She let go of his hand and went to find Dr. Möller. "Some of the patients that will not survive are asking for medicine. Can I give them some?"

"Don't waste it on them. You will give it to them, then they will be dead a few minutes later. Save it for the men who are going to survive."

"But they are in pain. Can't we ease their suffering for their last few minutes?"

"It would be nice if we could do that, but we need the medicine for the other patients."

She looked over at the man and felt so sorry for him. She went back to him, knelt beside his cot, and took his hand. "I'm trying to get some medicine for you, but it might take a while. Can I get you some water?" She didn't want to tell him that he wouldn't be getting any medicine.

Eva nodded, then went to the kitchen, retrieved a glass, filled it with water, and returned to the loading dock. But when she got to his bed, the man's eyes were closed, and his head tilted off to the side. She stood there, looking down at him. She was only gone for a minute. Her eyes blurred with tears. She didn't even get to give him his water. Sometimes, she wondered if she was really cut out to be a nurse. To work in a hospital, you can't cry over every patient who dies, especially in a time of war when so many of them will.

She sat the cup of water by the brick wall and moved on to the next patient. This man had his head wrapped in gauze, but other than that, he appeared to be okay. She unwrapped his bandage and looked at a bullet graze on the side of his head, with blood matted in his hair. She smiled at him. "You are going to be fine. The doctor will be here to look at your head soon, but first, he has to take care of the critical patients."

"The man next to me. Is he dead?"

She glanced over at the man she had brought water to. "He is, but don't worry about that. Only think about how you will get better and maybe even get to go home for a while and see your family."

"You think I will get to go home?"

"I'm not sure, but maybe. Now rest." She patted his hand, then went to the next patient. When she was done, she followed Dr. Möller into the operating room. She scrubbed in and assisted with four of the surgeries. All the rest of the patients were taken by the other doctors. When all the surgeries were finished, she and Dr. Möller sat on a bench outside the operating theater to rest.

"I saw you cry over that patient. I know it hurts. It's sad when you can't help them. I had to learn a long time ago that if I was going to do this, I could not let it get to me because I would lose people. It doesn't make it not hurt, but it helps me deal with it a little better." She met the gaze of his pale blue eyes and could see the sorrow in them. "You have a good heart, but you have to be strong," he continued. "If the war hasn't hardened you yet, it will." He patted her shoulder, then stood up. "Why don't you do a last round with the patients, then go home?"

"Thanks." Dr. Möller was one of the nicest people she had ever met, and she would miss him terribly if or when she went home. She returned to the patient ward, glanced at the charts on the beds, administered any medicines needed, and checked vitals. Bauer's mother had gone, and she was glad. She didn't like the attention his mother brought to her. She went to Bauer's bed and took the chart from the end.

"Your mother seems nice," she said.

"She is a remarkable woman."

"You don't feel bad that you gave all the credit to the doctor for saving you?"

"I thought that was what you wanted. You all but dismissed her praises."

"You could have agreed that it was a team effort because it was, and you know it."

"You specifically told her to thank the doctor and not you, so you cannot be angry with me for suggesting that she do so."

"That is where you are wrong. I can be angry. You didn't do it because you were taking my wishes into account. You did it because you can't admit that an American woman who you despise helped save your miserable life." She was shocked at her boldness. She wasn't used to talking to people that way, especially him. It could be because he was lying in a bed wounded and seemed less threatening at this moment, but she might pay for it later when he was well.

She took the syringe with morphine and squeezed a little out the top, then pulled the side of his pants down, exposing the top of his thigh, and jammed the needle in. He clenched his jaw, drew in a breath through his nose, and glared in her direction, his nostrils flaring. She pulled his pants back up and then took his temperature, blood pressure, and pulse. His blood pressure was still low, and he had a slightly high temperature. She looked at him puzzled, then lifted his shirt and pulled the bandage away from his side, inspecting it, but it appeared to be healing normally. Maybe it was a problem internally. She put the bandage back and pulled the blanket over him. “How long have you been feeling cold?”

He started to answer, but she cut him off before he could speak. “Don’t even try to deny it. You have an elevated temperature. That is why you have been feeling cold. I’m going to get the doctor and have him take a look at you.” She went to find Dr. Möller, but he was in another surgery, so she searched for one of the other doctors. She found Dr. Koch attending to a patient in the physical therapy wing. “Dr. Koch, do you have a minute?”

He looked up at her with his eyes but didn’t lift his head. “When I’m done here. What do you need?”

“One of the patients still has a fever, but I can’t find an obvious reason for it. I wanted to know if you could look at him. Dr. Möller is in surgery right now.”

“Give me ten minutes,” he said.

She waited for him by the entrance to the physical therapy wing. When he was done, he followed her to the patient ward, and she led him to Bauer's bed. She picked up his chart and showed it to him. "Do you see? It has been high for a while now. He had one right after surgery, and it went away a few days later, but it came back and has persisted since then, and I don't see the reason why. I checked all of his wounds, and they look fine."

The doctor pulled the blankets back and inspected him. After checking all the wounds, he stood and looked at Eva. "I don't see any obvious reason either. Make sure that you and the other nurses keep a close eye on him, and if it isn't better in a few days, let me or one of the other doctors know." He took her by the arm and pulled her away from Bauer's bed. "We need to figure out why this is happening. We can't ignore it if it persists. Whatever is causing it could kill him if left untreated, so for now, give him some acetylsalicylic acid to try to bring the fever down."

She nodded in understanding, then returned to Bauer's bed, got a spoonful of the aspirin powder, and put it in a cup of water, and stirred it with a wooden suppresser. "Here, drink this." She held the cup out to him.

He took it from her and put it to his lips while watching her. "Does your mom come and visit you often?" she asked.

He drank the medicine and held the cup in his hand, resting on his leg. "She does. She will be happy when I am no longer in here."

"I can imagine, won't we all be." He ignored her last comment. "I have never seen her here before," she commented, hoping to learn more about his mother's visits.

"She usually comes in the mornings."

"And your dad, does he not come and visit you too?"

"No. He is dead."

"I'm sorry, I didn't know."

"I'm not sorry, and you don't need to be either," he said with acid in his voice.

"Oh–you weren't close to him?"

"Don't you have something you need to be doing, Miss Abrams?" he asked, not hiding his annoyance.

She had forgotten how cold and unkind he could be, always with a wall up. What was he trying to hide? Did he wear a mask as a façade, or was it that there was really nothing to hide because there was nothing inside, no feelings, no emotions?

She jerked the cup out of his hand and wrote that she had given him aspirin on the chart and hung it back on the end of his bed. She walked away, not looking back. She could not wait to be rid of this place, especially him, for a while.

Chapter Twelve

✠

Thursday, April 3rd, 1941

Eva leaned against the wall inside the abandoned mill while waiting for the others to arrive. Bird poop covered most of the dirt floor, and the flapping of pigeon wings sounded in the rafters above, echoing through the empty building. All of the windows were broken out, and the breeze gently blew through, making the end of her dress dance around her legs. The sun was just beginning to shine through the east window as it rose higher in the sky.

Footsteps crunched on the gravel outside the doorway. Eva hurried to her feet, went to the window, and peeked through. Helmut was alone, approaching the building. He walked through the doorway and caught sight of her, his head jerking in her direction. "Eva, I wasn't expecting anyone else to be here. It's still early."

"I couldn't sleep, so I decided to come now. I knew I

would be the first one here, but I didn't mind waiting a while."

He nervously looked behind him. "What are you looking at?" she asked.

"I think they are on to us."

Eva tensed. "Why do you think that?"

"I have this funny feeling, and every time I leave my house, I swear someone is following me."

Part of her wondered if he was being paranoid or if he was right, and they really did figure out who was involved in the attack. As of now, she couldn't be sure which one was the truth, but every time he said something like that, it made her that much more nervous.

"Are you certain someone is following you?"

"I am fairly certain. Whenever I leave, I always take the precautions we have in place. I had to do it today as well."

"If you are being followed, we can't risk another attack," she told him.

"I know."

The thought of not doing another attack for a while made her feel better. She couldn't handle another experience like that. Inside, she was emotionally dying from the first one. She could never undo what they had already done, but she could prevent it from happening again. The German high command were terrible people, at least most of them, but trying to take them down also meant that innocent people would die because of it, and that was something she couldn't let happen again. Too many innocents had lost their lives in this war, and more were still to come, but hopefully not because of her.

"Frank and Thomas are here," Helmut said.

Eva peered through the window and watched as they walked up the gravel road, happy Lina wasn't with them.

Derek and Lina arrived a little after eight, and Helmut started the meeting. "Has anyone been followed over the past few weeks?"

There were exchanged glances, and they all responded with no. "That is good, but I believe I am being followed," Helmut informed them. "I think it is too risky to attempt any more attacks for a while. The first attempt was a success, and that will have to be enough for now. We should all lie low for a while and keep an eye out for anything suspicious. If you think you have been compromised, try to get the word out to everyone, providing it is safe to do so. And remember, if they come for you and there is no other way, you can't be afraid to do what needs to be done. If they catch even one of us, it is over for all of us." He passed out small tin cases that were used for pills.

Eva opened the lid, and a single white pill lay inside. She lifted her eyes to Helmut. "Is this a cyanide capsule?"

"Yes. If any of us find ourselves in a situation where there is no escaping, this is the last option left to us."

"Suicide?" Derek sounded disbelieving.

"Only if it comes to that," Helmut said, trying to reassure them.

Eva dropped he gaze back to the white capsule, and the sight of it terrified her. Her hand shook, the pill rattling in the tin. She couldn't believe she was holding one, the same pill that so many Nazis killed themselves with at the end of the war. There was no way it had come to this. She knew she didn't have what it took, even if she was arrested. She didn't think she was brave enough to take her own life.

Helmut continued. "Keep them with you at all times, in a place you can access easily. If we find out it is safe, we will start planning our next move. Maybe our next act will not be as big, but we could do something small, like dropping pamphlets at universities and other places where people gather."

"Pamphlets? What good will that do?" Eva asked.

"It's better than doing nothing," Lina snapped. "We probably can't risk another attack like the one we did for a long time, but at least we can try to make a difference."

"It will still be extremely risky with minimal effect. It isn't worth it."

"What would you suggest, then?" Frank asked.

"I don't know, but there has to be something better than that."

"You could kill the men that survived the attack at the hospital you work at," Lina said.

"What… no. I can't kill patients. They would catch on to that, and I would be shot," Eva told her.

"Not if you smother them in their sleep. Maybe you could overdose them on their pain medications. It would be so easy." Lina's lips pulled at the corners as a sinister smile formed.

"What part of 'they would find out' didn't you

understand." It should shock her that Lina suggested she kill helpless men in their beds, but she wasn't.

"Maybe there is another reason you don't want to kill them," Lina antagonized.

Eva looked around at the others to see their response to Lina's remark. They were all looking at the floor or in another direction, not wanting to get in the middle of another argument between them. The only one who was watching them was Helmut.

"If you want them dead, you kill them. I won't risk my life to murder wounded men while they sleep in their beds."

"Oh, you feel sorry for them."

"You are trying to put words in my mouth. That is not what I said or meant, and you know it."

"This is getting us nowhere," Helmut finally shouted. "No one is going to kill the patients. What we need to do is put our heads together and come up with an effective plan that will hit the Nazis where it hurts. Eva, I want you to talk to the patients in the hospital and see what information you can get from them. You will have to be discrete, but ask what you can."

"I can do that." Bauer would be a good one to get information from, but she knew that would never happen. He wouldn't even talk to her, much less tell her anything about his work. As soon as he was better, he would undoubtedly resume his harassment toward her.

"Derek, I want you to do the same. Try to obtain information that we can use." Derek nodded in response.

"Lina, I want you and Thomas to try to recruit more

people to our cause. Frank and I will go to the country and see if we can sabotage railroad tracks and bridges. If we can stall their supplies, it will slow down the army and hopefully give the English a fighting chance."

When Eva joined the resistance, she knew it meant entering into a world of shadows, lies, and secrets hidden behind a facade, but it was scarier than she had ever imagined it would be. It threw her into a dangerous game that she was sure she was losing. In her was a deep revulsion toward Nazis and their ideologies, and she felt compelled to act against them. But the things that should be done and how to accomplish them without being caught, tossed in jail, or executed weren't at all easy to determine. In the beginning, it felt like they were taking part in something unreal, like in a novel that tells of an exciting adventure. It, of course, was a good deal more exciting than most people's ordinary lives and probably enabled some to compensate for their shortcomings and inadequacies, which might have made them feel encumbered. But the truth was that they were operating in shadows fraught with danger, and most likely, reality would strike back with brutal effect. There was always the risk of being caught by the Germans. She didn't need any more excitement in her life. Time traveling to a period that was at war was exciting enough for her, but it was a little late to turn from it now.

"We will meet again soon if we can. Everyone will be informed of when and where right before the meeting is supposed to take place. It is safer that way. You can't tell what you don't know," Helmut said. "It won't be for a while, though."

Well, this was going to be interesting. How exactly was she going to get people to talk, and what kind of information could they actually hope for?

"Eva, Lina, can I talk to both of you for a minute," Helmut said.

She knew what this was about. She followed Lina and Helmut to the far end of the warehouse as everyone else dispersed.

"I don't know what is going on between the two of you, but it has to stop. We are all fighting for the same thing—"

"Are we?" Lina interjected, interrupting him.

"Yes, and this is what I am talking about. What is going on between you two?"

"I don't trust her. There is something not right about her," Lina said with venom in her voice as her eyes raked over Eva.

"I have never given you cause to not like me. You don't, for reasons unknown to the rest of us. I don't believe it's because you don't trust me. I think the real reason is you don't like me."

Lina chuckled. "No, my lack of trust for you is independent of my dislike for you, but it adds to it."

"Then why don't you trust me?"

"Because you were in love with a Nazi and then helped save the lives of men we all risked our lives to dispose of."

"I had to. It was my job. Don't you think it would look odd if I refused to help them? And he is not a Nazi."

"Eva is right, Lina. If she had refused to help any of

them, they would have had her taken in for questing," Helmut said.

"They have shot people for less," Eva added.

"But that doesn't explain you being in love with a German."

"We can't choose who we love, Lina. But that was a long time ago and is over now."

"Is it? So, you don't still associate with him?"

Eva quickly looked at Helmut, then back to Lina. "Yes, I have talked to him a few times, but we are not together. He is getting married soon. What does that have to do with it anyway?"

"Why do you still associate with him?" Helmut asked.

"I saw him at a ball, and he came by my apartment and the hospital once."

"He is getting married and still visits you. That is unusual," Lina pointed out.

"I agree. That is unusual, Eva." Helmut raised an eyebrow at her. "Why has he come to see you?"

"He said that he didn't like how we parted ways and wanted to make things right between us."

"Why would he care enough to do that? I don't believe that story," Lina shook her finger accusingly in Eva's direction.

"If you are not working with the Germans, then it means he still has feelings for you, neither of which is good," Helmut said. "It looks suspicious."

"So, you agree with Lina?"

"I'm only saying I can see why she is concerned."

“I didn’t realize I had to report every aspect of my personal life at the meetings. We all associate with Germans because we live in Germany. It’s kind of hard not to. You two are German, and you are pointing fingers at me?”

“None mingle with the German military in the same way as you, and where we were born has nothing to do with it. Being born in a certain country and loving a certain person are very different things; one you choose and one you do not.”

“I promise that what I am doing is not putting anyone in danger. I told you, it is over.”

“How can you know that for sure?” Lina asked.

“He doesn’t know that I work with the resistance, and even if he did, I’m not convinced he would turn me in. I was helping Jews in France, and when he found out about that, he still helped me escape.”

“Would he extend the same favor again if he found out you were part of the attack on his fellow officers?” Helmut asked.

“I don’t know…” Eva said, considering. She would like to say he would, but deep down, she didn’t know. “But he doesn’t know anything, and he won’t find out. He is not in the Gestapo or even a Nazi,” Eva said pointedly to Lina.

“What does he do?” Lina asked.

“Let’s either resolve why we’re really here, or I’m going to leave,” Eva said, finally having enough of Lina’s interrogations.

“You are right. You both need to get along. You don’t have to like each other, but you do have to tolerate one another when you are together, and no more provoking comments. If we start fighting amongst ourselves, this will fall apart. We can't afford to have discourse between us. Whatever thoughts you two have about each other, keep them to yourselves." Helmut turned without saying another word and walked towards the exit.

Lina stared at Eva and made no attempt to move. "What is your problem?" Eva asked.

"You are going to bring all of us down because of your recklessness. You care for only yourself."

"I don't know what I ever did to make you think that. But that's not the real reason, or at least not the only reason you don't like me."

Lina's expression changed. "You understand nothing," she said, brushing past Eva.

Eva was thoroughly confused. What did she mean by that?

Friday, April 4th, 1941

Eva pulled the curtains back and looked down at Sergei's car waiting in front of the apartment. He was standing outside near the back door, pacing. Eva put on her scarf, gloves, and hat, then picked up her suitcase, put the strap of her purse over her shoulder, and hurried out the door. As she reached the car, a person across the street caught in her peripheral, so she looked in their direction.

Gerhardt was standing near a light pole, watching her, and their eyes met. Why was he here? Had he come to talk with her about France? She didn't know, but she could not go talk to him now.

Sergei was holding the door open for her. "What is it?" he asked, noticing her distracted stare across the street.

"Nothing." She smiled and then slid into the backseat as his driver put her suitcase in the trunk. She turned and peered through the back window as they drove away, but Gerhardt was already gone. Not knowing why he was there troubled her, something she had not expected. She faced forward in her seat and settled in.

"We should be at the airport soon. Are you ready to see Russia and have a proper drink?"

"I thought I had one already when we were at the ball?"

He laughed. "No, what you had was not a real drink. And the parties, you will talk about them for weeks."

"Parties? I thought we were only going to another ball?"

"We are going to a ball, yes, but there will undoubtedly be a few parties while you are there."

That sounded like a lot of drinking and hangovers. She wasn't sure she wanted to do that again. She started feeling terrible at the ball even before arriving home, and the effects of the alcohol continued into the next day.

The car pulled onto the airfield and stopped next to a dual-engine propeller passenger plane. Eva leaned down and looked out the door window at it, the size making her a little worried. Even though it was a passenger plane, it was considerably smaller than the ones in her time.

"Is this the plane we are taking?"

"It is. Why?"

"It's kind of small, isn't it?"

"No, it's normal. It will get us there safely." He got out of the car and came around to open her door. She stepped out onto the asphalt, still looking at the plane. The whole situation made her nervous now that it was finally here.

"Are you alright?" he asked as she hesitated by the car.

"Yea. Flying sometimes makes me uncomfortable." She had never flown on a 1940s-style plane before and didn't trust them like she did the ones from her time.

"We won't crash, I promise," he assured her, and she gave him a forced smile.

The driver took their bags to the plane and sat them next to the stairs. The engines roared to life, and Eva jumped. "You really are scared of planes." He held onto her elbow as they climped the steps and let go when she entered the cabin, then went back down and got their bags, bringing them on board. He put them in the overhead bin, took the seat next to her, and buckled up.

"How long is the flight?"

"About three hours."

"What is Moscow like?" she asked.

"It is beautiful, but we are not going to Moscow. We are going to St. Petersburg."

"I thought we were going to Moscow. Why are we going to St. Petersburg?"

"Because that is where the ball is, and that is where I am stationed."

It had never dawned on her they might not be going to Moscow. She had heard that St. Petersburg was prettier than Moscow, so the idea of going there was more exciting.

She squeezed the armrest of her seat as the plane sped down the runway and tried to stay calm. The aircraft rattled, and a loud noise came from the engines. She looked out the window and watched as the plane got farther from the ground, everything becoming smaller. Her heart thudded, and she wondered why she was so nervous.

"Is it as bad as you thought it would be?" he asked.

"I'll let you know when we land."

He laughed. "Sit back and relax. We'll be there before you know it. You must have been terrified when you flew from America to England."

"I was." She thought of that journey so long ago. She was nervous, but not for the same reason she was now. "I think I will close my eyes and see if I can get some sleep. It will make the flight seem faster."

"If you think that will help, then go ahead."

She leaned her head back against the headrest and closed her eyes, hoping to sleep, but of course, her mind instantly started playing out memories, which eventually led to thoughts of Gerhardt. She couldn't stop thinking about what he asked and the things that could happen when she goes to France with him? What would they do, who would they see, and how would it be when they returned to Germany? All the things she didn't know pressed on her thoughts constantly.

She had been in and out of sleep when the plane started to descend. She opened her eyes and peered out the little window at the city below. It must be St. Petersburg she was looking at. The stereotypical Russian churches scattered across the city with their colorful domes.

"What will we do today?" she asked.

"When we land, I will take you to your hotel, and the ball is tomorrow. I think there is a party tonight. If there is, we can go, but even if there isn't, I will come and get you for dinner. Did you bring something to wear for the ball?"

"I have to admit that I didn't. The dress that I wore to the Ball in Berlin was loaned to me by my roommate. I brought one of the dresses from my closet, but it is not fancy."

"That won't do. You need something more fitting for a ball."

The memory of Gerhardt buying her dress for the opera rushed back. She didn't want that to happen all over again. "I will go shopping for one today," she told him.

"That's a good idea. It's probably best if you get it early. I know of a nice store where many of the officer's wives shop. I can give you the name and address when we land."

"That would be helpful, thank you." She was happy he didn't offer to buy the dress for her and relieved he didn't suggest coming. She would feel more comfortable shopping alone. The only thing that worried her was whether or not she could communicate with the person in the shop. She didn't know any Russian and wasn't sure if most people in Russia could speak German, French, or English. "Is it common for people here to speak a second language?"

“Some can. If you are worried about the people in the shop, most can speak at least one other language, and some can speak two. Polish and Czech are the usual, but some understand a little German and English.”

“I was a little concerned about that. I’m glad I can use at least one language I know.”

The wheels contacted the runway, the plane shook, and the overhead luggage bins rattled. It taxied for a few minutes before coming to a stop beside a building, and then the engines were cut. Sergei stood and reached for their bags in the overhead bin. He took her bag down first, sat it on the floor, and then retrieved his.

She scooted to the aisle seat and stood, picking up her suitcase. She had noticed the difference in treatment that he gave her compared to most of the men she encountered, like the German and French men. It probably had something to do with the way Russian men viewed women. In some ways, they were ahead of the times in how women were treated, but in other ways, they were still as behind as the other countries. A few years ago, while in college, Eva had a class with a Russian who told her about changes that took place during the early nineteenth century. Women in the workforce increased, and marriage was separated from the church, allowing a couple to choose a surname and give an illegitimate child the same rights as legitimate children. Rights were given to maternal entitlements, women finally got health and safety protections at work and were provided the right to a divorce with limitations. In the 1920s, abortions were also legalized, and they made marital rape illegal. Women had other equal rights to men as well, including paid holidays, equal minimum wage, and equal rights regarding insurance case illnesses. But, in the mid-1930s, they began taking steps backward, digressing. Abortion became illegal again, legal differences between legitimate and illegitimate children were restored, and divorce once again became difficult to attain. They also gave women lower-level jobs to encourage them to stay home and have more children. But Eva could tell that some of the older ways, when women had rights, were instilled in the minds of the men who grew up in a gender equal Russia before it changed.

She followed him to a waiting car, and he put their bags in the trunk. He then opened her door, which was not unusual for the time. He climbed in beside her, and the car left the airport. As they made their way through the city, she looked at all the rivers she had missed while they were flying overhead. St. Petersburg was on a lake, though she didn't know what it was called.

The car pulled in front of a hotel across the road from the lake shore. It was a multi-story, yellow-colored stone building with a green roof. It didn't have a unique shape and was on the square side, though it was a pretty building nonetheless.

She followed him to the front desk with her suitcase in hand and waited as he spoke with a man. He said a few things in Russian, then turned to her. "This is the hotel where I am staying. I thought it would be easier if you stayed here, too. That way, you don't have to find your way around town."

"Thank you. That does make it easier." She didn't feel as comfortable in Russia as she did in Germany or France. It differed from anywhere she had ever been.

The man at the desk handed Sergei a key, and he passed it to her. He said something else to the man, then started towards the elevators. She followed and set her suitcase on the carpeted floor once they were in the elevator.

"What is the plan for today?"

"Well, I have to meet with my commanding officer, so that would be a good time for you to get a dress. I can take you there when I leave and should be done in time to pick you up. But if I'm not, it's close to here, and you can walk. I will give you directions to the hotel. Hopefully, this evening, we are going to a party," he said, excited, a broad smile on his face.

It was obvious that he liked to party and drink, which did not surprise her based on the knowledge she had of the Russians, limited as it was. "Sounds like it's going to be an interesting evening."

"You might not remember it tomorrow," he said with a chuckle.

"Good, maybe I don't want to remember anything."

"You sound like somebody who knows a few things they wished they didn't."

"A few. I see things every time I close my eyes, and I wish I didn't, but maybe tonight I won't see them when they close."

"I think we have all felt that way." He tapped her arm

with the back of his hand. "I'll show you how to forget your problems like a Russian."

"I'm eager to learn." She was able to give him a genuine smile.

They got off the elevator and walked down the corridor until reaching a door at the end. "This is your room, and mine is the one across from it." He pointed to the door of the room they were standing in front of. "If you want to put your stuff inside, we can be on our way."

"Yes, of course." She put the key in the hole and turned it, pushing the door open. Immediately, the stench of stale cigarette smoke flooded her nostrils. She would ask for another room, except they all probably smelled that way. She sat her suitcase inside and closed the door, locking it, then turned as Sergei was pulling his door shut.

"Are you ready?"

"Yes. I'm actually excited to look at dresses."

He raised his eyebrows and nodded his head, obviously not sharing her enthusiasm for shopping. They went down to the car, and she admired the strange-looking buildings as they drove away from the hotel.

"I'm glad we are close. If I get done before you, I don't mind walking back to the hotel."

"If you walk back, wait in your room so I know where to find you."

"That shouldn't be a problem." She needed time to get ready for the party, anyway.

The car pulled beside a large store with dresses displayed on mannequins in the front windows. Above the door was a sign with something written in bold golden letters, but she didn't know what it said because it was written in Cyrillic. She stepped out of the car onto the sidewalk. "Do I need to wear anything special for the party?"

"No, come with what you are wearing."

That was easy enough. She closed the door and watched the car drive away, then went into the shop. The scent of new material mixed with perfume and cigarette smoke was heavy in the air. An older woman in a blue dress and hair in a tight bun looked up and said something to her in Russian.

"I'm sorry, I don't speak Russian. Sprechen Sie Deutsch?" she asked.

"I do," the woman spoke back in German with a heavy Russian accent.

"I'm looking for a dress for a ball. Do you have anything that would be suited for an occasion like that?"

The woman's eyes raked up and down her body, obviously trying to get a feel for size. "I think I have something that would be perfect for you." She pulled a long, straight, reddish-pink dress from a wall hook behind her. It sparkled as it caught the light from the window. It was fitted at the top, almost like a bodice, and silk hung around the arms. It was simple yet elegant.

"It's beautiful," Eva told her.

The woman went to a table and picked up a pair of white gloves. "These will go perfectly with it." She handed them to Eva.

The dress would show her shoulders and quite a bit of cleavage. Do you have something to cover my shoulders?"

"You don't want to cover the dress. Its design is what makes it so perfect for you. It will hug your waist while adding to your height and accentuate your bosom."

"That's exactly what I'm unsure about. I don't know if I want it to do that."

"Why? You have an elegant, slender body. You shouldn't hide it."

The woman was thick and muscular, and her body was nothing like Eva's. She wondered if the woman put emphasis on the dress showing her slender frame because she wished she looked that way. Eva personally didn't think she was at all unique. At home in America, many of the girls in her classes at the university were tall and thin like her, and a lot of them were also tan and athletic, which is how she wished she was.

"I guess I can wear it the way it is."

The woman smiled. "Good. Do you need any shoes?"

"No, I have a pair that will go with it."

Eva was directed to the back of the store to a small changing room and tried on the dress to make sure it fit. The cut and shape were almost perfect, so she changed back into her dress and brought the gown and gloves to the counter so she could pay. She had brought more money with her this time for an occasion like this. She had checked the price tag when the woman handed it to her, but it was in rubles, and she had no idea what it was worth. "Do you take German Reichsmarks?" she asked.

"We do." The woman did some calculations. "It will be thirty-five Reichsmarks for the dress and seven for the gloves." That was a more reasonable price than the dress in Paris. This was more in her budget. She paid the woman, then left the shop. She stood on the sidewalk in front of the store and looked for Sergei. She didn't see him or the car, so she decided to walk back to the hotel. It had not taken long to find a dress, so it was no surprise that he wasn't waiting for her.

When she got to her room, she hung the dress in the wardrobe closet and draped the gloves over the hanger. She tossed her purse in the corner and kicked off her shoes before falling onto the bed. Looking up at the ceiling, waiting for Sergei to pick her up.

She let her mind wonder to Gerhardt, and the thought of going back to France with him gave her butterflies. She was a little surprised by her excitement but also liked the rush. As she let her mind wander, her excitement turned to confusion, then morphed into fear as she remembered the attack on the German high command. The Gestapo was good at catching the people they were after. Panic formed in the pit of her stomach, moving up into her chest as a tightness took hold, and she had to push the thoughts out of her mind. She replaced it but only with another fear, the fear of what would happen when Bauer got out of the hospital. He would not give up on bringing his attackers to justice. "I have to get out of Europe," she said aloud. There was so much racing through her mind. The attack, the possibility of being captured, Bauer, Gerhardt, the rest of the war she knew was coming, her family, and finding a way home. She bolted upright, right now wanting a drink. The hope of drinking away her problems, even if only for tonight, made her happy.

There was a knock at her door. She slid off the bed and cracked it open. Sergei was standing outside. "Let's go," he said with enthusiasm that matched his smile.

"Alright, let me grab my purse."

She hadn't even taken her jacket off when she returned from the dress shop. She slipped her shoes on, tied them, and retrieved her purse from where she had thrown it in the corner. She stepped out into the hall with Sergei and locked her door.

"How long will this party go on for?" she asked.

"As long as we want it to," he beamed.

She looked at her watch; it was a quarter past six. She hoped that the rest of the evening would be a blur. She got into the car, and he came around the other side and slid in next to her. "I want to warn you, it will probably get loud tonight. When the guys drink, they start to shout, dance, or whatever comes to mind in their drunken state."

"Oh… I didn't expect anything less. There are going to be other women at this party, right?"

"Of course, but mostly men. The men are usually rowdier than the women, which is why I didn't warn you about the women."

"Well, there is a big surprise," she said in English.

"He gave her a funny look. "What was that?"

"Nothing," she assured him.

As the car traveled through the city, she tried to sort out what she was going to do when she returned to Germany. She really wanted to go to France with Gerhardt, and then she would dedicate her time after that to getting home. *Home…* she thought.

“Sergei, would it be possible to get to Alaska from Russia?”

“Alaska?”

“Yes.”

“Do you have any idea how much land there is between us and Alaska?”

“A lot. I don’t know the exact distance, though,” she admitted.

“Yes, a lot. It is only frozen land. There is nothing there. You would die before you reached Siberia.”

“Aren’t there people in Siberia?” she asked.

“A few, only military personnel, though. Civilians are not allowed in that area. It’s nothing more than prison camps there. Besides, as I said, you would die before you were even halfway.”

She felt discouraged; she hoped that this would be her ticket home. She turned and looked out the window so he could not see the disappointment.

“I know why you asked, but there has to be a better way to go home than crossing the breath of Russia to get to Alaska. Even if you made it to Alaska, could you survive crossing Alaska and Canada with no food, shelter, or a way to protect yourself?”

She looked back at him. “What better way? If there was a way home, don’t you think I would have tried it already?” she said, putting emphasis on “way.”

“I suppose. You know, this war won’t last forever, and

then you can return home."

"But that won't be for years. That is if I even survive it till the end."

"You don't know that. It could end soon, and you will survive."

"I know that wars are never a quick thing."

"Is it really so bad for you in Germany?"

"I am the outsider, and so many of them look at me like the enemy. You don't know how that feels."

"No, I don't know, but I have an idea, and I can imagine it isn't pleasant. There are Germans who seem to like you very much, though."

"A few, but the ones who hate me overshadow those who like me. I feel the darkness they cast no matter where I go. I can't escape it."

"They are simply asserting their power because they can. I wouldn't worry about them."

It was so much more than that. There were things he didn't understand, and there was no way she could make him. "I try not to," was all she could say.

They pulled in front of a large house with a covered area for the cars to drive under. A man standing out front opened the door for them. They both stepped out on the same side and she entered the house with Sergei. A maid inside showed them to a lounge that was already filled with people. Some were laughing over drinks as they stood in a group, while others were at tables drinking and playing games.

"Come over here. We can sit at one of the empty tables," he said as he walked to one near the middle of the room. On their way, he kept stopping and introducing her to different people. Most were in uniforms like him, but some were in suits. She only counted five other women in the room but countless men. The scent of alcohol permeated the air, and the cigarette smoke clouded the room. Her eyes watered, and her lungs hurt like she sucked in smoke from a campfire. It was an environment that she was not accustomed to.

They finally made it to the table, and as soon as they were seated, a man in a uniform brought them a bottle of clear liquid and two empty glasses, sitting them on the table. His jacket was unbuttoned, and a cigar hung from the corner of his mouth.

"And the party starts now," Sergei said.

"What is that?" she asked.

"Nastoiki, it's homemade vodka. You also need to try Russian wine. It's superb."

"I'm not so sure about the vodka."

"What—no. Come on, you said you didn't want to remember tonight, and this is what it's going to take to do that. It will leave you feeling like you are flying after about four glasses."

"That sounds interesting. Is the wine like other wines?"

"It's a little on the bitter-sweet side, but it's good."

"I'm feeling brave tonight. I'll try the wine and, I guess, the vodka, too."

"That's my girl." He poured some of the pungent liquid into a cup and slid it over to her, then poured himself a glass. "Sazdarovye," he said as he held up his cup, then poured the whole thing into his mouth in one swift move. He breathed loudly through his mouth and sat the cup back on the table. He nodded towards her cup. “Come on, now you.”

She picked up the cup, held it in front of her face for a few seconds, looked at the clear liquid, then tilted her head back, dumped the whole thing into her mouth, and swallowed. Her eyes immediately started to water, and the back of her throat burned like it was on fire. She coughed and tapped her chest.

“Oh my God, that was awful.”

He laughed. “Let’s get you another one.”

“No, I don’t think I can tolerate another one.”

“Sure, you can. We will have you drinking like a Russian by the end of the night.” He filled up her glass again, then his. “Let’s do it together this time.” He held up his glass, waiting for her to do the same. She lifted her cup, holding it in front of her like last time, and then they both drank them simultaneously. Again, she coughed, but somehow, it didn’t seem as bad as it did the first time. “Are you ready for another one?” he asked.

“Give me a second. My stomach is still trying to catch up to yours.” There was a lot of shouting coming from behind them. She turned in her chair and watched a group of men laughing and pushing one another, spilling their drinks in the process.

“Watch this. They are going to do the Hopak dance,” he said with excitement.

“Is that the one where they kick their legs while squatting?”

“Yes, that pretty much sums it up.”

Several men did what looked like a dance-off to her. It was so funny to witness, and they were so good at it. She turned to look at Sergei and realized that he had already poured her another drink. This time, she didn't hesitate to drink it, and when she sat the glass back on the table, he poured her another, and like last time, she threw it back.

"Do you think they would let me try the dance?"

"Usually, men do it, but I don't see why not." He yelled something in Russian to the men who had finished dancing. After he was done speaking, they all looked at her, then clapped as one man came to her chair and took her by the elbow, pulling her to her feet. She was tipsy and dizzy already. How was Sergei holding his liquor so well? The man led her to the middle of the floor, but after they were there, she no longer felt as brave as she did while at the table. She looked over at Sergei for some sort of support, and like she was hoping, he smiled and nodded his head in encouragement. The man showed her how the dance was done, then she tried. As soon as she lifted her leg, she fell on her butt and started laughing. "This is so fun, and I didn't even do it." She continued to laugh. Sergei stood from the table and came to help her off the floor, then took her back to her chair. "No, I want to try it again."

"Alright." He let go of her arm.

She got down and kicked up her right leg, but when she tried to do the second kick, she fell again. "I think I need another drink. Those last four didn't make me good at this."

"Unfortunately, the more you drink, the worse you will get at it. If I were you, I would quit while I was ahead." He helped her off the floor again and led her back to the table. "Do you want to try the wine now?"

"Yes, I do."

Sergei went to the bar, reached over the counter, and got a bottle of wine. He took a glass that was hanging over the counter and brought them back to the table. "Here you go," he said as he poured hers half full of a deep red liquid.

She took a sip. "You weren't kidding about it being bitter."

He sat down and poured himself another helping of vodka. "So, tell me about these people in Germany who think you are the enemy. The guy at the ball, is he one of them?"

She sipped the wine. "No, but he is like my enemy, in a way."

"How so?"

"He… it's actually a long story." She didn't know if she wanted to talk about it. Her head was so fuzzy that she wasn't sure she could even tell it right.

"We have nothing to do tonight but drink. I've got all the time in the world."

"Alright, but I'm going to give you the short version."

"That's fine. I've got time for the short version, too."

"I met him in France, and at first we didn't exactly like each other, well… actually it's more like I didn't like him. He was always friendly with me whenever we met. Sometimes, I think he tried so hard to be nice because he knew I wanted nothing to do with him. But, after a while, I relented, and we became friends, and after that, we became more than friends. I knew he had a fiancé, which is one reason I was reluctant for so long to have a relationship with him, but later, he broke up with her. She had nothing to do with the reason we broke up, though. It's because he caused the death of someone who was very dear to me. When I left France and came to Germany, I thought we might get back together, but I found out at the ball that he was back with his fiancé."

"It sounds like he is confused."

"I know. That is what I thought. He has now asked me to go to France with him?"

"For what reason?"

"He says for reconciliation."

"Well, I am not certain that he is being honest with you. It sounds like he doesn't want to let go of either of you. Take it from a man."

"I don't know what to believe, but I think I'm going to go. I want us to at least be friends again."

"I understand that. It's hard when people leave our lives for good. Have you ever met his fiancé?"

"No, I'm not sure I want to."

"Do you know why he chose her over you, even though you are back in his life?"

"I don't, maybe because he loves her more than me."

"Maybe it is out of a sense of commitment and also convenience. I'm sure he loves her, too. Do you think he loves you?"

"I believe he does, yes."

"And yet he is with her."

"I see your point. I guess there are more reasons to be with her than me."

"He has probably been with her for a while, and you can't take away that time they had together."

His comment hurt a little, even though she knew it was true.

"And what about the people who think you are an enemy of Germany?"

She huffed. "It's because I'm an American, among other reasons I don't even know, and probably wouldn't understand even if I heard them."

"Have you tried asking any of them?"

"One of them, but they won't tell me the actual reasons. And the other, he is not a nice person. He hates me and for no good reason."

"Maybe it is a valid reason for him, but like the other person, he isn't telling you what it is."

"His reason is that I'm American. He bases everything off that."

"Are you sure? It's likely that he is choosing not to tell you the other reasons? I doubt it's solely because of that."

"He says I stand for everything he opposes, simply by being me."

"What does he do for a living?"

"He is a Lieutenant Colonel in the SS."

"Sounds like you are at a disadvantage. You are in his country, and he is in a position of power, and you are not. You are probably resistant to his views and opinions of how the world is and should be, maybe without even realizing it.

And sometimes Germans can be stubborn in their ways," he said with a knowing look.

"This I am painfully aware of."

"Maybe you should find out if he truly doesn't like you. Maybe it isn't personal. Dig into the reasons he dislikes you if that truly is what it is. Is the feeling mutual?"

She laughed, sloshing some of her wine out of the glass. "It most certainly is."

"The reason I asked is that a lot of the time, a person is angry at the world, and it might not be personal to the person it is directed at. It really has nothing to do with you at all. But if he does dislike you, there is probably very little you can do about it. It is hard to change people's minds. They are going to dislike you no matter what you do. But I wouldn't worry about it too much. There is no way every person is going to like you."

"That is true, but he happens to be a person you really don't want to have as an enemy. Having him as your enemy is dangerous. He hates me because of his stupid prejudices. I don't know what to do about him, and I see him almost every day."

"Why do you see him every day?"

"Because he was one of the officers injured in the attack on the German high command weeks ago, and he is at the hospital I work at."

"You are a nurse?"

"I am."

"And you help take care of him like all the other patients?"

“I do, yes.”

“Then maybe he will be nicer to you when he is well again.”

“He won’t. He is still unkind, even in the state he is in. I am even the one who saved his life, and somehow that, too, makes him angry. He has told me as much. I’ve given up on trying to make him like me.”

“Maybe he really does hate you then,” he said, smiling as he emptied his glass.

“I know, but why? I have never done anything to him.”

“Like you said, simply because you exist. If people feel like their way of life is being threatened, they will go to great lengths to protect it.”

“But I’m not doing anything to endanger it. How do I make him see that?” She shook her head. “Stupid man.”

“I don’t know. Maybe you can’t. I have never been in your situation, but if I were, I would ask him what I could do to make the situation more bearable for us both. It might not help, but it is worth asking.”

“I haven’t tried that, but I doubt it will help. I look forward to the day I don’t have to worry about his opinion of me or ever see his face again.” The words were slurred as she spoke, then she finished the glass of wine. “Well, I have talked so much about myself, and my head feels like a balloon. You talk for a while. Any girlfriend, wife, fiancé… maybe someone who hates you, too?”

“None of the mentioned people, at least not the first ones.”

“What, why?”

"I haven't found the right person; besides, my career is my main focus right now. My only ambition at this moment is to do well in the eyes of the motherland."

"I guess that is a lofty goal."

"It is. How about another drink?"

She waved her hand. "No, my stomach can't handle more."

"That can't be all the drinking you can handle. We have only started."

"Oh no, I can't. You can drink some more, though, if you want." She already felt sick from the alcohol she had consumed, and her head pounded like a drum. She needed water, not more wine or vodka. At this point, she was fighting sleep and the urge to throw up. She checked the time. It was already past midnight.

"I think we should call it a night." She pointed to the large clock on the far wall.

"We usually party until the sun is up, but if you really want to go back, we can."

"I do."

He helped her to the car and told the driver to take them back to the hotel. She watched the buildings and lights go by in streaks before closing her eyes, pushing against the pain in her head that came in waves.

Chapter Thirteen

✠

Saturday, April 5th, 1941

Eva pulled on her gloves and admired the dress in the mirror. She rubbed her hands over the material and turned to one side and then the other, checking the fit. A knock sounded on the door, so she checked her watch. It was time to leave.

"Just a minute." She slipped her shoes on and grabbed her jacket and purse, figuring it was Sergei.

She opened the door and took in Sergei standing in front of her, impeccably dressed in evening attire. "I thought you would be in your uniform."

"Not tonight. I thought I would dress more the part. We have the option of wearing a tux or our dress uniform, but I thought this would be more fitting."

"Well, it certainly is fitting for the occasion," she said

approvingly. He held his elbow out for her, and she smiled, then looped her arm through his.

The ball was already well underway when they arrived. A doorman took their coats at the entryway, then they proceeded to the ballroom. There were people gliding arm-in-arm across the large wooden dance floor.

"I don't see any point in waiting. Let's go, shall we?" he said, holding his hand out to her.

"Why not."

They walked together to the middle of the room and turned to face each other. He put his right hand on her upper back and took her right hand in his left. His large, sweaty hand was stout. She placed her left hand on his shoulder, and they moved across the floor like the other couples. They danced the first song, then the second, and a third before she lost count. Being here tonight was amazing. It had a different feel to it than the ball in Berlin. This one made her feel as if she had stepped into a different world, a time and place from a movie. Maybe it was the building and the music, or perhaps the clothing. But what was happening tonight would be over soon and eventually feel like a dream, and Russia would not stay as it was now. St. Petersburg was so beautiful and unscarred by the war, like this room. They both had so much beauty and youth, full of life and elegance. The people were proud, and the culture was rich with traditions, but looming outside its borders was death and destruction waiting to crumble it, as the other Russian cities soon would be.

The people who danced in elegant dresses and fine suits

were oblivious to the dangers that awaited them, unaware that nights like this would soon be gone. They no doubt thought themselves safe, that their cities and their way of life would last forever and, together with Germany, would have their glory in the end. They thought, like the Germans, that they had a right to other people's lands and freedom as if it was given to them by God, which no doubt assured their already existing beliefs that their supremacy would never end. She wondered if they were so naïve as to believe they were immune to the horrible effects of this war. What they didn't know was that it would forever change their lives. At the end of it all, Russia would never again be the same. Power, the illusion of bliss, and security were all fragile things.

"I have to sit for a bit," she said, leaning in so he could hear her. "My legs are tired."

He led her to a table. "I'm going to get us some drinks," he told her before heading to the bar.

Tonight, she vowed to not drink copious quantities of alcohol like the night before. He returned to the table and set a glass of red wine in front of her, then took the seat beside her with his cup of clear liquid, no doubt vodka.

"I have enjoyed tonight more than I had expected. I rarely dance, but this has been fun," he said, then took a swig of his drink.

"It has been an enjoyable evening. I am impressed with this room." She let her eyes roam the room in admiration.

"It is pretty. I told you that you would enjoy this ball. I'm happy that you agreed to come. Now you get to see

Russia and all it has to offer. It is the best country in the world, and I mean no offense."

"None taken, although I'm going to have to disagree with you."

"As to be expected. Though, you have to admit that this has been amazing."

She tried to repress a smile. "It has taken my mind off of things, I will admit."

"I am happy that Russia has impressed you," he said, with his heavy accent as he rolled Rs that should not be rolled with broad intonations. He took a sip of his drink and then sat it back on the table. "You know that you will return to Germany alone tomorrow, right?"

"I do."

"I'm sorry that I cannot accompany you. But I would like to show you around St. Petersburg tomorrow before you leave. There is so much you haven't seen. It's an amazing city."

"I think I would enjoy that. So, what will you do when the war is over, Sergei?"

"Hmmm, I think I would like to get married and have a family and maybe a farm."

"A farm? You want to live on a farm?" she chuckled. "I can't see you living on a farm."

"Why not? It is good, honest work. Maybe I can grow some potatoes, cabbage, beets, stuff like that."

She laughed harder. "Besides potatoes, those are some of the worst foods you can eat."

"You don't like cabbage and beets?"

"No, I hate them."

"Well, I'm figuring out quickly that you will not be a beet or cabbage farmer. So, what do you want to do when the war is over?"

"Go home. That is what I want to do." She took a sip of her wine and looked at him over the rim.

"And what about this German that you know?"

"Well, he can't come with me if that is what you mean."

"Why not? Do they not like Germans in America?"

"No, of course, they like them alright, but after them starting another world war, I'm sure they would not be overly welcoming." She, of course, could not tell him the real reason. "It's not feasible. It would never work," she affirmed.

"I see how it could be complicated, and normally, I would say it would work even though you two are from different countries, but you had said that he is back with his fiancé. So, no, I guess it won't work. What will you do when you go home?"

"Go back to school, I guess."

"What do you go to school for?"

"I was going to go to nursing school."

"Aren't you a nurse now?"

"Yes, but the requirements in America are different than they are in Germany."

"So, marriage, children, and a farm are out of the question for you?" He gave a crooked smile.

"The farm, yes, but not necessarily the others. I can go to school and still get married and have children."

“I suppose you are right,” he said, and looked at the people dancing. “Shall we dance some more?”

“Yes, let’s.” She sat down her glass and put her hand in his, letting him lead her back onto the dance floor.

When the song was over, her legs were shaky, and her feet were sore from the shoes, but it was worth it. This was the most fun she had had in a while.

It was approaching midnight when they left the ball and half past when they arrived back at the hotel.

“I will meet you in the hotel restaurant for breakfast at 8:00 if that is not too early for you?” he asked.

“No, it’s fine. I should bring my things to the lobby with me then.”

“That is a good idea. My driver can take you right to the airport after.”

That night, Eva fell asleep quickly without the usual play-by-play of her life running through her head. That morning, she met Sergei in the restaurant, and they ate a quick breakfast.

“We have some of the most amazing buildings in St. Petersburg, and there is also a walkway along the lake that you should see,” he said before finishing off his glass of orange juice.

“I am happy to see whatever you show me. I always enjoy visiting new places.”

They walked along the lake, and he told her of the old shipping days when that was the primary way things were brought into St. Petersburg. He also told her of Catherine the

Great and how St. Petersburg was once the nation's capital when she was queen and that it later changed to Moscow. He explained the slow decline of the monarch and the immense power they formerly held.

After the walk, Sergei informed his driver that he was to take her to the airport.

"I have enjoyed having you here. I hope you enjoyed it as well."

"I have immensely. Thank you."

He kissed her hand. "Make sure and come back. Maybe next time you can see Moscow."

"I hope to one day."

She got in the backseat, and he closed the door, giving a quick wave as the car drove away. She had mixed feelings about going back to Germany. Not because she was particularly fond of Russia but because of all the things that awaited her there. Eventually, she would go to France with Gerhardt and that alone made her nervous. There was also Bauer to contend with. He was the wild card that she didn't know how would play out in the end.

The ground got farther away as the plane climbed, and she felt a twinge of sadness as it reminded her how far she was from her family. She was all on her own here and frightened of the unknown. She felt trepidation every day when she got out of bed, uncertain of what awaited her. Sometimes, she had to search hard to find things that got her through the day. That was enough to keep her going.

Unlike the flight to Russia, she was able to sleep on the way back. As the plane touched down, she was jolted awake.

She opened her eyes and looked around the cabin, then pulled herself up in her seat to wait for the plane to stop. As it was taxing to the gate, she noticed a black car with two small flags displaying the swastikas parked next to the airport entrance. She couldn't see who was in the car, only a shadowed figure in the front driver's seat. Once the plane had stopped, someone got out of the back of the car. They were wearing an officer's uniform and cap, but she couldn't make out their face. She put her head close to the window and squinted, but it was still to no avail. She knew they were there for her, and no matter if it was Gerhardt or someone else, it made her more than a little uncomfortable.

She stood and pulled the suitcase down from the overhead rack. Her hands were sweaty, and her pulse was racing. She put on her hat and retrieved her purse from the seat, then walked to the door, waiting for the pilot to open it. When he pushed the door open, her eyes locked on the man from the car who was standing at the bottom of the steps. She slowly descended, all the while keeping her sights on the man in uniform. He finally looked up to meet her gaze, and a smile cracked at the corner of his mouth. She was relieved to see Gerhardt staring at her with his penetrating blue eyes, and her heart sped even faster at the sight of him.

"Let me take that for you," he said when she reached the last step.

"Were you afraid I would not give you an answer? Did you come here to force one out of me?"

"No, I knew that you would give me an answer. But I didn't want to wait any longer. I had to change my plans, though. I will now go to France at the beginning of June."

"That is so far away."

He took her by the elbow. "Let's talk about it in the car." He put her suitcase in the trunk and opened the door for her. Once they were both in the car, he turned to face her, taking her hand in his. "Eva, it would mean a lot if you came with me. What do I have to do to convince you?"

"I had made my decision a while ago." Her eyes met his as he waited with anticipation. "I'll go with you."

His face softened at her answer. "I so wanted to hear you say that."

"Gerhardt, how could I have said no. I hope this trip will give both of us some peace of mind."

"I hope so, too."

As the car got closer to Berlin, Eva stared out the window at the smoke rising from all over the city, billowing into the sky like black clouds. She leaned forward to get a better view.

"What happened?"

"There was another bombing last night, one of the worst ones we have had yet."

"The hospitals must be struggling to accommodate all of those people."

"They are still trying to put out the fires, and many people are still missing."

"That's terrible."

"It is, but that is what this war has come to. Where Germany and the allies bomb innocent civilians."

She glanced at him, the strain evident on his face, and it

was what was happening in Germany that bothered him immensely. The car pulled in front of her apartment and stopped near the entrance. "What day do we leave?" she asked.

"I'm not sure the exact day, but when I find out, I will let you know."

"Are we flying there?"

"Yes."

"I'll see you then, I guess." She reached for the door handle, but he caught her hand.

"Then… am I to believe that you don't want to see me again until we leave?"

"I didn't mean it like that. It's that I was unsure if we would see each other again before it was time to leave. What are you trying to say?" she asked, unable to read the intentions from his expression.

"I'm not trying to indicate anything. I suppose we will have to take it one day at a time."

"I think that would be for the best." She got out, set her suitcase on the sidewalk, and watched the car pull away from the curb. Gerhardt glanced back through the rear window, and she held his gazer until his face disappeared. She was having a hard time sorting out her feelings. So many emotions were put into a pot and stirred together, blending into confusion.

She knew when she returned to work, it would be hectic, but it was worse than she had imagined. People were sitting in the lobby because there were no more beds available.

Some were bleeding on the floor, and others holding onto an injured arm or pressing a cloth to their head. There appeared to be whole families waiting to be treated. Helping wounded soldiers was hard enough, but this was indescribable. Seeing little children covered in blood and crying as they lay on the floor crushed her.

The day dragged on, and helping the wounded seemed endless. She didn't even have a chance to stop and eat or even check on the patients who had already been there. The firefighters constantly brought in new people that they dug out of the rubble.

The sun hung low in the sky when the arrival of new patients finally ceased, but it still took hours more to help find places to put them. She plopped down into a chair in the nurse's quarters, exhausted. Her whole body hurt, but mostly her feet and lower back.

"Eva, I need you to bring some food for the new patients. There are a lot of frightened children, I'm sure they are hungry, and food will help settle their nerves," Frau Wagner said, peeking her head in through the open door.

"I'll be right there." Frau Wagner disappeared again, and Eva sighed. She hoped to get more than a minute to rest but shouldn't be surprised that she had not. She got up from the chair and trudged down the hall back towards the patient ward, barely finding the energy to move one leg in front of the other. The sun had long been down, and the lights in the patient wings were dimmed so they could rest. People were still sleeping in the halls, some on beds and others on a blanket that had been laid out for them on the floor.

She opened the door of patient ward C to count the children. She didn't know how many of them there were, so she didn't know how many plates of food she needed to bring. She scanned the room for the children, finding some asleep in their beds and others sitting up, staring around the room, frightened expressions on their soot-covered faces.

Faintly in the room, there was a child's voice followed by an adult's voice. She looked for the source and saw a little girl sitting on the edge of another patient's bed. Quietly, she walked closer to see and hear better; she wanted to know who was talking with the child. She reached the storage cabinet and stopped beside it, peering around its corner. Her eyes widened when she saw the girl sitting on Bauer's bed talking with him. Why would he be talking with one of the children that came in? He was so off-putting and abrasive, at least towards adults. She could scarcely imagine him being tender towards children. Now, she had to know what they were saying. She came a little closer, but not close enough where they would notice her presence.

The girl looked no older than four or five. She was sitting on the edge of his bed in her tarnished nightgown, hugging a teddy bear that was blackened from the ash and smoke of the fires to her chest. Her voice was high-pitched and small as she spoke, and her blond hair was matted to her head, blackened from the smoke, as was her face, just like the bear.

"Did you get burned in the fire?" the girl asked Bauer, pointing to one of his bandages.

"No, I was being careless and hurt myself."

"How did you do that? Did you fall down?"

He faintly smiled. "Something like that. Where is your mom?"

"I don't know. I couldn't find her. I called for her, the… the loud noises scared me, but she never came." She stuttered some of her words. "Men took me away." The girl looked around the dark room. "But I don't see Mommy here," she said in her squeaky little voice.

"Were you at your home when the men took you?"

She nodded. "I was in my bed."

"No matter where your mom is, I know she loves you and thinks of you." He pointed to her bear. "What is his name?" he asked.

"It's a girl. Her name is Elsa." She looked down at the bear and picked something out of its hair.

"Does she help you when you are scared?"

"Yes. I don't feel as scared when I'm with her."

"You know, I feel afraid sometimes, too."

"When you fell?"

He smiled. "Yes, and other times, too. Do you have any brothers or sisters?"

"I have two older brothers, but I can't find them either."

"I'm sure they are safe."

"Do you have any brothers?" she asked.

"No, but I used to have a younger sister."

"Where is she?"

"Well, she is an angel now."

The girl's eyes widened. "How do you know she is an angel?"

"Because I watched her go to heaven."

"How did she go there?"

"One day, she closed her eyes to sleep, and then she floated up to heaven. She dreamed such wonderful dreams that it took her there."

"If I have wonderful dreams, will it take me to heaven too?"

"Someday, but not now."

"Do you visit her in heaven?"

He smiled. "No, I wish I could, but I am not allowed to visit her in heaven."

"Do you cry because you can't visit her?"

"Sometimes."

"Did Mommy and… and my brothers go to heaven?"

"I don't know, but if they are, they can see you and will never be far away. Your mom wants to watch you grow and see how wonderful your life will be, as do your brothers. Where is your dad?"

"I don't know, but Mommy said he went to fight."

"I'm sure he did. Your dad is courageous, and he loves you very much." She started to ask him another question, but he stopped her. "It's time to close your eyes. Save all your questions and ask them tomorrow."

"Can I sleep here with you?"

"The bed is kind of small for the two of us. I will be right here beside you, and if you should get scared during the night, you can come back to my bed. But you have to try and be brave, alright?" She nodded and slid off the bed, going to the one next to his, climbing in.

Eva waited until the girl was still before she approached Bauer. “Well, I didn’t expect that.”

“I don’t know what you mean.”

“Yes, you do. You are like Dr. Jekyll and Mr. Hyde. You treat me differently from everyone else. I don’t understand why, because I am trying to help you.”

He gritted his teeth. “How are you helping me? The thought of you here is nothing but an annoyance. You are trying to fit in somewhere you don’t belong.”

“You don’t think I know that. You couldn’t possibly understand what it’s like to walk in my shoes. I am trying to do the best I can, and you are making it harder.”

“Because you are not wanted here.”

“I can see that, but unless I can go home, I have to stay here, wanted or not.” She figured being cordial with him would be better than saying something mean, even if that was how she felt. “I heard you tell that little girl that you had a sister. What happened to her?”

The scowl on his face was gone, and his expression turned to fierce anger. “I will not talk about her with you.”

“I have an older brother. His name is Thomas,” she continued, still trying the nice thing to see if it got her anywhere.

“No doubt he is in the army now.”

“No, actually, he is a musician. A small-time one, but he enjoys what he does.”

For a minute, he was quiet, and she wondered what he was thinking. “If you don’t mind, I’m tired and would like to sleep.”

"Sure." She started walking away but stopped and turned back towards him. "It was nice what you did for that little girl. She is scared and alone, and you made her feel a little better."

"Children should not have to be subjected to this kind of thing, but they are. That's an unfortunate consequence of war."

So, he had sympathy for children. She could use that while trying to be nicer to him. "It is. One that's almost unforgivable."

Wednesday, April 9th, 1941

Eva ate her lunch with Heidi and Liesel at the Haus Vaterland in central Berlin. It was apparently the largest café in the world, and looking around, you could see Germans of all classes eating there or going to the cinema across the street. It was quite an impressive establishment, and this was the first time Eva had eaten there. Most of the time, they brought their own lunches to the hospital because they couldn't afford to go out, but today was Heidi's birthday, and they had to celebrate. Eva had asked if it was OK if she invited Ingrid. She felt bad for Ingrid because she was always alone, never meeting anyone at the hospital or eating lunch with the other nurses. She wondered if Ingrid had any friends.

"There she is," Liesel said, looking across the room. Eva turned and watched Ingrid walking through the crowded room towards their table. Ingrid smiled when she saw them.

She sat down next to Eva. "Thank you for inviting me. This restaurant is so nice. I've always wanted to come here."

"You are welcome." Eva gave her a little smile.

"We are happy to have you. Should we order now?" Heidi asked.

Eva counted the little money in her purse. She had to make sure she had enough to get something. This restaurant wasn't cheap.

"I have enough to get something good," Heidi said, laying some money on the table.

"We are going to get you something," Eva insisted.

"No, you guys will not spend your money on me."

"At least let us get you a drink and a piece of cake," Liesel insisted.

She smiled. "Thank you, you are all such good friends. I don't believe I've had cake since the war started."

"You should have cake on your birthday," Eva told her.

"So, do any of you have boyfriends?" Ingrid asked after they got their food.

"No, but I would like to," Heidi said thoughtfully, looking out the restaurant window. "Has anyone else noticed how cute some of the patients are?"

"That is what I have been saying," Ingrid chimed in. "There are so many of them that I would consider boyfriend material."

"I will worry about that when the war is over," Liesel stated, her words certain.

"Don't you want to live and not simply survive during

this war?" Ingrid asked.

"Whether we win or lose, I will worry about it then. Don't get me wrong, I notice the good-looking men who come in. If one asked me out, it would be hard to say no, and I would not be opposed to having a fling with someone, but I don't want anything serious until the war is over."

"Liesel likes to keep things simple," Eva told her.

"So, what will all of you do after the war?" Ingrid asked.

"Heidi smiled. "I want to have a lot of kids and a husband that will take care of me and treat me like a queen."

"I could definitely see you achieving that," Eva laughed.

"What about you, Liesel?" Ingrid asked.

"I could see myself living a quiet life out of the city on a farm with my husband and a couple of kids."

"Only two?" Heidi asked.

"Yes, I believe that is all I want."

"And why the county?" asked Ingrid.

"Because this city won't be fit to raise a family before too long, and things will be slower in the country and simpler."

"I can see the appeal to that," Eva agreed.

"You never said what you would do after the war," Ingrid said, focusing on her.

"I suppose I will go home."

"No one here has caught your interest?" Ingrid pressed.

Liesel and Heidi grew silent, chewing their food as they looked down at their plates.

Ingrid noticed the change in the mood. "What… did I say something wrong?"

"You said nothing wrong, Ingrid," Eva said. "Someone here has caught my attention, but even though we are in the same city, we are oceans apart. There are many reasons we aren't together and never will be. We are through. It was over the moment it began."

"It's not..." Ingrid trailed off, but the answer was written in the look she gave Eva.

"Oh God, no," Eva shrieked.

Liesel and Heidi gave each other a confused glance. "And what will you do, Ingrid?" Eva asked, trying to hurry and change the topic from her.

"I don't know. I guess a lot depends on the outcome of the war, but in an ideal world, Germany would win the war, and I would go to school and get married."

"Germany doesn't have to win, and it doesn't have to be an ideal world for that to happen," Eva told her.

"It's that I don't know what it would be like if Germany lost the war or if my future husband would want me to go to school."

"Your husband can't decide for you. Whether or not you go to school is your decision, Ingrid," Eva pressed.

"I guess."

A waitress brought Heidi's piece of cake and placed it on the table in front of her. "No singing," she said after the waitress left. "I want to enjoy my cake, and no one else here needs to know that it is my birthday except the people at this table."

When Heidi was finished with her cake, she stood, as did Liesel. "Are you guys ready?" Liesel asked.

"I think I will sit here for a while longer."

"Alright, we'll see you back at the hospital."

"OK," Eva shot her a smile.

Ingrid stayed seated at the table, too, and when Heidi and Liesel had disappeared through the front door, she spoke. "I'm sorry if I brought up a touchy subject for you."

"It's alright. I think I have come to terms with the way things are between him and me."

"Again, I'm sorry. It sounds miserable."

"It can be if I think too much about it, which is why I don't."

"I was going to tell you a few days ago, but I never got a chance. But while you were gone to Russia, the patient, Bauer, asked where you were. I guess your absence was noticed. I told him you would be gone for a while, and then he seemed indifferent, but when I told him you were in Russia, his attitude completely changed. He seemed alarmed by that. Do you know why that might be?"

So, he knows about the invasion of Russia. Of course he does. "I think I might."

"Why? What does that have to do with him?"

"It's delicate. I wish I could tell you, but I can't."

"Oh, I thought you said there wasn't anything between you two."

"I wasn't being completely honest with you. There is something between us. We do have a history, but not like what you think. We have a strong mutual dislike for one another." Eva stood from the table. "We better get back to work."

Ingrid followed beside her, and they walked to the tram stop. "So, if there really is nothing like that between the two of you, then you won't care if I pursue him?"

Eva stopped walking and eyed her in disbelief. "Yes, I would, but not because of any feelings I have for him. You don't know him like I do. He is not a good person, and you would be wise to stay away from him."

"Then why did you save him if he is so bad?"

"Because it was my job."

"That is not the only reason. Why did you really save him?"

"It is complicated. I can assure you there is no love lost between us. But Ingrid, you need to stay far away from that man."

"Sometimes you are confusing, Eva."

"Look, any relationship with him would be tragic. He would play you like a fiddle and discard you as soon as he tired of you. He is that kind of person, and I'm sure he has done that to women before. I like you, Ingrid, and would hate to see you get hurt. You should find someone who deserves you."

"You make it sound like he is evil."

"Because he is. We better start walking again, or we will miss the tram and be late."

While sitting together, Eva, out of the corner of her eye, noticed that Ingrid kept glancing over at her. It was obvious that Ingrid wanted to ask her more about it but wasn't sure if she should. Eva was happy she didn't. When they were at the hospital, they changed back into their uniforms, and then

Ingrid went to wash the bed linens while Eva filled a cart with plates of food for the patients. She pushed it into the patient ward and passed out trays. There was a patient who had been there a week now, and every time she came near him, he made her feel uncomfortable. Whenever she helped him, he would make some flirtatious comment or try to touch her butt. He was sitting up in bed, a smile on his face, watching as she came toward him like he was waiting for her. She took a tray off the top and sat it on the table next to his bed. “There you go.” She started to move on to the next patient, but he took her hand.

“If I wasn’t in this bed, we would dance.”

“I never agreed to dance with you.”

“You didn’t have to; your face says it all.”

“No, it really doesn’t.”

“Why don’t you sit, and we can talk for a while.”

“Because I have other patients to attend to, and I don’t date patients.”

“But I see you talking to the other patients.”

“Only when I have to. Look, I really have to go. So, if you would be so kind as to let go of my hand now.”

He didn’t answer but kept a hold of her. “No, you don’t. Come on, sit with me for a while.”

“She said to let go of her hand,” a man said in a steely voice.

He instantly dropped her hand, and she followed his gaze to the end of the bed. Bauer was standing in his light blue hospital pajamas a few feet from the bed, looking past her at the other man as if she wasn’t even there. They held eye contact for a few seconds before the other man dropped his gaze to the bed, and Bauer continued to his own.

What the hell just happened?

When Bauer walked away, the man looked up at her but didn't say anything. His gaze still made her feel uncomfortable, so she hurried and pushed the cart to the next patient's bed without looking back at him. She worked her way around the room, finally coming to the little girl's bed that she had seen with Bauer a few nights ago, but the bed was empty. Eva looked to see the girl sitting on Bauer's bed, leaning back against the pillow beside him. She went to stand by his bed and listened as the girl explained to him what she and her bear would do on a normal day, from playing in the backyard to having tea on her bedroom floor.

He looked up at Eva. "I think the nurse is here to bring us food."

The little girl looked at Eva and smiled with her round pink, dimpled cheeks, still sporting the pigtails that Eva had given her the day before. Eva handed her a tray of food and then gave one to Bauer. She sat on the edge of the girl's bed and watched her eat.

"So, Emilia, tomorrow you will get to leave the hospital."

She perked up. "Is my Mommy here?"

"No, I'm sorry. You will go live with some nice nuns and other children like you who can't find their mothers," Eva told her.

She looked at Bauer. "I don't want to go. Can I stay here?"

"No, I'm afraid not. You don't want to stay here with all these cranky sick men. You should go have fun with the other children. I can visit you at the orphanage if you want?" Bauer told her.

"Will you come and stay with me there?"

"It's only for children and the women who care for them. But I will visit you."

Eva waited for the girl to finish eating, then knelt beside her. "Do you see that nurse over there?" Eva said, pointing to the nurse standing near the door. The girl nodded. "Good. I want you to go over to her and tell her you are ready for a shower." The girl shook her head again, then hopped off the bed and walked to the nurse, looking back every few seconds. "Why did you do that?" Eva asked Bauer.

He laid his tray on the bed beside him where the girl had been sitting. "You mean telling that man to let go of your hand?"

"Yes, that."

"Because you asked him to, and he wasn't doing it, my reason seems pretty clear."

"You surprise me because if he had been raping me, I figured you would watch and do nothing."

"Is that the kind of person you think I am?"

"Yes, it is."

"Well then, you misjudge me like you do everyone else."

"I don't misjudge everyone else, and I certainly don't misjudge you. I see you for what you are."

"And I see you, madam. You are a fool, getting mixed

up in things you can't begin to comprehend."

"I don't know what you are talking about."

"I know you understand exactly what I am talking about."

"I'm afraid I don't."

"Then you are stupider than I thought."

"I don't know what trauma you suffered as a child, but whatever it was, you really should get some help."

He looked away from her and over to the window. "I believe they need you somewhere else."

"I believe you are right."

She picked up the tray from the bed and placed it back on the cart, then pushed it out of the room. Every time she tried to have a conversation with him, it always turned sour. He was definitely the anti-her. For a brief time, it seemed that he was trying to be nice to her by telling the other patient to let go of her hand, but of course, that went south fast. He wouldn't even admit that was what he was doing, being kind. He was a labyrinth that you couldn't find your way through, and she was sure he was evil with a black heart, but then he was kind to the little girl. There had to be some feeling buried deep in him. The way he talked about his sister sounded like love, but even psychopaths had moms and sisters and would occasionally help old ladies cross the street or do some other random act of kindness.

Chapter Fourteen

✠

Sunday, May 25th, 1941

Eva washed the blood from her arms in the large porcelain sink next to the operating room after a four-hour surgery.

"You would make a fine doctor," Dr. Möller said as he came to stand next to her at the sink.

"Thank you, Klaus. Maybe one day."

"Do you have any plans for the summer?"

"Yes, actually, I am taking a trip to France soon."

"Really? When are you going?"

She chuckled. "I'm not sure, actually. I'm going with a friend, but they don't know when they will have the time. I'm waiting for them to let me know so I can ask for the time off."

"That sounds exciting. Is it a gentleman you are going

with?"

Her cheeks turned a light shade of pink. "It is, but it is not what you think. He is only a good friend. Besides, he is getting married."

"Oh, I see. Would he be the same man you danced with at the ball?"

She watched the soap suds off her hands, not looking at him. "He would."

"You seemed quite upset with him, from what I remember. I'm surprised you are going to France with him."

"We worked things out, for the most part. This trip will be good for our friendship, I think."

He furrowed his brows. "Make sure you stay alert."

"For what?"

"Is it only the two of you going?"

"Yes."

"Often, I think men are less trustworthy than women."

"I know him. He is not like that."

"I'm not talking about only that. I mean about a lot of things. Situations rarely go as we expect them to."

"Thanks for the advice, but I'll be alright." She dried her hands and patted him on the arm as she walked past.

"Eva." Ingrid grabbed hold of her arm, pulling her into the linen room, then closed the door.

"Ingrid, why are we in the closet?"

"Did you hear?"

Eva shook her head. "Hear what?"

"SS Obersturmbannführer Bauer went home today."

"Seriously? That's good news." Eva's happiness faded

with her smile. If he went home, it meant he could go back to work soon, and he would no doubt come after her again. This, in fact, might be terrible news and not good news at all. "I need to talk to Frau Wagner about something. Thank you for telling me." She hurried out of the closet and went to look for Frau Wagner. She found her in her office, sitting at her desk, so Eva knocked on the doorframe and waited.

Frau Wagner looked up. "Come in, Miss Abrams." Eva walked in and sat in the chair across from her. "I'm glad you are here. I was going to find you, but you saved me the effort." She looked at Eva with an enthusiastic smile.

"Oh, what did you want to talk to me about?" The fact that she was smiling worried Eva. She never smiled.

"It's alright, Miss Abrams. You can go first."

"Alright, I was going to let you know that I will be going to Paris sometime in June. I'm not sure of the exact date yet, but I will let you know as soon as I do."

"As long as you don't tell me only a few days before you leave, it should be fine."

"Thank you."

"I'm sure you have heard that SS Obersturmbannführer Bauer has gone home today:"

Why was Frau Wagner asking her if she knew? Eva searched her face more closely. Something was amiss. "Yes, I have heard."

"We were going to keep him here at the hospital at least another week, but he insisted on going home. He said he had too much work to do and couldn't stay in the hospital any longer. He had to carry on with important business that needed his immediate attention, and he couldn't do it from here. We released him on the condition that he would work from home under the care of an in-home nurse for the first week before returning to full-time duty."

"Alright…"

"He has specifically asked for you to be the nurse that comes to his house." Frau Wagner put her thumbs and the tips of her fingers together and eyed her.

Eva blinked, and for a few brief seconds, she could not find her voice. "I… don't understand. Why would he ask that? He doesn't even like me." She nervously made a laugh and stared at Frau Wagner with conjecture.

Now Frau Wagner looked confused. "I don't know what you are going on about. All I know is he has asked for you."

Of course, he hasn't made his disdain obvious to everyone. "Do I get a choice?"

"You do, but why would you not want this opportunity?" She looked at Eva suspiciously. "To have the Obersturmbannführer asking for you personally is an honor. You must have done something to impress him."

"Oh, I doubt that. I am quite certain it is the opposite."

"Are you not going to accept his request then?" She looked insulted.

"What would happen if I said no?"

She leaned back in her chair, face flushed now. "Well… I'm sure it would offend him."

"It wouldn't be the first time."

"If you say no, it could jeopardize your trip to France."

"In what way?"

“How about we don’t find out, shall we?”

That sounded like a threat if she ever heard one. “It is only for a week?”

“Yes, one week.”

“Fine, when do I start?”

“Today, after you get off work.”

“And what exactly is it I need to do?”

“Mostly, the things you did while he was here. Taking his blood pressure and heart rate, administering his medication, and helping with anything he needs you to do around his apartment.”

“So, I’m going to be his maid as well as his nurse?”

“I guess if that is how you want to look at it.”

“How else is there to look at it?”

Frau Wagner shrugged. “I believe you are getting off about now, so you can head that way when you leave.” She slid a piece of paper across the desk in front of her. “This is his address, and there is a bag with the things you will need sitting on the floor by your locker.”

So, Frau Wagner expected her to say yes before even asking her the question. Eva picked up the piece of paper and peered at the address, then stuck it in her pocket. God truly was punishing her for what she did to him, wasn’t he? “I’ll head over there as soon as I finish up.”

She left Frau Wagner’s office, feeling a strange tingling running through her body. Was this his way of making her miserable, or was it so he could monitor her? She knew his suspicions of her never waned.

She went to the patient quarters and began stripping the

sheets from the beds. When she got to Bauer's empty bed, she jerked the sheets off and threw them in the basket with excessive force. She grabbed the pillow and pulled the case off, then smacked it back on the bed, again and again. She looked at the bed next to Bauer's, and the man lying in it was watching her. She looked around the room and realized that all eyes were on her now. She felt embarrassed by her actions, but she was so mad.

When she walked past the patient who took her hand, he called out to her. "Nurse." She stopped and looked at him. "Would you bring me some water?"

"Sure." She brought him a cup of water and set it on the table next to his bed.

"I don't know what he did to make you that mad, but I hope I don't."

"The two of you are not even comparable."

"I don't understand what happened the other night, but who is he? I don't know where he comes off thinking he can order me."

She put her hands on the end of his bed and leaned over it slightly. "First of all, when a woman tells you to let go of her, you let go. Second, I am as confused as you by the other night." She walked away but could hear him saying something behind her. She went to the laundry room and threw the sheets in the bin, then went to the nurse's quarters to change. Ingrid was also in there, changing to go home for the day.

"Eva, you left so suddenly. Is everything alright?"

"No, not really. I have to care for Bauer at his home for

the next week. I guess he asked for me personally."

Ingrid turned to face her. "What are you not telling me?"

"Ingrid," she yelled. "You know as much as I do about why he asked for me. He hates me and enjoys tormenting me."

"I only—"

"Look, I'm sorry. I didn't mean to snap at you. I'm a bit stressed right now."

"Sure, I understand." Ingrid lowered herself down into a chair at the table.

Eva came and sat next to her, putting a hand on her knee. "I'll see you tomorrow, alright?"

She gave her a faint smile. "Yeah."

Eva started to get up, then had a thought. "What if I could convince him to let you come instead of me? Would you be willing to do that?"

Her smile widened. "Of course, but do you think he would agree to that?"

"I don't know, but I don't see how it would hurt to ask."

"I thought you didn't want me around him?" Ingrid asked.

"He doesn't hate you, so I imagine he wouldn't treat you bad. But if you do this, you have to promise not to flirt with him."

"I can't promise that."

She sighed. "No, I suppose you being you, you can't. I'll see you tomorrow and let you know what he says."

"Thank you, Eva."

"No problem."

Eva put her jacket on, picked up the bag next to her locker, and hurried to the tram stop. She wanted to get this over with as quickly as possible so she could be home at a reasonable time. She was happy the weather was warmer now; it made waiting for the tram more bearable. When the tram came, she filed in with all the other people and found a seat.

It jolted forward, and she leaned her head on the window and closed her eyes.

"Papers Fräulein."

She lifted her eyelids, and towering over her were two men wearing suits and black trench coats, probably Gestapo officers. For a second, she stared at them but then quickly retrieved her ID from her purse and handed it to them.

"What's in the bag?" One of them asked, nodding towards the black leather bag on the floor by her feet.

She had not even thought that having it might look suspicious, but now, seeing it sitting there, she realized that it did. She tried to remain calm. "It's medical supplies. I'm a nurse and am on my way to a patient's house."

"If he requires medical attention, then why was he released from the hospital?" the taller of the two men asked.

She realized that being Gestapo, they probably would know Bauer. He might even be their superior officer. "I believe you might know him, SS Obersturmbannführer Bauer," she said, looking up at the man from her seat, feeling somehow empowered by telling them who it was she was going to visit.

The men glanced at one another before the taller one

spoke again. “SS Obersturmbannführer Bauer got released from the hospital today?”

“He did. He said he had work that needed doing and couldn’t do it from the hospital, so we released him if he worked from home for the first week.” She pulled the address of his apartment from her pocket and held it out for them. “Have a look. This is the address to his place.”

The shorter of the two men took the piece of paper from her and looked over it. “To be honest, I am not sure what his address is, so I cannot say that this is his,” he admitted.

“Here are the medical supplies I am taking with me.” She picked the bag up off the floor and set it in her lap, opening it so they could see the contents inside. “You are more than welcome to follow me to his apartment and explain all of this to him. He did ask for me specifically, so I’m sure he won’t be too happy to learn that you harassed me on the first day,” she said, trying to take control of the situation.

He handed her ID back along with the piece of paper. “I’m sorry to bother you.” They then moved on to the other passengers.

She sighed, relieved and surprised that it worked, even though she was telling them the truth. She closed the bag and set it back on the floor. Who knew he would save her from men in his own branch, unbeknownst to him, of course.

She got off the tram on the street he lived on and checked the numbers on the buildings to see which way she needed to go. She turned in the direction they grew larger because his address was four digits, then stopped in front of the building that had the same number as the paper. It was a modest, ten-story building made of red brick with rows of single windows running up the front. He lived close to the city center, yet his building and the surrounding ones survived the bombings. *How lucky for him*.

She pulled the front door open and stepped into the lobby. She looked for an elevator but didn't see one, so she climbed the stairs, panting by the time she reached the top. "Of course, he lives on the top floor of a building without an elevator. Yet another thing to make my life miserable," she said aloud, annoyed by the whole situation.

Three doors down the hall, on the left of the stairs, was his apartment number, written in bold, golden numbers on the door. She stopped in front of it, hesitating. She really didn't want to do this. The thought of her trip to France with Gerhardt gave her the motivation to lift her hand and lightly knock on the door.

A round-faced woman who looked to be in her early sixties opened the door. She wore a blue dress and had her gray hair piled on top of her head in a messy bun. "Can I help you?"

Eva instantly recognized her. It was Bauer's mother, the woman she saw at the hospital. "I'm sorry to bother you at such a late hour, but I'm the nurse from the hospital here to check on Obersturmbannführer Bauer."

"Oh, of course. I thought I recognized you. You are the nurse I talked to."

"Yes, that's me."

"Well, come in." She stepped aside so Eva could enter.

Eva stepped across the threshold, and the woman closed the door. “Come this way. He is in the living room.”

“Do you live here too?” Eva asked her.

“I do, but it is my son’s apartment.”

It was quite nice inside, spacious, and well-furnished. By the look of the furniture she could see in the living room, it could not have been cheap, and neither was the Persian rug it sat on. She assumed it was his mother who decorated it and picked out the furnishings because it was done in such an elegant way.

She followed the woman into the living room and looked around, only then noticing that Bauer was asleep on the couch with papers strewn on the floor, across the coffee table, and still on his stomach.

She turned back to the woman. “He is asleep. Should I come back tomorrow?”

“No, it would be silly to have come all this way for nothing. It won’t hurt to wake him up. He has worked all day on whatever that is,” she said, motioning to the papers with her hand. “That is why he is tired, I think. Since he is asleep, I suppose it wouldn’t hurt to have a cup of tea before we wake him.”

Eva did not expect that. If she agreed, it would make her get home even later, but how could she say no. She looked at her watch. Curfew started in twenty-seven minutes.

“I know it’s getting late, but I’m sure my son can give you a slip or something in case you are stopped. You won’t get out of here before the curfew starts even if you don’t stay for tea,” his mother said, noticing Eva glancing at her watch.

She looked out the window at the fast-growing darkness, then back at the woman. "I would love some tea."

"You can sit your bag there." She pointed to the side table at the end of the couch. Eva put her bag on the table, glancing quickly at Bauer, then followed her into the kitchen. She sat at the small square kitchen table covered with a white tablecloth and a lavender-filled vase in the center. "What kind of tea do you like?" she asked.

"All of it, really, but given the hour, I think I will take something without caffeine. I need to sleep tonight. I have to be up early in the morning.

"I'll give you chamomile, then." She filled up the kettle and set it on the stove, lit the burner, and then came to sit in the chair across from Eva. "So, how is my son?"

"I'm sorry?"

"They released him from the hospital early. I want to make sure that it is alright for him to be here."

"They did not involve me in the decision to release him, but I'm sure they would not have done so if he wasn't well enough. I saw him the last week he was at the hospital, and he seemed to be doing fine. Maybe that is why they allowed him to leave early."

"Well, I am thankful for all you have done for him."

"I assure you, I have only done what the other nurses have done."

"That is not what I have heard."

"I wasn't aware that you had heard anything different," Eva said, confused. Who had she been talking to, and why were they telling his mother about her and Bauer?

"Yes, my son told me it was you who saved his life."

"No, it was the doctor who saved his life. I only assisted."

"That is not what I meant."

"Oh, I see." Eva avoided her gaze. "He had told you what happened when he arrived at the hospital, then?"

"He did. My son would not be here with me now if it wasn't for your decision that day. I don't think I could make it without him. He is my son, and I love him, but it is more than just that. He takes care of me financially and is there as a companion. If anything happened to him, I would have no one, no income, and nowhere to go."

"I didn't know. Is it only the two of you, then?"

"Yes, it wasn't always this way, though. As the years passed, I found myself alone as a woman, and then my life less full as a mother."

Eva was pretty sure she knew what his mother was talking about, but she couldn't help but be curious. She wanted to know what had happened to his sister. Eva glanced into the living room to make sure that Bauer was still asleep. He was lying still with his eyes closed on the couch in the same position he was in when she arrived. She knew he would be upset if he heard her asking about his sister or anything about his personal life. "Less full as a mother?" Eva asked, turning back to her.

"Yes, I used to have a daughter, too, but she passed away years ago."

"What happened to her?"

"It was during the time of the depression while we were

living in a makeshift house."

"Makeshift house? You mean like a shantytown?"

"I have not heard that term."

"That is what we called them in America during the depression."

"You are American?" she asked.

The tone of her voice was clearly conveyed her surprise. "I am." Eva assumed she already knew that, but she obviously couldn't identify her accent.

"What brought you here?"

"It is a long story. I came to Europe for work, and then the war happened; that is it in a nutshell. So, you were one of the families that was hit hard during the depression?"

"We were, although everyone was having a hard time then, but we weren't doing well before."

"Was it because of the economic downfall that she died?" Eva pressed.

"I suppose it was, or maybe it only made the inevitable happen a little sooner."

"Inevitable?"

"Yes, she was a diabetic."

Eva was taken aback, even though she had heard that insulin had been invented in the twenties. "Didn't she have insulin?"

"She did when we could afford it. When Wilhelm was younger, and Charlotte was still a little girl, we lived on a farm, but their father drank and gambled all the money away, and we lost the farm. My husband was gone before we even left. I went into town with Charlotte to sell what I could, and when we returned, he was gone. Wilhelm told us he had left and that he tried to convince him to stay, but he couldn't. We were forced to move into a small, one-room apartment in town that we could barely afford. The children no longer had a father, and I no longer had a husband. He and the farm weren't the only things we lost. Most of our income went with him as well. Charlotte was only ten but was already sick most of the time, so Wilhelm, who was now twenty-three, had to support the family. As a child, he worked at the coal mine to help, but he did not have the responsibility of the breadwinner then as he did after his father left. Because then it was only the two of us, and he was still a boy, but when his step-father left, he was a man. Wilhelm spent most of his life in Cologne, as was most of Charlotte's childhood spent there, but after we lost the farm, we moved to Essen so Wilhelm could find work in the mines. I don't know how he managed it, but he stayed in school and worked evenings and weekends. I hardly ever saw him, but I was proud. When their father left, he kept a roof over our heads, food on the table, and was able to get Charlotte her medicine."

Eva turned in her chair, peering into the living room at Bauer, still sleeping on the couch. She would have never guessed that he had done that for his sister and mother. To her, he was vile and cruel, but to them, he was their savior, the one who loved and took care of them. She never really imagined him having a first name, either. Maybe always thinking of him as Bauer was more dehumanizing to her, and that is how she wished to view him.

"So, he supported the two of you?"

"He did."

The kettle whistled, so his mother stood and turned off the stove. She poured the water into two cups, setting one in front of Eva. She took her chair back at the table with her own cup.

"So, he went to college?" Eva asked, continuing the conversation.

"While he was a teenager, he worked the night shift in a steel factory after he was finished with his classes for the day. He continued working at the coal mine on the weekends, and despite all of that, he still managed to graduate at eighteen and start the fall semester part-time at the University of Cologne that year. My son…" She looked at him, sleeping in the living room with fondness. "He was always a brilliant boy. He even got into school on an academic scholarship." The look on her face gave away that she was in a different time. She turned back to Eva. "When the depression came, we found ourselves on the street." She took a sip of her tea, then set the cup back on the table, wrapping both hands around it. "He lost his job at the factory in twenty-nine, and we were forced to live in a makeshift house of small aluminum pieces, only held together with nails. He would do odd jobs here and there where he could find them. They allowed him to work at the school as a tutor, but that wasn't enough to support us."

"He continued to go to school even while you guys were homeless?" Eva asked, genuinely surprised and impressed.

"He did. He worked on farms and in fields in exchange

for food. Although I don't know how he would get the medicine for Charlotte, but he managed to for years somehow. Most of the time, we had barely enough to keep her alive. She was so ill, throwing up and sleeping most days."

"Is that why she died?" Eva asked, finally taking a sip of her tea which was now cool.

"No. Our makeshift house was next to another family on the outskirts of the city. One night, while Wilhelm was gone doing one of his odd jobs, the man came into our house and took Charlotte's medicine, no doubt to trade on the black market for food or sell for cash. Medicine was very hard to come by during that time, and it went for a lot of money on the black market. Early that morning, before the sun was up, Charlotte went into an insulin reaction, but I had no medicine to give her. There was nothing I could do for her. Wilhelm came home and saw what was happening to her. He rushed to her side, taking her in his arms, and asked me why I hadn't given her a shot. I told him we had no more medicine, and when he asked how that could be, I had no choice but to tell him that the man next to us had taken it. He watched as she died in his arms. He was frantic, stricken with grief. I watched my children suffer so much of their lives, but never more than that night. After she was dead, he laid her back on the blanket and left the house without saying a word to me, and came back late that night with bloodied knuckles, but it wasn't only on his hands; blood was on his shirt, his pants, and his face. I never asked him about it, and within the next few days, he moved us to another location and joined the officer training school. He was never the same after that. When his father left, he became a man, but this changed him in a different kind of way, more profound, I think."

A lot made sense to her now. She finally understood some of his anger and hatred. "I am so sorry. I honestly had no idea. How old was he when she died?"

She looked up at the ceiling with her eyes in concentration. "She died in November of 1931, so Wilhelm was almost twenty-eight, and Charlotte was fifteen."

"That is terrible." She wanted to lighten the conversation and the mood in the room a little. A lump had formed in her throat. "What did he study at school?"

A little smile broke across her lips. "He went to law school, and now he has a very important position in the Reich."

"Does he… and what does he do for them?" She sipped her lukewarm tea.

"He doesn't talk a lot about it, but I know he works for the secret police. He has to travel a lot for his job and lives in France most of the time, but I manage when he is gone." His mother lifted her head from the cup into the living room. 'Oh, he is awake. I think we can go back in there now."

"Who are you talking to, mother?" he called from the living room.

"It is the nurse that came to check on you."

He appeared in the kitchen doorway. "What is she doing in here?"

"You were sleeping when she arrived, so we had some

tea while waiting for you to wake up."

"You should have woken me as soon as she arrived."

Eva looked at his mother. "I didn't mind, but it is late now, so we better get started." By his expression, she couldn't tell if he was confused or angry, maybe both. He turned and walked back into the living room, and they followed. He sat on the couch as Eva retrieved her bag from the table. She sat on the couch beside him and took his blood pressure and temperature, listened to his heart, then checked his stitches. "Do you feel like you need any pain medication?"

"No."

"They told me at the hospital I would also do some cleaning and cooking, but no one mentioned your mother lived here. I'm guessing you won't be needing me to do any of that?"

"Normally, I wouldn't, but my mother is leaving tomorrow to visit with a friend for a week."

"Oh, OK. I will plan on doing that tomorrow, then." She stuck her stethoscope in her bag. "I really should be going now."

"Wilhelm, you need to give her a pass for being out past curfew," his mom instructed.

He stared at Eva for what felt like forever before speaking. "Sure, I can give her one." He got a blank piece of paper off the table with an official seal at the top and wrote something on it. "Here." He tore the paper from the pad and held it out to her. She took it and glanced over it. It said she had permission to be out past curfew for the following dates, and his signature was at the bottom.

That night, Eva found she couldn't sleep. The conversation with Bauer's mother kept running through her mind. She was surprised by all of it and felt sorry for him for the second time. Now that she knew such personal information about his life, it made her feel doubly bad for what she had done to him. It was amazing how you think you know someone, but you really don't. Learning about his past made her view life differently and people in general. She seemed to feel things more deeply lately, and she didn't quite know why. A suffocating feeling settled over her, and she struggled to breathe. "I need to get out of here. I need to go home." She sat up in bed. Why had she not gotten a letter from Jon? Tomorrow, she would send him another one.

The next morning, she changed and then ate cheese and meat on crackers. She wanted to go to the church and talk to the priest before work, so she had to hurry.

She took the usual route there and got off at the stop near the church. She pulled the heavy door open and stepped into the quiet chapel. It was empty as usual; she preferred it this way. It wasn't time for confession, so she walked the long hall to the priest's office and gently tapped on the door. Father Becker opened it and smiled.

"I was wondering when I would see you again. Please, come in." He moved aside and gestured with his hand for her to enter. She stepped past him and took a seat at his desk. "Nice to see you again, Miss Abrams. What brings you here today?"

"Confusion."

"About what?" he asked, sitting on the edge of his desk, folding his arms over his chest.

"Do you remember that terrible person I told you about?"

"I do."

"Well, I found out they are not as bad as I thought, and yet I still despise them, and they despise me."

"And what happened to make you rethink your negative opinion of them?"

"It's something they did for someone else. One of the people personally told me what he had done for them, and you would need to have a heart, even for a fleeting moment, to do what he did. Part of me is angry that I think that because I don't hate them as much as I once did, but I want to still feel that hatred for them."

"Even the smallest of things can make us feel something. It's amazing the depth of emotions humans can have. Love comes more naturally to us than hate. We want to love because it is the closest we can come to selflessness. Most of us go through life loving and wanting to be loved or trying to achieve it. It makes us feel better about ourselves."

"So, you believe that hating him a little less is the human thing to do?"

"In so many words, yes."

"But can't a person be a bad person and still be nice to some people?"

"Sure, it depends on how they feel about that particular

person or group of people."

"So, they are actually a bad person but can be good on occasion?"

"Good and evil can coexist in a person. It does in most of us. Who we are depends on which one we choose to feed. Our personalities, situations, and life experiences help determine what side we let be our dominant one. Now, it is true that some people harbor a darker psyche than others, and they will have to fight harder to stay in the light. But there are those that don't want to or find it too difficult."

"Can someone like that be anything other than what they have become?"

"It depends on if they think a thing or person is worth their time, but some people may be beyond hope. I believe you would be surprised by the things even a good person is capable of, given the right situation."

"I'm sure I would be surprised. And this person, I am certain, is beyond hope. I have only seen one side of them."

"But you know there is another side. There are many sides to us, and we show the one that best fits the situation we are in or the person we are with. Sometimes, though, it is best to not show any of our sides at all."

"Well, he chooses to not show most of them to me except anger. This person will come for me again, and I don't know what to do to get them to stop."

"Try talking to them again."

"I have."

"And you are certain that you are in danger from this person?"

"I am. I believe they might be the death of me."

"Then I would say getting as far away from this them as possible would be advisable. Do you have a way to do that?"

"I might."

"If you have a way, then do it, and when you are free from this person, forgive them for what they did to you, and try to only remember the positive things about them."

"If I make it out of this, I will work on forgiving them and forgetting them."

"Fair enough. Please come and see me before you leave if you find a way."

What he said caught her off guard, even though it must be obvious she was planning on going to America. "I will come and see you again, regardless. Thank you for lending an ear and advice."

"That is what I'm here for." He took her hand in his and patted it. "I'll see you again soon."

As Eva sat on the tram, she wrote Jon a letter, then dropped it off on the way to Bauer's house. She really needed to hear from him.

She remembered that Bauer's mother was going to be gone the rest of the week. That was going to be weird. It really was going to put her in an awkward situation.

Like the last time, she climbed the many flights of stairs to the tenth floor and knocked on the door. When it opened, he stared at her but didn't say anything, then stepped aside for her to enter. She walked past him but didn't remove her jacket or hat; she wasn't planning on staying long like last time. She went straight to the living room, put her bag on the floor, and then sat on the couch. He took the seat across from her and wasn't shy about looking her in the eye. It must be an interrogation technique he learned.

"Why did you ask for me and not one of the other nurses?" she asked pointedly.

"Because I don't know any of them. It made the most sense for you to be the one to come to my home."

"You don't even like me, and I'm sure it's obvious that the feeling is mutual. So, to me, it makes more sense for you to have asked for someone else." She was beginning to think that asking if Ingrid could come would be pointless. He would probably never agree to that.

"Maybe to you, it would have made more sense to ask for another nurse, but to me, you were the obvious choice. I am already familiar with you, as you are with me, regardless of how we feel toward one another. Nothing that has happened between us has been personal. It's not you; it's what you stand for. We went over this in France. I should not have to explain it again."

She stood from the couch. "Oh my God, are you for real?" He threw her a confused look, obviously not understanding the modern term. "I can't do this with you. You need to find another nurse to come to your apartment from now on." She reached for her bag on the floor.

"Sit down."

She glared at him. "No."

"Sit down!" he growled. His voice was laced with agitation. She slowly lowered herself back on the couch. "First, I told you that you would come to my apartment. That was not a request," he said, calmer now. "I understand we will never agree on most things, but that is not why you are here. You will come and do what is expected of you, then you will leave, that is all. You don't have to like it, but you have to do it. Second, you went behind my back and talked to my mother about my sister. I thought I made it very clear that you were not to ask about her, and yet you did. You will come to regret that. I know my mother left out a lot of what was discussed when she told me of your conversation. I also realize that you now know more about my life than anybody else and more than you should. If you ever speak about it with anyone, it will be the biggest mistake you ever make."

She was trying to be brave, but it was hard. He meant to frighten her and was succeeding. "Your mom was happy to talk about her daughter. Don't you ever let her vent?"

"Only this once will I discuss it with you, only this once. We thought about her and talked about her every minute of every day after she died, but after a while, we needed to move on."

"I don't think you have moved on. I think inside, you are still grieving because you didn't allow yourself to grieve properly when she died."

"What do you know about grief… or my grief," he hissed through clenched teeth.

"I know about grief. I have lost someone, too, but there is a wrong way to handle it and a right way. I understand you were robbed of your sister and why you were angry with the people who caused it. Your mom thinks the world of you and appreciates what you do for her, and she doesn't blame you for whatever it is you did because of your sister's death. She told me how your dad left and that you took care of them and provided for them during the depression, even while you went to school. I don't know if I could have done what you did. You were dealt a bad hand in life, given a raw deal, and for that, I am sorry, but don't let it make you bitter."

"It didn't make me bitter. It gave me clarity."

"Again, that is something you and I disagree on."

"Think what you like, Eva, but you will never know what it's like to be me, so don't presume that you do."

She realized that was the first time he had ever called her by her first name, probably to strike a chord, which he succeeded at. Her nerves were shot. "I need to go home. Let's get this over with."

She retrieved the things from the bag and rolled up the sleeve on his right arm. She did all the usual steps, then hurried and put her stuff away so she could leave.

"I know what you told me, but what is the real reason you saved me that day?" he asked as he rolled down his sleeve.

"Exactly the reason I told you."

"You know, it's my job to know if someone is lying, and I know you are lying now, but I don't know the reason. I will get to the bottom of it. Maybe not tonight, but soon. What you did screams ulterior motive."

She picked her bag off the floor. "I saved you because I felt sorry for you lying there on the stretcher, dying all alone. There was something in your eyes when you looked at me that made me think maybe you had a soul after all, but I guess I was wrong." She started for the door. She couldn't wait to get out of there.

"You didn't make dinner."

"Make your own dinner."

"I didn't say you could leave," he said in a raised voice as she opened the front door.

She intentionally slammed it behind her and ran down the hall, then the stairs. She couldn't take another second in the presence of that man.

The next few days were hard. Being around him made her hair stand on edge. He said little to her, but if looks could kill, she would be dead. All he did was glare at her while she took his vitals. She would make his food in silence and tidy the apartment. This had become their routine now. She only had one more day of going to his place, and she was beside herself with relief.

"Eva, there is a man here to see you."

Eva looked at Ingrid, who had come into the laundry room. Her breath caught in her throat. What if it was Bauer?

"It's not that officer that was here, is it?"

"No, it's some other man."

Butterflies formed in her stomach. Maybe it was Gerhardt. "Would you finish up here?"

"Sure."

"Thanks. Where is he?"

"He is in the main lobby."

She smiled at Ingrid and hurried past her, making her

way to the lobby. Her eyes caught site of Gerhardt in his officer's uniform, hat, gloves, and perfectly polished boots standing near the door. "Gerhardt," she called to him as she drew near.

He turned towards her, and instantly, his face brightened. "Eva." She embraced him, so needing this right now. To see his face again almost had her in tears.

He hugged her back but seemed taken off guard by it. "Is everything alright?"

"It is. I'm just happy to see you."

"Can we go out into the lawn for a minute?"

"Yeah." She followed him outside to a metal bench under a tree and sat down.

"I know now when we will go to France."

"Really? Please tell me it's soon."

"It's in two weeks. Is that soon enough for you?"

"It will have to be. What day do we leave?"

"June 13th. That is a Friday."

"Friday the thirteenth?" she repeated.

"Yes, is there something wrong with that day?"

"No, it's perfect. I can't wait. And what day will we be returning?"

"We will be there for a week, so we return on Friday the twentieth. I will be at your apartment early that morning to pick you up, probably around eight."

"I'll be ready."

His blue eyes bore into hers, then he leaned in and kissed her on the cheek. "I'll see you in two weeks." He stood and walked towards the street. She was on cloud nine. She could not wait to get away from Germany and see France again. Hopefully, being there with him would feel like old times, but not in all ways. Most of the time she had spent in France was less stressful than it had been here in Germany, even though she didn't realize it then. Time seemed to move slower there, like being in a field of flowers on a lazy spring morning. A breeze blowing in your hair as the sun caressed your face, warming your skin. She almost forgot what it was like to be in Paris, too, and how it made you forget your troubles.

She only had to check on Bauer one more time tomorrow, then it would be done. She never thought that Bauer returning to work would please her.

Eva arrived at his apartment and knocked on the door. She listened to his heavy footsteps, then the door opened, and he stood in the doorway. After a second, he moved aside for her to enter, again saying nothing. He followed her into the living room and took a seat on the couch. She sat next to him as usual and checked his vitals and stitches.

"You will be fine, returning to work tomorrow. I see no reason to think otherwise." She pulled a container filled with some soup from her bag and sat it on the coffee table. She didn't want to stay and cook for him. She wanted to check on him and leave.

"What is this?" he asked, looking at the container on the table.

"Potato soup. I brought it from home."

"You didn't use my food?"

"No, it's fine. I had a lot of potatoes that needed to be used before they went bad."

"Do you want some?" He nodded to the container.

"No, I only brought enough for you. I have more at home."

He took the lid off and sniffed. "It smells good. What's in it?"

"Ummm–potatoes, milk, onions, salt, and pepper. Sorry, I had nothing else to add to it. Things like butter and meat are scarce. I'll heat it up for you before I leave." She took it from him, put it in a pot, and set it on the stove. She waited in the kitchen with it, and once it was hot, she poured it into a bowl and brought it back into the living room with a cup of water, setting both on the coffee table in front of him. "If there is nothing else you need, I will go." He didn't speak, so she picked up her things and walked to the door.

"If I hurt you, I am sorry. I didn't know you then like I do now."

She paused at the door, feeling his stare boring down on her back, and slowly turned to look at him. She met the gaze of his tormented eyes, which showed a genuine emotion other than anger for the first time, but she could not identify it. His eyes burned a hole into hers so penetratingly that she swore he could see into her mind and all the secrets she hid there. She could only imagine he wanted to see into her soul all the times he took her in for interrogation. To say the least, this was an unexpected turn of events. She honestly didn't know what to do now. Should she leave or return to the living room?

"Do I frighten you?" he asked.

"Sometimes," she said without hesitation. In response to her answer, he looked away but didn't speak. "Why do you keep arresting me when I have done nothing wrong?" she asked, taking advantage of his silence.

He turned to her. "Because I have seen others like you who would tear the world down just so the Germans would fall to their knees, all the while letting people like the Jews and the Polish rise to the top."

"And the Germans aren't tearing the world down?" How many people have you killed or have died at the hands of the Germans?"

"In war, people die. You can't avoid that. It is a filthy game. But this is a cold and brutal world we live in, even without war. After the first war, Germany needed a savior. It was a broken country. Poverty and starvation were everywhere, and there was no law and order to speak of. The German people suffered greatly because of the Versailles treaty."

"But Germany set both wars into motion. How can anyone else be blamed for that?"

"It's not that simple. You don't understand what it's like to be German or the intricacies of war. It hasn't made you hard because you have been shielded from so much. You have to close off whatever you feel inside because you will be too fragile for this life of destruction and violence if you don't. You were about to leave. Go, I won't stop you," he said, looking away from her and back to his soup.

She hurried out the door and shut it, her heart racing in

her chest. Nothing with Bauer was ever simple. He was playing an angle, but she didn't know what. Their encounters always turned out badly for her in the end. He could not be trusted, even when he tried to put on the face of sympathy and civility. Underneath, he was still the same cold-hearted person. She couldn't pin him down, which was typical of a sociopath.

Chapter Fifteen

✠

June 13th, 1941

Gerhardt had a car waiting for them at the Paris airport when the plane arrived. It took them to a hotel comparable to the one she stayed at with Renee in size and elegance. When they got to their rooms, she was happy he was right across the hall from her. She didn't have to go far if she wanted to visit him in his room.

"So, what now?" she asked.

"I thought we could take a riverboat down the Seine after dinner."

"I have actually never been on the river. That sounds nice."

They put their bags in their rooms and walked the streets of Paris before eating. It was lit up exactly as she remembered it being. The sound of distant music flowed from the restaurants along the river. Faint conversations, barely audible over the music, streamed from somewhere not far off. Eva leaned over the rail and watched the waves as the lights of the city reflected off them, dancing with their movement.

"I was honestly so surprised to see you that night at the ball. I imagined you had made it home and settled back into your life there," he said, watching her intently. "Then I noticed you sitting at that table. I was happy to see your face again because I never thought I would, but that was a fleeting feeling. I couldn't fathom why you were in Germany. And sitting at a table with high-ranking German officers, no less, I couldn't comprehend how you got into that situation."

"Surprisingly, I know the men at the table. I would even go so far as to say one of them is my friend. He is a doctor who I work with, and I saved the other man's life. He was grateful to me, and that is why I was at the ball. He invited me. I will admit that I was surprised too when I saw you there. I knew you were in Germany, but I didn't expect to ever see you. What surprised me the most though was when you asked me to dance. I had told myself that you never wanted to see me again. At first, it was hard to accept that thought, but as time passed, I learned to cope with it. Then you asked me to dance, and it undid everything I worked so hard to accomplish. And when you told me you were back with your fiancé, it crushed me all over again. I would like to think that I'm dealing with it better this time than I did the first time."

"This is never how I wanted it to be, Eva. Sometimes, when you start a path in life, you have to see it through, and this is one of those paths. She will never be you, and I will never love her as I do you, but she doesn't deserve to be abandoned by me. She deserves better. We have been together for a long time and through a lot over the years, and no one can ever undo that."

His words hurt more than she thought they would. How come this was so hard? How come life was so unfair? "I understand, Gerhardt, but why are some of us doomed to love those we cannot have?"

"I don't know. It is not easy or fair. I wish we could give in, but I can never have that with you again. Even if Emma wasn't in the picture, I still don't think we could. We wouldn't be able to keep this up. I think we were doomed to fail the moment we met."

"I'm beginning to think you are right. What are we going to do now?" she asked, not meeting his gaze.

"Enjoy our time together while we can." He gave her an encouraging smile.

"I guess I won't be getting an invitation to your wedding, then?"

He chuckled but didn't answer. "I think you will be happy to hear that I have planned a few days in La Chapelle while we are here," he said, ending that conversation.

Her face lit up. "Seriously?"

He nodded. "Yes."

She was excited until the vivid memory of Sabina's death and her last day there played out in her mind.

"What is it? Your mood changed."

"I thought of my last day in La Chapelle."

"Oh Eva, I am so sorry. I didn't even think about that. We don't have to go."

"It's alright, I want to. Then, when I think of La Chapelle, it will be happy memories that will hopefully replace the old ones."

"That is a good way to look at it."

"When are we going?" she asked him.

"Any time you like."

"How about tomorrow?"

"If that is what you want."

"It is. I would love to see it again, and Renée and Adele."

"It won't be strange for you to see them again?"

"No, but they might not be too happy to see you, though." She nodded her head in his direction.

"You are probably right. They never were fond of Germans."

After dinner and the boat ride, they again walked the streets of Paris, simply enjoying each other's company. She wondered if this would be the last time they would ever spend together. Nothing in the world could prepare her for that.

Once back at the hotel, they stopped in front of her door. "Goodnight, Eva." He took her hand and kissed the back of it gently. "I'll see you in the morning."

"Goodnight."

When she was alone in her room, she lay on the bed and wept, hoping to cry herself to sleep. She knew now that they would never be together, so there was no reason to stay in Germany or even in this time. It was time she focus all her energy on coordinating with Jon on a way to go home if he would ever write back. She hadn't been putting her all into it before because some small part deep inside still hoped that she and Gerhardt would be together, but tonight, he crushed that fragile remaining belief. It was over. This was it for them.

June 14th, 1941

There was a knock on the door. She sat up in bed and looked at the clock on the side table; it was three minutes past eight. Throwing off the blankets, she got out of bed and went to the door, looking through the peephole. Gerhardt was standing on the other side of the door, staring down the hall. She opened it and sleepily gazed at him, waiting for him to tell her why he was there.

"Pack an overnight bag, and we will spend a night or two in La Chapelle. I had the rooms here held for us."

"Alright. Were you planning on us leaving soon?"

"Not unless you want to."

"Let me change and get some breakfast, then I'll pack a bag, and we can go. I hope you haven't been up long waiting for me."

"No, I haven't been up long. Take your time. I will be in

my room. Knock when you are ready."

When he went back to his room, she ordered room service so she would have more time to get ready. She ate while she dressed and put on makeup, then pulled her hair into a quick bun and threw a few things in her small bag. She went across the hall to Gerhardt's room and knocked on the door.

"You ready?" he asked when he opened it.

"I am." She noticed that he was not in his uniform. She held up her bag to show she was ready.

"Wait here." He disappeared for a second, then returned with his bag. "Let's go."

"Is there a car to pick us up?"

"No, I'm driving today."

"Oh, alright." She had never ridden with him before when he was the driver.

"You are not wearing your uniform," she pointed out, thinking how handsome he looked in civilian clothing.

"It's Saturday, and I am on leave, so I don't have to wear it."

"It's odd to see you out of it."

"I'm sure it must seem a little strange to you."

He was wearing brown pants with suspenders pulled over a thin, white, long-sleeved cotton shirt with the sleeves rolled up. It suited him. He could have been any man on a normal day, one without the worries of a soldier. She followed him outside to a small silver car. He put the bags in the backseat and opened the passenger door for her.

"Thank you, good sir," she said, teasing.

"Madam," he curtsied to her, and she laughed. He always knew how to make her smile. He got into the driver's seat, and they headed east out of town, letting the warm June air wash through the open windows.

"What were you like as a child?" she asked, wanting to know more about him. If she could not have him, she could at least take as much memory of him home as possible.

"An absolute angel," he said with a half-smile.

"The devil's angel, maybe."

He laughed. "Probably. No, I was quiet when I was young and did a lot of things on my own. My dad focused more on my older brother, and my mom babied my younger brother, so that left me to my own devices most of the time. I got into trouble a lot as a child. I was always doing something ornery, so I kept my parents on their toes."

"What kind of things would you do?"

"Well, one summer when I was about ten years old, I had become bored with school being out. My older brother was on a trip with our father, and my younger brother was sick with croup, so I would hang out with my schoolmates most days. One of them had gotten hold of some fireworks. I don't know how he managed that, but I wasn't too concerned about the details. We, of course, couldn't let good firecrackers go to waste, so we concocted a plan to get the biggest bang from them as we could. The neighbors next door had bought a new car, and of course, to a bunch of ten-year-old boys, the back of the car looked like a great place to put firecrackers. After the sun had gone down, we snuck outside, put them in the trunk, and then lit them. We ran to a nearby bush to watch the spectacular event, and it was spectacular, at first. They were whistling and shooting through the night sky in a beautiful array of colors, and it was amazing until it caught the carpet in the trunk on fire. Of course, we panicked and ran, but it didn't take long for my father to figure out I had something to do with it. He had had enough of my mischief, so no more nannies for me. It was going to be boarding school from then on. I guess he figured I couldn't get into as much trouble there, especially since I was no longer around my friends. We tended to get into more trouble when we were together than we did on our own, so there was some logic to his thinking."

"Oh my gosh, you were so bad. I would be livid with my child if they ever did something like that," Eva said, laughing so hard she had to take a moment to catch her breath.

"Come on, I know you caused mischief when you were a kid? All kids do."

"Yes, but nothing like what you did. Is that the only thing you did?"

"Sadly, no," he said, now laughing at himself.

"Noooo, what else did you do?"

"Oh no, it is your turn to spill."

"Fine. But I did nothing even remotely close to that."

"Doesn't matter."

"OK. The thing that is coming to mind is when I broke my mom's favorite lamp."

"Come on, you have to give more detail than that."

"I will." She waved her hand at him. "It was Christmas

Eve, and I really wanted to know what I got because that year I had an enormous present, and I had to know what it was. I snuck out of bed, went downstairs, and tried to pull it out from under the tree. It was near the back, so it was very difficult to do. Well, I tripped on the cord to the lamp while trying to pull the gift from under the tree and fell against it, knocking it off the table and shattering it. My brother heard the noise and came downstairs to see what was going on. Of course, he figured I was trying to open gifts and yelled at me. That woke Mom and Dad, who came down to see what the commotion was about. Thomas told them that I was out of bed trying to open gifts, but when they asked about the broken lamp, he told them it was him who broke it while trying to take the gift from me. He knew if they found out that I broke it trying to open my gift, I would not get that gift anymore. Even though they thought he broke the lamp, they would probably still take away the gift I was trying to open. He obviously knew what it was and didn't want me to lose it, so when my parents asked which one I was trying to get, he took a small package from under the tree and handed it to them."

"What was in the packages?"

"The small one was a neckless, but the big one was a rocking horse that I had wanted all year."

"How old were you?"

"I'm not sure, maybe five or six."

"That was nice that your brother did that for you."

"He has always been like that, looking out for me."

"I'm sure you miss him."

"All the time." She thought about how different Gerhardt's childhood must have been from Bauer's. Gerhardt never wanted for a meal or a roof over his head. Nor did he have to take care of his mother or brothers. His dad was strict, but he would not have left them. She didn't know how Bauer's dad treated him or his sister because his mom didn't say, and hell would freeze over first before he told her. She wondered why the thought of him popped into her head.

"That, Eva, is another reason we can't be together. I will not be the one who keeps you from your family."

"You know that people move all the time, and more often than not, it is because of someone they love?"

"Yes, but I will not move to America when my country needs me, and my family is here, and I know that you would not want to leave your family in America and move to Germany, not even for me."

"How do you know what I want? You forget that I have lived away from my family and country for years now. It has not even been my choice, but I have been fine. What better reason to live abroad than of your own choosing for the person you love?"

"That is debatable whether or not you have been fine, but I understand that would make more sense than the reason you are here now. However, it still wouldn't be ideal." He pulled off to the side of the road, shutting off the engine. He turned in his seat to look at her. "Eva, in an ideal world, we would be together, but we don't live in one. When we first met, and I was getting to know you, I understood that what we had was mostly because of me because I pursued you even though you continued to tell me that it would never work, but at the time, I didn't want to admit it. I wanted what I wanted, and I ignored the cost, mostly the cost to you. It took you fleeing to make me see that you were right and I was wrong. I finally understood what you were saying, that there was too much keeping us apart. I was being selfish. I see that now, and I am sorry."

"I know I told you that, and there is a lot of truth to what I said, but we could make this work if we really tried. I will not lie to myself and say that it would be easy because it wouldn't, but it would be worth it, at least to me. But I think that ship has sailed for you, and I respect that. I can let mine sail, too, but before I do, I need to make sure that there is really no hope left for us."

"I don't see how it would work, and I'm not going to lead you on. So yes, my ship has sailed." There was a sadness beneath the reassurance in his voice.

"I guess you and I have different ideas about what is possible and what isn't, but if that is how you feel."

"Please believe me when I say that I am doing this for you and not for myself. Do you believe me?" he asked in a low, soft voice.

"I think so. I want to."

He leaned over and pulled her in his arms. "I am so sorry. I wish it didn't have to be like this," he whispered in her ear.

"I know you don't, but it still hurts. What matters the most is what you think of me. In you, I have found something I don't believe I will ever have again. I can only hope you think the same of me. Someday, when I'm old, I want to look out on the horizon and know that you are somewhere there and that you still love me."

"You will always have my heart, even though we're not together, and it doesn't matter if you are on the other side of this world." He released her. "Why don't we focus on the good things? We are here together now, and you know what? Neither of us knows what lies on the other side of this war or what its end will bring. Who knows. Anything is possible, right?"

With the back of her hand, she wiped a tear from the corner of her eye. "Sure."

He started the car and pulled back onto the road, and they arrived at Madam Blanc's a little after six. The rest of the car ride had been quiet. She didn't feel much like talking after their last conversation. They pulled in front of the house, and then got their bags from the trunk. They walked up the steps and rang the doorbell.

"Is she expecting us?" Eva asked.

"No, I thought we would surprise her." Eva suddenly had butterflies in her stomach, along with apprehension. She had not seen Renée or Adele in a very long time.

The door opened, and Adele was standing in front of them. Her eyes widened when she recognized them. "Oh, my God. Eva…?"

"Yes, it's me," Eva said, smiling at her.

"You are alive." Adele embraced Eva, a tear rolling down her cheek. "Come, Renée will be so happy to see you."

She glanced over at Gerhardt. "Why is he here?" she asked, wiping the tears away.

"He is the one who had helped me escape. I'll explain it all, I promise."

They followed Adele to the parlor. "Sit in here, and I will fetch the Madam for you," she told them, then hurried out of the room.

Eva looked around the elegantly decorated parlor. "It's like I never left."

"It does seem the same. Nothing has changed since I lived here."

Adele appeared in the entryway with Madam Blanc. "Oh lord, I thought you were dead. You are like a ghost standing in my parlor." Her eyes moved from Eva to Gerhardt. "Adele tells me that you are the one who helped her?"

"I am."

"Then you are welcomed too. Please, have a seat. Why are both of you back? I didn't think it was safe for her here anymore?"

"I live in Germany now," Eva said. "So does Gerhardt. We are actually here on holiday. He thought enough time had passed, and the soldiers who were stationed here had already moved on."

"You are not here for work?" she asked Gerhardt.

"No, Madam, I'm only here for a week."

"The two of you are together, then?" she asked, still unsure of the situation.

Eva and Gerhardt exchanged a glance. "No, he is getting married, and I remain single. We are here only as friends,"

Eva told her.

"You are not with the same Germans you were here with last time?"

"No, I now have a different job."

Renée cleared her throat and met Adele's gaze before looking back at them. "Eva, you will stay in your old room, and he can stay in the room at the back of the house on the main floor. His old room is not available."

Eva suspected that it was now filled with junk, like so many of her other rooms. They ate leftovers from dinner while Renée and Adele kept the questions coming. It shocked them that she lived in Germany, but the fact that they had not arrested her surprised them even more.

"I was certain that some of the Germans stationed here were after you," Madam Blanc said.

"So was I," Eva admitted.

"Is it the same in Germany?"

"In a way. Some think that I'm a spy."

"I remember it was mainly that one German officer," Adele said.

"Yes, he was persistent. He is actually in Germany, too, but lately he is a lot less intrusive. He had been wounded and only recently returned to work. He was actually a patient at the hospital where I work, and I was one of the nurses who assisted with his surgery and tended to him."

"Was it about two weeks ago that he returned to work?" Renée asked.

Eva found her question a bit odd. She thought about it for a second before answering. "Yes, I guess it was. Why?"

“Because he is here.”

At first, her words didn’t register, and Eva didn’t break her gaze from Renée, waiting for what she said to process. Eva thought for a second she might faint after digesting the information. “Here… as in La Chapelle?”

“Yes, and staying in my house.”

All Eva could do was nod in response to this. She stood from the table. “I’m actually feeling tired. I think I’ll go to my room now.”

“Of course. Adele, help her to her room, then show Hauptmann von Schulz to his.”

“Please, call me Gerhardt.”

“Show Gerhardt to his room,” she repeated.

“I need a moment with Eva if you’ll excuse me,” he said, and Madame Blanc nodded.

He led her out into the hall, away from the dining room. “Eva, he will not do anything to you here. You have seen him in Germany and helped him while he was in the hospital. I can’t imagine he will do something now, plus I am here.”

She swallowed hard and nodded her head. “I need to lie down.” She fought the onset of dizziness, trying not to faint.

“I understand.” He looked at her, worry written on his face. “I’ll see you in the morning, then.” He kissed her on the cheek and watched her walk upstairs while waiting for Adele to show him to his room.

Adele led Eva up the stairs to her old room and opened the door, gesturing for her to enter. Eva walked past her and sat on the bed, trying to keep it together. “I thought you should know that officer is staying in the room next to yours. That is why it wasn't available."

Eva looked to the joint door, then briskly walked over to it and turned the deadbolt. Do you think that tomorrow maybe you could find me another room?"

"I will see what I can do."

"Thank you." Eva glanced at the door, then back at Adele. "Is he here now?"

"No, he is still in town for work, I believe. You said he had been injured?" Adele asked.

"Yes, he was. In an explosion."

"And you helped him while he was in the hospital?"

"Yes, why?" Adele's nervousness and questions were worrying her.

"Has his opinion of you changed because of that?"

"No, I don't believe his opinion has changed at all, but if it has, I would say it has been for the worse, not better. Will you do me a favor?" Eva asked.

"Of course."

"Would you not tell him we are here and ask Renée to do the same? And tell Gerhardt not to say anything, at least not tonight. I would also appreciate it if you would ask Gerhardt to hide the car somewhere out of sight?"

"I will."

"What time does he usually get back?"

"It's never consistent. He rarely comes back at the same time," Adele told her.

"Alright, Gerhardt has the keys to the car. I'm going to go to bed and try not to think about tomorrow."

Adele left the room, and Eva sat on the bed again, staring at the joining door as if he would disappear if she looked at it long enough. He must have done this on purpose. He had to have known they were coming. She was so angry she could hit him. Could he not let her have this, not even for one week? That is all she wanted. She stood so she could get ready for the night. Fuming over Bauer would not solve anything. She put on her PJs and crawled into bed, falling into a restless sleep.

It was the early hours of the morning when a door opening and closing echoed from the hall, and then the floorboards in the next room creaked under the strain of someone's weight. Slowly, she pulled herself up in bed and rubbed her eyes, listening, but didn't dare turn the light on. There was random clinking and banging on the other side of the wall. Then, bedsprings squeaked and popped, indicating that he had laid down. He still didn't know she was there, in the room next to his. She gently laid back down so the springs in her own bed didn't squeak. She faced the joining door, wondering if he would be gone before she or Gerhardt was out of bed. He came in so late they might be up before him, but she hoped he would have to be back at work early. In the morning, they were going to stay with someone else or go back to Paris. She didn't care how much Renée complained. She would not remain in the same house with him another night.

Eva tried to fall back to sleep, but soon after she closed her eyes, he coughed. Her eyes flew open, and she lay there, listening to the on-and-off coughing for over an hour. It kept her up, and she wondered how Renée and Adele could sleep through it. This was going to be a long night. Her bedroom door opened, and a shadowed figure entered the room. She jumped, sitting up in bed.

"Eva," Adele's voice whispered in the darkness.

"Adele, you scared the crap out of me," Eva breathed.

"Sorry, but I didn't want to knock because he would hear, and I didn't want to alert him to the fact that you are here. I had forgotten to tell you that this has been going on since he arrived. I know you can hear it, so I wondered if it was keeping you up too?"

"Well, it's kind of hard to sleep through that, Adele."

"I know, I'm sorry. I have often thought of offering him something to help, but I have not found the courage. Do you think you could do something if you see him tomorrow?"

"I have more reasons than you to fear him," Eva reminded her.

"You seem to be more comfortable around the Germans, and you have more experience with them. Besides, I'm not a nurse."

"I'm not comfortable around that German. I have never met a person who made me feel more uncomfortable in my life."

The coughing started again, and they both looked to the door.

Adele turned back to Eva. "Please, help him. It will help the Madam and me."

"Fine," Eva gave in, throwing off the blanket. "Go heat

some milk and put a spoonful of honey in it. I will also need a cup of warm water with a lot of salt added, and stirred well. And if you have any ginger and peppermint, grab that, too, and take it to his room."

"Wait, you are going to help him tonight?"

"Might as well. If it helps all of us sleep peacefully for the rest of the night, then I will. Besides, unless he goes to work early tomorrow, I don't know how I can avoid an encounter with him."

Adele was surprised. Eva knew she hadn't expected her to do it now. Adele quietly left the room, leaving Eva to think about how she wanted to approach the situation. She got out of bed and put her robe on, then went into the hall, stopping right outside his door. She could hear him turning in the bed. It seemed so odd being back at this door, but Gerhardt was not the one who would answer it. She knocked lightly and waited for him to open it. The weight shifted on the bed, and then footsteps moved on the creaky old floor. Light came from under the door, then it opened.

Bauer first looked annoyed, but it was quickly replaced by complete surprise at the sight of her. "Eva, what the hell!" He looked up and down the hall like he was checking to see if anyone else was there. "What are you doing here?"

"I'm not happy to see you either, but you are keeping everyone awake with that awful coughing," she said to him in German.

"You are staying here?" he asked slowly, as if she might not understand his words.

"Yes, like you didn't already know that. Unfortunately,

I'm in the room next to you. Gerhardt is staying on the main floor."

"Gerhardt…?" His tone and demeanor changed in an instant.

"Yes, we came together. We, however, did not know that you would be here, or we would not have come. As it is, we will leave in the morning."

"You're leaving?"

"You are here, so yes."

"You don't have to leave on my account."

"Oh, but I do, and I want to."

Adele came up the stairs with a tray of the things Eva had asked for.

"What is this?" He pointed at the contents on the tray.

"I had her bring some things up for you to help with the cough. Thank you, Adele," she said, taking the tray from her. Adele walked past them, returning to her own room, never looking at Bauer. He continued to stand in the doorway without attempting to move. "Can I come in, or are we going to do this in the hall?"

"Do what?"

She nodded to the tray in her hands. This."

"What is all of that?" Still, he didn't move.

"Things that will help. Now, can I come in? My hands are getting tired."

He looked at her for a moment longer, then moved out of the way. She walked past him, setting the tray on the nightstand. "Sit down," she told him. He closed the door, then came and sat on the edge of the bed, still a little unsure.

"Here, I want you to gargle this saltwater and spit it in the bowl. Do it several times." She handed him the cup with salt water and a bowl. He took the cup from her but didn't look away as he poured some into his mouth. He gargled the water for a few seconds, then spit it in the bowl, repeating the process a couple more times. He set the cup back on the tray. "Good," she said. "Now drink this, and then you are going to take a hot bath with ginger and peppermint mixed in. It will help open your airways." She handed him the warm milk with honey. "When did the cough start?"

"About a week ago." He lifted the cup to his lips and took a sip.

"Is that the only thing, or are there other symptoms accompanying it?"

"Headaches and general body aches. Why?"

She ignored his question. "Do you have any pain in your upper chest or wheezing with the coughing?"

"Some…" He glared up at her.

She suspected her questions were getting on his nerves. *Good.*

"I think you have an upper respiratory infection. You need to go to the doctor, and I don't mean it as only a suggestion. You really do need to go. First thing tomorrow would be best. If you don't get it taken care of, it could turn into pneumonia, and you could die. I am going to run the bath and put the ginger and peppermint in. Come in when you are done with the milk. After the bath, you can go back to bed, and the coughing should be better. It won't be gone, but hopefully, you can at least get some sleep. As will the rest of us."

She went to the bathroom and turned the knobs, filling the tub, dropping in a couple tablespoons of ginger and a handful of peppermint leaves. She turned the hot up high, hoping it wouldn't be too hot. The mirror over the sink started to fog. She turned around to tell him that the bath was ready, but he was standing only inches behind her; she hadn't heard him come in because of the running water. She gasped and almost fell into the tub, grabbing onto the edge with one hand as the other hand went in the water, splashing some over the side. "Jesus Christ, you scared me," she said in English.

"All I did was walk into the bathroom."

She glared at him but said nothing, then stood and took the towel from the rack to wipe the water off her hand and arm. He pulled his PJ top off and threw it on the floor next to the tub, then reached for his bottoms. "I'm going to go," she blurted out, not wanting to stay in the bathroom with him a minute longer. She hurried out and closed the door quickly behind her. She went back out into the hall, then to her own room, and shut the door, locking it this time. She crawled into bed, feeling extremely uncomfortable with everything that had happened. She should have told Adele no, but it was too late to change her mind now.

June 15th, 1941

The sun poured through her window. Another day had dawned, and the melodic birdsongs sounded outside. Eva stretched and rubbed her bleary eyes, then slid out of bed and walked to the window. There was a pearly glow in the sky, and the just-risen sun shone softly on the ground, bringing with it a flurry of early-morning activity from the squirrels and birds. It was odd that she woke prior to everyone else. She focused on the clock next to her bed; it was a quarter to seven. Eying the bed longingly, she wondered if she should crawl back in and try to go back to sleep but decided against it. She realized she had slept through the rest of the night and didn't hear Bauer coughing. Her remedies were a success. She folded her arms across her chest and went to the joining door, putting her ear to it as she listened for any movement coming from the other side, but there was nothing. She tiptoed downstairs and peeked into the dining room. Seeing that it was empty, she stepped softly to Gerhardt's room and cracked the door open. He was still asleep, lying on his side, an arm hanging off the edge of the bed. She couldn't help but admire his sleeping form, the muscles in his arm and shoulder softly flexed, and the muscles in his back visible through his thin undershirt. She closed the door before the temptation was too strong, and she went into his room. That would not end well. She crept back to the kitchen to look for some food. She gathered up whatever she could find in the pantry that didn't need to be cooked. She would wake Gerhardt after breakfast if he wasn't already up by then.

She jumped, the slice of bread falling off her plate, when she caught sight of Bauer sitting at the table in the kitchen, eating.

He looked up at her with only his eyes, then back down at his food. "Jumping at the sight of me again, I see."

"I didn't know anyone was up," she said, feeling ridiculous.

"I have work."

"You got in early this morning."

"It's a war. It doesn't stop because we go to sleep."

"I get that." She awkwardly stood in the doorway, trying to decide what she should do. "The stuff I gave you seemed to help," she said, trying to break the heavy silence in the air.

"I guess." He took another bite of his boiled egg.

"You guess? You slept without coughing the rest of the night."

"I don't remember one way or another." He buttered his toast but still didn't look at her.

"Have I done something to make you mad?"

"Now, that is a complicated question," he said, still not looking at her.

"No, it's not. It is a yes or no kind of question."

"He smirked. "It most certainly is not."

"How so?"

"I trust you can figure that one out yourself."

"Why did you come here?" she asked. "Is it because you knew I would be here?"

He laid his toast on his plate, brushing the crumbs from his fingers. "Don't flatter yourself. I'm here because France is the country they have assigned me to, or have you forgotten? I didn't even know you were here until last night."

"Then why were you in Germany?"

"It is my home country, and the country where the German military headquarters is based. I have to go between both countries, so sometimes I'm here, and sometimes I'm there. It depends on what I'm doing and where I am needed."

"I find it a bit coincidental that you happen to be here in France at the same time as me."

"It is strange, I admit, but I suppose you will say the same thing when I'm back in Germany again."

"Well, it doesn't matter anyway because we will be leaving today."

"Back to Germany? Didn't you arrive yesterday?"

"No, I mean leaving this house."

For the first time since they had been talking, he looked up from his plate. "Because you are ignorant. You think you know about things when you don't, and then you form an uneducated opinion of them."

His comment confused her and seemed unnecessarily harsh. "You think you know me and the things I do and do not understand, but you don't. You know nothing at all about me." She turned to leave. She would eat later.

"And you do not know me, but maybe you would if you weren't so close-minded," he said.

She stopped but did not turn to face him. "I am not the close-minded one. That is you. You are prejudiced and hateful all the time." She left the kitchen and went back to her room, closing the door in case he decided to follow. She sat on the bed, trying to figure out what to do. Maybe she should wake Gerhardt now so they could leave. She went back downstairs to Gerhardt's room and gently knocked on the door. He opened it in his PJs, and by the look on his face, he was not expecting to see her.

"What is it?" he asked, rubbing his eyes with the back of his hand.

"I want to leave."

"Now?"

"As soon as you dress and pack your things."

"He knows we are here then?" he asked, realizing that must be why she wanted to go now.

"Yes. I barely interacted with him, but it was enough to make me not want to stay here. I have already told him we are leaving today."

"You told him we are leaving?" There was an inflection in his tone that betrayed his concern.

"I did."

His expression changed. "Eva… I'm not so sure that was a good idea. He has to know we will be doing it because of him."

"He does because I told him. And I don't care. I don't want to stay in this house another minute with him here."

"I am going to talk to him. We are not going to do anything until then, alright?"

"Why? There is no need to explain this further. I'm sure my reason was pretty clear."

"I understand, but I don't want to make him angry. Why don't you go change and I will do the same. I think it will be best if I speak to him alone, though."

"I agree. We don't do so well together," she admitted.

"I'll come to your room after I talk to him, then we can decide what we are going to do."

She went back to her room to wait for news from Gerhardt. She lay on the bed and closed her eyes for a minute but was jolted awake by a knock on the door. She had not meant to fall asleep. She slid off the bed and went to the door, cracking it open. Seeing that it was Gerhardt, she opened it all the way and let him in. They both sat on the bed, and she waited for him to speak.

"He said that he will not bother us while we are here. I told him we would be leaving to go back to Paris in a day or two."

She sensed that he was not saying everything that was talked about. "That's it? You spoke to him, and he simply agreed to behave?"

"More or less. I don't know all of his reasons, but I wasn't going to press him for them."

"Did he give you any reason at all?"

"He said he understands why you want to leave, but it makes little sense for us to since we only arrived yesterday. He didn't know we were coming, and you didn't know he was here. I was told that he would be gone most of the time anyway, so there won't be many situations for the two of you to interact. I think he feels a little bad that it has to be this way."

She huffed. "I don't think he feels bad. He knows that he is the one who made it this way between us, so he has no one to blame except himself."

Gerhardt looked at the floor as he spoke. "Either way, he

has agreed to not make your time here miserable."

"I'm a little surprised but glad he is willing to do that."

"So," Gerhardt smiled, "what would you like to do?"

"First, I need to eat, then maybe we can go swimming at the pond you took me to on our picnic."

His smile grew wider. "That seems so long ago now. I would like that. It will be like old times."

"Not like old times, but close enough," she said.

He patted her hand. "Eat, then we'll go."

"Has he left yet?" she asked.

"I believe so. I'll go and let you get ready." He stood and left the room.

She changed, then went to the kitchen to eat, happy that Bauer had left for the day. When she was finished, she packed some food for the trip, remembering the food Gerhardt brought the last time they were at the pond. Gerhardt was waiting for her by the car when she went outside. She put the food in the back and got in the passenger seat, happy to be spending this time with him.

Chapter Sixteen

✠

June 16th, 1941

Bauer was true to his word. Over the past day, he had left them in peace. She barely even noticed his presence, but it would be short-lived.

Eva and Gerhardt sat at the kitchen table eating breakfast as they looked across at one another. She smiled at him, remembering the day before when they went swimming. It was not like the first time. There was not the same sexual tension, flirting, or uncertainty about what would come next, but it was fun and relaxing. This time, she knew they were there only as friends, and nothing physical would happen between them, but it was enjoyable being in his company all the same.

They looked into each other's eyes as they ate but looked away as someone entered the kitchen. The person walked to the side of the table and stopped, waiting for them to look up. Eva and Gerhardt lifted their heads at the same time to peer at Bauer, who was standing over them. Gerhardt instinctively stood because Bauer was his commanding officer, even though neither of them were in their uniforms.

"There are some things I need to discuss with you." He turned to Eva, then back to Gerhardt.

"Of course."

"Let's do it out here," he said, gesturing towards the hall.

She kept her eyes on both men as they walked through the entryway, disappearing into the hall. Faint voices echoed back, but she couldn't understand what they were saying. It worried her that Bauer wanted to speak to Gerhardt. What could he possibly need to talk to him about alone? She anxiously waited for them to return, tapping her feet on the floor while keeping her gaze fixed on the doorway. Finally, Gerhardt walked back into the kitchen without Bauer.

"What did he want?" she asked, a little too quickly, her voice shaky. Gerhardt had a different look on his face, and she could not make out what he was thinking. "Gerhardt," she said again, trying to pull him out of his thoughts so he would answer.

"He said that I would be going back to Germany today. I have been re-assigned."

"Re-assigned? Re-assigned to do what… where?"

"I can't say, but I can tell you that you won't see me again for a long time."

She tensed at his words. "What do you mean… why do

you say that?" He briefly met her gaze, then looked down at his hands. "Gerhardt… what are you not saying?" She stood from the table and came to stand in front of him.

"Eva, I can't tell you what the assignment is. I wish I could, but I can't."

She racked her brain to remember what in world history happened in June 1941, and then her breath caught in her throat as she remembered. It was the invasion of Russia. Her eyes bore into his, horrified at what this meant for him. There was no way they were sending him to the Russian front for the invasion. He was an intelligence officer that worked at a desk in Berlin. Why would they be sending him there? Maybe they needed him to help with the analytical part of the invasion. Yeah, that made sense to her because nothing else did.

"Eva, why are you looking at me that way?"

"What?" she asked, not realizing she had been staring at him without seeing him. "I was thinking about how different things will be in Germany now that you won't be there."

"You are strong, Eva. You will be alright." He rubbed her arm. "You were looking at me so strangely a minute ago. Was that all you were thinking?"

She nodded and swallowed. "Uh-huh." She forced a smile.

He took her hand. "Eva, look at me." She lifted her gaze from their joined hands to his face. "I will be alright, you know that," he assured her.

"Do I?"

"I will." He gave her a reassuring smile.

“Do you even know what you will do?”

“Not yet, but I will when I get back to Berlin. Speaking of Berlin, I need to get ready. I have to take the car back with me, so you will need to catch the train home. I’m sorry about that.”

“It’s fine. I don’t mind the train.”

“When will you leave?” he asked.

“I don’t know. Maybe I will leave today too.”

“There is no need. Why don’t you stay and enjoy your last few days here.”

“I don’t know if that is a good idea.”

He put his hand on her cheek. “You will be fine. Remember what I said. You are strong, one of the strongest people I know.”

He moved his hand and let it drop to his side. “I have to go pack now.”

When he turned to leave, she grabbed hold of his sleeve. “Please, Gerhardt. You say that I am strong, but I’m not. I am weak, and if you go, I don’t think I will make it.” She knew what potentially lay ahead for him, and that thought was grim. She could not tell him that she knew where he was going, but she had to try to stop him from going if she could. Even though it was inevitable that he would go in the end, and her efforts would be in vain.

He turned to face her. “Eva, no matter what happens in this war, you will make it out alive. I would bet the odds against anything. You are a survivor, and you don’t need me for that. When I leave, it will be hard at first, but with each passing day, it will get easier.”

“You might be right, but I don’t care. Knowing you are in danger somewhere is what I can’t take. I can’t imagine a world where you no longer exist.”

“You have to trust me when I say that I will be alright. You will not be alone in Berlin. You will have your friends and the hospital. You will forget about me in time. Besides, I will be back. You must believe that. I really do have to go. They are expecting me this evening for my briefing.”

“I know,” she said. “I know.”

He walked out of the kitchen without finishing his breakfast. She sat back in her chair and looked down at the plate in front of her with partially eaten scrambled eggs, a slice of cheese, and a half-eaten croissant. How quickly things had changed. She no longer felt like eating, so she pushed the plate away and then went to Gerhardt’s room; she needed to spend every minute with him that she could.

She stood in the open doorway as he packed his things. “Would you like some help?”

He glanced over his shoulder briefly, then turned back at the bed, poking a shirt in the duffle bag. “I’m all but finished now,” he said, zipping it up. “But you can walk me out to the car.”

She nodded and followed him outside in silence. What could she say? Nothing would keep him here, so there was no point in wasting her breath.

He put the bag in the back seat, then turned to her. “I’m sorry for breaking your heart. I know I have in so many ways. Our lives have been entwined and might always be, but they are on very different paths.” He leaned down and gave her a soft kiss on the lips, then planted one on her forehead before getting into the car and driving away.

In her mind, this was the worst thing that could happen to him. The Russian front was a brutal place, a slaughterhouse for boys and men. She could only hope he would be behind the lines as one of the strategists for operations, but even that was not a safe place to be.

As she turned to walk back into the house, Bauer was leaving. Their eyes briefly met as they passed, and in his were things she could not discern. They were full of secrets and hidden emotions, none of which he would divulge to her. But she did not care to venture into the depths of those hazel eyes. She stared at the ground and continued to the front door.

"Are you going to stay or go home today?" he asked, causing her to halt a few inches from the door.

She didn't look at him. "I haven't decided yet."

"You don't have to leave. As I told Gerhardt, I will stay out of your way."

She finally turned, focusing her gaze on the bottom of the steps where he was standing. "Did you know about this before today?"

"If you are talking about his re-assignment, I only received the orders late last night but decided to wait and tell him today. I didn't want to wake him. There was no point."

"So, you didn't re-assign him?"

He chuckled. "We are not in the same unit or even the same posting, Miss Abrams. And we have completely different jobs. His re-assignment came from Berlin."

She hated to admit it, but he was right; he was in the Gestapo, and Gerhardt was in the Wehrmacht.

"As much as I enjoy our little chats, I really must go now," he told her in a monotone voice, like their conversation bored him.

He walked to the car that was parked out front and climbed in the backseat. His orderly closed the door and went to the front. She watched the shiny black car pull away, leaving a cloud of dust behind it. The small red flags with swastikas flapped in the wind as if they were trying to fly away. That was twice this morning that someone told her they had to go. Somewhere deep inside, she had a sense of abandonment and a strange, lonely feeling that settled in her chest.

She went to her room and sat on the bed. *Now what?* She thought, wondering what she should do. Did she go home or stay like Gerhardt and Bauer suggested and try to enjoy her last few days here? She focused on the wall, the rays of light dancing on it like diamonds. A gentle breeze coming through the open window made the thin white curtains flutter. The atmosphere in the room was serene. The feeling of familiarity was overwhelming. She loved this room and this house. It still looked the same as it did when she would stay with Madame Blanc. This room and the rest of the house had remained the same, but everything else had changed. Almost nothing was as it used to be. She lowered herself onto the bed, pulling her legs into the fetal position. She would see what Renée and Adele were doing later. They would almost certainly want to do something with her. Maybe sleeping would help clear her mind so a decision could be made whether to stay or leave.

That morning, after getting out of bed, Eva went downstairs and looked for Renée and Adele but couldn't find them. She walked to the window and peered out over the gravel driveway, noticing the car was gone. They weren't home, so she decided to walk into town. This would be her first time in La Chapelle since leaving. She wondered if it would be the same as the house, comforting and familiar, or if it, like most things, had changed.

It was such a lovely June day. The breeze made the walk comfortable, but soon, the air would be hot like the summer days. Eva's hair blew around her face, caressing it, tickling her skin. The sweet, earthy smell of the wildflowers from the un-sowed fields and meadows was strong in the air. This place felt so far from the war, the same as it did when she lived here. It was almost impossible to imagine one was raging across Europe or that France was occupied by the enemy. Eva loved everything about it; she missed the sweltering, humid summers spent in the fields, the long walks, and laying in the grass as the sun was setting. Its delicious, fragrant scents that started in the spring and lasted through the summer were some of her favorite things. It was one of her most cherished places on earth, and yet it brought her so much pain now. The road into town was also a reminder of the past, still lined with the white French lilac bushes she used to pick on her way home to brighten up the rooms. She would try harder not to remember that time and strive to live in the present.

As she entered the town, people standing outside the shops looked at her curiously, but none seemed to recognize her, and she was glad. She went to the fountain in the middle of the town square and sat on the edge. Closing her eyes, she imagined that Gerhardt was standing not far away, calling her, and then the memory of Sabina tossing the flower in the fountain to make a wish was vivid. Her eyes flew open. That was something she did not want to think about. There was a tightness in her chest already, and the tears burned her eyes as she blinked them away. She knew this would happen if she came here, yet she chose to, anyway.

The fountain was a place that brought back happy but painful memories, so she left and wandered through town, looking at the goods in the shop windows and those displayed out front. She bought some strawberries and savored their sweet flavor as she continued down the old, cobbled streets. She stopped in front of the city hall where the Germans were operating from. She shielded her eyes from the sun and focused on the building, recalling how scared she was as she waited in line to register and how Gerhardt frightened her when they first met. It was almost laughable now.

The front door opened, and Bauer came out with several other men following on his heels down the steps. He stopped when he noticed her.

"Did you need something, Miss Abrams?" he asked. "I don't have a lot of time."

"No, I don't need anything from you," she said, leaving

her meaning open to interpretation.

His expression didn't change, like what she said didn't faze him. He walked past her along with the other men, and they climbed into two cars and drove away.

There was a small La Chapelle cemetery on the other side of the river from the main part of town, and Eva wondered if Sabina was buried there. She made her way down the hill and crossed the bridge over the Ruisseau de Mohimont river towards the cemetery. She stepped through the opening of the small rock wall that surrounded the graveyard and walked up and down the rows. Sabina's grave would have a smaller headstone than most of the others in the cemetery. Would Fabien's grave be there next to his daughter's? She scanned the rows, looking for newer headstones. The cemetery was small but densely packed with some stones broken or fallen, moss and lichen covering the fronts and backs, and high grass surrounding the bases. There were several newer-looking stones a few rows to her right. Stepping over a fallen headstone, she made her way to them and squatted so she could read the words. None of them were Sabina's or Fabien's, so she stood and continued searching the rows again. She had almost checked the entire cemetery when two newer-looking headstones at the back came into view, near the rock wall. Slowly, she made her way towards them, this time feeling some trepidation in doing so. Somehow, she knew these were their graves, and she wanted to see them, but, at the same time, she didn't. Seeing their names on the headstones would solidify their deaths in her mind. Until now, it was feasible to keep them alive in her memory, as if she had only left and they were still here waiting for her.

She stopped when she reached the headstones but didn't look at them. Instead, she peered beyond the wall at the trees, needing a moment before reading them. Finally, she lowered her eyes on the larger stone, then the smaller one beside it. As she had known, they were indeed Fabien and Sabina's. She got down on her knees and sat on her feet. She reached out and touched the small white stone first, tracing the engraving of Sabina's name with her index finger. It was hard to read the writing through the tears. She remembered her little face, the freckles on her nose and rosy cheeks, her eyes blue like the sky, and her hair the color of gold. She was always happy with a natural lust for life.

"Oh, sweet Sabina," she said through tears, her hand still resting on the cool stone, her throat closing. "I am so very sorry. Your life was taken from you at such a young age. You barely lived before it was snuffed out. I wish I could change that, but at least you are with your father." She turned her gaze to Fabien's grave now. "You were so good to me, better than I deserved. You both are dead because of me, and I can never undo what has happened. I only hope you can forgive me." She finally moved her hand from Sabina's stone to his and pressed her fingers against it, wishing she had picked flowers to put on their graves. "I will come back and leave flowers before I go. It is the least I can do." She lifted her head and gazed across the cemetery, taking in all the headstones, wondering if Ezra was buried here too, but of course, he wouldn't be. He was a Jew. The

Germans probably dug a hole somewhere obscure and threw him in. They would not have marked it, so she couldn't visit him even if she wanted to. Maybe Madame Blanc knew something about it.

She kissed the tips of her fingers and placed them on both of their headstones, then stood and headed back to wait for Adele and Madame Blanc. When the house came into view, the car was already parked on the grounds. She walked through the front door and called their names as she removed her hat, laying it on the entryway table with her purse.

"We are in the lounge," Madame Blanc's voice echoed down the hall.

Eva passed through the large entryway that led into the lounge. Adele and Madame Blanc were sitting on the Victorian couch, drinking tea.

"Come and join us," Madame Blanc said. Eva poured herself a cup and sat across from them.

"I can't believe that you could face that German and I'm even more surprised that you could bring yourself to help him, though I am thankful you did." Madame Blanc raised her cup to her lips.

"I know what he can be like. This was not my first rodeo with him." Adele and Madame Blanc's gazes were fixed on her, perplexed. "It's an expression," she told them. "I couldn't sleep, and I'm sure you guys couldn't either."

"No, we could not," Adele said. "I think he has been doing what you suggested. The herbs in the kitchen that you used are depleted now."

"Do you know if he ever went to the doctor?" Eva asked

out of curiosity, wondering if he had taken her advice on that as well.

Adele turned to Madame Blanc to see if she knew, but Madame Blanc only sipped her tea. "I don't believe so, but he could have while he was gone during the day."

Eva nodded and took a sip of her lukewarm tea. She had a nagging suspicion he didn't follow her advice about going to the doctor. Did she confront him about it or let it go? She honestly didn't know. "How has it been living with him?"

"It has been bearable. He is very different from Hauptmann von Schulz, but honestly, we don't see him most of the time. He hasn't been here long and leaves for work when the sun is still rising and rarely returns before the early hours of the morning. That is all we see him do is work. Whatever his job is, he is very dedicated to it," Madame Blanc said. "But I don't think he will be here much longer. When he arrived, it was made clear that he would only be here for a short time. If my memory serves me, he told us after a couple of weeks, he would be returning to Paris."

Eva rolled her eyes. "Yes, he is dedicated. It's good that you don't have to put up with him for long. He is the Gestapo officer overseeing France. So, he will probably come and go from La Chapelle. I know the main Gestapo headquarters in France is in Paris, so he will probably be there most of the time. He did say that he has to go back to Germany for work, but it's usually only for a few weeks at a time."

"Better here with us than in Germany with you," Adele said.

“You are right,” Eva agreed. She drank the rest of her tea and set the cup and saucer on the coffee table. “I think I will go to my room now and read.”

“How long will you stay?” Madame Blanc asked.

“I don’t know. I had thought about going back early, but I still have another day here. I might stay.”

“We would love it if you did.”

“I will think about it. Thank you for the tea.” They gave her a smile before she left the room.

She sat on her bed and leaned against the headboard. On the side table was the book she brought. She picked it up, opening to the marked page, ready to read when a car pulled up outside, tires crunching the gravel. She slid off the bed and peeked out the window. Bauer’s orderly was holding the door for him, and once he was out, shut it and followed behind him. They came up the steps, and the front door opened then closed. Brief words were exchanged in the foyer, then the front door opened again and closed while heavy boots clicked on the stairs, the boards creaking under the weight. For some reason, the thought of him seeing the light under the door made her skin prickle. Turning the light off crossed her mind, but she realized it wouldn’t matter because he was already coming down the hall, and she would never make it to the light switch before he passed in front of her room. The footsteps were at her door when they stopped. She held her breath and waited for something to happen. The seconds seemed to pass by like minutes when, finally, there was a faint knock on the door. She closed her eyes and blew out the breath she was holding, then closed the book and laid it on the bed beside her. She considered not answering, but he knew she was awake. Sliding off the bed, she went to the door, cracking it open just enough to peer out.

"Yes?"

"I was going to ask you what you needed in town today?"

"I didn't need anything. I was out for a walk."

"You walked all the way to town?"

"Yes, I used to do it all the time when I lived here."

"That is quite the distance."

"Not really, only if you don't like to walk or it's cold or raining. I wanted to ask you something, too."

His demeanor grew guarded. "Alright."

"Did you ever go to the doctor like I suggested?"

"No, I haven't had the time."

"Time... if you don't make the time, it will only get worse, like I said. And it has no regard for your work or opinion."

"The time," he emphasized, "I spent in the hospital set me so far back I now have to work seven days a week and fourteen to sixteen hours a day so I can stay on top of things."

"Keep this up, and you will get pneumonia. If that is how you have been carrying on the whole time you've been back in France, it is no wonder you are sick."

"War waits for no one."

"No, but a man waits for sickness. You act like you don't even care."

"Do you?" he asked.

"What, no. I mean, yes, I care when someone gets ill. That is why I am a nurse. It is my job to care." His eyes were fixed on her, burning a hole as she spoke. "If you don't want to go to the doctor, then don't, and if you want to continue to work yourself into the sickbed, then go ahead." He still didn't speak, and she wanted to smack the expression off his face. It was unnerving. She hated his piercing eyes and the stern expression he always wore. He stared down at her, his square jaw tense from clenching his teeth. She decided this conversation was over and started to close the door, but he put a hand on it, the action making her jump. She did not know what he was going to do next. His preventing her from closing the door had been so unexpected.

"What can the doctor do for me that you can't?"

"He can prescribe the medicine you need. I cannot do that."

He finally broke their gaze. "You will go with me and my orderly tomorrow to see a doctor."

She opened her mouth to protest but didn't when anger flashed in his eyes. "Fine. Can I close my door now?"

He removed his hand and walked to his room. She closed the door and locked it. "Bastard," she whispered under her breath. Him telling her she was going to come must be his way of saying, if I have to suffer, you have to suffer.

June 17th, 1941

She sat on the front steps, waiting for Bauer's car to pick her up. She checked her watch; he was already ten minutes late. Bauer told her the car would be there at three to get her so they could drive to Sedan, the nearest city. La Chapelle was a tiny village and was too small to have a doctor.

Fifteen after three, a black car came up the drive. She picked her purse up off the stone step and stood. It pulled in front of the house and stopped, then the orderly got out and came around to open the back door for her. She did not know his name like she did Gerhardt's orderly and wasn't too concerned with learning it either; she would not be seeing much of him, anyway.

"Where is Obersturmbannführer Bauer?" she asked, noticing the backseat was empty.

"He is not ready yet. I'm afraid he is caught up at work right now, but he should be finished soon."

"Why would he tell me to be ready by three, then?"

"He didn't know his work would run so late, but it has taken longer than expected."

She was annoyed; he had stressed the fact that she needed to be ready to go by three, and then he was late. Again, it was probably something he did on purpose. She slid into the backseat, and Bauer's orderly closed her door and got behind the wheel. They drove down the long dirt road towards La Chapelle in silence. Her mind drifted to Gerhardt. She never fathomed that he would ever wind up on the Russian front. It made her feel sick every time she thought about it. Maybe if she contacted Berlin, there would be some way to keep him from going, only they could not find out that she knew about Operation Barbarossa, which was the name for the planned invasion of Russia. If they learned of this, she would be arrested for sure.

The car pulled in front of city hall, and the driver turned the engine off. "I am going to go in and let him know that you are here. Please wait in the car," he told her.

She didn't answer but stared out the window at the white plaster-covered building. The car shook when he closed the door, and she focused on the back of him as he ascended the steps. A tinge of fear crept over her, remembering the last time she was in a car with Bauer. He scared her most of the time, but maybe, just maybe, he would be nicer to her on this car trip, given the things that had transpired between them since their last car ride together.

It seemed much later in the day than it was; the clouds were thick, grey, and hung low in the sky, threatening rain, rolling over the countryside. She caught sight of Bauer and his orderly coming out of the building together. The orderly opened the back door for him, and he slid in across from her. She deliberately didn't look at him but continued to stare out the window, focusing on the clouds. The car began to move, and the sensation of his eyes on her was uncomfortable, so she dared a glance in his direction. She couldn't tell for sure, but he seemed angry when he flashed a sideways glance at her. She turned her head to look him square in the face. Why the hell was he giving her that look? She had not done anything to him. As they stared at one another, her gaze was drawn to the darkness under his eyes. It was clear he wasn't getting enough sleep. His skin was a pale ,ashy color, and little beads of sweat had formed on his forehead. He looked worse for wear. *Idiot*, she thought. *You should have listened to me and gone to the doctor sooner.* She turned away and peered out the window again.

"I apologize for being late, but I could not help it," he finally said, breaking the silence.

She turned back to him. "And what about tomorrow?"

He furrowed his brows. "What about it?"

"Well, I suspect the doctor will tell you to rest for a while until you are better, and I'm guessing you will not do that, so of course, you will return to work tomorrow."

"You have guessed correctly."

"Would work really suffer that much if you took a day or two to rest?"

"It's not that I do all the work. It's that certain decisions can only be made by me. My officers can't make some of them, so they must get my approval. If I missed work a few days, they would be coming to the house for my signature or for meetings. So, as you can see, it would not be all that restful to stay at the house."

"More so than going in to work tomorrow or the next day. At least you would get some rest."

"I doubt I could take that much time off. I have to go to Paris soon, anyway."

She knew that he traveled around France but didn't know how often it actually was. "And do you get to choose when you go?"

"Sometimes, but other times, I'm instructed to go. However, I do get to choose this time, but it still needs to be soon."

"So, make it in a few days, then. You know what? I don't care what you do after we leave the doctor. I am going back to Berlin in the morning, and I'm not going to concern myself with what you are or are not doing here."

"Then why did you tell me to go to the doctor?"

"I have never seen a person care so little about their own wellbeing. All you care about is your work. That is all you do. You don't like anything else."

"You obviously don't know me well because if you did, you would know that I care about a lot, and I like many things."

"You care about your mother, that much I figured out when you were in the hospital, and your life is devoted to Germany, but outside of those things, I can't see you caring about much else. And, likes, I've never seen you do anything but work."

"I like to ride horses. I find playing the piano relaxing. I often go for walks. I enjoy dancing, carpentry, and boxing, amongst other things. Being in the military is not the only thing I like. You would have considered that I had other interests if you ever took a second to look past my uniform."

"It's kind of hard to when you are wearing it."

"That's because it's what you choose to see."

"Why are you not getting transferred too?" she asked.

"Because I am needed here. I know it upsets you that Hauptmann von Schulz is being transferred, but like me, he has a job to do. You are not the only thing in his life."

She tried to not let his comment wound her. "No, you are right, and I'm not the only one in his life, either. Did you know he was back with his fiancé?"

"I did, yes."

"I thought when he found out that I was in Berlin, he would still want to be with me." She had no idea why she was talking about this with Bauer. But she felt the need to vent.

"He has a history with her."

"You don't know him like I do. I was sure he would choose me, but instead, he chose her, and now he is gone, and I might never see him again." She looked down and folded her hands in her lap. "He has her, and she has him, and they will write each other letters and share their feelings and experiences, and when he returns home, she will be the one that gets to hold him, kiss him, watch him shave, hear his laugh, to hold his hand, all the small things that are actually big things, then they will marry and have children. At the end of all of this, she gets him, and I get nothing, I get…" She trailed off, tears rolling down her cheeks. She had not expected to tell him so much, especially with such powerful emotions. By the time she stopped talking, she realized she was yelling at him more than talking.

Bauer said nothing while she was speaking. He simply listened. Finally, he did speak. "Love is not something that you take; it is something that is given. If he did not give you his love, there is nothing you can do."

"But he did give me his love."

"He showed you his love, but he didn't give it to you. He gave it to her."

She wasn't sure how to feel about what he said. It could be true, but it could also be that Bauer was trying to be cruel. She forcefully wiped away the tears, embarrassed that she allowed herself to cry and in front of him. She was silent for the rest of the car ride.

When they arrived at the hospital, the doctor told Bauer to take a few days from work to rest, as Eva had expected. He gave him antibiotics and some pain medication. The doctor said her advice was good and that he should continue doing it along with taking the medicines prescribed.

As they drove back to La Chapelle, Eva remembered that she needed to put flowers on Sabina and Fabien's graves before leaving in the morning. When they got back to the house, she went right to her room and didn't come out for the rest of the night. She could not handle another second with him.

Chapter Seventeen

✠

June 18th, 1941

Bauer had offered to take her to the train station, but she objected, saying it would not be conducive to him getting better, which was true, but of course, it wasn't the real reason. She packed her things and then walked into town, picking flowers to put on Sabina and Fabien's graves. She placed the most colorful ones on Sabina's grave and the white ones on Fabien's. Before leaving, she quietly stood, staring down at the headstones, wishing things could be different. Forcing herself to leave their graves, she returned to the house and retrieved her things, then walked to the train station with her small bag.

She boarded the train and took a window seat in an empty box. Staring out the window, she watched the steam rise from the engine, finding herself all alone again. How did it come to this? She came to France with Gerhardt but was leaving without him. There was a sensation deep in the pit of her stomach, an uneasy awareness that this was the last time she would ever see him. She was so lonely and missed him more than could be said with words. She closed her eyes and imagined his lips against hers one last time. It almost felt real as she envisioned his arms around her, making her feel safe as they always did when he held her.

There was no end to this misery that she could see or these feelings. So much time would pass by without him, and though they say time heals all wounds, there was no certainty it would heal this one. It hurt her every time she thought of him, but now the wound was reopened. She wanted him in her life but wasn't so sure he felt the same.

She was glad to be returning to Germany and happy to leave France, and that was surprising. She never imagined that would happen, but Bauer was in France and not Germany. The emotional effects of the last few days culminated, and the exhaustion swept over her. She closed her eyes and laid her head on the cool glass, hoping sleep would come. On days like this, she craved affection from another person. If Liesel or Heidi were here now, she would hug them and cry. Inside, the emptiness swallowed her up like a black hole, dark and alone.

The train cars jerking and grinding as they pulled into the Berlin station ripped her from sleep. She opened her eyes, groggy and confused, as muffled voices sounded from the other side of the window. She sat upright, blinking against the bright sun, unable to remember any of the trip except when they left the station in France. She collected herself and retrieved her small carry bag from the overhead compartment. Knowing she would see Liesel and Heidi soon was already making her feel better. Even the thought of going back to work brought her a small amount of joy. To help get her mind off Gerhardt, she craved routine and normality.

She walked into the apartment and went straight to her room, tossing the bag onto the bed and her purse next to it.

It was barely past three, and Liesel and Heidi were still at work, so she had some time to herself before they got home. She lay on the bed, tapping her hands up and down on the mattress, trying to figure out what to do. She turned her head to the left, her gaze drawn to the music box on the corner of the dresser. She got off the bed and walked over to it, taking the box from the top. She turned it over in her hands, reminded of the day he gifted it to her. It was given to him by his mother, intended for the woman he would marry, except that woman wasn't her. *Perhaps I should give it to his fiancée,* she considered. It was decided. She would return the music box to the person it really belonged to. She picked her purse up off the floor and stuck the music box under her arm. She remembered that his fiancé's name was Emma, but she didn't know her last name, but hopefully she could find out. Maybe Oberst Heinrich Schmitt could find out for her.

She waited for the tram to take her to the Reich Security Main Office. She hated that building; it was the headquarters of the SS and Gestapo, and it was the building where Bauer worked when he was in Berlin. There were so many reasons not to go there, but at last, this was her best chance of finding out Gerhardt's fiancé's last name. The compelling need to give it to her was unclear. Maybe it was because she felt guilty that he gave it to her and not his fiancée, or perhaps the truth was she wanted to meet her. There was a strong desire to see what she looked like, to know who this person was that he would spend the rest of his life with if he ever returned from the front.

She got on the tram and took a seat across from an elderly couple. The tram moved but came to a stop shortly after. A loud commotion sounded in the street. The cries of a woman wailing mixed with shouts and yelling male voices.

Eva craned her neck, trying to peer in the direction of the commotion. People lined the sides of the road and stopped on the sidewalks, watching something that was taking place in the middle of the street. A crowd of people surrounded something, so Eva moved her eyes to the middle of the circle. A man was lying on the road, and a woman stood close by, screaming and crying. There were three German soldiers standing over the man. He was on his knees as one soldier held his pistol to his forehead. The woman continued to cry and plead with them, especially the one who held the gun. Another soldier held her back, and the third stood nearby, looking on. The soldier with the gun laughed at the man's apparent misery, yelled that he was a Jew, and spat in his face. The man cupped his hands together, holding them up, begging the soldier to stop, but he didn't. He hit the man in the face with the butt of the pistol, knocking him to the ground. Blood from his forehead dripped onto the pavement. The soldier kicked the man a few times in the stomach.

"Get up, you filthy Jew," he yelled. The man was

struggling to stand, so the soldier lifted his gun, aiming it at his head again, and pulled the trigger. Blood splatted on the soldier's face, and several of the people standing close, including the woman crying in the circle. The soldier holding the woman shoved her to the ground next to the man. She crawled on her hands and knees over to his lifeless body in hysterics, cradling him to her. The soldier lifted his gun again and shot her in the back of the head, then she slumped on top of the man's body.

Eva was shocked but couldn't look away. The sheer horror of it kept her transfixed. Her hands covered her mouth as she held her breath. Her head spinning, and the contents of her stomach were making their way up her throat. She leaned to the side and vomited on the floor of the trolley.

It had never dawned on her that there were still Jews in Berlin, but the Germans must not have cleared them all out yet. This was the first time she had witnessed something like this in Berlin, though she was sure there were Jews rounded up daily, only she didn't see it. The urge to run as far from the gruesome sight as possible took over. She stood, making sure to not stand in her vomit, and squeezed through the people until she reached the door, nearly jumping off the tram. As soon as her feet hit the ground, she ran in the opposite direction as fast as her legs would carry her. When she could no longer see the tram or the people, she stopped to catch her breath, putting her hand on the wall of the building next to her for support. Inside was numb in every possible way. She was beginning to regret returning to Berlin but then remembered what she had been running from in France. At this moment, she didn't know which one was worse, what she had been running from, or what she was now running from.

She decided to visit the priest instead of trying to find Gerhardt's fiancé. She really needed to talk to someone. Someone who would listen and say the hard truth that she needed to hear. Friends would tell her what they thought she wanted to hear or be overly critical to protect her. Neither of those things would be helpful right now. She would go to the Reich Main Security Office another day. She didn't have the stomach to step foot in it after what she had witnessed.

The sun was warm as she made her way across town, yet a chill ran over her, only not from the air. She passed women and children on the sidewalk but not a single man. The absence of men was even more noticeable than usual. It could only be for one reason. The invasion of Russia that would take place in a matter of days. The city felt different. There was a change of mood in the air. These women who passed on the street were aware something serious was happening. Information about of the coming events had been kept from them, so all they knew was they had to tell the men in their lives bye. Berlin was now a city of women, children, and old men.

She pulled open the large outer door of the church and entered the chapel through the smaller inner door. The church was empty, and her footsteps echoed on the stone floor. She went to the hall leading to the back of the church where the clergy office was, knowing that Father Becker should be in his office because it wasn't the time for confessions. The door to his office was cracked open a few inches, but not enough to see inside, so she knocked on the doorframe.

"Come in," a voice said from the other side.

She pushed the door open and peered in. Father Becker's back faced her as he put books on the bookshelf. "Father Becker."

He turned to look at her and smiled. "I am happy to see you again, Eva. Please, have a seat. He extended his hand to the chair across from him. She sat down but waited for him to speak. He laid the last few books he was holding on the desk. "How did the trip to France go?"

"It was fine… at least in the beginning." Father Becker didn't speak, so she continued. "We talked about the things we needed to, and I believe we came to an understanding. While we were in France, though, I had the misfortune of lodging with a person who hates me and, I believe, wishes me harm." She looked away from Father Becker, down at her lap, focusing on the pattern of her dress. "It was the person I told you about, the one I didn't think could be forgiven. His being there tainted the rest of the trip, but what really made it bad was that Gerhardt had to leave suddenly. He had been deployed but couldn't say where. I have this overwhelming feeling that I will never see him again. It is undeniable. I never will. There is no feeling that compares. It is a pain like no other. Losing the little girl in France was one of the most painful things I have ever experienced, and yet I can't compare it to this because they are so different. I don't even know how you measure pain because I've never tried to before."

"Why was him leaving, and the thought of never seeing him again so painful for you this time?"

"I think because I feel he is in danger, but it's not only that. I might never see him again, and I struggle to accept that."

"Why do you think he is in danger now and you didn't before?"

"Because they have sent him out of Germany. I didn't have to ask to know that, it was obvious. Something is happening. Have you noticed the absence of men in the city? I mean, more than usual?"

"I have."

"What do you think is going on?" She wanted to see if the people of Germany suspected another invasion was getting ready to happen.

"I believe we will soon be invading another country, or the war is doing badly somewhere, and they don't talk about it on the radio."

"I'm inclined to agree with your first thought."

"And you think he will be in harm's way in some foreign land which will result in his death?" he asked, regarding her.

"Yes, I do."

"You know, Eva, you nor the man you speak of will escape this war as if it never happened. None of us will."

"I understand that. Today I saw them kill a man and woman in the street because they were Jewish. They shot him in the head as she watched, then shot her."

"It is awful that these kinds of things happen. We are all God's children, only they don't see it that way, Hitler, I mean, and his loyal followers. Someday this will end. The hate and brutality though, not for a long time. But the memory of it will last forever. Unfortunately, the end of the war will not be the end of the suffering for the ones who lose, for them it will only get worse."

One thing that most Americans knew was how the Germans were treated at the hands of the Russians. "I know that. I can't even imagine what it will be like for them."

"Eva, I think you should go home. If there is a way, that is what you should do."

"I agree. There is nothing left for me here."

He stood. "I have to get ready for confession now, but I want you to come and see me again before you leave. And if there is anything I can do to help, please don't hesitate to ask. Remember, you are loved, and that is reason enough to not give up."

"I'm not sure there is a way for me to leave. But I won't stop looking."

He walked her to the front of the church and took her hand. "You will be alright."

His voice was kind and reassuring. "I hope so. Thank you." She left the church and stepped out into the warm summer sun, feeling a little more hopeful.

June 19th, 1941

Heidi and Liesel were excited to see her when they got home and found her sleeping on the couch. When Eva woke, she recounted her trip to France but left out some of the events that had taken place. She decided to tell them what she witnessed on the street with the Jews. They were as horrified as her but didn't seem to be surprised by what had taken place. When Eva returned to work, it was the most normal thing that had happened to her in over a week. The hospital was not as busy as it had been, but that would soon change.

She had worked alongside Dr. Möller most of the day, and every time she passed by Frau Wagner, she would give her stern, disapproving looks, but Eva didn't care.

"You have been gone a lot lately. I have missed seeing your face around here, and some of these new nurses are not catching on fast enough," Dr. Möller told her.

She watched him eat his dinner while he talked. They sat in the small wooden chairs next to the equally small table in his office, as they did so often.

She smiled. "Thank you. I have missed you, too. It has been crazy this last week."

"In what way?"

"The trip to France was not as I expected…"

"Of course, you went to France. What did you expect?" he said, half-serious, half-joking.

"Well, it wasn't because of France. It had more to do with some of the people there and the fact that the person I went with had to leave early because he was being deployed. It was sudden and very secretive. I don't understand why he had to go or what is going on." She did know where he was going and what was going on, but she couldn't figure out why he was going. It didn't make sense for his job. "What do you think is happening?" she asked.

"I honestly don't know what they are doing. I'm not sure any good will come of it, though."

She wondered if Bauer knew about the Russian invasion, then immediately wondered why she thought that. Did Gerhardt know about it but didn't believe he would be going? She wanted to change the subject. "So, how has Ingrid been doing?"

"She has done pretty well. She is one of the better nurses."

"I'm glad to hear you say that. I feel like she really tries hard."

"It's interesting that you say that because when she first came to work here, I assumed you were not too fond of her."

"At first, I wasn't, but then when I got to know her, I realized I had been wrong."

"I think a lot of times we misjudge people in the beginning, and sometimes we misjudge them repeatedly because we don't really know who they are or what drives them. If we are lucky, we might eventually figure it out."

"True, but you can often tell a lot about a person right after meeting them."

"This friend of yours, is he the man you danced with at the ball?"

"He is."

"And you love him?"

She almost choked on her food. "Ummm, he is engaged and will marry his fiancé when he returns."

"I didn't ask if he was getting married. I asked if you love him?"

It must have been evident at the ball that there was something between them. "I did, and I suppose I still do."

"So why is he marrying someone else, then? Does he not feel the same about you?"

"He does, but he loves her too and was with her first. He has known her a lot longer."

He leaned back in his chair and pushed the glasses up on the bridge of his nose. "I didn't realize it was like that. I'm sorry. Eva, there are other men out there who will give you what you need and share their love with only you."

"Well, if there is, I haven't met him yet."

"Maybe because you don't know what that looks like."

"What, no! I know what love looks like, and I'm not blind to it. It's that I haven't seen it directed at me except from him."

"You know, not everyone shows love in the same way."

"If there is a man out there that will love me, he isn't here in Europe. He must be somewhere else because I haven't met him."

"And you want to wait until you return home before finding this man?"

"Yes, I do."

"I can see the logic in that, but I also think if you believe you know where and when you will meet this person, then you never will."

"I don't think I know when or exactly where, but I'm sure it will not be in Germany. Besides, I really shouldn't be with someone here."

"Pain has a way of making us view the things around us differently."

"Right now, I'm done with men."

There was a knock on the door, and Ingrid poked her head in. "Frau Wagner wants me to do the rounds with Eva." She looked to Dr. Möller, making sure he was fine with it.

"We are finishing up," he told her.

Eva cleared the table, putting the dishes back in the bag she brought. Most days, she and Dr. Möller shared their food. He reminded her of her dad. Even though they didn't look alike, they acted similar in many ways.

She followed Ingrid to the east wing, not looking forward to doing the night rounds. They did it with the lights off so they wouldn't wake the patients, which made it harder to see what they were doing. Eva went to the first bed and took the clipboard off the end.

"So, how was France?" Ingrid whispered.

"It was fine."

"What did you do there?"

"I visited some old friends."

"Did you find it hard to resist the French men when you lived there?"

"I don't know that I would say it was any harder to resist them than men of other countries."

"Come on, with their dark hair, blue eyes, and silky voices, you could resist that? Besides, aren't they supposed to be romantic?"

"Silky voices…?" Eva asked, giving her a sideways glance.

"You know, because they speak French."

Eva chuckled. "Your ideas of men are amusing but mistaken."

"Why are you laughing? I'm being serious."

"I know you are, and that is what makes it so funny. There is more to a man than his looks. Of course, that helps, but that is not the most important thing."

"Then what would you say is?"

"I would say the way he treats you. Does he really listen to what you have to say and try to understand you, take an interest in things you like, and go out of his way to be kind? Does he do nice things for you, make you feel safe and protected, and look out for your well-being? Things like those are important, as are his character and his values. Does he make you feel loved?"

She blinked at Eva. "Those are things you look for in a husband, but I'm talking about a sexual partner."

"I know you are, but I have never been with a man only for that. Every man I have ever been with, I was in a relationship with."

"You have never wanted a man only for that?"

"Not really."

"I have been with men for what they could offer me, then when they had nothing more to give, I would leave them."

"That seems cruel," Eva told her. She didn't agree with men using women, and she also didn't think it was right for women to use men.

"Is it? But men do that to women all the time."

"I suppose they do."

"What if there was a man that you didn't like, but it benefited you in some way to be with him? You wouldn't sleep with him to get what you wanted?"

"You are talking about using people, and I am not comfortable with that, Ingrid. Have you ever had an actual relationship with someone?"

"Not one that lasted long." She fiddled with her fingers.

"Have you asked yourself why that is?"

"No, because I haven't wanted something serious yet."

"Well, OK then."

"You should really try it sometimes," Ingrid said with a childish smile on her face.

"What?"

"Being with a man for the pleasure of it and nothing more."

"I don't know…" She trailed off, not wanting to have this conversation anymore. Eva hung the clipboard on the end of the bed and then went to the next patient. "Anything exciting happen while I was gone?" she asked, wanting to change the topic.

"Not really, the usual. However, there was a Jewish woman who was escorted out of the hospital. She was in here seeking medical care, and they told her we can't help her kind, her kind being a Jew, I mean."

"I knew what you meant, Ingrid."

"Dr. Koch called the authorities on her."

"Of course he did," Eva said. She was not fond of Dr. Koch. He had an air about him, and there was always arrogance in the way he talked to people.

She changed bandages and administered medicine, then went to the different operating rooms to make sure they had all the supplies they would need for an operation before she left. "I'll see you tomorrow," she said as she walked past Ingrid.

"You work tomorrow?"

"Of course." She went to the nurse's station to change. While she was putting her skirt on, Frau Wagner came in and closed the door. "Eva, I should not have to remind you that nurses are not supposed to fraternize with the doctors."

"I am not fraternizing with any of the doctors. Dr. Möller and I are only friends. There is nothing romantic going on between us."

"I know that is what you tell people, but I have my doubts."

"I am telling you the truth. It is not like that between us. He is old enough to be my father. I am in love with someone, but it's not him."

"Even that kind of relationship at work between the doctors and nurses is not permitted."

Eva buttoned her skirt but didn't look at Frau Wagner. "We are not doing anything wrong."

"It can interfere with work and the proper functioning of

the hospital."

"It doesn't, and you know that. We both perform at our peak, and our friendship does not impede our work."

"Make sure it stays that way." She shot Eva a warning glance before leaving the nurse's station.

June 20th, 1941

Eva focused on the music box in her lap, hoping this time she wouldn't witness something as unpleasant as the last time she rode the tram. She was using the time it took to travel across Berlin, hoping to muster the courage to see Gerhardt's fiancée. There is no way of knowing what to expect when they meet. Would she be pretty? What would his fiancée think about her showing up on her doorstep? Eva didn't even know what to say. But before she worried about that, she still had to go into the Reich Main Security Office to get the address, that is, if it was even possible to.

Eva was checking the street signs, and when Prinz-Albrecht-Straße came into view, she stood. She cradled the music box in her arm and stepped off the tram in front of the five-story building that stretched the entire block. It was an impressive structure, fitting for the purpose it was used for. The sight alone was intimidating. She could only imagine the things that went on inside. At the front of the building were two guards, one on each side of the door. They were the uniforms of enlisted soldiers, holding rifles to their sides like statues. Neither of them moved as she passed to enter the building. She obviously didn't look intimidating enough for them to worry about.

The inside of the building matched the outside in color and panache. It had high ceilings with arches and a balcony overlooking the main lobby. Eva went to a desk near the front to figure out where she needed to go but then realized she didn't even know what to ask.

"Can I help you, Fräulein?" the man behind the counter asked, eyeing her suspiciously.

"Well, I am trying to find someone. I have something that belongs to Hauptmann Gerhardt von Schulz's fiancé, but he has been deployed elsewhere. I only know her first name but not her last name or address. I thought I might get that information here."

"Did he work here?"

"No."

"Then how will I know that?"

"I know someone who works here that I believe could get it for me."

"Who do you know?"

She actually knew two people who worked here, but she would never ask for Bauer. "Oberst Heinrich Schmitt," she said, weirdly wishing she hadn't asked right after saying the words.

"You know the Colonel?"

"I do. Is he here today?"

"Yes, but he's in a meeting."

"I can wait."

"If you like. You may sit over there." He pointed to a bench in the hall opposite the doors.

She forced a smile and went to sit on the bench. Over an hour passed before the man at the desk came over to her.

"They are out of the meeting now. He has been told you are here and instructed that you wait for him in his office, so I will take you to the second floor."

"Thank you, but if you tell me how to get there, I'm sure I can find my way."

"I'm sorry, but I have to escort you there. Civilians are not allowed anywhere other than the lobby unless being escorted in the building."

"Oh, I didn't know."

"This way." He gestured down a hall towards a set of elevators, and she followed. They took it to the second floor and stepped out onto a hall, stuffy from the stale cigarette smoke. It was not as impressive as the lobby, with off-white walls and light grey carpet covering the floor. The doors lining the hall were finished in a glossy chestnut brown, making them stand out in contrast to the walls.

He opened a door halfway down the hall. "In here," he indicated with a wave of his hand. She entered the large, spacious room, and he came in behind her. "Sit here at the desk, and he should be in soon. When you are finished, I will escort you out."

She nodded and took the seat he pointed to. He left the room, and she leaned back in the deep, soft leather chair to wait. It was an elegant office with a single, large window overlooking the street, a substantial mahogany desk in the center, and a fireplace at the back. A portrait of Hitler framed with gold edges hung on the wall to the right of the desk. It took up a large portion of the wall, and beneath it was a serving table with crystal bottles filled with liquor, lined with four cups neatly beside them.

The door behind the desk opened, and Heinrich walked in, his face lighting at the sight of her. "Eva, how nice to see you again. To what do I owe the pleasure?" He sat in his chair, and she took the one across from him.

"I need some information and thought maybe you could help."

"Tell me what it is, and I will see what I can do?"

"Do you remember the man I danced with at the ball?"

"I do." The words were drawn out.

"Well, he is engaged, and I have something that I believe his fiancé should have, but I don't know her last name."

"What is his name?"

"Hauptmann Gerhardt von Schulz."

"The name does sound familiar."

"His fiancé's first name is Emma," she added.

"What department did he work for?"

"He actually didn't work here. He worked at the Reichstag."

"Should you not have gone over there? I'm glad to see you, but you probably will have better luck at the Reichstag."

"I had thought about it, but I didn't know who to ask, and they might not tell me, even if they knew. That is why I came to you."

"I will be glad to help if I can, Eva. Let me go talk to some people, maybe I can find something out."

"Thank you."

He disappeared behind the door, and she took a minute to ponder what she would say if successful in finding his fiancée. She kept turning it over in her head but every time arrived short of an answer. Heinrich wasn't gone long before he came through the door again.

"I have her last name. It actually was easier to get than I thought."

"Oh…" Eva was surprised.

"Her name is Emma Weber. She lives on 742 Kanalstraße in Oranienberg."

"How did you find out so fast?"

"It so happens that he knows a few people here who also know his fiancé." He held out the piece of paper to her, and she rose from the chair, reaching across the desk to take it.

"Thank you so much." She took it from him and put it in her purse.

"It is not a problem. So, I hear that you recently went to France with this man. Can I ask what that was about?"

"You can. We used to be together, but not anymore. We went as friends to France because that is where we met. I guess you could say we were nostalgic for the way things used to be."

"But he is gone on deployment now, you say?"

"He is. I know that we are not together anymore, so it is not my place to be worried, but I do. I don't know what he is doing or where he went, so I can't say how much danger he is in."

"He is your friend, and it is only natural to worry. I'm

sure he is fine, safe, and well behind a desk somewhere."

"I would like to think that, but because I don't actually know, it is hard not to worry."

He gave her a slight smile. "Put your worries to rest. He will be alright."

She didn't have to ask. It was clear there were things he wasn't saying. He was trying a little too hard to reassure her, which meant something was possibly amiss. It was likely he knew if Gerhardt was going to Russia, but of course, he couldn't tell her that. But did he know more?

"I'm sure you are right. I have to go to work tonight, so I better get this to her soon. Thank you again for getting the information for me."

"You must come back to see me again. I am having a get-together at my house in a few weeks. I would love it if you could make it to the gathering. It will be fun."

Surrounded by German officers in a room filled with cigarette smoke, what would not be fun about that? she thought sarcastically. "I will have to see if I can make it. That's too far away right now to know my schedule."

"Think about it." He took her hand and kissed it the old-fashioned way men did in those days.

Chapter Eighteen

✠

June 21st, 1941

A large gilded door knocker shaped like a lion's head stood in contrast against the massive oak door. Eva took the ring hanging from the lion's mouth and rapped it several times. After a few seconds, a woman in a black and white maid's uniform pulled open the heavy door. "Yes?"

"Is Emma home?"

"Who is asking?"

"I am a friend of her fiancé, Gerhardt, and I have something that I would like to give her."

"If you give it to me, I can take it to her."

"No, I need to give it to her myself. Please, is she home?"

"She is." The woman looked Eva up and down as if unsure whether she should let her in but finally stepped aside. "Wait in the drawing room, and I will retrieve her.

What is your name so I can tell her who is calling?"

"Eva Abrams."

She led Eva to an ornate room decorated with rare items that had to come from as far away as Africa. Eva sat on a light violet-colored satin couch. On each side were two tropical trees in porcelain pots. This was an imposing house with expensive furnishings, but none of which surprised Eva. Gerhardt came from a wealthy family, so it was no wonder that she did as well. Her house was a stark comparison to Bauer's nice but humble apartment, which he shared with his mother.

"Wait here," the maid told her and disappeared out of the room.

While Eva waited, she removed the music box from her purse and set it on her lap. She wanted to hear it one last time before she gave it up, to think of him and the time they had together. She twisted the small crank at the bottom and opened the lid, closing her eyes, the lullaby filling the air, taking her to a different time. Goosebumps spread across her body as the image of their time in the meadow lit in her mind. She suddenly felt hot, and her cheeks pricked with the memory of his touch.

"Hello," a smooth, high-pitched voice interrupted her thoughts.

Eva's eyes shot open, and she closed the lid a little harder than she had intended, the loud bang echoing in the room. "I'm sorry I didn't see you come in," Eva said, standing from the couch.

"My maid said that you know Gerhardt and have

something for me."

"Yes, I do." Eva pointed to the couch across from the one she had been sitting on. "If you will have a seat, I can explain."

The woman looked curiously at her but went to the couch and sat. She was tall and thin, with golden blond hair that fell in ringlets around her slender shoulders. Her eyes were the lightest blue Eva had ever seen, and her skin the complexion of cream with the slightest hint of peach in the apples of her cheeks. There was not a single scar or blemish on her skin, it was perfect. Eva had expected his fiancée to be pretty but was a little perturbed that she was this stunning. Of course, she was. Why would she be anything else?

"Gerhardt gave me this music box that belonged to his mother, but I thought you should be the one to have it."

"Why would he give it to you?" The way she eyed Eva was questioning but also scrutinizing.

"Because—"

"Wait, you are the one he had a fling with while in France," she said, cutting Eva off.

How did she know about that? He must have told her. And fling, was that all it was to him?

"Yes, we were together for a time in France while you two were separated. I don't know that I would say it was a fling, though." The way his fiancée described her and Gerhardt's relationship was upsetting. She tried her best to push it aside and extended her hand, holding the music box out.

Emma stood and came to stand in front of Eva, taking

the box from her hand. Emma spoke as she looked down at it. "You know, I didn't know what you looked like or even what your name was, but ever since I found out you existed, I have known that he loved you more than me."

Her words surprised Eva. "I don't think that is true. He chose you, not me," Eva reminded her.

"He did choose me, but you are his real love. When he looks at me, I think he is really seeing you." She moved her gaze from the music box to Eva. "But that is fine. I can live with it. I can live with the thought that you will always have a part of his heart. Do you know why?"

Eva shook her head. "No."

"Because I have a part of his heart too, and I have him, and that is more than you ever will."

Eva knew exactly why she told her that. She wasn't trying to be kind. The intentions were clear, and she meant to wound. Eva decided to play off that assumption, and instead of responding defensively, she would be nice. "I know, and that is why I am giving the music box to you. You are the one he is marrying, so you should be the one to have it."

"You are right. It should belong to me. I suppose you know they have deployed him?"

"Yes." She concentrated on the patterns woven into the rug. "Do you know where they sent him?"

"Sadly, no. But I hope he comes home soon."

A lump formed in the back of her throat. She knew he would be gone for a very long time and possibly would not return at all. "You never know. This war is crazy."

"Indeed, it is."

Eva stood. "I am sorry to show up at your door like this and then leave, but I have to be at work soon."

She glanced at the box in her hand. "I understand."

Eva was led to the door by the maid and shown out. It had gone better than expected. Actually, she didn't know what to expect. But Emma spoke the truth. He would be hers someday if he returned. All she was left with was the memory of their time together.

June 21st, 1941

After work, Eva caught the tram to Grunewald Forest to meet with Helmut. It had been a long time since their last meeting. The attack put all of Berlin on alert, forcing them to keep a low profile.

Helmut was standing by the shore of the lake inside the park. "You look worse for wear," she said as she approached.

"I have been moving from place to place and have had little time for personal hygiene."

"What have you heard about the attack? Do they suspect anyone?" she was afraid they had.

"They don't seem to, not yet, at least. We are planning a new assignment. We want to blow up some rail lines out of Berlin. You won't be going with us to do this, but we wanted to see if you can get any information on troop movements in the area."

"What part of Berlin were you thinking?"

"Probably the west side. That is where a lot of their supplies come in."

"Maybe you should focus on the rails in the east."

"Why?"

"Because a little birdie told me they will attack Russia in a few days?"

"What…!" Shock resonated in his voice. "Who told you this?"

"I can't tell you, but the source is reliable."

"This could change the whole outcome of the war." The thought of this reflected on his face, in the way his lip pulled at the corner, and his eyes stared past her.

"It absolutely will." It was crazy how much more she knew than him, and the Germans too, for that matter."

"I need to tell the others. We will need to rethink our plans. Meet me back here at the same time a week from today."

"I'll be here." She turned and walked back to the tram stop. She sat at the back, not noticing the familiar rocking of the car as she replayed the meeting with Helmut. His reaction did not surprise her. It was going to take him and the others a while to wrap their heads around that news.

As the tram approached her apartment, she stood and waited by the door until it came to a stop. Stepping off onto the sidewalk, she entered her building and climbed the stairs two at a time. When reaching the apartment door, she took the key out, but something white on the floor poked part way under caught her attention. She bent down and picked up an envelope with the Red Cross symbol stamped on the back.

She turned it over; Jon's name and an address in England were stamped on the front. Her heart skipped a beat. *Oh my God, he has found me a way home.* She unlocked the door and hurried into the apartment, throwing her purse on the floor. She tore the letter open and dropped down on the couch.

Eva,
I believe I might have found a way for you to come home. I know this will be difficult, but you need to get to France. We are planning a night trip by boat over the English Channel on Monday, June 30th. We will leave from Dover and should be at the Sangatte beach by midnight. If we are not there right at midnight, wait half an hour, and if we still are not there, leave. It will be too dangerous for you to stay any longer. If we do not come, it means that something has gone wrong, and another coordinated pickup date will be planned. If the trip is successful, you should see a flashing light coming from the beach. It will blink SOS three times. Please remember the information I have given you and destroy this letter.

-Jon

Eva read over the letter several more times, then took it to the kitchen and lit it with a match, watching it catch fire, turning to ash as it fell to the counter. She was excited and nervous, her hands shaking and her palms sweaty. She almost didn't dare hope that this plan would work. She was finally going to go home, but how would she get another pass to France? Gerhardt was always the one who procured them for her. Maybe Heinrich could get her one. She hated asking him for another favor, but she absolutely had to have it. It was only three days until Germany invaded Russia. Maybe she could get one before then because if she waited, everyone would be too busy to worry about a pass to France for a nobody.

She scraped the ashes into the trash, then went to the desk in the living room, taking a pen and paper from the drawer. She wrote a letter telling Jon that it was unlikely she could get a pass to France that quick, but she would try. She asked if he could change the date and that she hoped to have a pass by the end of next week. She folded up the letter and put it in an envelope, licking the flap and sealing it. She wrote the address that was on Jon's envelope onto hers and put it in the care of the Red Cross. She grabbed her purse off the floor, stuck the envelope in it, and then hurried out the door.

After dropping the letter off at the nearest Red Cross office, she took the tram to the Reich Main Security Office. It gave her chills every time she entered that building. To her, it was the worst place in Berlin. It was where they dealt with overseeing foreign affairs, including the Jews, and she knew what that really meant.

The same man who helped her last time led her to Heinrich's office and left her there like before. She had to wait longer this time for Heinrich. He seemed hurried and preoccupied when he entered.

"Eva, it is nice to see you again, but now really is not a good time."

"I am sorry to bother you, but I really need a pass to France that is good through June. I have a friend that is sick and might not make it. They have asked that I be there." She hated lying to him, but it was necessary.

"I am so sorry to hear that. I would love to help you, but right now, I can't. I have a meeting that I am already late for. Why don't we discuss it at the party? I should have more time then."

"The end of next week?" she asked, the panic rising.

"Yes," he said, surprised at her sudden alarm at waiting.

She faked a smile. "Yes, we can talk about it then. It is not a problem." She stood from her chair.

"Great, don't forget to come," he said, pointing at her as he turned to walk around his desk.

"I won't." She could not afford to now.

He hurried past her, this time not stopping to take her hand. It must be the invasion tomorrow that had him in a tizzy. As soon as the door closed behind him, she quit smiling, and her emotions settled into panic. This was disconcerting.

June 26th, 1941

There was excitement in the city. The invasion of Russia was on all the radio stations and everyone's lips.

"What do you think about Germany going to war with

Russia?" Ingrid asked.

"I think Germany doesn't need to be fighting a war on another front."

"Don't let anyone else hear you say that," Klaus said behind her, causing her to jump.

Her heart beat like it was going to jump out of her. "Give a warning next time you come up behind me."

"Be glad it was me and not someone else." He focused on her, his face fixed in a stern expression. "How is he doing?" he asked, referring to the patient she was helping, not giving her time to counter his warning. It was a young man missing his right arm, face charred and no hair on his blackened, scabbed scalp, leaving him forever deformed. The wounded men were already pouring in from the front. It was already taking its toll on Germany and would only get worse with time. She worried every day that one of the patients would be Gerhardt.

"He is doing as well as can be expected."

"We can only presume that this is the kind of thing we will see from now on," he said.

"Do you think it will always be this bad, men coming in with wounds like this?" Ingrid asked.

"No, I think it will become much worse." A hint of sadness seeped through in his baritone voice.

He didn't know how right he was. "Ingrid," Eva said.

"Yes."

"Liesel, Heidi, and I are going dancing tomorrow night. Do you want to come?"

"Yeah, of course, I want to come. Where are you guys

going?"

"We haven't decided yet. If you want to meet us at our apartment at seven, we can all go together. Here is our address." She handed Ingrid a folded piece of paper.

Ingrid took it from Eva's outstretched hand and stuck it in her apron pocket. "Thank you for inviting me."

Eva flashed her a smile. "You are welcome."

It was two days until the party at Colonel Schmitt's house, and she was going to make it a point to go. She needed that pass. Literally, her future depended on it.

After work, she took the tram to Potsdam, then walked to the small grocery store near their apartment. When she arrived at the store, there was already a line of people outside. Now, with the war raging on the eastern front, food was rationed even more, and people wanted to make sure they got their grain, loaf of bread, roll of cheese, pint of milk, eggs, sugar, oil, butter, and cube of meat, making the queues even longer. It wasn't much, but it had to last. People only got to use their food coupons once a week. The little food was for her, Liesel, and Heidi, so they had to stretch it the whole week. Hopefully they weren't out of what she needed by the time she reached the front. Almost every day, Eva was hungry. Not the kind that made your stomach cramp, but the kind that was constantly there in the back of your mind.

When it was finally her turn, she handed over the coupons and smiled at the clerk. He was a young blond-headed boy, probably in his early twenties, who was always kind when she came in. She often wondered why he was not fighting with the other young men his age but always decided not to ask.

"How are you doing this fine evening, Miss Eva?" He always used her first name instead of her surname, which made her feel more welcomed.

"I am doing alright. It looks like you have been busy this last week."

"Oh yes, with the war now in the east, people are concerned that they won't get their food, and they worry it will be rationed again. They are trying to get as much as they can while it's still available."

"I understand. That is what I am doing."

"These are hard times."

"They are and will probably get worse."

He didn't respond but quickly looked away and put the food in the mesh bag she brought. I'll see you again next week."

"You can count on it."

She walked down the narrow street back to the apartment, the mesh bag digging into her fingers. It reminded her of her second encounter with Gerhardt, which felt like a lifetime ago. She retrieved the key from her purse, not knowing if Liesel or Heidi were home. When she reached the door, she tried the knob, and it turned. She pushed the door open, and Heidi and Liesel's voices echoed in the apartment. The smell of food wafted in her direction. She carried the bag into the kitchen and set it on the table.

"What are you making?"

"Soup with the remaining vegetables before they go

bad," Liesel said. "Did you go to the market?"

"I did."

"Oh, good. I was going to go but haven't had the time."

"I invited Ingrid to go out with us tomorrow," Eva blurted.

Liesel stared at her while stirring the soup, completely silent. "That should be fun. Has she been to any of the clubs before?" Heidi asked.

"I'm not sure. I didn't ask."

"Will she be meeting us here?" Liesel's expression was unreadable.

"She is. I gave her our address. I hope it's alright. I didn't even think to ask you guys first?" Eva wasn't sure they liked Ingrid, especially Liesel.

"It's fine. I know that you work with her a lot. We should get to know her better, too," Heidi said. "Oh, and you had a letter at the door when we got home," Heidi said, exchanging a glance with Liesel.

"What?" Eva asked, excited. She hoped it was from Jon, then remembered she had only recently sent him her reply.

"Who is the letter from?" Heidi handed the envelope to Eva, the back facing up.

She hurried and turned it over to see where and who it was from. The stamp on it was from St. Petersburg, Russia, as was the sender's address. "It's from Sergei," Eva said, a little surprised.

Liesel looked up from the pot of steaming soup. "The man you went to Russia with?"

"Yes, but I don't know why he is writing me a letter,

especially now."

"Well, open it and see what he wants," added Heidi, the anticipation in her voice unmistakable. It was so easy to get Heidi excited.

Eva tore the letter open, pulled out the paper, and unfolded it.

Eva,
I wanted to ask you about something you had said to me that night at the ball. We were discussing the German man that you had been with when you made a comment that the...

She trailed off. "I think it is best if I read this alone."

"Why?" Heidi whined.

"Because some of it is personal." The truth was, she would have been fine reading them the whole letter if he had not mentioned her saying not to trust the Germans. She had completely forgotten she had even said that.

"Alright, have your secrets then," Heidi said, a little upset she would not read the rest of the letter aloud.

"It's not that, Heidi. It's something I would rather keep to myself. It's not like you don't keep things from Liesel and me."

"She is right, Heidi. We both know you don't tell us everything. No one does. She is allowed to have her secrets, like the rest of us," Liesel interjected.

"Fine," Heidi grumbled, still annoyed. She slid off the chair and moved to the counter to put away the food.

Eva went to her room, closed the door, and sat on the

bed, continuing where she had left off.

...Germans could not be trusted. At the time, I didn't think much about what you said, but now I have to ask myself why you said that. How did you know they couldn't be trusted? You are not German but only live among them. Perhaps there is more that you have not said. If there is, I implore you to tell what you know; you could save many lives. I don't know if you can get a letter to me, but I ask you to try.

-Sergei Ostrovsky

She refolded the letter and held onto it. Why was she so careless? How could she let something like that slip from her lips? There had to be a way to explain what was said. She hid the letter under some clothes in her drawer and retrieved a piece of paper and a pen, then sat at her small desk in the corner to write an explanatory letter. She kept it short, writing she only said those things because of all the alcohol, coupled with anger towards a German at the time, so she felt resentment towards all of them. She explained that what was said meant nothing, that it was only the ravings of an angry woman who was intoxicated and to give it no more thought. She folded the paper and put it in an envelope, sealing it. She would mail it tomorrow on the way to work but didn't know if any mail would reach Russia now. She had hoped the letter was from Jon. She was worried that he could not schedule the rescue for another date. She understood how hard it must have been for him to set that one up and how risky the whole operation was. Jon would not be the only person coming, so planning another landing could be difficult.

She lay on her bed and curled into a ball, hugging one of her pillows. It was no surprise that her thoughts turned to Gerhardt. What was he doing right now? Was he safe? Was he happy? Was he alive? Did he have enough food? Was he getting ready for bed and thinking of her the way she was thinking of him, or was he thinking of Emma? Her mood shifted with the belief that he was thinking of Emma and not her. The wave of sadness that always came when she thought of the two of them crashed over her. She knew it wasn't fair that the thought of them together made her feel bitter. They both deserved to be happy, independent of her. Because she was miserable, it didn't mean they had to be.

"Whatever," she said, tossing the pillow behind her. She slid off the bed, deciding that her time would be better spent getting ready for bed than bemoaning the loss of Gerhardt and thinking ill thoughts towards him and his fiancé.

June 27th, 1941

The loud music and excitement helped keep Eva distracted and her thoughts off Gerhardt. They filled the room with drinks, laughter, and dancing. When men asked her to dance, she didn't tell them no this time. Who cared if they were German? They were still men. It wasn't like she was going to sleep with any of them, and they were the only men around, so what was the harm in dancing with them? She already worked with them, lived amongst them, and cared for them at the hospital, so why not this? No one could accuse her of fraternizing because she was already doing that simply by being in Germany.

"I'm glad to see you are finally getting out there," Heidi said when Eva returned to the table from the dance floor.

Eva tipped her head back and took another shot of whisky. "I figured, why not? There is nothing stopping me."

"Exactly, that is what I have been saying," Heidi reminded her.

Tonight, she was freer and more alive than she had been in a long time, and she had to admit that some of the men who asked her to dance were cute. Maybe dancing with the Germans was a mistake, but right now, she didn't care. She was having fun.

"Eva, come dance with me," Ingrid called from the dance floor.

Eva slid off the chair and met Ingrid in the crowd. The room looked like it was spinning, and she loved it. She wanted to be daring and seductive but recognized it was mostly the alcohol talking. As they danced, she rubbed against Ingrid, and the men watched in awe. She doubted that any of them had ever seen someone dance like that. She was doing a kind of dance you would see in the movie Dirty Dancing. The look on Ingrid's face was of intoxication and confusion, but she seemed willing to go with it. Eva stood with her legs apart and squatted close to the floor while holding her dress up to her thighs so she wouldn't stand on it, then slowly rose as she rubbed her hand through her hair, brushing it away from her face. It was not in a bun like usual but hung freely around her shoulders. She rolled her hips and rubbed both hands down her sides and over her otter thighs. All eyes in the room were on her, and it felt strangely alluring. The music she was dancing to was not being played by the band in the club but in her head. It was music from her time, music you could really dance to.

Her whole body was feverish from the constant movement and proximity to Ingrid. She normally didn't like this kind of attention, but the alcohol in her system made her brave. She didn't know exactly how much was running through her veins right now, but it made her feel good.

Ingrid was trying to keep up with her moves but was struggling, so Eva took one of Ingrid's hands in hers, put her other one on Ingrid's hip, and began to move Ingrid's body in sync with her own. Ingrid's cheeks were flushed, and not only from the alcohol.

"Where did you learn to dance like this? I have never seen anything so provocative."

"I don't know. I think it must be the alcohol, but I'm enjoying it while it lasts."

"And it doesn't bother you that all the men in the room are watching us?"

"Not right now, it doesn't, but it probably will tomorrow."

"I think all the men in the room want to have sex with you."

"Maybe, but none of them are getting any." It made her feel powerful, knowing she could have that effect on most of the men in the room and yet deny them. It was the first time since she came to this time that she felt powerful and in control. It gave her a sick sort of pleasure to know that she could play with the emotions of the German men. They were the enemy, strong and powerful, yet they were still simply men, like any other, and tonight she could bring them to their knees.

She danced until she was tired, then returned to the table. The sweat on her body was making the dress damp, causing it to cling to her in a strange way as she walked. It was only then that she realized the room was quiet, deafeningly silent. There wasn't even music playing, and no one spoke, but all eyes were on her. The men and the women both. That is when a twinge of embarrassment for what she had done started to surface. Many of the men in the room had suggestive looks on their faces, lust in their eyes, and some simply looked confused. But the women looked shocked, angry, or perhaps disgusted.

Heidi cleared her throat, but it was Liesel who spoke. "What the hell was that?"

"Honestly, I don't know. Maybe we should go." Eva glanced around the room again, no longer wanting everyone staring at her.

"You think?" Liesel said sarcastically. "Besides, it is one-thirty in the morning, and we are out way past curfew without permission."

They got their purses and left the club, keeping to the

shadows on the walk home, trying not to be seen. If a patrol didn't drive by, they would make it without any consequences.

After they were back at the apartment, Eva lay in her bed, staring at the ceiling as she played the night's events over in her mind. Now that some of the alcohol had worn off, she was horrified. Why had she done that, and why did the other girls let her make such a fool of herself? Even worse, she had drug Ingrid into it. She would never go back to that club ever again. At least she didn't know anyone there except for Ingrid, Heidi, and Liesel. She remembered Ingrid's question on the way home. "Why did you do that?" she had asked.

"People who are in pain do stupid things." That was all Eva could say in response. What she did was stupid, but dancing like that felt good at the time. It felt exhilarating. It was such a high, like being on drugs, but unfortunately, she was now experiencing the low that followed the high.

Chapter Nineteen

✠

July 5th, 1941

The party was already well underway, and Eva had yet to see Heinrich. She was starting to worry that he wasn't at his own party. She needed him to be there. He was her best chance of getting home. He had the power to get a pass to France and was the most likely person to do so, especially now.

She stood near the open window. Car fumes and factory smoke drifted inside, and the faint hint of cooking food from one of the nearby houses traveled with it. All the outside smells were still more tolerable than the thick plume of cigarette smoke that polluted the room. It wasn't as strong near the open window, and the gentle breeze felt nice. It was suffocating being in a confined space with that many people smoking. Besides, most of the men in the room made her skin crawl, anyway. She didn't want to mingle with any of them. She was happier alone by the window and was only here for one reason. Then she planned to leave shortly after getting what she had come for.

Searching again for Heinrich, she spotted him near the door on the far side of the room, talking with someone. She sat her drink in the windowsill and was getting ready to walk over to him but stopped, noticing that he was talking with another officer. The man's back was turned towards her, but judging by the expression on Heinrich's face, they were having a conversation he did not like. She decided it was best to wait until they were done before approaching him. She went back to the window and watched the men talk, sipping the champagne she had left on the windowsill. Heinrich's face was austere, and he nodded his head a lot during the conversation. He pushed his round, wire-rimmed glasses up on his nose with his index finger, then patted the other man on the upper arm. The man walked out of the room without ever turning around, and she realized he never removed his cap or uniform jacket. Obviously, he had not intended to stay. She was happy that Heinrich was now free to talk.

She sat her glass back on the windowsill and made her way across the room towards him. When she was almost to him, he turned, smiling warmly at her.

"Eva, I am happy to see that you could make it. Have you been here long?"

"Yes, but I only noticed you a few minutes ago. I would have come over sooner, but you were talking with someone."

His smile faded, and he took her arm, leading her to the

edge of the room. “Eva, I wanted to tell you that I tried to get you a pass to France but could not secure one.”

“What… why?”

He opened his mouth to speak but was unsure how to answer her question. She anxiously waited as he struggled to choose his words. “Eva… I was informed when I inquired about a pass that there has been a travel ban placed on you.”

She tried to process what he said. The panic was forming in her chest, rising to her throat. “A—what?” she asked in a slightly higher-pitched voice than usual.

“It means that you cannot leave Germany or even Berlin.”

She tried to think past the fear that was clouding her mind. “Why would there be a travel ban on…” she paused mid-sentence, nervously rubbing her forehead, rethinking her question. “Who would have done that?”

His hesitation did not go unnoticed. “I’m not sure who gave the order, and I was not told why there was a travel ban placed on you.”

“So you don’t have any idea who it was?” If he had even a suspicion, she wanted to know.

He contemplated his words carefully. “I can’t say for sure. It was probably no single person who made the decision, but was decided based on a file they must have on you.”

“A file?” This night was going from bad to worse. The Germans having a file on her had never crossed her mind. “Do they have a file on everyone?”

“No, I suspect not.”

"Why would they have one on me, then?"

"Maybe because you are American, or something you have done has made them suspect you."

"I haven't done…" She trailed off, remembering the times that Bauer had taken her in for interrogation. "If they had interrogated someone in the past, would there be a file on them?" she asked, already suspecting the answer.

"Yes. Have you been brought in before?" His face was one of surprise, and his tone was disbelieving.

She was sure he must be a little shocked at that knowledge. "I have, on several occasions, actually." She averted her gaze.

"Oh, for what?"

"I honestly don't know for what. The same person has brought me in every time. He is convinced that I am guilty of something, even though he has no proof. The officer's name is SS Obersturmbannführer Bauer. Do you know him?"

His eyebrows shot up. "I do know of him."

"Is he the one that put the travel ban on me?"

"I believe he is, yes." He said the words slowly, like he was unsure what he should say.

"But… but he is in France." She struggled to finish the sentence.

"He doesn't have to be in Germany to give that order."

The sudden need to sit down hit her. She took a few clumsy steps to the nearest chair and plopped in it. *That bastard.* Of all the times he could have put the ban on her, it had to be now, right as her way back home was finally at hand.

"I will see what I can do, but there is no guarantee I can get the ban lifted," he cautioned.

"But you outrank him."

"It doesn't matter. That is not my department, so he has more say regarding things like that than me. I can maybe go over his head and talk to his superior and try to have him apply pressure, but I'm afraid that will be my only option. If he says no, there is nothing else I can do. My hands will be tied. That is really our only avenue."

"So, how would you get it removed?"

"I can only ask them to remove it, but it has to be someone in that department who actually does it."

"You mean the Gestapo," she said with acid.

"I understand your anger, Eva, I really do, and I wish I could do more to help, but this is war, and they have to take every precaution they feel is necessary."

"Do you know how tired I am of hearing excuses because of this war!" she hissed. First Gerhardt and now this, things couldn't be worse. She hated that she snapped at Heinrich, but this was so unfair.

"Look, why don't I take you home. I'm sorry that the party had to end this way. And as soon as I know anything, I will let you know."

She nodded and stood, almost wishing she didn't know the truth.

On the ride home with Heinrich, she couldn't shake the feeling of being pulled down into the quicksand that was this war. The pressure was crushing her, and soon her head would be under, and the air would be gone.

The car pulled in front of her apartment, and Heinrich put his hand on top of hers. “I don’t want you to worry too much about this. I hold a lot of sway in the Reich and with the high command. I’m hoping I can pull some strings and get the ban removed, but I also don’t want to give you false hope. Remember what I said at the party. It might take some time and possibly won’t happen at all.”

“I remember, and I appreciate you trying.”

He patted her hand. “Have a goodnight.”

She smiled and stepped out of the car. She watched it drive away, then went up to her room and closed the door, not wanting to talk to anyone. She was so mad that she could break something but knew it wouldn’t help. What she really wanted was to punch Bauer in the face and hope that it knocked out a few of his teeth. She wanted to scream, fight, and cry, but all she did was lay on her bed and stare into the darkness. Tomorrow, she was going to write to Jon and tell him what had happened. How was he going to get her out of here now? More like, could he get her out at all now?

July 6th, 1941

Work passed in a blur. All she could think about was how trapped she felt.

“Eva, where are you at today?” Ingrid asked.

“I’m here.”

“In body. But in your mind, you are somewhere else,

somewhere far away."

"Is it really that obvious?"

"Yes, it is."

"I'm sorry. I have a lot on my mind right now."

"Do you want to talk about it?"

"Not really."

"Well, whatever it is, you don't seem to be happy."

"I'm not, and I'm trying not to think about it."

"Alright, I will distract you. Do you remember the guy that asked me to dance before our… whatever that was we did on the dance floor?"

Eva couldn't help but smile at Ingrid's words. "Yes, I remember."

"Well, I have been seeing him since then, and I think it is getting serious."

"Oh, really? That is exciting. I'm happy for you." Eva tried to show interest, but it was hard to focus on anyone or anything right now.

"Last night we were together, and we… well, you know."

"I take it you are saying you had sex with him?"

She giggled. "Yes."

"We are two adults. You can say what you mean. You had sex with him, and you only now think it is getting serious?"

"Yes, and we are serious, I think."

"Was this your first time?"

She looked insulted. "No!"

"I hope you were being careful."

"You sound like my mother."

"I am older than you."

"Not old enough to be acting like my mother."

"You are right, but I am old enough to know more about life than you. Look, I'm not trying to tell you how to live yours, but I do say what I see as obvious to those I care about."

She smiled. "You care about me?"

Eva held her hand up with her index finger about a quarter of an inch from her thumb. "Maybe this much."

Ingrid swatted her on the arm. "I know you are joking."

"Are you sure about that?"

"Yes, I'm sure."

Eva smiled and went back to taking inventory of the medicine. Without warning, the memory of her parents, brother, and her friend, Jenny, assailed her, intruding into her thoughts. She had not allowed herself to think of them in... well, to be honest, she could not remember the last time. Frankly, it was too painful, so she suppressed the thought of them most of the time. Maybe it was because Ingrid reminded her in some ways of Jenny. She was younger and a lot less mature, but she did have personality traits that were the same. Eva wished she could see their faces again and hold each of them. Her chest tightened as tears stung her eyes. She wanted to sit on the floor and cry. The feeling she had tried to hold back for so long hit her like a raging bull. When they said bye, she didn't know it might be the last time. In the beginning, it was easier to hold back that fear because the belief that eventually, she would go home sustained her, but now the doubt was growing that it would ever happen, and for the first time, that fear was real and not simply in her head.

“Eva… are you crying?” Ingrid gently touched her arm.

Eva rubbed her cheek, the tears wetting her fingertips. “I guess I am.”

“What happened? You were fine a minute ago, and now you are crying.”

“I remembered my parents. It’s been a long time since I’ve been home, Ingrid, and I miss them.”

Ingrid rubbed her back. “It will be alright. You will see them again.”

“No, Ingrid, I don’t think so.”

“Why would you say that? Of course, you will see them again.”

Simply knowing how the war ended wasn’t enough. It was all the things that happened in the middle that she didn’t know or understand that would govern her life now and determine if she lived or died. Sure, the war would end, and the allies would come out victorious, but would she emerge from the smoke and debris of this war also victorious? Doubtfully. She had already given up too much to reach the other side, the same as she was when she entered. She had lost so much, like a soldier who was missing a limb, only her pain could not be seen with the eye. Yet she felt that phantom aching of something that had once been there.

“No, Ingrid, for far too long now, I have been staring into the abyss, and I am exposed and vulnerable. I no longer see the light, only this seemingly bottomless chasm.”

"What are you talking about? You have the gift of happiness. You cheer me up in a way that no one else does. Yeah, this war is awful, but spending time with you helps me forget that."

"Ingrid, I am so happy that my presence makes this war easier for you to bear. I only wish someone was able to do that for me."

"I thought you had someone who did."

"Once, but he is gone now."

"Doesn't your shift end soon?" Ingrid asked.

"It does."

"Why don't you go home, and I will finish up here."

"I don't mind staying."

"No, get some sleep. There is not a lot left to do, anyway."

Eva wrapped her arm around Ingrid's shoulders. "You are a good friend."

"I try. Now go."

Eva laid the rolls of gauze back on the cabinet shelf and picked up her purse. The trams didn't run this late, so she had to walk home. She was in her uniform and felt safe being out after curfew, but if they still didn't believe her, they could ask the hospital.

Chapter Twenty

✠

July 6th, 1941

The hot summer wind blew the bottom of her uniform, flapping against her knees. She lifted her head upward towards the blanket of stars. Under normal circumstances, you couldn't see the stars while in the city, but with the war, you could always see them after nine on a clear night because of the lights out and curfew the Germans imposed on everyone. The city was quiet and calm, and she enjoyed her time alone. She felt like it gave her a little bit of clarity. Now that she had time to think, she realized that she should not give up hope of going home. The war was still going to end, and the Germans were going to lose. That much she knew. If it meant waiting until the end, then that is what she would do.

Engines rumbled behind her, and the headlights from the vehicle shone on the road in front of her. She looked over her shoulder to see who was driving by. A government car, followed by a covered truck, was only a block behind her. The car and truck pulled to the side of the road and stopped. *Keep walking unless they tell me to do otherwise. They can see that I am in a nurse's uniform, and they won't bother me*, she told herself. She looked forward and kept walking, hoping she wasn't wrong.

Doors opened and closed, and then footsteps clicked on the sidewalk behind her, but no one spoke. It was uncomfortable now, so she picked up the pace. Because no one told her to stop, she wondered if they were there to put posters on the walls or something of that nature. Out of nowhere, she felt her body roughly being pulled backward and struggled to get free, but it was useless. She was quickly overwhelmed and stunned by an open-handed blow to the side of the face that knocked her to the ground. Then, it was over as soon as it had begun. A hood was pulled over her head, then two men escorted her to the car and threw her into the back seat. A chill traveled down her spine, and her heart beat a heavy thump against her ribs. This could not be happening again. What had she done? Did this have something to do with her wanting a pass to France, or could it be about the bombing? She didn't know what else to do except scream, so she shrieked so loud it hurt her ears, and then she was met with another blow to the head. Her eyes watered as pain shot through her face. This was different from all the other times they had taken her in. Never before had they hurt her like this. She was more frightened now than she had ever been. This time was going to be much worse. Her heart beat so fast it felt like it might explode, and she was close to vomiting, partly from the pain in her head and partly from fear.

The car drove for a while, then stopped, but she didn't know how much time had elapsed. It seemed like forever and only seconds at the same time. They pulled her from the car, her feet dragging on the pavement. She could tell that they were going up steps but didn't know where, although she had an idea. She pulled against the powerful grip of the hands, but they dug their fingers harder into her skin.

"Stop," one of the men yelled, jerking her so hard that her arm popped at the shoulder. They took her to a room and roughly shoved her into a chair. They removed the hood, and standing in front of her was a large man in black slacks with suspenders over a half-unbuttoned white shirt. His sleeves were rolled up, exposing muscular arms. His hands were on his hips like he had been waiting for her. One of the men who had drug her into the room started ripping her uniform off, throwing it to the floor. When he was done, she was only left with her thin white shift. Tears streamed down her cheeks freely, her throat closing as she struggled to breathe, but she pulled in as much air as she could, willing herself not to faint. The man in the suspenders came to stand in front of her and, without so much as a word, punched her in the stomach with his large-fisted hand. She doubled over, her head almost between her knees, and lost the contents of her stomach on the floor, some splatting on his shoes. He hit her again. This time, her vision blurred as her breaths came in sharp, stabbing gasps. She fell out of the chair onto the cold floor.

He pulled her up by one arm as if she was a doll and sat her back in the chair. “We know that you are in the resistance. Tell me the names of the other people and what you are planning next, and this will all stop.”

“But I’m not in the resistance,” she choked out. “I’m a nurse. I know nothing of plans or names of people in the resistance.”

He slapped her hard across the face, her neck popping as her head snapped to the side. “Tell me their names,” he yelled, putting his face close to hers. The stench of his hot, putrid breath was unbearable, turning her stomach.

A painful burning sensation radiated from her cheek up the left side of her head, and she cried uncontrollably. Her mouth had gone dry like it was full of cotton, and when she swallowed, her tongue stuck to the roof of her mouth, making a clicking sound when she pulled it away.

“I don’t know,” she said through aching, deep sobs.

He slapped her again. Blood ran from her nose onto her lip, the metallic iron taste seeping into her mouth. “But you do know.” He kicked the chair, and it tumbled backward, hitting the floor, her head making a loud thud as it impacted the concrete. The pain at the back of her skull pulsed a throbbing that caused a loud ringing in her ears. The drumming of her heart pounded against her temples.

He lifted the chair with her in it, then pulled it across the room with one hand to a sink, tipping it forward. She fell out of the chair onto the floor. He lifted her, then dunked her head in a tub filled with water. He held her under with one hand and the other he had on her upper back to make sure she couldn't get up. As the breath she held burned her lungs, she wondered if he was going to leave her there to drown. Her lungs hurt more with every second, and she was about ready to take a breath full of water when he pulled her up. She sucked in a gulp of air and then another. He grabbed her hair and jerked her head back with his powerful arm. He put his face next to hers again. "What-are-their-names?" he intoned.

He was inches from her, and body odor, coupled with the stench of his breath, washed over her in an unpleasant squalor. "I don't know." Her body shook, making it hard to speak.

In one sudden movement, he submerged her head again, and this time, he kept her under for longer. She finally could not hold the air in anymore and took a breath, sucking in water. The burning of holding her breath was nothing to the burning in her lungs now. She fought wildly, her feet slipping in the water that had splashed on the floor. When he pulled her up the second time, she could hardly take a breath. Finally, she drew in a long, sharp gasp that seared like hot coals. It hurt so badly, and she didn't think it could get worse until the muscles in her stomach cramped, and she started coughing up water. It was like razors in her lungs, scraping and cutting.

"Are you going to tell me now?"

"I don't know anything." Her voice was weak and hoarse.

"Fine, we can do this the hard way." He squeezed his fingers around the back of her neck and walked her to the middle of the room as another man pulled the chair. He forcefully sat her back down, then went to a table covered with tools and began selecting one from the row. He picked up a pair of pliers and walked back to her. "Maybe if I take a fingernail, you will remember their names."

Her heart was thudding painfully, and the now slow beats were like a muffled drum in her chest. She was on the edge of her endurance; her maximum limit had been reached. She choked back another sob as the fear consumed her, and the control she had over her body was gone. The tears poured down her face, and she could no longer hold her bladder. The warm pee soaked into her shift and ran down her legs, forming a puddle on the floor between her feet. He came up beside her, grabbed hold of her right hand, and took one of her fingers. She screamed when the pressure of her nail pulled against the skin, and then the darkness swallowed her.

She opened her eyes, vaguely remembering being dragged through a corridor to a cell. She blinked against the darkness and could barely make out a concrete wall in front of her. The only light came from a tiny window on the outer-facing wall. The rough cement pressed against her back, and the hard, cold, concrete floor beneath her felt like ice, and she couldn't control her body from shaking. Every part of her throbbed, and her hand was covered with fresh and dry blood. She sat up, leaning against the wall, crying as the room spun around her. She tried to clean her hand with her shift, but it was covered with dirt and smelled of stale urine.

Footsteps echoed from down the hall, and she was overcome by panic. She slid to the corner at the back of the cell and wrapped her arms around her knees. The sound of a key being put in the lock clinked through her cell, and then the heavy door groaned as it opened. Two men came in and walked straight toward her.

"Nooo," she screamed when they took hold of her arms. "No, not again, no!" She fought as hard as she could, but they didn't loosen their grip, and her muscles were weak.

The men took her back to the room she had been in before, and the same man was in there waiting. The sight of him scared the hell out of her. She was like a wild animal that had been cornered and thrashed against the grip of the two men harder than before, not caring anymore if she hurt herself in the process. The large man came over to her, and with one punch, she was out. She was brought to by a bucket of water being poured over her head.

"You didn't think you would get off that easy, did you?" He picked up the pliers and came towards her.

She thought death would be better than this, although that is how she was sure this was going to end. Helmut's words telling her that everyone breaks eventually sounded in her mind like he was there telling it to her now, and then she remembered the pill he had given all of them. She did not have hers there now and was surprised to find herself wishing that she did.

She fought against the restraints they put on her, the rope cutting into her wrist, and only succeeded in tipping the chair over. He went to her side, knelt, took her hand, and then pulled another fingernail off. She screamed and cried, wishing that the darkness would take her again, but it didn't this time. He set her chair up and stood in front of her, holding up the pliers with her nail still in them so she could see.

"Next time, it will be a finger. Now, what are their names, and what are their plans?"

Trying to talk through the tears and snot, she faintly said. "I don't know anything. You have the wrong person." She honestly didn't know how much longer she could hold out.

"Do you know how we found you? One of your buddies gave you up, and another one of your buddies gave them up. That's right; you are not the only one we have here. One of you will eventually tell us who the leader is, and all the rest of the names will follow, as well as all the plans."

She understood now why people broke. She was seriously contemplating giving up their names so it would stop. Before she could speak, or he could take another fingernail, or worse, a finger, the door opened, and two men entered. The large man with the pliers went to talk with them. She listened to them talk, but one voice stood out over all the others, Bauer's voice. She lifted her head and turned towards the door. Bauer was speaking to the man who had only seconds ago been torturing her. Bauer looked right at her, but his face was expressionless; his eyes betrayed no emotion. He held her gaze for a fraction of a second before turning back to the man. She could not hear what they were talking about because they kept their voices low, but she had a foreboding in the pit of her stomach that one of the others broke, and that was what they were speaking about.

Without a second glance in her direction, Bauer left the room, and the man in the suspenders came back and stood next to her chair. He untied her hands and told the other two men to take her back to her cell. They each took an arm and pulled her down the hall, her feet dragging on the ground, then dropped her on the cell floor before closing the door, leaving her in the dark. She didn't even try to move from the spot where they left her. She hurt so badly and didn't care if she lived or died at this point. She was thirsty, hungry, and beyond exhausted; they had not given her food or water since they brought her in, and she wasn't even sure how long ago that was. This had to be what it was like if you were kept awake for a week. She closed her eyes and squeezed the tears from them. There was such a foul smell in the air, but she didn't know if it was coming from her, the cell, or both.

She jolted awake when the cell door opened, but she was too tired to fight this time. They hauled her off the floor and dragged her down the hall, but instead of bringing her back to that room, they took her down a flight of stairs and through a door. Soon, she was in the night air as they escorted her to a car. They put her in the back seat and threw her clothes, shoes, and purse in with her but did not get in. The only other person in the car with her was whoever was driving. They shut the door, and the car began moving, but she didn't sit up to see where they were going. Her mind was clouded, and even though she was lying down, disorientation, like wading through a bog on a foggy night, surrounded her.

Though the seat was soft, it hurt to lie there no matter how she turned. Her body throbbed on the outside and the inside, especially her fingers, stomach, and lungs. The car finally came to a stop, and the man who was driving got out and opened the back door, pulling her into a sitting position. He grabbed her things and helped her out of the car, supporting her up the steps to the front door of the apartment building. He took the keys from her purse and unlocked the door, then helped her up the flight of stairs to her apartment. He handed her the keys, bag, torn clothes, and shoes. Then, without saying anything, he turned and walked away. Once he disappeared down the stairs, she let the tears flow, sliding down the wall. She cried and screamed, pounding the floorboards with her fist, even though it hurt. She did not know what else to do; the emotions were too overwhelming; she felt like she was drowning in them. So badly, she wanted something to numb the pain, all of it.

The door opened, and Liesel and Heidi paused in the doorway, looking down at her. “Oh my God,” Liesel cried out, hurrying to her side and kneeling. They both took an arm and helped her into the apartment, sitting her on the couch. “Eva, what happened?” Liesel asked softly.

Through the tears, all she could get out was Gestapo and torture. “Let’s get you cleaned up.” They helped her to the bathroom, turned on the tub faucet, and then pulled her shift over her head. Eva stepped into the warm water, and it felt strange, like she hadn’t bathed in years.

“I’ll get you some clean clothes, and Heidi will make you something to eat,” Liesel said.

They closed the door, and Eva slid into the water. Her head, being shoved into a tub, came rushing back. Her lungs still hurt and probably would for a while. Lifting her fingers to eye level, she focused on the missing nails, then dropped her gaze to the bruises covering her body. Even though the nails would grow back, it was like a part of her was missing that she would never get back, and she cried at the loss.

Heidi had brought her some food as Liesel bandaged her fingers and face. All she wanted to do was sleep because she didn't have the energy for anything else. Her body was bruised, and her mind was spent. Her emotions were a whole other thing, muddled and beyond comprehension. They were there, swirling and raging inside, but she blocked any attempt they made to rear their ugly heads. She would work on processing them later. Because the only way to sort out each emotion and deal with it was to compartmentalize everything that happened.

Chapter Twenty-One

✠

July 9th, 1941

The last few days blended together, blurring into one long block of time. Eva, neither physically nor mentally, was ready to face the world or the emotional trauma that would eventually need sorting. Sleeping away the hours kept the haunting memories at bay. Heidi and Liesel insisted that she go to the hospital and get checked by a doctor, but Eva refused. The desire to not interact with Germans was stronger than her need for medical attention. They made Dr. Möller aware of what had happened, and he asked to visit her at the apartment, but they told him it was too soon.

Heidi and Liesel finally convinced her to leave the apartment and go on a walk with them to the nearby park. They thought some fresh air and a little exercise would do her good. Eva was starting to feel a little better until she caught site of two soldiers patrolling their street on the walk back and panicked.

"Eva, you need to talk to someone about what happened," Liesel insisted.

The night they found her, Eva decided to leave out most of what happened while detained. It was painful to talk about, and it would be painful for them to hear.

"I can't, Liesel."

"Do you know when you will return to work?" Heidi asked. "You are missed."

She shook her head. All she wanted to do was hide in a dark corner and cry, but that wasn't healthy or sustainable.

They returned to their building, and when Liesel put the key in the lock, the elderly woman who lived in the apartment next to theirs opened her door and stepped out into the hall.

"I was waiting for you all to return. There was a gentleman at your door. I could hear the knocking from my apartment. I asked if he needed anything, and he said no but inquired if Eva was home. I told him that you were all out. He gave me this letter and stated that I was to give it to you, Eva." She held an envelope in her thin, wrinkled hand.

Eva's heart raced, thumping hard against her ribs, a bout of dizziness washing over her. The Gestapo had been here for her. "You said, man, there was only one?" Liesel asked the woman.

"Yes, only one man. He wasn't in a uniform. He wore a suit, but the way he carried himself, I could tell he had to be military."

"Did he give a name?" Asked Heidi.

"No, I asked his name, but he never told me. He simply said for me to give you this letter, then left." The woman held it out, and Eva's hand shook as she reached for it. "It's alright. I didn't get the impression this man was here because you were in trouble. But he was very insistent that you get the letter."

"Thank you," Eva told her. Once they were inside, Eva went to her room and closed the door. This time, Heidi and Liesel didn't ask her why. She held the letter but was afraid to open it or even see who it was from. After several minutes had passed, she mustered the courage, broke the envelope seal, and unfurled the thick parchment paper.

Miss Abrams,
If you will allow me to visit with you, I would like to clear up some things. I know I'm probably the last person you want to see right now, but I feel I should explain some of the events that have taken place as of late.

SS Obersturmbannführer Bauer

She tore the letter into tiny pieces and threw it on the floor. No doubt this was some kind of trick. They probably released her, hoping she would lead them to the others. She was not about to suffer the company of Bauer, not after what happened. The look on his face when he saw her in that chair told her all she needed to know, that he was the one who put her there. He had to be the reason she was arrested. He certainly didn't seem to be surprised when he saw her, and the chances of her making it out alive if arrested again were slim. After everything she had done for him while he was hurt, this is how he repaid her? How could someone be that heartless? Was anyone really that cold and callous? She hadn't thought so before, but he sure changed her opinion about that. That night he proved to her that someone could be. She would never help him ever again, and the priest was wrong about everyone deserving forgiveness. He did not deserve her forgiveness or her kindness. *I should have let him die on that stretcher. I know that now. I made the biggest mistake of my life by saving him.*

She picked the pieces of paper off the floor and threw them in the trash can. She decided to go to bed early because she wanted to return to work tomorrow. She wasn't planning on going back so soon after what happened but needed some normality in her life. She put on her PJs, slid under the covers, and pulled the chain on the lamp. Her thoughts wandered to what the man torturing her had said about having caught others from the resistance. Who had they caught? It could not have been Helmut because he said they were still looking for the leader. A fear built in the pit of her stomach like acid that, by now, all of them had been arrested, which meant they would be coming back for her. She tried to push the worry away but knew she would eventually have to find out what happened to the others. This must be why Bauer had a travel ban put on her. He did not want her to escape.

July 10th, 1941

The following day, Eva dressed and ate her breakfast in a rush, hoping to visit the church before work. She rode the tram to the stop where she always got off. Unlike all the other times she visited the priest, walking to the church now made her uncomfortable. Anywhere in Berlin made her paranoid now, always worrying the Germans were watching, and any minute, someone would grab her from behind and put her in the back seat of a car again. It was like waiting around for your own death; you know it is coming, but you don't know when or where, and there is nothing you can do to prevent it.

She continually looked over her shoulder, checking to ensure no one was behind, but no one was even close. She looked forward but stopped in her tracks, the air hitching in her throat. Two soldiers were near the church doors talking while they smoked. They didn't seem to be on the lookout, simply conversing with one another.

She considered turning and going home, but thought it was silly to believe they were there for her. How could they possibly know that she would go to this church on this day and at this exact time? She hadn't told anyone and only decided to go this morning. She drew in a deep breath and sauntered forward, trying to appear casual, but her pulse increased the closer she got. When she reached the door, the two soldiers stopped talking, turning their heads in her direction, and she froze.

"Fräulein," one of the men said. "Is everything alright?"

She honestly couldn't speak. She was paralyzed with fear. She looked at them, panic in her eyes. She was like an animal who just walked into a trap. Their concentrated stare was suspicious, and her eyes were fixed on them, too, not moving.

"Can I see your papers, Fräulein?" one man asked, stepping towards her.

In an instant, her mind snapped to flight mode, and she bolted. She pushed her body, her feet pounding the sidewalk in the opposite direction.

"Stop," one of them called from behind.

She didn't stop or slow. Instead, she sprinted across the street, almost getting hit by a car. It came to a screeching halt before honking, but she barely noticed. All she focused on was the thumping in her ears and the clicking of the heels on the pavement. Her muscles hurt, her lungs burned, and her mouth was dry, but she didn't care. There was no way she was stopping. She was beginning to think there was a chance of escaping until colliding with three more soldiers who were waiting to cross the street. One of them grabbed the back of her dress, almost tripping her, and held the fabric tightly until the other two soldiers caught up.

She screamed and struggled in the man's grip, but it was no use. Her strength could not compare to his. He probably had a foot or more on her and weighed one and a half times what she did. When the other two men reached them, one of them yelled at her.

"Why are you running, huh?"

"I didn't do anything," she hollered.

"You didn't show me your papers when I asked, and then you ran, and someone only does that if they have something to hide. Let's see what you are hiding." He pulled the purse from her shoulder and opened it, taking out her ID. "Eva Abrams. You are an American." He glanced from the ID to her. "Maybe that is why you ran."

"It is not a crime to be American," she voiced.

"No, it is not, but maybe that's not why you ran. Judging by the bruises on your face and the bandage on your hand, I'm guessing this is not the first time you have been apprehended."

"What should we do with her?" the man restraining her asked.

"Take her in. Let them deal with her at the Reich Security office."

"No, don't take me there, anywhere but there, please!" She could not go back to that place. She would rather jump off the bridge than go back into that building. In a moment of overwhelming panic, she tried to punch the man holding her.

"Don't do that," he hissed, grabbing her wrist. "Stop struggling, or I will have to add to those bruises on your face," he threatened.

They took her to a car parked a few blocks away and put her in the backseat, a man sitting on each side while the other one slid into the driver's seat. For the first time, she noticed people had stopped on the street to see what was happening and felt a little like the Jewish people.

The car stopped at the front of the building, which had become so familiar to her now. They took her to a small, dimly lit room and pushed her into a chair, then left. She frantically scanned her surroundings but couldn't see a sink or table with tools. They must not use this room for torture, only interrogations. She had been left alone, sitting there, not knowing what was going to happen next.

She waited for what seemed like forever. No one came in, but shoes clicking on the shiny marbled floor echoed on the other side of the door, but that was it. They would be wondering at the hospital where she was, but there was nothing she could do. She stood from the chair they sat her in and eyed the door, apprehensive at first, but ran to it, pausing only inches away. She leaned forward, putting her ear to the cool wood. Muffled voices of people walking by filled her ears. After they were gone, she gave it a few more seconds to be safe, then tried the knob, and to her surprise, it turned. She peeked her head around the door and stared down a long, well-lit hallway but saw no people. The idea of escaping was tempting, but she would never make it. She didn't even know where in the building she was. Maybe it was worth it anyway? It was better than staying here to be tortured and possibly killed. It was odd that she hadn't been cuffed and was left unguarded. She opened the door wider, but voices came from the stairwell. Instinctively, she closed the door, hurried back to the chair, and sat down. The panic rose, pressing on her ribcage, as her sweaty palms gripped the armrests of the chair. The pin and needle sensation that always accompanied a spike of adrenaline spread across her body. An anxiety attack was building, and she concentrated on her breathing, trying to even it. She wouldn't survive a repeat of last time.

The door opened, and a man in an officer's uniform came into the room and then closed it. She didn't look in their direction but could see him in her peripheral. She stared down at the glossy wood of the table, close to hyperventilating as tears blurred her vision. The man came and sat across from her before laying down a folder and opening it.

"Why did you not show your ID when you were asked?"

She tried to catch her breath and speak. She lifted her eyes from the table to the man who was burning a hole in her.

"Because they scared me," she managed to say through tears.

"Why did they scare you?"

"Because men like that, and men like you, are the ones who did this to me." She pointed to the bruises on her face. "And this," she said, holding up her hand to show him the bandage.

He didn't say anything but looked down at her folder. He picked up a piece of paper, the words handwritten and not from a typewriter. He scanned it, then returned it to the folder and closed the flap. He scooted his chair back, the feet screeching on the floor, and stood up, giving her a side glance as he walked past. He opened the door and called to someone in the hall. A man in an enlisted uniform came into view, and the officer leaned close to him and said something in a low voice. The man nodded, then disappeared, and the officer stepped into the hall and closed the door behind him, but there were no retreating footsteps. He was waiting on the other side.

Not long after the soldier left, multiple footsteps approached in the hall, then men's voices sounded on the other side of the door. She didn't know what was going on, but it was making her more nervous by the second.

The voices stopped, then footsteps leading back down the hall grew faint. The door opened, and Bauer stepped into the room, the sight of him causing her to jump out of the chair, stepping away from the table. He went to the chair that the other man had been in and took a seat.

"Sit down, Miss Abrams."

Warily, she sat down out of fear of what he would do if she didn't.

"Somehow, I am not surprised to find you here again," he said, going through the papers in her folder.

"I did not do anything," she said in a shaky voice. She hoped he could not tell how terrified she was.

"I hear that you ran when asked to show your ID. You can see how that would look suspicious." He lifted his head from the folder and focused on her face, occasionally glancing down at her hand, so she moved it off the table and laid it in her lap. "Why did you run?" he asked.

"Why do you think?"

"I don't know. That is why I'm asking."

"Because I didn't want to be brought here again."

"And yet running was the very thing that brought you back."

"You and I both know me being brought in again was inevitable."

"Do I… is there something you want to tell me?"

"You want me to be guilty of something and always have. You will stop at nothing until I'm in prison or dead."

"What a wild imagination you have." He closed the folder and rested his hand on top of it. "Did you ever get the note I left for you?" he asked, dismissing her accusation.

"I did, and then I tore it up and threw it in the trash."

He pursed his lips, a slight furrow between his brows as he stared pointedly at her, an icy coldness in his demeanor. "Did you read it?"

"Yes. But I don't care what you have to say."

"Well, seeing how you are the one being detained and I the one with the power to release you, I am going to tell you, and you will listen. I know you believe me to be this awful person who has a stone heart, but you are wrong. For the record, I am not the one who had you arrested. I am the one who had you released. You are lucky. I had only just arrived in Berlin when I was made aware of your arrest. If I had not gotten here at that time, you might have been shot or, at the very least, still be in prison."

"I don't believe you, or if you did, it was for some ulterior motive."

"Of course, you think that. Like I said, you can be one of the stupidest people I have ever met. You can't see what is right in front of you, and you think what you see is reality. I know your kind."

"You don't know me," she said with such venom it surprised even her.

"I believe I do quite well, actually," he stated, unphased by the contempt directed at him.

"If you are the one who had me released, then why did you have a travel ban put on me?"

"As long as there is a war, you will not go home. Need I remind you that you are a prisoner here in Germany, even if you are not in a cell."

She was not sure what he meant by that exactly, but at the same time, it made a certain amount of sense to her. Since being here, she has felt like the people in the song Hotel California. You can check out, but you can never leave.

"What do you mean by that?" she asked.

"I mean, there are too many things that make you look guilty, so why would I let you leave?"

"Then why have me released?" She was so confused by his actions.

"I am not at liberty to discuss that with you. I'm afraid it is classified."

"Classified? Oh my God, you are so full of shit."

He leaned partway over the table and spoke in a lowered voice. "You know, one of the reasons I had you released is because of how you treated me while I was at the hospital and then at my home. The fact that you saved my life is something I still grapple with, but regardless of how I feel, it is you who is ultimately responsible for that. So, I thought I would return the favor. Don't make me regret that decision, or next time you find yourself here, I might treat you like any other prisoner." He stood. "You were supposed to be at work already, correct?"

She nodded. "Come with me, and I will have my orderly take you there."

"Why are you not in France? Aren't you supposed to be the head Gestapo officer there?"

"Yes, but right now, I'm needed here." His tone suggested annoyance at her question.

"Why are you here, and Gerhardt is not?"

"Do you really think that I am going to discuss military decisions with you?" His piercing eyes glared at her as if she just asked him to divulge Hitler's next move. It was silly to think he would actually give her an answer.

She followed him into the hall and to the elevator. When the door opened, they both stepped in, and she made sure to stand on the other side, as far from him as she could get in the confined space.

"One more thing," he said. "My mother has taken ill. I want you to go to the apartment each day to check on her until she is well."

"Maybe she should go see a doctor."

"There is no reason. She only needs someone to help with things around the apartment while she is unwell because I'm gone most of the time. You can monitor her and make sure her condition doesn't worsen."

Did she say no or give in, accepting that he now felt like

he had complete control over her? He has made that abundantly clear time and time again. “For how long?” Like a fool, she decided to ask instead of saying no.

“I don’t know, it depends on the length of time it will take for her to get better, so however long she needs. She will let you know when your services are no longer required. You can start tomorrow.” The way he worded it was so matter-of-fact. He led her to a car waiting out front, and his orderly opened the back. “Take her to the hospital.”

“Yes, sir.”

As the car moved through the streets of Berlin, she tried to wrap her head around the events of the past hour. How could anything he said be true? It didn’t make any sense. It all must be part of some greater plan of his, but that still doesn’t explain what the other man said. Who had they caught from the resistance?

After the car dropped her off at the hospital, she hurried inside and went to the nurse’s quarters first to put her purse away.

“Eva, where have you been?” Ingrid said surreptitiously as she entered the room. “Oh, my… your face, Eva.”

“I know. It looks worse than it is.” In truth, it felt worse than it looked, but she didn’t want to tell Ingrid.

She took Eva’s hand and inspected it. “Heidi told me that they pulled out some of your nails.”

She snatched her hand away. “Yes, they did, but the nails will grow back.”

“Where have you been today?”

“They arrested me when I ran from some soldiers who

asked for my papers."

"Why did you run?"

"Because they scare me, Ingrid," Eva yelled, not trying to be mean, but Ingrid didn't understand. "I can't see any of them now without being consumed with dread, so much so that I struggle to breathe."

"What about the patients and the doctors?"

"I don't know, but I'm sure I will soon find out."

"How did you get out? Were you able to prove to them your innocence?"

Eva wasn't sure she wanted to disclose the details of her release to Ingrid but then decided she might be the one person she could tell.

"Remember that man you asked me to help you with, the one whose life I saved?"

"Yes, I remember him."

"I told you I knew him a little before that day. I actually knew him when I lived in France. He is the head of the Gestapo there, and he spends his time between France and Germany."

"I knew it. I saw that you knew who he was when he came in."

Eva folded her arms and paced. "He found out that I was being detained and decided to have me released as a favor for what I did for him."

"See, saving his life paid off."

She stopped. "Did it? Maybe he only said that, and it's not even true, or he had me released, hoping that I would lead them to someone or something."

"No, I don't think so."

"Ingrid, sometimes you can be so naïve. You don't know him like I do. He is a snake. No, that is too good for him. He is like a parasite."

"Why do you hate him so bad?"

"He has had me arrested in the past."

Ingrid's eyes grew wide. "I… didn't know that."

"Yes, and he probably had me arrested the last time too, not today, but the one a few days ago."

The door burst open, and Frau Wagner walked in. "Should you not be doing something other than gossiping in the nurse's quarters, Ingrid?"

"Yes, Frau Wagner." Ingrid hurried past her out of the room.

"Why were you late today, Miss Abrams?"

"I am very sorry, Frau Wagner, but I was detained this morning because I did not show my papers when asked."

"Why would you not show your papers?"

"I don't think there is even a point in trying to explain my reasons."

"Why don't you try me."

"They scared me, so I ran. Men in suits and uniforms frighten me now."

"I see. I understand why you would feel that way, but it is an irrational fear. Unwarranted."

"No, see, that is where you are wrong. It is not unwarranted. They are the ones that had me arrested. Who else besides old men, little boys, and men in the SS and Gestapo are left in Berlin? I have no reason to fear the boys and old men, but I do have an excellent reason to fear the men of the SS and Gestapo. And don't tell me it was my fault that I got arrested all those other times. The only time it has been my fault was today. There is a reason they have released me every time. Because their accusations against me were unfounded."

"It indeed appears you have been mistreated by some of them, but not all, and they are only doing their job."

"I don't want to hear how they were simply doing their job, or it is their duty, or it's the war. I am so sick of hearing that." She slammed the door to her locker and walked past Frau Wagner, who did not try to stop her. Eva went to Klaus's office to look for him, but he was not there, so she went back down to the main floor and inquired about his whereabouts. One of the other doctors told her he was near the back-loading dock sorting the many wounded men who had come in that morning. She went to the rear of the hospital and out on the loading dock, witnessing the chaos unfolding before her. Doctors and nurses were running around in a flurry, trying to check on each patient.

She spotted Klaus at the far end and hurried over to him. "What can I do?"

"Eva," he seemed surprised to see her, and the sight of her face and hand registered quickly on his face.

"Please, tell me how I can help. Give me something to do, and I will do it."

He pointed to some patients near the open doors of the loading dock. "Check them over and see which ones need surgery first. And Eva, come and see me in my office once this is sorted out."

"I will." She started with the patient nearest to her. When she saw his wounds and the blood-stained clothes, the image of her fingers, bloodied and without nails, appeared in her mind's eye. She flinched. *Can I do this?* she asked herself. *Of course, I can. I am strong. I am strong. I am strong,* she repeated over and over in her mind like a mantra.

Eva could not help with the surgeries because of her fingers, so she waited until Klaus was done and met him in his office. He put his hands on her shoulders and stared down at her face. He then took her chin between his fingers and turned her head from side to side, inspecting her bruises. "I am so sorry, Eva. I wish I could say that I'm surprised they did this to you, but I'm not."

She was able to fight back the tears until he pulled her from the chair, taking her in his arms and hugging her tightly to his chest. They flowed down her face, soaking into his shirt.

He put one of his hands on the back of her head and held her tighter. "Shhhhh," he said softly. It only made her cry harder.

"I don't like it here, Klaus. I want to go home."

"I know, and I wish you could."

"I can't do it anymore. He is squeezing the life out of me little by little."

"Who is?"

"SS Obersturmbannführer Bauer."

"Who?"

"That man that I asked you to save."

"Why would he do that?"

"Because he hates me."

He pulled her away from his chest to look at her face, dropping his arms to his side. "Why would he hate you, Eva?"

She told him about what happened between them in France and then here in Germany.

"But he wants you to take care of his mother?"

"Yes, only I don't understand why. I think he wants to keep an eye on me."

"Maybe he thinks you will do a good job based on your care for him."

"No, I don't think that is it."

"Did you ever consider that maybe he is a private person and you are the only one he has allowed into his home, and so he feels more comfortable letting you tend to his mother than he would a new person?"

She sniffed. "No, I have not considered that. I have only considered the fact that he is a seriously disturbed individual."

"Maybe if you do this, he will leave you alone."

"He will never leave me alone. All I know is that I should have never saved his life."

"Eva, you cannot be saying these things, not even around me."

"I don't care anymore. Maybe it would be better if he hurried and killed me, putting me out of this misery I am in every day."

"You don't mean that."

“I do. Life is not worth living when it is like this.”

“Things won’t always be this way, Eva. It has to get better, and it will.”

“It doesn’t feel like it ever will.”

“Not right now, but if you give it time, things always get better. Come here.” He motioned for her to return to his arms. She gladly went into them with a shuddering sigh as his fatherly arms wrapped her in love and safety. He reminded her so much of her dad, and she was thankful for him. “Maybe you can kill him with kindness,” he suggested.

“I tried that when he was here in the hospital, but he continued to be mean and hateful towards me.”

“But he released you because of what you did for him. Even though it didn’t seem like it at the time, you had an effect on him. Continue to treat him with kindness, and maybe he will keep you from being arrested again. You could have died in there if he hadn’t gotten you out. People who are arrested for suspicion of spying or being in the resistance don’t make it out of there alive. They usually torture you until you talk, then put you up against a wall and shoot you, and that is if you are lucky.”

If Klaus was trying to scare her with what could have happened, he succeeded. She hated this country and could not wait to leave and be free of this awful entanglement she found herself in. Maybe she didn’t need Bauer to lift the travel ban if someone could forge the documents for her. Why hadn’t that thought come to her sooner?

Chapter Twenty-Two

✠

July 11th, 1941

Lifting her hand, Eva reluctantly knocked on the door to Bauer's apartment. The trepidation was mounting at the idea of him being there, but because it was midday, she was counting on him being at work. She held her breath as footsteps approached from the other side but relaxed when his mother opened it.

"Miss Abrams, Wilhelm told me you would be here today. Please, come in." Eva stepped past her into the apartment and waited for his mother to tell her what she wanted. "Oh, don't just stand there, dear. Take off your shoes and have a seat." Eva promptly slipped off her shoes, went to the sofa, and sat at one end, leaning against the armrest. She expected his mother to sit at the other end, but instead, she took the middle cushion close to Eva.

"Is your son here?" Eva asked, discretely glancing around the room.

"Oh no, he is working. He is always so busy."

"When does he go back to France?" She hoped the answer would be soon.

"You know, I am not sure. I think he might be here for a little while longer. He never told me exactly what he was doing, but he said something about there being a lot of things that needed taking care of in Berlin."

Of course he does. "He said you have not been feeling well. Have you seen a doctor?" Eva asked.

"Yes. I have an upper respiratory infection. He gave me medicine for it. He told me to get a lot of rest, and I do, but I still get worn out easily during the day."

"Your son said you would let me know what you needed help with."

"Yes, it would be nice if you could assist me around the apartment."

"Around the apartment?" Eva asked, the anger beginning to boil deep inside.

"Yes, he said you offered to help when you learned I was ill."

"Did he… well, he must have been mistaken. You realize I am a nurse, not a maid?"

She eyed Eva with conjecture. "Yes, of course. So, you didn't offer to assist?"

"Nope." Eva could hardly keep the anger out of her voice.

"Maybe he misspoke, or I heard him wrong."

"Let me tell you what he told me. He said I was to come to his apartment because you were sick, so of course, I was led to believe that it was to check on your health."

"He did say that you would be doing that as well. You don't have to stay if you don't want to or have other things you need to do. I didn't know there was a misunderstanding."

Eva regarded the apartment. It could use a little tidying up. The sink was half full of dirty dishes, and laundry was piled in a basket in the hall. "No, I don't mind helping. I will do the dishes and laundry. Are you hungry? I can make you something to eat?"

"That would be nice, but I think I can manage that. I know you came over here under false pretenses, and I am sorry. It's that he worries about me. We are all each other has."

Her words made Eva feel bad, but she understood it wasn't intentional. His mother made some for both of them while Eva worked on the dishes.

"Tell me a little about your family, Miss Abrams?"

"Please, call me Eva."

"Eva. What a pretty name. Mine is Marie, and you may call me that."

"Well, Marie, my mom and dad are still alive, and I have one older brother."

"Oh, what is his name?"

"Thomas."

"And is Thomas in the military?"

"No, because he is an only son."

"What does he do then?"

"He is a musician and plays the guitar in a band."

"Does he make a lot doing that? How can he support a family with that kind of work?"

"He doesn't have a wife or children, so I guess to him, there is not much incentive to make lots of money right now."

"I suppose if he only supports himself, then there is no need yet. What about you? Are you married or have children?"

"God, no." After saying it, she realized how it sounded. "I mean, not right now. I feel so young and would like to finish school first when I go home, then I will worry about that. Maybe one day, but I prefer my independence."

"I see."

"What about you? Do you have any grandchildren?" Eva was curious if Bauer had any kids running around somewhere.

"No. I'm sure you remember me telling you about Wilhelm's sister, Charlotte, dying when she was fifteen."

"I do remember."

"So, no, I don't have any grandchildren. I would love to have some one day, but who knows, I might not live to see that happen. I know Charlotte would have gotten married and had children by now if she were still alive, but I often wonder about Wilhelm."

"He doesn't want to get married or have kids?"

"He does, I think, but he is far too busy, focused on his work right now."

"Well, he won't be giving you grandchildren until the war is over then," Eva told her.

"Sadly, no."

Eva finished the dishes and laid them out to dry on the counter. "How do you wash your laundry, Marie?" Eva called over her shoulder.

"Oh, I have a washing machine now. Wilhelm bought it for me last year. I love it so much. Have you ever used one?"

Eva smiled at her question and how funny it sounded. "Yes, I have." The apartment she lived in with Heidi and Liesel had one that they all shared. Eva took the basket full of clothes to the washing machine that barely fit inside a hall closet. "Do you separate them in any kind of way?"

"I separate the colors from the whites, but that is all. Wilhelm gets his uniforms and shirts dry cleaned and pressed."

"Right." Eva dumped the clothes from the basket on the floor and sorted them into two piles, one with whites and one with colors. She started the first load, then went to the kitchen and sat down at the table to eat the soup his mom made. It was potato soup with a side of bread. "It looks very good, Marie. Thank you."

"It's the least I can do." Marie looked around the table. "I forgot the butter." She rose from the chair and returned to the table with a butter dish in her hand. She placed it in front of Eva, then sat back in her chair. "You look skinny; do you get enough to eat?"

"I do." Eva was taken off guard by her remark. Marie's motherly demeanor was fitting; she looked the type.

“Your weight would suggest otherwise. Let me get you some food to bring home.”

“No, I couldn’t take your food.” She really didn’t feel comfortable accepting their food, but more than that, she didn’t want Bauer to notice any missing and learn she was the one who took it. And the notion of bringing food home that he paid for made her sick. She wanted nothing from him or the knowledge that he somehow supported her in any kind of way, even something as seemingly trivial as taking a loaf of bread. Eating food while here was bad enough, but she would not take any home.

“It really is no trouble. We would hardly notice it was missing. We have plenty of food.”

“Thank you again, but no. I don’t want to take your food.”

Marie fixed her gaze on Eva’s face. “How did you get those?” she asked, pointing to the bruises on Eva’s face with a hand that was starting to show wrinkles. Eva’s face was a ghastly sight, with the blackish-blue circle around her partly closed left eye and the deep-set cut above her eyebrow. Her cheek was twice as round as it should be, and her nose was still healing after being broken.

“Men like your son.” Eva thought perhaps she should feel bad about what she said but couldn’t bring herself to.

Marie looked momentarily confused but quickly realized Eva’s meaning. “The Gestapo did that to you?”

“Some of them did.”

Her face grew serious. “Was my son one of them?”

Eva didn’t think it was right to tell Marie what her son

had done to her in the past, so she chose to conceal most of the truth and only tell the part that was positive. “No. He is actually the one who had me released.”

Relief washed over her face. “When Wilhelm wasn’t working in the mines, he would take Charlotte outside to play,” she began. “One winter, I noticed them outside in the snow, catching snowflakes with their tongues. It was the funniest thing to watch as they told each other what their snowflake tasted like.” She chuckled. “I don’t know if Charlotte actually thought the snowflakes tasted like something or if it was only in her head because Wilhelm told her his had a taste.”

Eva suppressed the urge to smile at how Marie’s face lit while telling the story. She suspected his mother was trying to lighten the mood and tell of the kind, human things that her son did.

“Did they spend a lot of time together?” she asked.

“Oh yes, almost every day. In the summer, he would catch frogs in the pond with her, and then she would bring them home and ask to keep them. Bugs were something else that they enjoyed catching. I would have thought that Charlotte would be afraid of insects, but she wasn’t. She was fearless, very much like Wilhelm in many ways, which I attribute to the fact that she tried to do everything he did.”

“They sounded like quite the duo,” Eva said.

“They were. The day she died was the worse day of his life.” She rubbed her hands together in her lap. “Wilhelm has always been very fond of children. He used to make things from wood or paper for the kids who lived on our street and for Charlotte."

"I wouldn't have guessed that he liked kids," Eva admitted.

"Even as a small boy, he loved them. He always wanted to go see the new babies and hold them. He would stand on his tip toes and stare down at them in their cribs, hold their tiny hands, and sing to them in his sweet child voice."

"That doesn't really sound like him, or at least not a side of him I have witnessed." Eva then thought of the little girl in the hospital.

"He was caring then and still is now. He has a tender soul."

Eva almost choked on her food at Marie's comment. She patted her chest to help the food come back out of her windpipe.

"I know you don't see him as I do, but I can assure you that I know my son better than anyone."

"I'm sure you do. I was not trying to be rude or disrespectful. That is just not what I've experienced."

"How closely acquainted are you with my son?" she asked inquiring.

"Not well, aside from the experiences I've had with him, which haven't been many."

"As an adult, he can be quiet, but when he was a child, he always talked and asked so many questions. Once, after he drank a cup of water, he came to me and said, 'Mama, why do we hiccup?' I told him I didn't know. 'Mama, if the sun is so big, why does it look so small? Do bugs know they are going to die when the winter comes?' Or, 'Mama, why does the sky look blue? Why can't we see the wind?' He asked so many things that I could not answer, but he was so sincere when he asked them. Some of my favorite ones were when he asked, 'why do we dream? If we can see our dreams, can blind people see theirs too? Mama, why does glue not stick to the inside of the bottle?' I would always laugh. He was so curious. I believed in him. I always knew he would do great things."

Eva didn't know what to say to this. Hearing about Bauer as a child was uncomfortable. It was difficult to think of him ever being one at all, especially one like his mother was describing. "Was his sister as inquisitive?"

"She would ask questions like all kids do, but not in the same way as Wilhelm. He was a kid beyond his years, and even as an adult he is mature for his age. I think Charlotte knew that, and maybe that is why she would cling to him."

"Cling to him?"

"She was his shadow. At night, after I had gone from their rooms, she would sneak out of bed and into his room and into his bed, and of course, Wilhelm couldn't say no to her. He would lay awake and tell her stories, or sometimes he would light a candle, and they would lie in his bed and draw on a piece of paper he found in the garbage. They had to share a single graphite pencil that he had traded a carrot or potato for, but they didn't mind. I often knew they were awake because I could hear Charlotte giggle or her footsteps on the creaking floorboards above as she went to Wilhelm's room. Most young men his age would not have spent so much time with their little sister, but he adored her and was devoted to her."

"I did not know he was so fond of her," Eva admitted.

"She was the love of his life. I knew that would change someday when he found a wife, but all the things I thought would happen never did. She died, and he never married. How things change," she mused. "They usually turn out so different from what we think."

Eva almost felt sorry for him, almost. "You must miss her a lot."

"I do, but I have learned to live without her now. Do you want to see some pictures? I also still have some of the things they drew together."

Eva looked at her watch. She had already been there for over an hour and feared that he might return soon. "I can, but I really should go after I hang the laundry."

"Oh, I didn't realize that you had work today. I'm sorry I kept you so long."

"I don't work today, but I need to meet someone later, and I don't want to keep them waiting." The truth was, she wanted to see the priest, who didn't actually know she was coming, but his mother didn't know that.

"It's quite alright, dear. I can show them to you tomorrow if you come?"

"Did you want me to come?"

"If it is not too much trouble."

She knew Bauer would be upset with her if she only checked on his mother one day. "I don't mind. I can come by tomorrow."

"I can show them to you then," Marie said.

Eva hung the wet laundry and gathered up her things. "What time does your son usually come home?"

"It's never the same time, but I would say usually around ten or eleven, although some nights he doesn't come home at all."

Out rounding people up, no doubt. She had the morning shift tomorrow, so she told Marie she would be there around seven-thirty after her shift ended.

The closer she got to the church, the faster her heart raced at the memory of the last time. She surveyed the area, checking up and down the street, but there were no soldiers this time. She made her way across the street to the church and entered through the large wooden doors that adorned the front. Her shoes on the floor echoed off the stone walls and high ceiling. The burning candle wax permeated the air of the chapel. She strolled down the familiar hall to Father Becker's office and tapped on the door. It was shut all the way, which was unusual, making her wonder if someone else was with him, but when he opened the door, he was alone.

"Eva, come in." She went to her usual chair at his desk and sat down. "I'm glad to see you, but honestly, I expected to sooner."

She didn't know why, but tears welled in her eyes, brimming over. He didn't say anything but took the handkerchief from his pocket and came around the desk, laying it in her lap. Then, he sat in the chair next to hers.

She picked it up, dabbing at her eyes, and they remained that way for a while before she finally spoke. "I'm sorry. I don't know why I'm crying."

"Does it have something to do with the bruises on your face and bandaged hand?"

"That, and many other things, things I thought I wanted to talk about, but now I'm not so sure."

"You don't have to say anything if you don't want to. We can sit here for as long as you need."

"I know that you are a priest, but would it be inappropriate if I asked for a hug?"

He smiled, his round ,red cheeks lifting. "No."

The tears came fresh again before they embraced, and her body shook with every wave of sobs as he held her. She was crying for everything that had happened to her over the last few years. The tears flowed freely, yet they did not take away the pain inside. His embrace eased it the way medicine would, but it too only lessened the torment inside. Only time could do that. But it offered a small amount of catharsis.

She was not sure how long they stayed that way when she released him and straightened. He focused on her tear-stained face, sympathy in his eyes. "This war is hard on all of us, but if we stay strong and lean on those that are willing to help us, and help others, then we can make it through. I know that right now it might feel like you can't go on, even though you try as hard as you can. There are cruel people in the world, and the way they treat you makes you think there is no hope left. But you know what? All storms pass, and the rain eventually stops. And when that happens, the darkness will fade, the sun's brightness will shine through, and the heartache that you feel now will fade away with it. I'm telling you not to despair."

"It is so hard not to."

"Keep looking because there is always hope. People find strength in times of crisis they didn't even know they had."

"I thought so too, but when I tried to get a pass to France, I learned they put a travel ban on my name. Now I don't know what I am going to do."

"Do you know why?"

"Yes, that awful man I told you about put it on me so I couldn't leave Germany. He even went so far as to tell me I was a prisoner here, even though I was not in a cell."

"Do you know why he would do that?"

"He doesn't want me leaving because I'm sure he is planning on another arrest. He is the reason I have this." She pointed to her face, though right after saying it, guilt reared its head. She wasn't sure he was the one who had her arrested and he was not the one who hit her. He had released her, so she might have just lied to a priest.

"This is a very unusual situation you are in. I don't know how much I can find out, but I will ask around for any information that might be helpful to you."

"Thank you. And I promise I will not be upset if you can't find anything."

"Come and see me in a week or two, and I might have something then."

Chapter Twenty-Three

✠

July 12th, 1941

The wind blew from the west, and carried with it the smell of charred buildings, burning her nose as she walked the few blocks to the hospital. There had been another raid that night close to Potsdam, too close. She had curled up in the bathtub to make herself smaller, covering her head and body with pillows as the building shook. Smaller, broken pieces of plaster fell from the ceiling, hitting her like balls of hell. She thought of her parents' dog every 4th of July when he would hide in their bathtub, terrified of the fireworks.

She really didn't want to live in Berlin anymore, even if she had to stay in Germany. The countryside sounded more and more appealing with each passing day.

She turned the corner and a few blocks away was the

large white hospital looming, the tall trees on the grounds lining the walkway to the front. She would be there in a matter of minutes but was stopped short when someone pulled her roughly by the arm with such force that she almost fell to the ground. The only thought going through her mind was to fight, so she swung her right fist as hard as she could while turning, expecting to hit a member of the Gestapo, but her fist contacted Helmut Mayer's face. Immediately, the pain in her hand radiated up her arm. She shook it and cradled it with her other hand. "Owww, that hurt, Helmut. Why the hell did you grab me?"

"Where have you been? I've been trying to contact you for days," he spat, holding his hand to his cheek.

"You didn't know? Six days ago, the Gestapo had me arrested. They beat and tortured me and said another member of the resistance they had already captured gave me up."

Helmut shook his head, confused. "No… that can't be right. Frank and Thomas were arrested only three days ago by the Gestapo. The rest of us are in hiding. I was searching for you so you would know what had happened, but you were nowhere to be found. I thought you had been arrested, along with Frank and Thomas."

Now Eva was confused. "No, as I said, they arrested me six days ago. They told me others had been arrested, but were still looking for the leader. If Frank and Thomas were only arrested three days ago, then who else could they have?"

Helmut grew agitated and turned away from her, rubbing his forehead with the palms of his hands, then turned to face her again. "Eva, it was you!"

"What…?" she choked, shocked, her voice going up an octave.

"The Germans didn't release you because of their kindness. They are not known for that. The Germans let you go because they wanted you to trust them and confide in them. They knew that if they could get you to, then you might tell them things or lead them to the rest of us, and it looks like that is what happened. Who else could have informed them about Frank and Thomas? They didn't know about them until you were arrested, then they were picked up after they released you. And that is another thing. Why did they release you? How did you manage that? They don't release members of the resistance. Hell, they rarely release anybody. They shoot them when they are finished, once they have extracted all that is useful."

"I don't—" she began saying, but he cut her off.

"You gave them up in exchange for your life, didn't you?"

"No!"

"You did, but that still doesn't explain why they would let you go. They lie to you and say they will free you if you give them names, but then they shoot you anyway. No, you must have been a spy this whole time. Could Lina have been right about you all along?"

"Helmut, look at my face. Why would they arrest me and torture me if I worked with them?" She pointed at her swollen face with her index finger.

"Why did they let you go, then?"

"I don't know the answer to that."

"And how do you explain the fact that Frank and Thomas were picked up shortly after they released you? The Gestapo can find all of us through one member of our network."

"I can't explain that either. I'm as much in the dark as you are."

"Lina, Derek, and I are meeting on the 18th at the place you and I usually meet in the park near the lake. We will convene before sunrise, and you should be there. We need to learn who is at fault. One of us had a hand in this. Someone talked." He paced in agitation.

"It wasn't me," she pleaded.

"I'm sorry, Eva, but all the cards point to you."

She inhaled deeply, then spoke slowly, her voice deepening. "Am I going to my trial on the 18th?"

He didn't speak but bore a hole in her with his deep-set grey eyes. She took a few steps back from him and shook her head. "No… I won't go and be judged by you or anyone else for something I didn't do, especially Lina, who we all know hates me."

"If you don't, you will be admitting your guilt by omission."

"So, I'm dammed if I do and dammed if I don't. Is that how it's going to be?"

"You knew what you were getting into when you joined. You understood what would happen if it ever came to this. If we don't weed out the traitor, we all get caught, and the mission fails."

"I am not a traitor, no more than any of you. What will happen to me if I don't come?"

"I think you know."

"And if I do?"

"We will decide if you are guilty or not."

She laughed sardonically. "You said everything points to me being guilty, and I have no way to prove that I am not, only my word. We both know what will happen if I go." Her eyes teared out of fear, anger, and frustration. "It's ironic. All this time, I had been worried about the Nazis when it was the people I allied myself with and thought of as my friends that I should have been worried about."

"You know that one of them will give all of us up. Everyone breaks, so even if you are really not a spy and one of them mentions your name, you are a dead woman, anyway."

"So, I'm dead no matter what?"

"Unless we can get out of Berlin, but before you even think about that, we need to decide if you are indeed the traitor. I know Lina won't believe you, but Derek might. And if your argument is compelling enough, I might believe you too."

"I will come, but I will not die that day. I have not put up with all the shit that I have to let you, any of you, take my life." She turned and hurried from the alley, her hands trembling as she squeezed them together in front of her to hide that they were shaking.

She was no longer safe anywhere or from anyone. The walls were closing in, and she had nowhere to run. She was trapped in Berlin, and the city's two opposing sides both wanted her dead. She had no idea how she was going to get out of this. She needed Jon to come through now more than ever. She had already written to him, explaining that there was now a travel ban placed on her and that she could no longer go to France. They needed to find a different way, but she had not heard back from him. She suspected that all her correspondence was being monitored now, so it was difficult to say everything she wanted in the letters. If the Germans weren't checking her mail before, they certainly were now.

After putting her things in the locker, she went straight to the operating room to assist with surgery. Shortly after arriving, Frau Wagner told her she was needed in surgery. When she entered the operating theater, she saw that it was not Dr. Möller at the table but Dr. Koch. *Great, one more thing to add to my already bad day*, she thought as she scrubbed in.

Dr. Koch glowered as she approached the table. "You are late. Did you think I was going to wait to do the surgery until you decided to come to work?"

"No, Dr. Koch. I'm sorry, it won't happen again."

"See that it doesn't. Later today I need an assistant to help with something I'm working on in the lab. After your shift, I want you to meet me there."

She was supposed to be at Bauer's house after work. "There is somewhere I need to be after work," she informed him.

He scowled, his light brown eyes peering above his surgical mask at her. "Is there someone dying?"

"No."

"Good. Then I expect to see you after work." Without saying another word, he looked back to the patient. Dr. Koch was very different from Dr. Möller. He was a stern, abrasive man, whereas Dr. Möller was kind and gentle. He did not like to be told no and thought he was always right. He constantly disagreed with the other doctors over one matter or another. Dr. Koch was an intelligent man and a brilliant doctor, which added to his arrogance.

Through the rest of the surgery, all she could think about was if it was possible to convince the resistance of her innocence. And then there was Bauer; how was she going to explain why she didn't tend to his mother. She knew now that the Gestapo lied about capturing another member of the resistance, thinking it might get her to talk, but the question was, who informed them about her, Thomas and Frank? Because someone had. Was it the same person? That made sense to her, but why was there so much time between Thomas and Frank's arrest and hers?

"Eva… pay attention. I said to use the apparatus and give me some drainage."

Dr. Koch's loud voice jolted her out of her thoughts, and after a few seconds of processing what he had said, she picked up the apparatus to drain the blood from the wound.

"What the hell were you doing back there? I need you to be alert when you are in the operating room, not taking a stroll through your head," he snapped as they walked to the sinks. He pulled off his gloves, smacking as he stretched them, then threw them in the trash as he concentrated on her, waiting for an answer.

"I'm sorry, it has been a stressful day, but I know that is no excuse, and I will do better."

He glared. "Don't be late to the lab." He pulled open the door next to the sink. "I know your shift ends at seven. I expect to see you there no later than ten minutes past the hour," he called to her as the door swung shut behind him.

Eva barely made it through the lab door at eleven past the hour. Out of breath, she focused on Dr. Koch, sitting in his chair with a glass slide under a microscope, expecting him to yell at her for being a minute late, but he never even looked up.

"I need you to take a vial of blood from the rabbit in the cage behind me."

"Yes, of course. What are you using it for?" she asked while retrieving a needle off the table beside him.

"Make sure that you wear the gloves beside the cage," he told her but didn't answer her question.

She picked up the larger leather gloves on the table to the right of the rabbit's cage and slid them on her slender hands, taking care not to bump her fingers that were still bandaged. When she opened the cage, the rabbit ran towards the back into a corner and huddled there, breathing rapidly. It reminded her of when she was in the jail cell. "Sorry, little one," she whispered, then reached to the back of the cage and took the rabbit by the scruff on the back of its neck. Gently, she poked the needle into its white fur and pulled the plunger of the syringe, the vial filling with dark red blood. When it was full, she pulled it out and released the rabbit. Immediately, it ran to the back of the cage again, and she closed the door and picked up the vial, taking it to Dr. Koch.

"Here," she held it out to him.

He leaned away from the microscope and opened his hand, waiting for her to place it in his palm. She handed it to him and then sat in the chair beside him.

"What are you going to do to that rabbit?"

"Nothing. As doctors, we are not allowed to do testing on the animals themselves, but we can use their blood for research."

"Why can't you test on the animals?"

"In 1933, Hermann Göring banned vivisection and experimentation on all animals. The leaders of Nazi Germany believe in the welfare of animals. They took a variety of measures to ensure animals were protected. Even the hunting of animals has been banned, and anyone who violates these laws will be sent to a concentration camp. Göring said that he wanted to show sympathy for their pain and that they passed these laws for the sake of humanity itself."

She could not believe what she was hearing. Did they really value animals' lives above that of the Jews? What a sick view this was. Not that animals didn't deserve to be protected, but to be put above human life was wrong.

"Perhaps the same measures should be taken to protect all human life."

He looked at her, forehead creased, but didn't say

anything. After a few minutes of her watching him put drops of blood on a small glass tray, he finally spoke.

"I will not have time to clean the lab before I lock up. I need you to do that and feed the animals; then you may go."

She checked her watch; she was already late in going to Bauer's apartment. Hopefully, he was not home, so he would not notice her absence. His mother would be forgiving of her tardiness, but he would not.

She did the things Dr. Koch told her to as fast as she could, hoping there would still be enough time to swing by Bauer's apartment and then go home unnoticed. Doubt loomed heavy over her, though. She didn't think that would happen. By the time she would get to Bauer's apartment, he would undoubtedly be home, that is, if she had time to go there at all, given the hour.

She said bye to Dr. Koch, then slipped out, grabbing her purse but not bothering to change out of her uniform. She looked at her watch and decided that a quarter past ten was too late to go by Bauer's apartment. She would have to explain why she never came, a thought that caused her stomach to twist into knots.

July 13th, 1941

After work, Eva arrived at Bauer's apartment and slowly climbed the stairs to the top floor. As she ascended the steps, she would think, *please don't let him be home* in her head as if it was a prayer.

She stood at the door, taking in a breath before knocking. It was late, but not so late that it wouldn't be possible for Bauer to still be at work. Bauer's mom opened the door and paused, a confused expression set on her face.

"Eva, what are you doing here?"

"I'm here to see how you are and to check on you, remember?"

"You didn't come yesterday, so I thought you had changed your mind. It's alright if you did. There was no need for you to come today."

"No, that's not it. I wanted to come yesterday, but I was unable to leave work. By the time I got off, it was too late to come by, but I knew I could explain the reason why today when I came."

Marie stepped to the side. "Come on in. You know, Wilhelm seemed surprised when he learned that you had not come by yesterday. It almost seemed like he was upset, but he never said if he was or not. I told him I didn't need you checking on me. He didn't answer but kissed me and went to bed."

Eva knew he was mad but didn't want to let his mother know. "What time will he be home today?"

"I'm not sure, but I expect to see him soon."

Eva needed to check his mother quick and be gone before he came. She didn't want to suffer any more of his wrath. "How have you been feeling?"

"A little better than the last time."

"Let me have a look at you." Eva retrieved her stethoscope from the little brown leather bag and listened to

Marie's heart and then her lungs. Her heart was strong, but her lungs sounded a little congested. Some wheezing happened whenever she breathed.

"Did your son say how long you would need my assistance?"

"He didn't, but I suspect only while I'm feeling unwell."

"I'm sure you will be feeling better in a few days. Have you eaten? I could make you something?" Eva suggested.

"Thank you, but I have already had dinner." She glanced around the room, then settled her gaze on Eva. "I want you to know that I tried to raise my children differently from other German mothers. I didn't leave them in their cribs when they cried or immediately lay them back down after feeding them. I held them and hugged them. I wanted them to know that they were loved. I never agreed with this ideology that you had to raise your child to be tough and never show emotions. To not cry and have a stiff upper lip. No, I didn't want them to be numb inside. I didn't want unpleasant situations to be more than they could bare. I wanted them to feel even if it hurt. However, their father had a different idea about how they should be raised. He agreed with the traditional German teachings of child-rearing. And so, a little of both of our views stayed with them."

"Why are you telling me this?" Eva asked, surprised by Marie's sudden comment that came out of nowhere, having nothing to do with what they were previously talking about.

"Because I can tell that you feel disdain for my son. He is not always as he seems. He is very guarded, holding many of his emotions in, even when around those he cares about.

I'm not sure if it is because of the trauma he endured as a child or as a result of the work he does. It is not clear to me. It did not happen all at once but over a long period of time, and I believe it is a combination of his father leaving, his sister dying, and now his work. He was such a loving little boy, always there for others. He will do anything for those he loves."

"I believe we all face things that change us, and after, we are never again the same." Eva put her stethoscope in her bag and closed it.

"Charlotte idolized her brother, and she knew he adored her. Whatever Wilhelm was doing, Charlotte always wanted to be with him. She loved to draw pictures of Paris and always said that one day she was going to go there. That is why Wilhelm asked for a posting in France after his promotion and station in Poland. In the winter, even though it was cold outside, she still wanted to come with him when he went to see if he could find more food. He would pull her in a wagon from our apartment up and down the streets so they could check the trash cans for anything worth selling or maybe scraps of food that were still edible. Despite the circumstances, she still enjoyed going with him. That is why I say don't judge him by what you see on the surface because that kind tenderness he had as a boy is still there underneath that uniform and his tough exterior."

"I'm sorry if you think I have misunderstood your son, but he has given me many reasons to think differently of him. I don't believe he retains any of the innocence he once did as a child. Somewhere along the way, he has lost it."

"No one can know a person quite like their mother, and I assure you that it is still there, somewhere."

"Why do you care what I think of your son?"

"You said you don't have any children?"

"No, I don't."

"Then let me explain this to you. A mother hates to see someone think ill of her child, especially when she knows they are wrong about them."

"But I am not wrong. I would tell you the things your son has done to me, but I don't want you to think differently of him. But know that I have good reasons for how I feel."

The front door opened then closed, and Bauer walked into the living room but stopped mid-entry. After staring at them sitting on the couch for a few seconds, he took off his hat, laying it on the hall table. He removed his jacket and then the shoulder strap with his gun and hung them on the rack, too, before sitting in the chair across from Eva and his mother.

He looked directly at Eva. "Why did you not come yesterday? I told you every day. I thought I made that abundantly clear."

"I'm sorry. I could not leave work until after ten. I didn't think you would want me to come by at a late hour."

He considered for a minute. "You are right, I would not, but you should have let me know. You could have called me last night from the hospital. While you are caring for my mother, I expect you to call if, for any reason, you are going to be late or can't make it."

"I will."

"There is some food in the fridge I can heat up for you. If you like," his mom asked, looking at her son. She didn't say anything to Wilhelm about what he said.

He never looked away from Eva, not even when his mom spoke. "No, I think I will go out and eat tonight," his eyes still focused on her, breaking down the defenses she so desperately tried to hold. "Eva is going to accompany me."

"What…?" Her head snapped towards him, and then steadily, she looked to his mom, searching for an answer, but there was none offered from either of them.

"You heard what I said." He stood, going to the coat rack, and retrieved his jacket and shoulder holster. He was not in his uniform today but in a suit.

Eva got off the couch and strode over to him. "I don't know what you are expecting of me, but I need to go home. I have work in the morning."

"I am expecting nothing of you but dinner. Get your things," he told her as he buckled the shoulder holster.

She focused on his face, her mouth slightly ajar, trying to figure out if he was serious or only messing with her. Then it hit her. Maybe he wasn't really taking her out to dinner but back to prison. That thought overcame her, and once again, the panic rose in her throat like bile. She turned her attention to the door.

Noticing the change in her and said calmly. "We-are-going-to-dinner."

His reassured voice calmed her a bit. Nodding once, she got her things from the couch, then left with him.

Chapter Twenty-Four

✠

July 13th, 1941

It was quiet in the car as Eva sat across from Bauer in the backseat, trying not to look in his direction, instead focusing on the headlights on the buildings. Occasionally peering to the left, she tried to determine if he had been telling the truth. Her heart still racing, pounding her rib cage, breaths coming fast and hard as she waited to see if he was lying.

Sometimes, when Eva would glance in his direction, he was looking at her, too, so she would quickly turn away. She didn't want to go to dinner with him, but it was the lesser of the two horrible things that could come from this night. It was only them and the driver in the car, so if he was going to have her arrested, the other Gestapo members must already be wherever he was taking her.

She waited, expecting the car to approach the Reich

Main Security Office, but she could not see the building through any of the windows. “Where are we going?”

“I told you.”

“What is the restaurant called?”

“Does it matter?”

“I think it might.”

“It is called Sucre et Sel.”

He came up with the name quickly, making her wonder if maybe he was actually telling the truth. “Why are you taking me to dinner?”

“Because you obviously want to know about me, and this will give you the chance to ask questions when I’m not busy with work or relaxing at home.”

“Why do you think I want to know about you?”

“I know every time you come to the apartment, you talk about me and my private life with my mother.”

“She volunteers the information,” Eva made sure to point out.

“I know my mom likes you. I don’t understand why, but she does. And because of that, she feels comfortable talking to you about personal things she shouldn’t. You ask questions too. I am aware that not everything she says is voluntary.”

“Yes, I have asked her a few questions. I want to know who the man is that hates me so much and would love nothing more than to see me gone.”

“I hate your values and beliefs. That hasn’t changed.”

“And I hate yours. That feeling is mutual.”

“Indeed. I’m glad we got that out of the way.”

The car pulled in front of the restaurant, and the driver got out, opening the door for her, but not Bauer. She stepped out and looked up at the name on the front of the building; it read *Sucre et Sel.* He had been telling the truth about the restaurant.

He followed her into the lobby, and they waited for a table. Of course, it didn't take long for the host to seat them, even though the restaurant was full. Bauer pulled a chair out for her, then went to his own. He laid his hat on the edge of the table and combed his shiny brown hair back to fix any stray pieces.

"So, Eva, ask your questions."

Hearing her first name roll off his lips sounded strange. This was only the second time he had ever called her by her first name. He put her on the spot, and now she didn't know what to ask, or maybe it was that she didn't know what she felt comfortable asking. "Alright… what do you do for fun when you are not working?"

"Really? That is what you are going to start out with?"

She shrugged her shoulders. "I don't know what else to ask."

"How about the kind of questions you ask my mother?"

"Maybe I really do want to know what you do for fun."

He let out a breath. "I don't have a lot of free time, but when I occasionally do, I often enjoy horseback riding and playing football. I have told you some of this before."

She knew he was talking about soccer and not American football. "I enjoy riding horses too, but I'm not very good at it. I went on a group ride one time in Bryce Canyon. It's in the state I'm from," she said.

"In Utah?"

"Yes, how did you know that?"

"I have read the file on you, remember?"

"I had forgotten. That information must have come from my identification papers?"

"It did."

"Are those the things you do to relax?"

"No, not usually. There is something far more effective to alleviate stress," he said, rolling a cigarette between his fingers.

"What is that?"

"Fighting."

She raised an eyebrow. "Fighting…?"

The left side of his mouth lifted into a smirk. "Yes, fighting."

"Like boxing?"

"Sort of. Instead of wearing gloves, we wrap our hands in cloth, which is the only thing between our fists and the other person's face, and a lot of times we don't even do that."

"So, you do bare-knuckle fighting?" The movie Fight Club immediately came to mind. She didn't know why anyone would want to do that. It seemed so violent and uncivilized.

"Yes."

"And does that actually help?"

"It does. When I feel stressed or angry, there is nothing better than hitting something. That dull throb in your fist after it impacts someone's skull sends a rush of excitement, power, and a sense of control, knowing that you caused more pain to the other person than you are in. Sometimes it's liberating to feel pain and to cause others pain. It lets you know your limits and allows a heightened awareness of your body and mind."

She stared at him, unblinking. She was finding it hard to understand how that was something to be desired. She recalled being hit, and the intense pain that came from it. "Is that how you feel about most people?"

"What?"

"Wanting to cause them pain?"

"Of course not," he said, agitation thick in his voice. "I would not get in the ring and fight you."

"Why not?" she asked. "I thought I would be the one person you would get the most pleasure out of beating."

"You have affirmed how little you really know me."

"Did I?"

"Yes. For starters, I want the fight to be equally matched. If it wasn't, I might as well hit a punching bag. Second, I don't think you could understand the feeling two men get when they are in the ring together. Anger rises to the surface, testosterone peaks, and the need to win and dominate the other drives your every emotion and sensation. It gives you a high as the adrenaline surges through your body like it does for an addict on drugs," he said, looking past her, obviously lost in his thoughts.

"You are right. I do not understand. Maybe because I have never been in a fight. Also, why would you want to feel what an addict does?"

"It's different for men than it is for women. Your nature isn't the same as ours. And to answer your question, it's not the drugs that make a drug addict; it's the need to escape reality. Fighting is the same in some ways as drugs, yet different in others. I'll admit it is an escape for me, but it doesn't leave my mind hazy and confused like drugs; it makes my focus sharper. In that moment, my mind is clear, and my senses are heightened. So, you see, Eva, that is one of the many reasons I choose that over drugs when I need an escape. Really, in a lot of ways, it is more of a high because it is something real, and not simply tricking the mind into thinking things are better by numbing it to reality."

She contemplated what he said. "I'm sure you are right about that. Although I still find it hard to believe you would not get some sick pleasure from hitting me."

He leaned forward, putting his arms on the table, crossing them. "I would not say pleasure is what I got from fighting with another man. It's more of a release. So, no, I have not thought about hitting you."

She blew out a long breath; she didn't believe him for a second. "That is not the impression I got when you were trying to scare and intimidate me all those times I was in custody."

"I didn't need to hit you to get the information I wanted. Scaring you was enough."

"Are you saying I'm weak?"

"Not exactly, but I could tell right away that you didn't do well with intimidation and almost certainly wouldn't with actual pain. I knew you would break under that pressure alone."

"Who said I broke. Besides, who wouldn't? I think anyone does after prolonged treatment of that kind. But I didn't break when they punched me, dunked my head underwater, making me suck it in, or even when they pulled out my fingernails," she snapped back.

"You are right. Everyone breaks eventually," he agreed, his voice remaining calm and level.

"Have you ever been in the shoes of the man who did this to me?" she asked, holding up her hand.

"At times. That is not part of my job, though. We have people who do that. But I am often present."

She noticed he never looked at her hand or even at her face but focused on his hand that was resting on the table. "And when you do that, torturing people, does it make you feel the same way you do in the fighting ring? Did it give you pleasure?"

"As I have said, I do not get pleasure from it, but there is a sense of gratification. It's different from fighting in the ring, though, because it's done for a very different reason. The gratification I get is that I know I'm doing it for my country. The purpose is duty. Violence used as a solution to problems is interlaced with human nature. We need it like we need the blood that flows through our veins. Now, if I wanted to get pleasure from something that could cause me pain, then that is something I would do with you if I was willing to lower myself to that."

"Excuse me?" she was shocked and horrified by what

thought came to her mind.

He laughed this time. "I'm sure I know what ran through your mind, and no," he said, shaking his head, "that is not what I am talking about. Abusing a woman would not give me pleasure of any kind in any situation."

"Then what did you mean? And why would you say lower yourself to that?"

"I see that you are naïve about a lot of things. Let me explain. I meant lower myself to be with someone like you."

"Someone like me?" She knew exactly what he meant now. She gave him the most hateful stare she could. "I should have let you die on that table. I wish I had," she spat.

"I know you do. Honestly, I'm still surprised that you didn't. It only confirms that you do dumb things. You can be so ignorant."

Her mouth dropped, and she grabbed the cup to dash the water in his face but realized it was empty, so she slammed it back down on the table. "I hate you!"

"I would, too, if I were in your shoes. And I was referring to relationships when I said it was something I would do with you, not abuse. The correlation between pain and pleasure is very similar. There is a fundamental connection between them that I don't think anyone completely understands. Relationships are as profound as they are complex, and one with you would be as painful as it would be pleasurable, believe me."

"I am so confused by what you are saying right now." She would have left the restaurant already, but she needed him to get home. The last thing she wanted was to continue this conversation.

"I guess to you, this is not the easiest thing to explain," he continued. "I don't mean pain in the sense that we usually think of. I mean that people avoid anything that involves pain, yet they might enter into a relationship that can have the potential to release an untapped capacity for pleasure and happiness, though that is usually only after they cross over from friends to lovers. That is also when they have the greatest capacity to hurt one another." He waited for her to respond, but she didn't, so he continued. "I believe love, sex, pain, and violence all stimulate and release the same feelings in the human body. Sometimes pain is perceived as pleasure and the other way around, but I believe for each of us, it depends on the kind of pain. I don't find pleasure in the pain I feel when I'm in the ring, but there is a complex and mysterious link between them."

"I still don't know what the hell you are talking about."

"Let me explain it this way, then. Think about how our sexual experiences are mirrored in our emotions and at the very core of our relationships. It offers an enlightening perspective. When you love someone, it can create emotionally the same pain or pleasure experience it does when you make love to them. They are both moments of deep connection and intimacy. Their vulnerability and nakedness are matched, even though they are opposite experiences. Pain doesn't have to be physical, either. You could be deeply hurt by someone because of what they said to you or equally as hurt by what they didn't say. The act of loving in whatever form requires a willingness to experience both the pain and the pleasure that comes with it."

"You said a lot of crap that I don't believe anyone on this planet would understand."

Despite her obvious anger, he chuckled. "A lot of people understand it, Eva."

"Twisted people, maybe."

"You said that I hated you, but your hatred for me is far more profound than any feeling I have for you."

"Do you want to know the maddening thing about this? The truth is, I want to hate you, I really do, but if it wasn't for you, I would probably be dead now. That being said, it doesn't mean I don't still think you are an awful person with a black heart and an all-around asshole. Truthfully, somewhere deep down, I think I do still hate you."

He peered intensely at her. "You have a pretty face but such a cruel tongue."

She tried to meet the intensity of his gaze, then held it. Everything Bauer did or said seemed so chillingly rational yet morally disgusting. "Only towards you," she said.

He looked at his plate of food and let out a long breath. "Let me put it into simple words that you can understand. To be in a relationship with you would cause me more pain than pleasure, thus not making it worth the effort. So, if I wanted to feel pleasure and pain from the same thing, I would date you. I have never felt both from one thing, but you would definitely fit that narrative."

Eva was dumbfounded. She didn't even know what to say to that. He noticed the utterly confused look on her face. "All relationships can be good and bad at the same time.

That is one of the many reasons I'm not in one. But you, Eva, you would truly bring both of those emotions to a relationship."

"Are you saying I'm the reason Gerhardt went back with his fiancé?"

"I didn't say that."

"Let me see if I can understand this. You think that being in a relationship would be more painful than being in a fight?"

"Yes, only not in the same way."

"That is such a messed-up way to view relationships. It's no wonder you are alone."

"I am alone because I choose to be."

"I know that is what you said, but it isn't the reason. I think it's because no one wants to be with you."

Anger flashed in his eyes before he concealed it. "There are plenty of women I could date. I know a woman who has wanted to be with me for years, but I have shot down all her advances. I have no desire to be with her, especially now with so much going on."

"Someone wanting to be with you. There must be something wrong with her."

He hadn't responded to her snide remark like she thought he would but went back to eating. Neither of them spoke to one another as they finished their food, but Bauer regarded her every move.

"You should come and watch sometimes," he said, finally breaking the silence.

"Watch what?"

“A fight.”

She pulled the fork slowly from her mouth. “I don’t think that is a good idea.”

He took a swig of his water. “Why?”

“I mean, do I really want to see two people hurting each other.”

“Have you ever witnessed it?”

“You mean besides having it done to me?” He glared at her, and his look was answer enough. “No, I have not. Besides, do women really go to those things?”

“Come then. I’m fighting on Friday. And a few women do, but not many. Most nights, it’s only men there.”

Friday. Why did that day have significance for her? Then she remembered it was the 18th, the day she was meeting the resistance. “I can’t. I already have plans for that day.”

“Maybe another time, then.”

She chose not to answer and put another fork full of food in her mouth so she didn’t have to talk to him.

Chapter Twenty-Five

✠

July 15th, 1941

Eva's eyes were fixed on the letter from Jon in her hand. The last time she wrote, she had to tell him that going to France was impossible, that she couldn't even leave Berlin. She could only wonder what Jon had to say about that. She was nervous about opening the letter, not wanting to read that going to France on that date was her last chance or only hope.

Finally, she mustered the courage and tore the envelope open, unfolding the piece of paper that had been neatly placed inside. She stared at the words on the page, but her shaking hand made them difficult to see, so she held the paper with both hands to steady it.

Dear Eva,

I received your letter and, to put it mildly, the news upset me. I don't know that I can get you out of Germany without a pass. I cannot stress this enough. You have to keep trying to get one. But while you wait, I will caution you to be alert. Although I believe it might be a little late for that now.

I didn't know how I was going to tell you this or if I was even going to need to. I had hoped that the course of events would change without me saying anything, but I fear now I have waited too long.

If you remain in Germany and things stay as they are, you will die. I know that a German has helped you in the past. I will explain how I know this when I see you again. You will have to rely on the protection he can offer if you wish to stay alive. I don't know his name. I only know that a German officer has helped you before, and I believe that he can help you again. You will be shot, but by who I am uncertain. It could be the Gestapo who will arrest you and have you shot, or it could be someone else. That is what I see if you do not seek his help. I have seen both outcomes, and both, as of now, still remain possible. There is not much about you I can find in history, but the little information available shows that the Gestapo arrested you, which led to your death, and other sources say you survived the war. I think that both are still there because you have not decided what you are going to do, or maybe this person will not help you again.

I said that I didn't know his name, but I believe you will know who this person is with the limited information I have given. Eva, you need to seek him out because I can no longer help you, not right now, at least. I will never stop trying, but you have to survive long enough for me to figure out a new way to get you home.

- Jon

She laid the letter on the bed beside her and tried to process the information and what exactly it was that Jon was telling her. Could he really be telling her that Bauer was her only hope of survival? *No... that can't be it.* She picked the letter back up and reread it and then again, making sure she didn't miss something, but she hadn't read it wrong. That seemed to be what Jon was saying.

Bauer almost certainly would not save her again. What he had done for her was an exception. It was not in his nature to be kind or generous. He was only trying to pay off what he felt was a debt to her. She saved his life, so he saved hers, and now the transaction was completed. Besides, she had clearly stated at dinner a few days ago that she still harbored resentment towards him. And he made it abundantly clear that she would make his life hell.

Eva folded the letter and slid into back in the envelope, then stuck it in the drawer with her undergarments. She put on her hat and gloves, then grabbed her purse. She needed to figure out what to do, and the only person she could think of who could help her make sense of this was the priest.

She entered the chapel and looked around at the few people sitting in the pews. Some were sitting with their heads down as if praying, and others looked on, staring at the giant cross with the sickly Jesus hanging from it. It always disturbed her a little when she saw it. Jesus looked more frightening than he did inspiring. He was thin and frail, with blood running down his head as the crown of thorns tore into his skin. She quickly walked by the Jesus statue and down the hall to Father Becker's office. It was not confession hour, so she assumed he would be there.

She knocked on the doorframe, and as usual, he smiled when he saw her. "Come in, Eva."

She walked in, closed the door behind her, then sat in her usual chair without being told to. "I'm afraid I have found myself in a terrible situation and in need of your advice."

His expression turned serious. "Of course. What has happened?"

She tried to think of the best way to explain this to him. She dropped her gaze to his desk and then spoke. "I received some information this morning telling me that my death is certain unless I seek help from the man I hate. The man I have been telling you about. But father, I am certain he will not help me. He would sooner see me in a grave than lift a finger to help." Father Becker chastised her with a look. "Sorry, Father, but it's the truth."

"Have you tried asking him?"

"No, and I don't want to."

"Who told you this, that you will die without his help?"

“I can’t say, but the source is reliable.”

He nodded. “I understand. Did this person say in what way this man will help you?”

“No, and they didn’t say how I was to get him to help, either. I do have an idea, and it would not directly require me to ask him for it.”

“What way is this?”

“Trying to be his friend.”

“I think that is a good place to begin. Start slow, and get to know him. Let him trust you. And remember, in the end, it is God that rights every wrong.”

“Rights every wrong… is that why I cannot be with the man I love? His fiancée getting him is not fair. It’s not a wrong that has been righted.”

“And him breaking her heart is?”

“I know you are implying that life is not fair. Of course, I know it’s not, but lately, it has been extremely unfair to me.”

“Maybe that is because you can’t see what is in front of you. From what you have told me, there has been someone every step of the way to help you. You have many people that are willing to put forth the effort to make sure that you are safe, including this person who has warned you.”

Eva sensed that he was trying to tell her she was feeling sorry for herself. “What are you saying?”

“I’m saying that you need to ask for this person’s help. No matter how you feel about them, you need them. It really doesn’t matter if you hate them or if they hate you. If there is the slightest chance they can help, then you need to try. It doesn't mean that it will be permanent. There are other ways too. Have you thought about a false ID?"

"I have, but they know my face here. It wouldn't work if I stayed."

"Is it possible to get a fake ID and go to Sweden or one of the other neutral countries?"

She met his gaze, his deep-set blue eyes gazing across the desk at her. She had not thought about that. "It might be, but I would have to get into contact with the same friend who warned me in order to get one. They are not in Germany, so it would take time, and I don't know when the Gestapo will come after me again. It might take too long. That is where the confusion comes in. I don't know what to do right now, in this moment."

"I think you should do what your friend told you to do."

"How would I even accomplish that?"

"What connections do you have to this person, the German?"

"Not many. I have been tending to his mother. I go to his apartment every day after or before work."

"How did you start doing that?"

She hesitated before answering. "He asked me to, more like he demanded that I do."

"Why would he do that?"

"Because he helped me when this happened, and now he thinks I owe him," she pointed to the now healing bruises on her face.

"I see."

"I think to him it is a payment for helping me."

"That is possible, but I don't believe so. If he asks or tells you, as you have said, to go to his home and help his mother, that sounds more like trust and respect."

"What? No. I told you, he hates me."

"Does he? I'm not saying that there is no dislike towards you in some way, but that doesn't mean you cannot respect your enemy. And if you are his enemy, it goes to show that what he has done demonstrates his respect towards you even more. As a person or professionally as a nurse, I'm not sure, but he does in one way, or perhaps both." Eva didn't answer. "He is the one you saved at the hospital, isn't he?"

"Yes."

"Maybe that was your first foot in the door."

"If I had not saved him, he would have let me die. He all but told me that. He said that it was to repay what I had done for him."

"That's fine. It has put you on the path you need to be on. These two events have placed you in a unique situation, where you now run in the same circles as the one person who can help you."

"So, what now?"

"Maybe try to be nicer to him next time you meet, like you had said. Don't come across as standoffish."

"The last time we spoke, he told me I cause people pain." She knew that wasn't exactly what he said, that he was suggesting she would cause him pain, but she wasn't going to tell the priest that part.

He rested his chin on his fist with his elbow on the table. "That is harsh, I agree."

"You think?" her comment oozing sarcasm.

He did not acknowledge her sarcasm. "But that doesn't mean he didn't say it out of anger."

"I'm sure he did not."

"His actions and words are conflicting. Can you see that they are?"

"I guess. But it doesn't make a lot of sense."

"It does if you really think about it. If a person you hate helps you, it lessens the hate you feel for them, even if only a little, and that is enough to tug the strings of your conscience. What you did has allowed him to see a different side of you, a side he chose not to see before."

The memory of how she had witnessed him treating other people had always been so different from his treatment of her. "So, he does have a heart."

"Try it. Do you go to his home tonight?"

"I do, but he is usually not home when I'm there. It is typically only his mother."

"When you see him again, act solely with kindness."

"I will try."

He stood and came around the desk to stand beside her. "I know it is scary, and he is the last person you want to rely on. But sometimes God puts people in our path for a reason."

"One of those 'God works in mysterious ways,' huh?"

He squeezed her hand. "Exactly. It is not always easy to figure out life or God's ways."

She stood, retrieving her purse from the floor. "Thank you. I will give it a try."

"You will be alright, Eva."

Her eyes teared. “You don’t know that, and neither do I.”

“That is where faith comes in. He will help you.”

“I hope you are right.”

Chapter Twenty-Six

✠

July 17th, 1941

Eva waited on the bench in the hospital's main hall, staring at the white paint that was starting to chip and fall on the floor. Although, calling the wall white was being generous because it didn't look like it had been white in many years. It had yellowed some time ago from the sun that shone on it every day, streaming through the adjacent windows as well as the smoke that lingered in the building from the patients' and doctors' cigarettes.

She glanced over at Frau Wagner's door, and like the last time she checked, it was still closed. Frau Wagner had said she wanted to meet with her, telling her to come by her office after lunch. The door was closed when she got there, so she knocked, but Frau Wagner had said she would be right with her and to wait in the hall. That was over half an hour ago.

Frau Wagner's office door finally opened, and she stepped out into the hall. "Miss Abrams." Eva stood from the bench and followed her into the office, and then Frau Wagner shut the door behind them. "Have a seat, Miss Abrams."

She took the visitor chair and waited to hear whatever Frau Wagner had to say. She always felt as if she was in trouble when she had to go to her office, like an insolent child going to the principal's office.

"Miss Abrams, have you noticed that supplies have been disappearing for a while?"

Eva tensed a little but tried to stay calm. "I have noticed that the supply cabinet in the nurse's quarters has seemed low on many things."

"And do you know where these things might be going or who has taken them?"

"No. I have not seen anyone take anything." Eva didn't think that Frau Wagner believed her.

"If you happen to notice anything strange or see something that leads you to suppose a certain person is taking them, whether they are acting differently than usual or anything else that might tip you off, I want you to tell me immediately."

"I will."

"Just to let you know, everyone is a suspect."

"I understand. I would suspect everyone, too, if I were in your position."

"You are free to go," Frau Wagner said. Eva stood to leave when Frau Wagner spoke again. "You and Miss Braun will work in the psychiatric ward together today."

Eva turned back to her. "But I am not qualified for that. I have not had any training."

"We are down four nurses up there, and I told them I would send them two of my nurses. You and Miss Braun work well together, so I am sending them both of you. Don't get me wrong, I need all my nurses today, but they need you more than I do right now. Miss Braun is already there. Find her when you go up."

Eva nodded. "I will go straight away." She left the office and headed to the stairs.

"Eva." She heard her name echoing down the hall. She turned and spotted Liesel putting folded sheets on the metal rack. "Where are you going?"

"Frau Wagner has me working in the psychiatric ward today."

Liesel wrinkled up her forehead. "Why?"

"I guess they are short four nurses. She is sending Ingrid and me up there for the day."

"What time do you get off?" Liesel asked.

"At six."

"Good. You can go out with Heidi and me tonight. It has been forever since we all hung out together."

Eva thought about what was going to happen tomorrow, and not knowing what the outcome of that would be, she decided it would be good if she went. "I know. We have all been so busy lately. Are we going to leave from here or go home first?"

"Go home, of course. We have to doll ourselves up

before we go out," she said with a chuckle.

"Alright, I'll meet you in the nurse's quarters after work."

"I'm curious to see if you are going to be as brave as last time," Liesel teased.

Eva's face blushed. "No, I don't think there will be a repeat of last time."

"I was almost hoping there would be. I had never seen anything quite like that before."

"And you will never see it again. Maybe you can do it, and I will watch this time."

"No, I don't want to bring that kind of attention to myself, but maybe Heidi will," Liesel joked.

"Maybe. I better go up. I'll see you later."

Eva hurried to the third floor and found Ingrid. She was kneeling next to a man in a chair who was scraping the bottom of his bowl with a spoon over and over, even though it was empty.

"Ingrid."

Ingrid glanced up. "Oh good, I'm so glad that it's you. I hate being here. At least you will make it tolerable."

"Have you been up here long?"

"No, only about twenty minutes."

"What are you doing with him?"

"They said he is shell-shocked, whatever that means. He doesn't talk or do anything. Mostly he stares at the wall and obsesses over things, like that bowl." She nodded to the bowl in his hand that he was still scraping with the spoon. "There is nothing left in there, but he keeps trying to get something out anyway."

Eva knelt beside him, touching his hand. He stopped scraping and jerked his head towards her, his piercing blue eyes boring into hers. They were intense yet hollow at the same time, and the whites of his eyes were completely bloodshot. The way he stared unnerved her, and she flinched. He turned away from her and went back to scraping the bowl.

She looked at Ingrid. "I think he has an extreme case of PTSD along with something else I can't identify."

"Of what?" Ingrid asked, the pitch of her voice rising at the last word, obviously confused.

Eva was not sure when they learned about PTSD, but apparently, it wasn't that well-studied in 1941. "It's when someone suffers from severe stress because of something that happened to them. It usually happens to people who have fought in a war."

"Oh," Ingrid said and looked at the man. "And you think that is what he has?"

"Yes, I do."

"Will he get better?"

"He might. I think most people do eventually, but sometimes it can take a very long time. Are we only giving them food and helping with bathing?"

"Mostly. They also have us playing games with them. They said that the interaction will help them get better faster."

"That is probably right, but I am not as familiar with mental illness as I am with physical ones."

Eva played cards with a couple of the patients, but her mind was not on the game. It wandered to how she had not seen Bauer since the dinner. She needed to know if her being nicer to him would change how he treated her. She needed him to be receptive to her kindness, and soon.

Ingrid walked over to Eva's chair and leaned in close to her ear. "They are all so delicious," she said, quiet enough that only Eva could hear.

"Who?"

"The soldiers. Aren't they?" Eva stared at her with raised eyebrows. Ingrid rolled her eyes. "Not these men, the ones downstairs. Don't tell me that you don't go home a little bothered?"

"No, I don't. Can we talk about this later?" With only her eyes, she looked over at the men sitting at her table, then back to Ingrid.

"Fine," Ingrid said, turning on her heels.

A few hours passed, and Eva was making rounds when Ingrid walked quickly in her direction, concern carved on her face. "Eva."

"What?"

"There is a man here who says he needs to talk with you. There is something not right about him."

Eva followed Ingrid's gaze to the door. Derek Brunner was standing in the entryway, holding his hat with both hands, looking around the room. His eyes darted from side to side, and he seemed uncomfortable. *What is he doing here? This can't be good*, she thought.

“Excuse me,” she told Ingrid, getting ready to go to Derek.

“Do you know him?”

Eva didn’t answer but set the chess piece on the board and walked to Derek. She searched his face and observed his body language, wanting to know why he had come to the hospital. “What are you doing here? You should not be here,” she said in a low voice. She took him by the arm and pulled him out into the hall.

“I had to come and see you and could not consciously wait any longer.”

Eva shook her head in confusion. “What are you talking about? I’ll be there tomorrow.”

“I know. That is why I came to see you today.”

She blinked, taking a step back. “Derek, you are worrying me.”

“You can’t come tomorrow. If you do, you will die. They don’t believe you. They are already convinced you are the traitor. Their plan is to kill you tomorrow when you arrive. I’m not even sure if you will be allowed to defend yourself. After tonight, I wouldn’t go home either.”

Eva stared at him in shock and disbelief. “What am I supposed to do, Derek?”

“I’m not sure. Go into hiding, maybe.”

“How? I can’t do that. I don’t have anywhere to go. There is a travel ban on me. I can’t even leave the city.”

“You need to have it figured out by tomorrow. I’m sorry. I wish I could be of more help. We are all keeping our heads low. We believe the Gestapo knows who some of us are, if not all of us."

"What about work? I can't stop coming in."

"I think you are safe at work for now, but probably not as you go to and from the hospital. I would take a different route every day if I were you. Look, I have already lingered too long. If they find out that I warned you, they will kill me too. I need to go. But please, be careful. And whatever you do, don't go to that meeting tomorrow."

He turned to leave, but she caught his arm. "Wait, why did you warn me?"

"Because I don't think it is you. I think you should know that Helmut wants to believe you, too, but he has to do right by the others. If there is a threat and all the signs point to one person, he feels his hands are tied."

"I understand, really, I do. But I feel like I need to tell you this, that if my life is in danger from the resistance, I might have to turn to the Germans for help."

The horrified look on his face suggested that he had not expected her to say that. "What…?"

"I'm not talking about turning anyone in. What I mean is, if they think I have the protection of the Germans, perhaps they won't come after me."

"But how would you do that?"

"I have a plan. All I need to do is make it appear that way. It doesn't have to actually be true." Eva wasn't about to tell him that she might have to seek the assistance of a Gestapo member and that she needed his help from the Germans as well as the resistance.

"Are you familiar enough with a German to do that?"

Eva stared at the floor to avoid his gaze but didn't speak. "I see. So, it is true."

She looked at him. "What is true?"

"Lina said she thought you saved the life of that Gestapo officer, SS Obersturmbannführer Bauer. He was one of the names at the top of our list. We know that all the high-priority officers we targeted died in the attack, except for him. It was apparent that he would succumb to his wounds. There was no doubt of that. But he was brought into the hospital for surgery and not left outside to die like the others in his condition. Now I am not a doctor or nurse, but I know a little something about procedures. If it is thought that someone is too far gone and the chances of survival are slim, they will move on to the ones who have more of a chance. For some reason, he was chosen above the others, but we never could quite figure out why."

Eva didn't answer. What would she even say? She didn't want to lie to him; he was trying to help her. "It is true. I did ask the doctor to operate on him. Seeing all that death was more than I could take, I didn't want one more life on my conscience. I did not save him because of his rank or position. I would have saved him, even if he was a lowly private. How did you know of this, anyway?"

"It came down the line of information and somehow got back to Lina. By saving him, you might have undone all that we tried to accomplish. I am sure he is the one heading this operation to find us, and he is good at what he does. There is a reason he is one of the Gestapo officers overseeing an entire country. But it is personal for him now. You need to be careful that he doesn't find out you were involved. If he did, he would no longer help you but pursue you like a wolf on the hunt. You would be on the run from him, like the rest of us. He has smelled blood in his nostrils, and you could be next."

"I know now that I should have let him die that day."

"The only way they would believe that you are not the traitor is if you exploited or killed him. He would be an excellent source of information. If you could do that, I think I could convince them to give you more time, and there might not be a need for the meeting at all. Do you think that is something you could do?"

Eva honestly didn't know if she could kill someone, and Bauer would never give up information. She was there when the bomb went off and was an accessory to murder but not the one doing the actual killing. She really was only a passenger. "Ummm… I'm fairly certain that we won't get anything from him, and I'm not sure about the other thing. Will I have time to think about it?"

"Only today. The meeting is tomorrow morning. I could meet you early before the sun is up, and you can tell me your decision. But if you have decided that you can't do it, I recommend you follow my suggestion." Eva nodded. "I really need to go. I will see you tomorrow at six at the front entrance of the hospital. Remember, don't go home."

Eva nodded again. She couldn't even bring herself to answer. She continued staring down the hall long after he was gone.

"Eva?" Ingrid said, putting a hand on her arm.

Eva jumped at the touch. “Ingrid, what is it?” she said, breathless.

“What is it? I should be asking you that. What did that man want?”

“Noth… nothing,” she said, struggling to say the word.

Ingrid peered down the hall, then back to Eva, who still had her gaze fixed on it. “It doesn’t look like nothing. Eva, you are not alright.”

Eva quickly turned to Ingrid. “I’m fine. I need to be alone for a minute. I need to think.” She walked swiftly through the psych ward towards the stairs that led to the roof. She had an overwhelming urge to be alone. She did not want to see or talk to anyone. She was afraid it would bring on an anxiety attack. One was starting already as a twisting began deep in the pit of her stomach, reaching her throat, but she could keep it at bay as long as she didn’t have to interact with anyone. She hoped that no one noticed her uneasiness and the pace of her walk. She hurried up the stairs until she reached the door that led to the roof. When she pushed it open, the warm evening air caressed her face. She closed the door behind her and walked across the roof of the hospital until she reached a corner. Then sat down, leaning against the wall. She closed her eyes and drew in a deep breath.

She wasn’t sure how long she had been up there, but when the sky went dark, she knew it must be after curfew because the city lights had gone out. Berlin was now blanketed in an inkiness as if it wasn’t even there, except for the lights that were in constant search for planes.

There was more of a breeze at the top of the building

than on the ground, and it blew loose pieces of hair around her face. Her eyes brimmed with tears and dried on her face as the air hit them. She stood, then paced back and forth. Her mind was spinning, and she was unable to focus on a single thought. She squatted and pounded her temples with her fist, trying to get her head to stop swirling and the thoughts to make sense. "Think, Eva, think," she cried, trying to figure out exactly what her options were. As her mind slowed, she considered what lay before her. *If I show up tomorrow, they will kill me, and the only other option is to kill Bauer.*

The tears ran faster, wetting her cheeks. "After all that has passed between us, I'm no longer sure that I can take his life, nor that I want to anymore." She shook her head fast back and forth. "No, I can't kill him; I don't want to kill him; I don't want to kill anyone. But I should want to kill him, and at one time, I did wish him dead. But now I can't because I need him to keep me safe." She laughed, choking on the tears at the same time. "Are my only options to kill him or rely on him? Has it really come to that?" She wiped the tears from her face roughly with the back of her hand. "No, I'm not sure I can do either of those things. I can't kill Bauer, but I don't think I can go down the path required to save my life, either. If I killed Bauer, then who would protect me from the Gestapo? No one." Tears continued to pour from her eyes. "I am screwed, no matter what I do. If I choose to seek his help, would he? Even if it was in his power to do so, I don't think he would," she said aloud to herself as she continued pacing.

Eva walked to the edge of the building and leaned over,

peering down into the darkness. She had no guarantee that Bauer could or would do either of those things, and so the thought of dying peacefully in her sleep or the quick death of falling from a building was more appealing than being tortured, shot, or hung by the Gestapo. Or being beaten to death or shot by the resistance. "This is the best way," she told herself. She knew that she was probably crazy, but it felt like the world was on her shoulders, and this was her only option now because she could see no other way out. It was ironic that she might be better off dead than alive.

She climbed up onto the ledge of the building and held her arms out to her sides for balance. She was like a bird preparing for flight. She dropped her gaze over the side again. It was an ocean of blackness, and she could hardly make out the ground. She lifted her head to the stars, the weight of them crashing down on her, and she knew this was the choice that had to be made if she wanted to be free. The images of the people she loved played through her mind like a slide. Gerhardt's face was the first she saw. His deep ocean-blue eyes and blond hair swept to one side. Her heart hurt, the aching for him throbbing in her chest. Then, her parents' warm smiles and tenderness, and her dear brother. They had a special bond like no other, and it pained her that she would never see him again. Then there was Jenny, the best friend anyone could ask for, and she missed her motherly advice and witty personality. For some unknown reason, Kevin's face played in this reel of images. Why was she thinking of him, and now of all times? She didn't love him, not anymore. He was a chapter of her life, a closed one, but a chapter nonetheless. *Maybe this is what they talk about, how your life and the people in it flash before your eyes before you die*, she wondered.

She closed her eyes and prepared for her last few seconds on earth when a scream echoed behind. The sudden sound caused her footing to falter, and she started to fall forward until someone grabbed onto her dress, pulling her backward off the ledge. She fell on the roof, landing on her back, staring up at a figure leaning over.

Ingrid's face came into focus, hovering over Eva's as she stood frozen, gaping in horror down at her.

"What the hell were you doing, Eva? What were you thinking?" Ingrid slapped her hard across the face, taking her by surprise.

Eva could not feel the pain in her cheek from the shock of everything that had taken place in the last few minutes. Her whole body was numb, as was her mind.

"I don't know." The sound barely escaped Eva's lips.

"Pain makes people selfish. I knew that something was wrong, and I chose to ignore it. It's obvious that you are hurting, but you are foolish to think that this is the way. You are selfish because you are only thinking of yourself. Did you even consider for a second how this would affect other people?" Ingrid yelled, becoming breathless from all the shouting. Ingrid's eyes glistened, tears streaming freely down her face.

"I… I didn't," Eva trailed off, not knowing how to answer.

"Why would you do that, Eva? Why? What could be so

bad that you felt like your only way out was to kill yourself?"

"I want to tell you."

"Then tell me."

"I can't." She shook her head, sitting up. "I can't."

"You will never do that again. Promise me you won't?"

"I promise."

"I will not say anything, but you have to get some help. And if I ever suspect that you are going to try this again, don't think for a second that I won't tell someone."

Eva sniffed and wiped her nose on the back of her hand. "I won't."

Ingrid helped her to her feet, and they walked together back to the roof door.

Chapter Twenty-Seven

✠

July 18th, 1941

Heidi and Liesel were disappointed when Eva canceled their plans. She felt bad for bailing on them, but there was no way she could go to a club, dance, laugh, and enjoy the evening as if nothing had happened. She almost died, and she needed to emotionally process that and come to terms with what she had done. Then, there was the matter of dying at the hands of others. She still didn't know how to prevent that from happening.

Eva had watched the sunrise from her bedroom window, feeling surprisingly calm. Maybe because almost dying helps you put things into perspective. When she came to terms with the fact that she would die, it made her no longer fear death. Accepting it made her feel at peace, at ease with the idea of leaving this life for what waited on the other side.

She no longer wanted to die, but the thought of the Gestapo or resistance coming after her wasn't frightening. She attributed it to shock because it would terrify any normal person. She didn't know what would happen when the shock wore off, though. There was a high chance that the fear would be worse than before.

It was long past the time of the meeting with the resistance, and she understood it was too late to fix it. That ship had sailed. As far as the Gestapo, that was yet to be determined.

She stood up and carefully went to her bedroom door, turning the knob slowly, trying not to wake Liesel or Heidi. Derek had told her not to go home, but that would have meant sleeping on the street. If she left now, where would she go? Could she come back? Would she tell Heidi or Liesel? Could she keep up with an elaborate lie without it spiraling out of control? That is if she could even think of one? She needed to have something to tell them soon, but right now, she needed to leave and go somewhere the resistance would not find her.

She peeked out into the living room; it was empty and quiet. She closed her door back and went to her bed, pulling out a small bag from underneath. She gathered the things she would need for a few days and poked them in haphazardly, pushing the contents down so she could close it. Now, she had to figure out where to go. *I could go to Ingrid's*, she thought. *But I don't know where she lives. I can ask her tomorrow at work, but that still leaves today.* She had the day off and needed a safe place to hide for the next twelve hours, which made her remember what Derek said about them trying something when she was going to work or coming home. Maybe she could sleep at the hospital tonight, then ask Ingrid in the morning about staying with her. She no longer checked on Bauer's mother since she had been doing better, but that didn't mean she couldn't stop by and see her anyway. Bauer would be at work, so she didn't have to interact with him.

She picked her bag off the floor and left the apartment, heading towards the tram stop. She constantly checked over her shoulder, half expecting someone to be following her. She scanned the faces of every person who passed on the street to make sure they weren't members of the resistance. To her surprise, none looked familiar, but that didn't mean they weren't watching her from the shadows.

She didn't slow her pace until arriving at the tram stop. Nervously, she shifted her weight between her feet while waiting, and when the tram came down the street, she relaxed a little but kept a watchful eye. It stopped, and she hurried on, finding a seat near the front. She set her bag on her lap, lacing her fingers together, and rested her hands on top of it. She scanned the outside from the window, but still, there wasn't anyone she recognized. She closed her eyes and drew in a deep breath, relieved she had made it this far.

A sudden idea came to her. She would not go to Bauer's apartment. She would go to his work and ask him if he would remove the travel ban and give her a pass. It was a long shot, but she had to try. What did she have to lose? She was already in over her head.

When the tram finally arrived at the Reich Main Security Office, she stepped off onto the sidewalk in front of the building. She gazed at the structure in the bright sunlight and suddenly wasn't so sure about her idea. She had only been here once since that fateful night and had hoped to never step foot in it again. But here she was, going in of her own free will. She gripped tighter to the handle of her bag, hoping that somehow it would help calm her.

Oberst Heinrich Schmitt was in this building, but it wouldn't do any good to see him. He would only tell her it was out of his hands and that it was the decision of the Gestapo. If they weren't at war with Russia, she was confident he would try harder to do something, but as it was now, he had better things to do.

Eva stopped at the desk between the two flights of stairs, but the secretary didn't look up and instead continued writing. "Excuse me?" Eva said.

The woman stopped writing, looking from her paper, considering Eva. "Yes." She was a thin, blond-headed woman in a uniform, and that struck Eva as odd. The last time she was here to see Oberst Heinrich Schmitt, the secretary was wearing civilian clothing and was a man. The woman scowled at Eva, waiting for her to speak, obviously annoyed that she had to stop what she was doing.

"I'm here to see SS Obersturmbannführer Bauer."

"Do you have an appointment?"

"No, but—"

"Then I'm sorry. He can't see you." She turned back to her paper and began writing again.

"He knows who I am. If you tell him I am here, I'm sure he would want to see me."

The woman slowly looked back up from her paper. "If you do not have an appointment, then you cannot be admitted."

"He could come down to the lobby. I'll wait."

The secretary motioned to a guard. "Escort this woman out of the building." She cast Eva a skeptical eye.

He took Eva by the arm, but she jerked it away. "I know my way out." She looked into the woman's ferret-like eyes. "Bitch," she said before turning and walking away, hoping she couldn't speak English. As Eva was getting ready to go through the front doors, two German officers walked into the building, passing by her.

She turned on her heels. "Excuse me?"

The two men stopped and turned to her. "Yes?" one closest to her said.

"Do either of you know Obersturmbannführer Bauer?"

"Yes," both men said simultaneously.

"I came here to see him, but that woman at the desk won't even tell him I'm here." She nodded toward the secretary.

Both men turned their attention in that direction, then back to her. "Does he know you are here?"

"No, but we are acquainted. He would want to be told."

"Well, I would gladly tell him, but he is not here right now."

Eva's face fell. "Oh, where is he?"

"He left for an early lunch."

"Do you know where?"

The men looked at each other. "Doesn't he usually go to that café on Unter den Linden boulevard?" the man with light brown hair asked the other.

"I think that is where he usually goes," he agreed.

The one that had mentioned the café spoke again. "I believe it is called the café Kranzler, and it is in the central Mitte district," he told her.

"Thank you." She flashed him a smile, then looked at the secretary, who had been watching the whole thing. Eva felt victorious. It made her happy that they told her what the woman would not.

Eva left the Reich Main Security Office and took the tram to Unter den Linden Boulevard. When she stepped onto the street, she was amazed by the surrounding buildings. She had never been to this part of town before. White pillars lined both sides of the road, each with a bronze eagle on top and the red flags hanging down the poles. It was this way for as far as she could see. About every six feet on the front of the café Kranzler also hung the Nazi flags, with the black swastikas in the middle. It was suffocating, and at this moment, she felt more intimidated by the German people than she ever had. Nazi symbols were everywhere, and the people walked around like it was so normal, and to them, it was. But to her, they were a symbol of evil, and she felt sick to think of the pride they obviously took in it.

She inhaled and walked across the street towards the café. It had three floors, each packed with people. She didn't know how or if she would find him amongst the crowd, that is if he was even at the restaurant. There was a waiter close by putting cups and plates on a tray from the outside tables.

"Excuse me," she called, hurrying in his direction.

He turned to her. "Yes?"

"I am looking for a specific officer. His name is SS Obersturmbannführer Bauer. I have been told he comes here often."

"Yes, he does."

"Do you know if he is here now?"

"He is." The waiter laid the tray on the table and motioned for her to follow, then stepped inside the café. He pointed towards the back of the room. "He is sitting there."

Eva's gaze followed his finger to Bauer, sitting by himself at a table near the window. He was eating and drinking something while he read the paper.

"Thank you."

"No problem."

The waiter went back outside, and she made her way through the crowded room. She was glad he was there and that it hadn't taken long to find him. He continued to read the paper as she approached his table, not once looking up. She stopped a few inches from the end but didn't speak.

He lowered his paper to take a sip of coffee but paused, the cup midair as he did a double-take, surprise clear on his face. "Miss Abrams. How did you know I was here?"

"I asked around."

His expression didn't change from the usual calm and controlled one it had gone to after his temporary bout of surprise. He looked at the bag in her hand, then back up at her. “I hope you aren’t planning on going anywhere, Miss Abrams.”

Without asking, she sat in the chair across from him and put the bag on the floor beside her feet. “Actually, that is what I wanted to talk to you about. I came to ask if you would have the travel ban removed?”

He gave her that smile that always made her feel uneasy. He folded the newspaper and set it off to the side. “Why would I do that?” He took a sip of his coffee.

“Because I want to go to France.”

“What is in France?”

“Nothing in particular. But I would rather be there than here.”

He eyed her as though his bullshit meter was ticking in the red. “Well, I am afraid, Miss Abrams, that you have wasted your time.”

“Why, you could have it removed so easily?”

“Who said it is easy?”

“I know you could if you wanted to.”

“True, I could.” He took another sip of his coffee.

She leaned back in the chair. “But you don’t want to?”

He checked his watch. “I hate to cut this chat short, but there is somewhere I have to be, and I can’t be late.”

She wanted to yell at him about Germans always having to be on time, but that would not help her get what she wanted. “Can we talk about it later?”

“Two days.”

She furrowed her brows. “What?”

“Meet me here in two days, at nineteen hundred hours.”

"What time is that?"

He closed his eyes, momentarily letting out a breath, then opened them, his cold gaze fixed on her as she anxiously tapped her left foot. "Seven, Eva. I don't understand you, Americans. All you have to do is count up from twelve until you get to nineteen, twenty, twenty-one, or whatever number is given to you."

If he was trying to make her feel stupid, then he succeeded. "Sorry, civilians don't go by that time in America, only the military."

He took his hat from the table and pulled it low on his head. "I'll see you in two days." He brushed past her without saying another word, and she squinted out into the crowd.

She couldn't believe how uncaring he was most of the time, but what he said gave her something to think about. If he was willing to meet with her again, that meant she had a chance, even if a small one.

Eva left the café and took the long way to the hospital, hoping that no one from the resistance would be watching that route. She was counting on Ingrid to let her stay at her apartment. She could not keep sleeping at the hospital.

Eva put her bag under one of the extra beds they kept stored in the basement. She had less chance of getting caught if she slept there than if she took one of the beds on the hospital floor. She lay on the bed, covering up with the blue blanket, and kept quiet. The doctors and nurses rarely came into the basement, especially at night. She drifted in and out of sleep, the footsteps and rolling beds overhead waking her, but it was still better than going home.

July 19th, 1941

Eva woke early in the morning as the sound of people hurrying coupled with the moans and yelling of men in agony. She wondered if another group of wounded had come in from the field hospitals at the front. She would have changed and gone up, but everyone would wonder why she was there so early, so she ate the bread and cheese she brought instead.

When it was finally time for her shift to start, she climbed the stairs, cracked open the door, and peeked out. The hall was empty, so she hurried and closed the door, smoothed down the front of her apron, and walked to the emergency ward.

As she expected, it was utter chaos. Doctors and nurses rushed around, and patients lay on beds, chairs, and the floor. The beds in the basement would probably be brought upstairs now, so it was good that today she would ask Ingrid to stay with her.

Eva found Dr. Möller attending to a patient. “What do you need me to do?”

“I need you to assist me in surgery. I’m going there now. I want you to take this patient into the operating room one.” He pointed to a man lying on a bed to her right. He had bandages wrapped around his head and torso.

Without saying a word, she took the bed, pushed it to operating room one, and began preparing for surgery.

"Eva," Dr. Möller said as he walked in. "I need to talk to you about something." He went to the sink, picked up the bar of soap, and lathered it over his hands under the running water but continued talking. "Many of us are being asked to go to the Russian Front to assist in field hospitals there. I am one of the doctors who is going, and I thought I would ask if you wanted to come as well. Is that something you are willing to do?"

His request shocked her. Eva had never considered that; it changed everything. Maybe Bauer would remove the travel ban if she told him she was going to help on the Russian front. He would finally be rid of her and never have to see her again. If she went, she risked being captured by the Russians, and that would be bad. But she could look for Gerhardt there, which would be a positive aspect of going.

"I don't know. I need to think about it. When do you leave?"

"In a little over a week."

"It won't be the same here if you are gone," she told him.

"I know. That is why I thought you might want to come with me."

"I would, actually, but I'm not sure I can go. That is something I need to find out."

"Why couldn't you go?"

She chuckled out of the irony of the whole thing. "It's a long story. I should know soon, though, and then I will give you an answer."

After surgery, she searched for Ingrid. "Ingrid, I'm glad

I found you. I wanted to ask you something."

"No, I didn't tell anyone."

"Thank you, but I wasn't going to ask you about that. Something has come up, and I need a place to stay for a while."

"Did you get kicked out of your apartment?"

"No, nothing like that. I just can't go home right now."

Ingrid studied her with a level gaze. "Trouble with Heidi and Liesel?"

"No. I understand that you want to know what it is, but I would ask that you not push me for an answer right now."

"Alright. How long do you need a place to stay?"

"I'm not sure, but hopefully, only a few days. Also, if Heidi or Liesel ask you about it, I want you to tell them you invited me to stay with you."

"OK… why?"

"Because I want them to think that is why I won't be home for a few days. Or they will ask if something is wrong."

"Is something wrong?"

Eva hesitated. "Yes… but I'm working on fixing it. I don't want them to worry, though, while I try to figure out how to do that."

"Are you coming over tonight?"

"Yes, if that's alright."

"It is."

"Thank you so much, Ingrid. I owe you."

"I will think of a way you can repay me, believe me."

"I know you will." She found Heidi and Liesel in the

nurse's quarters eating lunch.

"Hey, guys." She sat down next to Liesel.

Both of them looked at her and stopped chewing. "Why were you gone yesterday morning when we got up? Where did you go?" Liesel asked.

"I couldn't sleep, so I went for a walk, then I visited a friend. While I was out, I ran into Ingrid, who invited me to stay with her for a few days. I told her yes. That is where I was last night and will be the next few nights."

"Why didn't you tell us that you were staying with her?" Heidi asked.

"Honestly, I didn't think about it until I was already there. I knew I would see both of you today, so I didn't worry about it too much. I'm sorry if I worried you."

"It would have been nice to know. If you ever do something like that again, please tell us first."

Obviously, they were not happy with her, and they had a good reason. She would be mad at her, too. She might as well tell them about possibly going to the Russian front. There was no sense in waiting. "There is something else. Dr. Möller asked me if I wanted to go to the Russian front with him to work at a field hospital there."

Heidi laid her sandwich on the table. "What, no. You can't go there. Do you know how dangerous it is? It won't be like Berlin. Even with the bombings here, it is so much worse there. It's not only soldiers that die; everyone is in danger of being shot, blown up, or worse, captured."

"I know. I have thought of that. But they are in more need of doctors and nurses there than we are here," Eva told her. “Sometimes I feel more in danger here than I would if I were fighting the Russians myself.”

“Why do you say that?” asked Liesel.

“Forget it. I don’t know if I am even going. I should know in a few days, and I’ll tell you what I have decided.”

Eva was happy to be going home with Ingrid. The resistance didn’t know where she lived, so they wouldn’t know where to look. The only way they would find out is if they followed her there from the hospital. Ingrid’s apartment was tiny, with a single room. The bed, kitchen, and couch were all in the same space. Only the bathroom was separate. “I’m OK sleeping on the couch,” Eva told her.

“It doesn’t matter,” she said.

“Do you work tomorrow?” Eva asked.

“No. Why?”

“Because I have to be somewhere tomorrow at seven, and if I’m done in time, maybe we can hang out.”

Ingrid smiled her usual innocent smile, her round, pink cheeks pushed up, showing her white teeth. “That would be fun.”

“I will try to hurry, but I honestly don’t know how much time it will take.”

“Do I get to ask what it is you are doing?”

Eva thought about that for a minute. She didn’t see why it would hurt to tell her. “Well, I’m meeting someone.”

“Oh, a man?”

“Yes, but not what you are suggesting. Remember that officer I saved?”

Her smile grew. “Yes….”

“That is who I am meeting. And don’t look at me like that. He would sooner kill me than date me, and the feeling is mutual.”

“Then why are you meeting him?”

“Because he has something I need. It is a long story, but it has to do with why I can’t go home right now.”

Her smile faded. “Oh, I see. And you think he can help you?”

“He can. I’m just hoping he will. I have to convince him that it is worth his time.”

“How are you going to do that?”

“I have no idea. I have until noon tomorrow to figure it out, but I won’t know until seven when I meet him, and then it might be too late.”

“You are smart. You will figure it out.”

“Thank you, Ingrid. I think it’s less about my intelligence and more about how strong his dislike for me is.”

Chapter Twenty-Eight

✠

July 20th, 1941

Eva waited at the café for Bauer, impatiently tapping her foot up and down under the table, as she often did. She was already on her third cup of tea, and still, he had not shown. She didn't know what could be keeping him; he was usually so punctual. *Of course, he is not on time when meeting me,* she thought.

Almost half an hour later, she noticed him making his way through the restaurant towards her. He had a severe expression on his face, almost bordering anger. She knew this could make it harder for her to convince him to remove the travel ban. He sat down in the chair across from her and put his hat on the table, running a hand through his hair. Like Gerhardt, he kept his hair in a deep side part and combed until it was smooth. She wanted to say something about him being late but decided against it.

"Sorry, I am late. I could not get away from work."

He looked at his watch, and she wondered if he was already in a hurry to leave. "I will get right to the point. The last time we talked, I asked if you would have the travel ban removed, and you told me to meet you here today. My reason for wanting it removed has changed, though. I am no longer going to France. I have been asked to work at a field hospital on the Russian front."

His eyes widened. "You want to go to the Russian front?"

"It's more like I'm needed at the Russian front."

He rubbed his hand through his hair again and licked his lips. "I cannot give you an answer now, but you will have one soon."

Her shoulders dropped in disappointment. "How soon?"

His eyes shot up to her, cold as ice. "I don't know, but the worst thing you can do right now is to keep asking me about it."

She nodded. "I will try not to. The doctors and nurses are leaving in a little over a week, so I would need it removed before then."

She reached down, got her purse off the floor, and stood to leave, but he caught her hand. "Where do you think you are going?"

"Home." Her tone alluded to her confusion at his actions.

"I didn't say you could leave."

"I didn't know I needed your permission."

He let go of her hand and nodded to her chair, indicating that she needed to sit back down. She lowered herself into the chair but didn't move the purse from her lap. "I am going to have a cup of tea, then we are going somewhere."

"It's late, and I need to get back. I already told someone that I would do something with them tonight."

"I'm sure they will understand."

"But—"

He held up his hand to stop her from talking, then leaned back, eyes locked on hers like a magnet. The silence between them was heavy as they waited for his tea. He didn't speak or look away, so she focused on the skull pinned to the front of his hat that he rubbed with his finger. The waiter finally brought the tea, and he took a taste of the steaming liquid. She watched as he sipped it slowly and deliberately.

"Where are we going?" she finally asked.

"You will see when we get there."

"That is so informative," she said sarcastically.

"You know, if you want me to even consider removing that travel ban, you need to stop with the sarcasm. The next sarcastic remark you make, my answer will be no."

She folded her arms across her chest. Going to the front had to be easier than this. At least she could understand the enemy there. She would know what they were going to do because they made it obvious. With Bauer, she was always confused. He loved to play mind games and was deliberately vague about what his intentions were most of the time.

He finished his tea, then put his hat on. "Let's go." He stood and started for the door, not even waiting for her. She sighed, then stood and followed him outside. His driver opened the door for them, and Bauer waited for her to get in first, then slid in beside her. He gave the driver an address, but she didn't know where it was.

She chose not to look at him but instead opted to stare out the window, but could feel his eyes on her.

"I didn't realize the streets of Berlin were that interesting," he said.

"They're not. It's just…" she stopped, remembering what he said about her being sarcastic.

"Miss Abrams, I believe you were going to be sarcastic."

"No, I was going to be truthful."

"And what is the truth?"

"Are you not going to consider removing the ban if I tell you?"

"No, it will not change my decision." She met his gaze, not quite believing him. "I promise," he assured her.

"I would rather look at what is out there than in your direction. Plus, it makes it harder for me to talk to you."

It did not seem to anger him at all by what she said. Instead, he smiled. She turned back to the window, but her thoughts went to him. She wondered why he smiled at her obvious disdain for him, and it bothered her.

They finally arrived at their destination. It was a large building that could have been a warehouse once, but she wasn't sure because it was hard to see it in the dark. What were they possibly going to do here? Her uneasiness was growing, and she worried what she had gotten herself into.

"We're here," he said. The driver opened the door for them, and Bauer stepped out of the car, but she didn't. She stayed still in the seat, like he had invited her to join him in a snake's den.

"What are you waiting for?" he asked, agitation in his voice. "Get out of the car."

She slid over to the open door and slowly stepped out. "Is this going to end badly for me?" she asked, not moving from the car.

He chuckled. "No, Eva. No one is going to hurt you. Now let's go."

Reluctantly, she followed him into the large building. It was open with no rooms, and in the middle was a boxing ring. Immediately, she understood why they were there. He had brought her to watch him fight. This would be her first time, and she didn't know how it would be for her. Violence was not something she was keen on, especially after what she had been through.

"Sit here." He pointed to an empty chair in the front row.

She sat down and glanced around the room, noticing that she was the only woman there. An uncomfortable tide engulfed her, making the uneasiness she already felt worse. She now wished she could leave.

Bauer climbed between the ropes, then went to the other side of the ring and unbuttoned his uniform jacket. Eva watched as he took it off and handed it to a man standing below, then he removed the suspenders from his shoulders, unhooked them from the pants, and gave them to the same man. Eva didn't break her gaze as he did all of this but finally averted her eyes when he reached for the buttons on his shirt. She didn't know why she felt the need to look away; obviously, there was a chance of seeing him shirtless if she watched him fight, and she had seen him without a shirt before when he was in the hospital. She had seen much more than that, but it somehow seemed different now. She couldn't look at the floor the whole time. Slowly, turning back to him, she watched as he wrapped his right hand with a long, white cloth. She allowed her eyes to roam the rest of his body, not sure how she was supposed to feel. Her mind went to confusing places, and swirling emotions fused into a haze of bewilderment. She was tense, fingering the lace on her shirt, but then folded her hands in her lap and tried to relax her body.

He was surprisingly in good shape, and that is not how she remembered him. He had muscular arms, well-defined abs, and incredibly low body fat. His bone structure was of medium build, but his muscles were toned and visible under the skin. She realized he was stronger than she had given him credit for, but then again, she had never really thought of his body at all before now. He looked to be around six feet tall, so a little shorter than Gerhardt but still quite a bit taller than her five-foot-seven frame. Something else she noticed were the moles on his chest, neck, arms, and back. She found herself searching for them, but when her eyes caught the hair that ran from the bottom of his belly button down into his pants, she paused. That is when she looked away. Her eyes had drifted too far south for her comfort.

The man that Bauer was going to fight stepped into the ring. He was shorter than Bauer but bigger in sheer body mass. She didn't know if Bauer would win the fight. *Good. Maybe he will beat the shit out of him*, she thought, but immediately the guilt crept in at the thought.

The men acknowledged one another, then began circling. Both had their fists raised in front of them. The other man took the first swing, and Bauer dodged it by moving his head quickly to the side. Eva gasped, covering her mouth, then immediately felt embarrassed by her reaction to what had almost happened. She put her hand in her lap, hoping no one noticed. There she was, gasping when Bauer almost got hit, and all of the men around her were yelling and whooping, obviously enjoying what they were seeing.

Bauer took a swing at the other man, but he, too, dodged it. This happened a few times before the other man's fist contacted the side of Bauer's face, his head snapping to the side. She gasped again and almost stood from her chair before stopping herself. There was blood on his teeth, his bottom lip, and coming from one nostril. He wiped it away with the back of his hand, getting it on the white cloth that it was wrapped in. He looked at the blood on his hand and smiled, making it easier to see all the blood on his teeth. He spat, then swung his left fist so fast she almost missed it, hitting the other man squarely in the jaw, and he staggered backward. Immediately following, Bauer swung with his right fist, delivering a blow to the man's stomach. He doubled over slightly but jumped to the side to avoid another hit.

"Come on," Bauer yelled as he got into position. The guy took a swing at Bauer, hitting him again in the face, and Bauer countered by hitting him in the face again. It was easy for Eva to hear both men breathing heavily and their fists hitting each other's skulls. It was a dull thud, bone of the hand hitting bone of the head; it sounded painful. Both of their hands were already bloody, but it didn't seem like they noticed, or at least didn't care.

The referee stepped in and told them to go to a corner, then announced that it was the end of the first round. *First round, how many rounds are there*?

She leaned close to the man sitting to her right. "How many rounds are there?"

"Nine," he answered.

She was aghast. "Nine? They have to do nine rounds of this?"

"Of course. That is how it is done. If only one man is left standing, then he has won, but if they are both still standing at the end of the ninth round, then it is a tie and goes to the judge to decide."

"Right." She leaned back in her chair. The fact that anyone would be willing to do this puzzled her. She watched them go round after round, both men bloodying the other, grunting as they hit or got hit. When it was close to the end of round eight, Bauer had the other man in the corner. Bauer took hold of him with one arm and repeatedly administered blow after blow to his side with his other fist. The man had both arms up, trying to shield himself, and by the labored breathing, she thought they both must be getting tired and worn out. She could not watch anymore. She turned her head to the floor, but it did not stop her from hearing what was happening. She stood up and yelled. “Isn’t anyone going to stop this?”

Almost all the men in the audience turned to look at her, and Bauer also stopped hitting the other man to look out of the ring in her direction. There was a look in his eyes that she had never seen before, and his face took on a strange appearance, covered in blood, but whose blood though she didn’t know. He looked wild, and at this moment, he frightened her a little, as he narrowed his eyes at her, studying her with a predator’s unwavering attention. Now she understood why he said he would not compete against her in the ring. It would indeed be an unfair fight.

While everyone was distracted looking at her, including Bauer, the other man seized the opportunity and swung, knocking Bauer back and almost causing him to fall. She jumped at the sudden movement of the other man but decided to sit back down, glad the attention was back on the fight, but worried that Bauer would be angry at her for causing him to redirect his attention, allowing the other man to get the upper hand. After a few minutes, the referee had them both go back to their corners, and they wiped their faces and hands with a towel and drank some water. As Bauer drank, he glanced down at her, shaking his head in obvious annoyance at her outburst. Finally, they began the ninth and final round, and it wasn’t long before Bauer had the man cornered again. It was obvious his opponent was growing more distressed and worn out with every punch, but

Bauer still didn't stop. He continued to hit him, again and again, until the referee finally came to break it up.

"Hey-hey-hey-stop." He took ahold of Bauer and pulled him off the other man. After a cool-down period, Bauer and the other man said a few things to each other and shook hands.

Eva was confused by their exchange. The other man did not go down, but he obviously wasn't winning, so who won? And why did they shake hands as if nothing had happened? She leaned over to the man on her right again. "Who won?"

"That man." He pointed to Bauer. "Because the other man would have gone down if the referee had not stopped it or conceded. Sometimes, they break it up before someone gets seriously injured, but they decide when that is necessary. I can't believe you yelled for someone to stop it. If you knew who was up there fighting, you would not have interrupted."

"Him?" she pointed to the other man in the corner.

"No, him," he pointed again to Bauer.

"Him…?" She questioned.

"Yes."

"What is so special about him?"

"He is a good fighter. He usually wins, even if the other man is bigger. He fights often, so he has learned the techniques and moves. And he has crazy endurance."

"You must come here often to watch the fights?"

"I come to see most of them, and he is at many of them. I have never seen you here before. Is this your first time?"

She smiled uncomfortable, having a hard time believing she was there now. "It is."

"Are you here with someone? I mean, you don't see women at the fights if they didn't come with a man."

"Yes, I am here with someone."

He peered over her shoulder at the man sitting to her left. "Right."

Eva turned to the man on her left, then back at the man she was talking to. "No, I'm not here with him."

"Oh, my apology. I assumed because you were sitting next to him. Who are you here with then?"

"Him." She pointed to Bauer.

The man's smile faded. "What… no, not Obersturmbannführer Bauer."

"Why is that surprising to you?"

"Because he never brings anyone here, least of all a woman."

"Why least of all a woman?"

"Well, for one thing, women are not actually allowed here, although we make exceptions for the officers, but they usually don't bring women, anyway. I think besides you, it has only happened once, and Obersturmbannführer Bauer is the last person that would bring a woman."

"And yet here I am."

He leaned away to get a better look at her and wrinkled his forehead, squinting his eyes. "Why would he bring you?"

"I don't know. He told me about it a while ago and said I should come when he learned I had never seen a fight before."

"How do you know him?"

"Well, that is a bit of a story, one too long to tell tonight. To make a really long story short, we met in France."

"Ahhh, are you his…?"

"No… not in a million years."

He frowned. "Why would you say that?"

"Again, a very long story. Let's leave it at how we came to be acquainted is complicated."

Bauer went to the side of the ring and motioned for Eva to come over. "Excuse me." She stood and walked to Bauer, looking up at him.

"What the fuck was that stunt you pulled? You never distract someone when they are in a fight unless you want them to lose."

"I wasn't trying to make you lose, but I didn't want to see that other man get hurt too badly. You had him in the corner, and he seemed defenseless. It was awful. I had to look away. I couldn't watch anymore, but I still heard all of it. After listening to you hit him again and again, I had to do something."

"Spoken like a woman." He leaned over and climbed between the ropes, stepping out of the ring. She backed away from him, but he didn't seem to notice. He walked past her and went to a sink on the wall. He removed the wraps from his hands, then cleaned the blood from his face, and put his undershirt, shirt, suspenders, and jacket back on. She came over to him as he was pulling on his hat.

"I can bandage those for you if you want." She gestured to his hands.

He inspected his bruised and bloodied knuckles. “They are fine.”

“They won’t be if you leave them like that. They will get infected.”

“Maybe later.”

“Do they always get like that after a fight?”

He looked at his hands again. “Not this bad. The fight rarely makes it to the ninth round.”

“Why is that?”

“Because someone usually goes down before that. Come on, let’s go.” He took her by the arm to pull her along but let go when they started walking. Men who had been watching the fight patted him on the back or shook his hand. This went on until they reached the door.

“Is it always like that?” she asked when they were finally in the car.

“Usually. There is a lot of excitement during a fight, especially one that lasts all nine rounds.

“Why did you ask me to come tonight?”

“You said that you had never seen a fight.”

“Why would you think that is something I would want to see or enjoy?”

“I didn’t say I thought you would like it.”

“Then why bring me?”

“I wanted you to understand, to witness what it was like when two men fought in the ring. I have tried to explain it to you, but words will always fall short. You have to see it to understand what I was talking about and why I said a fight with you would not be equally matched in the ring.”

"I do understand now, and I agree. I don't have the experience needed."

"That is one reason, yes."

"Is that what you did to the man who stole your sister's medicine?"

Fire flashed in his eyes. "Why would you ask that?"

"Because your mother told me that after she died, you disappeared, and when you returned you had blood on you, but it wasn't yours."

He turned away from her and peered out the window. His face hardened in concentration.

"You beat that man to death, didn't you?"

"Maybe you shouldn't judge someone unless you've walked in their shoes."

"I am sorry for what happened to your sister," her voice was gentle.

He finally looked at her. "I don't need your pity."

"I wasn't trying to—"

"Don't." His low, rough voice broached no argument.

She didn't want to push him. Even though he said he wouldn't hit her, the memory of him in the ring still made her uneasy around him. "I have my medicine bag at the apartment. I can bandage those for you when we get there."

"If you want."

Eva took in a deep breath. She remembered that she shouldn't be going back to her apartment, but she could not tell him that. He would wonder why. Her heart raced, her palms were clammy, and she tried not to worry about going to the apartment. Perhaps they weren't there, and she would be safe.

The car pulled in front of her apartment complex, and they both got out. She instantly looked around for anyone who could be watching her and checked the street for any cars parked near by. There was a car across the street with two people sitting in it, and her breath caught in her throat. She knew right away that it was not the Gestapo. The car was too old and not the right make to be theirs. Her hands were shaking so much that she could hardly unlock the outside door. Bauer carefully watched as it took her several tries to put the key in the lock, and she continued to glance behind her. He turned his head and looked at the car sitting across the street that she kept peering at. He faced the road and started towards the car. The engine roared to life, and the headlights flicked on, then it wheeled away, the tires screeching on the pavement. Eva watched as it disappeared around the corner, knowing it would be back but grateful that Bauer got them to leave, even though it was unintentional.

She unlocked the door, and he followed her up to the apartment. This time, unlocking the door was a little easier. "Sit there," she told him, pointing to the couch. She made sure to shut the door after they were inside. She went to the bathroom, retrieved her medical bag, and brought it out to the living room. She sat on the couch next to him and took his left hand, laying it on her leg. She applied medicine to his wounds, then got some gauze from the bag, and gently wrapped his hand, then tied it off. She placed his hand back in his lap and took the other hand. He watched her every move, letting her wrap his hands without saying a word, even though his eyes spoke volumes. It was a horrible, uncomfortable situation. She had to break this silent tension.

"Do you feel bad about what you did?"

"Do you feel bad about things you have done?" he asked, turning it back on her.

"Sometimes. Would you ever do something like that again?"

"Well, I think a lot of what we do comes down to guilt, really. One can take on different degrees of guilt in a single moment of thoughtlessness or in months of premeditated planning."

"Are you trying to say you feel guilty about it now but that you didn't, then?"

"No, I'm telling you that if you feel guilty enough about what you did, you probably won't do it again. But I don't feel any guilt about what I did. I would do it again. Only one death was too good for him."

She stopped wrapping his hand and met his intense gaze. There was no remorse on his face as a shadow passed over his eyes, the light fading from them until they were dark and empty, and she knew he was telling the truth.

"Don't look at me with those judging eyes. You don't have it in you to do what needs to be done."

She now realized he could not see the monster he had tragically become that day, and neither could his mother, or maybe she chose not to see it. It was also possible that he was a monster long before that incident.

“I am not like you,” she said, almost in a whisper.

“No, you are not. I suppose that is not a bad thing.” She finished his hand and placed it back on his lap. “Thank you,” he said, checking his bandaged hands.

“You are welcome.” He stood up to leave, and the fear returned, the fear of what would happen after he left. She found herself wishing that he would stay so that she would be safe. She thought of the letter from Jon and how it said he would protect her. She could see it now, how being near him kept others away, and she wished that she had been nicer to him. She could not be nice in the next five minutes and expect him to save her in some way. She was going to have to let him go and get herself out of this one.

“Well, don’t hit anyone for a while,” she said.

He looked at his bandaged hands again. “I don’t plan on it.”

When he left the apartment, she ran to the window and watched him get into the car, then it pulled away. No sooner than it turned the corner did the other vehicle return, and this time, it pulled in front of the apartment, and two figures stepped out. It was too dark for her to see who it was, but she could guess. She knew that they would have to break the front door down in order to enter the building, which would give her some time to try to flee through the fire escape at the back of the building. She went to the door, pulling it open, not bothering to close it behind her as she ran out into the hall. She heard a crash come from the main floor; they had made it in. When she reached the end of the hall, she pushed the window up, which led to the fire escape, and crawled out onto the platform. She started lowering the ladder when two figures running down the hall came towards her.

“Shit.”

It was only halfway down when they reached the window. It was too late. She couldn’t finish lowering the ladder. She had to go now.

She started her descent down the ladder and jumped to the ground when she got to the last rung. Her ankle twisted when she hit the ground, and she immediately felt the pain, but she could not stop now, even though it throbbed. She stood up and ran the best she could down the alley. One of the men shot at her from the window. She instinctively covered her head with her arms as she limped away, trying to do what she could to protect herself. They were coming down the ladder behind her, and that is when the doubt that she could escape filled her with terror.

She could no longer go to Ingrid’s apartment. They would follow her there, and it would put Ingrid in danger, so when she turned the corner, she headed east towards Berlin and tried to stay in the shadows. She did not want the patrols spotting her on the streets after curfew, either. She came upon a car parked on the side of the road and did the only thing she could think of. She laid on her stomach and crawled underneath it, holding her nose and mouth with her hand, trying to muffle her breathing. The footsteps of the two men ran past, but she did not move, suspecting they might come back, and she was right. The footsteps returned after a few minutes, and her heart raced painfully fast. She worried it might give out when they stopped close to the car. Her eyes were locked on their shoes as they stood no more than a foot or two from the car. Their pant legs were the only other part she could see of them from where she was lying. Her chest hurt from the continued pounding of her heart against her ribs, as a wave of dizziness from the fear and panic washed over her. They started back towards her apartment, and she let go of her nose and removed her hand. When the footsteps were only a faint echo off the buildings, she crawled out and ran in the opposite direction. Eva couldn't let the pain and swelling of her ankle slow her down, even if it hurt like a bitch; she had to get off the street. She had no idea where she would go. She could not return home, and she couldn't go to Ingrid's now, either. The hospital was the other way, the direction the men were running, plus they might look for her there.

She could only think of one place, Bauer's. She knew where he lived; it was in Berlin, the opposite direction the men were going. They didn't know where he lived, but they wouldn't try to get her there even if they did. What would she say when showing up on his doorstep? She couldn't tell him she had lost her key because they had been in the apartment. But she could tell him that someone had broken in. That would probably be the most believable story.

Headlights coming from the cross street shone on her, so she hurried and ducked behind a trash can in the alley. She watched the patrol truck drive by, shining its spotlight around, checking the streets for anyone that was out past curfew. After it had passed, she stood to leave but realized when she squatted down to hide part of her skirt hung in something that leaked from the bottom of the trash can. “No,” she cried, pulling the back of her skirt around to inspect the wet spot. It smelled of rotten food and was now yellowed. “Dammit.” She let go of the fabric and hobbled out of the alley back to the street.

When she got to Bauer’s apartment, she remembered that it did not have a lock on the front door like hers. She went into the building and up to the top floor, stopping in front of his door. She struggled to find the courage to knock. She considered sleeping in the hall on another floor or in the utility room if she could get it open, then knocking on his apartment after he had gone to work when only his mother was home. She decided against it, mostly because she was so tired and felt like she might fall over from exhaustion, and right now, she wanted to sleep somewhere soft, warm, and safer than the hall. Plus, she needed to bathe and get out of her smelly clothes. She also needed to eat something, although she was not sure she could eat right now. *You can do this, Eva,* she told herself, hoping to find the fortitude to knock. She balled her hand into a fist and tapped loudly several times on the door. The front door to the apartment building opened, and voices echoed in the stairwell, and then footsteps started up the stairs. It sounded like they were taking two steps at a time.

She pounded harder on the door. “Oh God, please open.” The footsteps on the stairs grew closer. They were almost to the top floor.

She beat both fists against the door now, and it flew open. Bauer stood in front of her, his face pulled into a scowl of annoyance. His eyes carried a mixture of concern and barely contained anger, but it faded once he registered who it was, and then it turned to confusion.

"Eva…?"

Her eyes blurred with tears. "Please, can I come in?" His mom came up behind him, tying her robe.

"Wilhelm, who is it?"

He hesitated before answering. "It's Miss Abrams."

"What does she want?" she asked, sounding confused but not upset.

"I don't know, mother."

Eva turned when the footsteps on the stairs reached the top level, and the silhouette of a man at the end of the dark hall came towards her. She screamed and stepped into the doorway next to Bauer, the blood draining from her head right before everything went dark.

Chapter Twenty-Nine

✠

Voices filled Eva's ears, but they sounded distant. Far away, like it was coming out of a tunnel. Slowly, her tired eyes fluttered open, blinking heavy eyelids against a blurry, scratchy feeling. The room she was in was dark, but a dim light came from another room. She blinked a few more times, then looked around. The last thing she remembered was running down the hall and pounding on Bauer's door. Eva realized she was on the couch in Bauer's apartment, and the voices were coming from the kitchen. It was Bauer and his mother speaking low and probably about her. She was sure they were trying to figure out what to do with her.

She lay still, contemplating her situation. She wanted to pretend to be asleep until morning because Bauer would have questions for her if he knew she was awake, but at the same time, she really needed a bath, and she had to go to the bathroom. She could hardly stand to smell herself. She tried to listen to what they were saying, but it was too quiet and muffled for her to make out any words. She sat up on the couch and peered through the kitchen entryway. They were sitting at the table, speaking to one another.

She carefully stood from the couch when the pain in her ankle registered. It had not been as noticeable when she was scared, the adrenaline numbing it, but now it was excruciating.

"Oww." She caught herself on the side table next to the couch, and then the lights came on in the room.

"No, no, you need to sit back down," his mother said, hurrying towards her with her arms out to catch her if she fell. She helped Eva back onto the couch and then sat down beside her.

Eva dared a glance at Bauer, and he did not look happy. "Mother, can I have a word with Miss Abrams alone, please?"

"No. She is in no shape for you to berate her right now."

"I am not going to berate her. But I need to find out why she is here. Can you give us a minute?"

"It's alright," Eva told her. His mother stood and, as she left the room, looked at her son, their eyes locking in a shared understanding. She went to her room and shut the door, leaving Eva alone with him.

He came and sat on the end of the couch opposite her. "Eva, you seemed distressed when I was at your apartment. Then you come to my apartment well past curfew, covered in what smells like rotten food and a banged-up ankle. What has happened?"

"I knew there was something not right with that car. When you left, they got through the door to the building, came to my apartment, and tried to break in. I fled out the back window and down the fire escape, but I had to jump off the ladder because I didn't have time to lower it all the way. That is how I hurt my ankle. They pursued me down several streets, and I had to hide under a car and behind a trash can. They went back in the direction of my apartment, and I didn't know where else to go, so I came here. When I heard the man coming up the stairs, I thought they had followed me here. That is why I screamed."

"And fainted," he added.

"Yes, that too. I did not expect that to happen. I'm sorry."

"For what? Passing out on my floor?"

"Well, yes." She was so embarrassed by what had happened.

"And you think I want you to apologize for that?"

"Yes, I mean, I don't know. I'm sorry for all of this."

"Eva, I'm not mad at you, and you need to stop thinking that I am all the time."

"You are so often."

"I get upset with you often, I admit, but I am not angry with you now. I think you did the right thing by coming here if someone was after you. They committed a crime and need to be caught. Tomorrow, we will go to your apartment together and see what we can learn."

That thought scared her for many reasons. One was that they were still there waiting for her, the second was that there might be something that would tip him off as to who was chasing her, and the third was what Heidi and Liesel would think. She also remembered that Ingrid was probably wondering where she was. What a mess. "That would be good," she told him, finally.

"Alright, well, it is late, so we should get some sleep. My mother already has a gown for you to wear in the bathroom. You probably want to take a bath. When you are done, you can have my bed. I will take the couch."

"No, I couldn't take your bed. I'm fine out here."

"Eva, damn it. Why can't you listen to me even once? Now, go take a bath and go to bed. I am not going to do this with you tonight."

The change in his demeanor and the harshness in his voice made her jump. He held a sense of authority and knew when and how to dish it out. It probably made him effective at his job. You needed to be scary and intimidating when you were in the Gestapo. Holding onto the armrest of the couch for support, she pushed herself up.

"Here, let me help you."

When he touched her arm, she involuntarily flinched. Anger flashed across his face, but he quickly replaced it with his usual calm expression. "You are sweating, and your pulse is racing," he said after touching her arm.

"I'm fine."

"You are scared, and you don't need to be. I know that this has been a trying night for you, but nothing will happen to you here."

She tried to relax and let him take her arm this time. He put his other arm around her back and led her to the bathroom, sitting her on the toilet. "I'll get my mother."

"No, I can do it. Don't bother her. Is this the gown?" she asked, nodding to a pink folded fabric on the side of the sink.

"Yes. My bedroom is at the end of the hall. I can help you there when you are finished." He stepped out of the bathroom, closing the door.

She turned on the tub faucet, then realized how awkward this was. She was in Bauer's bathroom preparing to take a bath, then she was going to sleep in his bed. It was unreal. She never could have imagined this a year ago or even a few months ago. She had helped him, and he had helped her twice now. What a crazy thought that was. Maybe all of what was happening tonight would get her where she needed to be with Bauer. Perhaps now he would keep the Gestapo off her back and, without realizing it, the resistance too.

She carefully got into the tub, trying not to slip and fall from the weakness in her leg. She lowered herself into the warm water, considering her situation, and was disgusted with herself that she depended on a German for protection. But the truth was, she was in an enemy country and understood that anything could happen to her. Who else did she have to rely on, if not the enemy? She depended on them for everything at the moment. If it meant using one of them to save her life, then why not? How was that a bad thing?

There was a knock on the door. "Eva, I need to go to bed soon." Bauer's voice came from the other side of the door.

"I'm sorry. I'll get out now." This was all so strange and awkward. She had forgotten that he was waiting for her to get out so he could help her to the bedroom. She pulled the plug and stepped out of the tub, drying off with the towel that was under the nightgown. She put on the same underwear she had been wearing and slid the gown over her head. It was too big for her, but it was clean and smelled fresh, so she didn't care. She picked up her dress and opened the bathroom door. Bauer was leaning against the wall in the hall, obviously waiting for her.

He came to her side and put his arm around her shoulders again to help steady her. "Nope, leave that." He took the dress from her hand and tossed it back in the bathroom on the floor. "My mother will wash it in the morning."

"She doesn't need to do that."

"She will wash it with our clothes." He led her to the bed and helped her sit on the edge. "If you don't need anything else, I will go to the living room now."

"I'm fine. Thank you." He nodded, then left the room, shutting the door behind him. She sighed and lay on the bed, covering up with the thin white duvet. She pulled it up to her chin and closed her eyes, ready for sleep. The scents in the room and the duvet filled her nostrils. She pulled it closer to her nose and inhaled. It smelled of cologne, soap, and cigarette smoke. She had forgotten that he smoked, but most men did in this time. It did not smell like the smoke from cigarettes in her time. The scent was not as strong or as repugnant. It had more of a sweet smell, like a cigar.

She looked around the room, but it was too dark for her to really make out anything. She would have to remember to look when the sun came up. She hoped that she could learn something about him from the contents of his room. Even the smallest detail about his life could be helpful in securing his trust and protection.

Chapter Thirty

✠

July 21st, 1941

The scent of coffee brought her out of the dream state she was in. Being chased by the two men had played in her dreams throughout the night, and then she would wake up confused about where she was, only to remember that she was in Bauer's apartment and his bed. That realization caused her to dream of being tortured by the Gestapo. It seemed those were the only two things her mind would replay while she slept, causing her to feel tired when she woke.

She sat up in bed and rubbed her eyes to clear her vision. She threw the blanket off and checked her ankle. It looked more like a cankle now than an ankle, and she knew it would need to be wrapped. She slid her legs over the side of the bed and slowly put her weight on her one good leg. She hobbled to the door and cracked it open, peeking out, but she couldn't see anyone. Again, voices traveled from the kitchen. Bauer and his mother were already awake.

She looked at her watch; it was not even a quarter past seven, and she wondered why they were up so early. She remembered Bauer would probably already be gone if it wasn't for her. She didn't know if he was planning on waking her up or if he was going to let her sleep until she woke on her own. Now that the sun was up, she wasn't sure she wanted him to see her in the thin pink nightgown she was wearing but she didn't have anything else to wear or put over it. She closed the door, went back to the bed, and sat on the edge. She looked around the room, now noticing how empty it was. There were a couple of things on the dresser and the walls, but on the desk in the corner was a picture frame with a photo in it. She slid off the bed, went to the desk, and picked up the frame. It was of a young blond girl with her hair in braided pigtails, tied at the end with ribbons. She looked to be around fifteen or sixteen, wore a checkered dress, and displayed a big smile, dimpling her cheeks.

This must be his sister. She sat it back on the desk and scanned the room again. She didn't dare open any of the drawers. With her luck, he would come in right after she opened one. It seemed like such an intimate thing to do, going through his things, sleeping in his bed, seeing him naked. She never thought she would ever be in the position to do these intimate things in Bauer's life.

She went back to the door and opened it again. She was going to have to come out, eventually. She slowly walked down the hall to the kitchen with her hand on the wall for support. Bauer and his mother were sitting at the table, drinking coffee. His mother looked up when she caught sight of her.

"Good morning. How did you sleep?"

"I slept alright."

Bauer turned in his chair to look at her when she entered. "I didn't know you were awake yet. If I had, I would have come to help you into the kitchen."

"It doesn't matter. As you can see, I managed to get here on my own."

"I can see that." He stood up and pulled a chair out for her. "Sit down. I'll get you a plate of food." He put some meat, cheese, and a piece of bread on a plate and sat it before her, then returned to his own chair.

She quietly picked at the food, feeling the constant gaze of their eyes as she did. "Your dress is drying. As soon as it is ready, Wilhelm will take you to your apartment," his mother informed her.

"Thank you. You didn't have to do that."

"I did. It really smelled awful."

Eva's face flushed. "I bent down by a trash can last night, and my dress hung in something that had leaked out."

"That's alright. It's clean now."

"How long until it's dry?" Eva asked.

"It should be ready when we are done with breakfast."

"That's good."

After a relatively quiet breakfast, Eva was given her dress and went to the bathroom to change. It felt good to be in her clothes again, and even better that they no longer smelled. She combed through her hair with her fingers and swished water in her mouth. She was finally ready to go.

She met Bauer in the living room. "I'm ready."

He stood and went to the door, holding it open for her. They didn't speak to one another as they descended the stairs. Eva didn't because of how awkward the situation was and because it made her feel uncomfortable to spend this much time with him, but she didn't know his reasons.

She could not help but wonder if the men were still there waiting for her at the apartment as the car grew closer. She needed to go to Ingrid's and be prepared to give an explanation because Ingrid would ask. Her plan was to tell Ingrid that she spent the night at Bauer's, but she wasn't sure what reason she was going to give as to why she spent the night there.

They entered the apartment together and looked around. Nothing seemed to be out of order, broken, or taken. There was no sign that they had been in the apartment at all.

"It doesn't look like they were in here," he said.

"No, I don't think they were. I was supposed to be spending the night with a friend, so after you left, I was going to head that way when I saw them coming down the hall, so I ran. That is when I escaped through the window and down the fire escape." Her story was not the total truth, but it was close enough.

He looked at his watch. "I really need to be at work now. Do you want to stay here, or I can have my driver take you back to my apartment if that would make you feel more comfortable? I could also take you somewhere else if you like."

"Can you take me to the hospital?" she didn't want to stay here, but she also didn't want to go back to his apartment. She needed to talk with Ingrid and apologize for last night.

"Sure. I will be working out of the office today, but I need to swing by the building for a few minutes first if you don't mind waiting."

"I don't mind."

"Alright, let's go then." The first part of the drive was quiet, but Bauer finally broke the silence. "I have to ask. Do you know what those men wanted because they didn't rob you or take anything from the apartment? To me, it doesn't appear that they were after anything that you had, but rather they were after you."

"I never saw their faces, so I don't know who was chasing me. I don't know why someone would be after me."

"You have no idea at all?" he asked accusingly.

She knew he didn't believe her but wanted to see if she was going to be honest with him. How could he think she would tell him the truth, especially if it implicated her in some way? She did not trust him, not even after all the times he helped her. "No. I don't know what they wanted."

"Alright. Well, when you decide you want to tell the truth, you know where to find me."

She looked at him, taken aback by his honesty. "I told you the truth."

"Just remember that we have ways of getting the facts

from someone."

"Are you threatening me?"

"No. I'm reminding you of what could happen. I'm not the only person in the Gestapo, and I won't be in Berlin much longer."

"You are going back to France?"

"Yes."

"When?"

"Probably in the next few weeks."

Eva faced forward in her seat and looked out the windshield. Why did this information bother her? Because if he left and she didn't go to the front, there would be no one here to protect her anymore. That seemed like a logical explanation for the feeling she was having.

They pulled in front of the Reich Main Security Office, and he opened the door to get out.

"Do you want me to wait in the car or in the lobby?" she asked.

"Whichever you prefer," he said.

"I think I will go in."

"Alright." Once he was out of the car, he held out his hand for her to take. She hesitated for a second, then took it. He helped her out, then let go of her hand and walked ahead of her. They entered the lobby, and he told her to wait in a chair off to the side of the room, and then he disappeared up the stairs. The same woman who tried to have her escorted out of the building last time was at the front desk. Eva noticed she was staring at her, and she also knew the secretary had seen them come in together.

She could not help but smile, knowing that it had to annoy the hell out of her. Eva made eye contact with her briefly. The woman looked like she might jump over the desk and attack her if she thought she would get away with it. For the rest of the time, Eva tried to not look at the woman. She was not in the mood to have a stare-down battle with her.

Bauer was gone for longer than she had expected, and she found herself wishing she had stayed in the car. Every time she heard someone coming down the stairs, she would look up, hoping it was him, and every time it wasn't. Finally, she spotted him descending the stairs.

He did not stop at her chair but walked past her as he said, "Let's go."

He was in a hurry and different to when they came in. She wondered what had happened while he was up there. She stood and tried to keep up with his fast pace, but he reached the car long before her. She hobbled the last few feet, and as she was getting in, he put his hand on the small of her back to try and get her to move a little faster. *What is going on? Why is he in such a hurry*?

He slid in beside her and told the driver to go before he even had the door closed. "I'm afraid I can't take you to the hospital, but I will drop you off at the next tram stop."

"Alright."

"I'm sorry I can't take you all the way, but something has come up."

She didn't even ask him what because she knew he wouldn't answer. "I wanted to tell you that I removed the travel ban on you," he said.

She almost couldn't believe her ears. "Thank you!" she said, overwhelmed with gratitude, the words almost catching in her throat.

"You are welcome," was all he said.

As they drove, he tapped his knee with his fingers, a nervous gesture, she thought.

"When do you leave for the front?" he asked, finally breaking the silence.

"In a little over a week, I think."

He put his elbow on the windowsill and gripped his chin, rubbing his lips with his finger as he stared out. What she told him didn't seem to sit well.

"Is something wrong?" she asked.

"No," he said curtly. The car pulled off to the side of the road. "This is the tram stop."

"Right." She got out, and the car pulled away. *What was that about?*

As soon as she was in the hospital, she looked for Ingrid, spotting her restocking the medicine cabinet in the nurse's quarters. "Ingrid!"

Ingrid's head jerked around. "Where have you been? I waited up really late for you, but you never came back."

"I know, and I am so sorry. I spent the night at Bauer's house," she admitted sheepishly."

"What…? No. You have not been honest with me. There is more going on between you two than you let on. Did you go over there seeking pleasures in the night?"

"I did no such thing. It was not like that at all. We

weren't even in the same room, and his mother lives with him. I ran into some trouble after he took me home. Someone tried to break into the apartment and chased me. They were looking for me in the area of the apartment, so I couldn't go to your place. His home was the only other place I knew to go, so that is where I went."

Her eyes were wide, and her mouth ajar. "I didn't know. I'm sorry that happened to you. Are you alright?"

"I'm fine. I wanted to talk to you about something. Dr. Möller asked if I would accompany him to a field hospital on the front, and I decided I would go. Do you want to come too if he says you can?"

"Do I want to go to the front? No, but… I know doctors and nurses are badly needed there, and if you are going well, I'll go too."

Eva gave her a hug. "I'm glad you will be coming with me. It will be harder there, and I will need a friend."

"Of course, you need someone to save you the next time you decide to kill yourself."

"There won't be a next time."

"Well, you will need saving somehow, that I'm sure," she chuckled, trying to lighten the mood.

That I do, you have no idea, Eva thought.

She found Liesel and Heidi and told them of her decision, and of course, they thought she was crazy. Then she went to Dr. Möller. "Klaus, I have decided to go with you."

"That is good news. I knew you would come." He beamed warmly at her.

"I asked Nurse Ingrid Braun if she would like to come. I hope that is alright. I know I should have asked you first."

"No, it's fine. We can use all who are willing to go. It is pretty bad there, from what I hear."

"I can believe that. There are so many men coming in daily it makes me wonder what is happening there." Of course, she knew how bad it actually was and how much worse it was going to get. The poor men and boys on both sides had not even seen the worst of it yet.

"I got word an hour ago that we leave in two days."

"I thought you said we didn't leave for another week?"

"I did, but the orders have changed. It must be worse there than I thought because someone high up gave us the order to leave as soon as possible."

This whole thing seemed strange, and she couldn't help but wonder if Bauer had something to do with it. Right after he removed the travel ban on her, the orders to the front were changed from a week to two days. Why would he be in such a rush for her to leave for the Russian front, the most dangerous place to be right now? Maybe he was hoping she would die there, but why would he help her if that is what he was hoping would happen? This made her think perhaps he had nothing to do with it, and it was only a coincidence. There was more to the picture than meets the eye that much she was sure of. She just didn't know what it was that she couldn't see. Maybe it was Bauer, but he was about as hard to crack as the enigma, possibly even harder because he was not set to work in a logical pattern. Whatever the reason, she was happy to be leaving Germany. For her, this was probably the most dangerous place to be right now.

July 23rd, 1941

She sat in the seat next to Ingrid, and Klaus sat across from them as they waited for the plane to taxi down the runway. Her hands were cold but sweaty, and she felt lightheaded from the excitement and anticipation of it all. They knew now where they were heading. Klaus told them that they were going to a field hospital in Crimea at the southernmost tip of the Ukraine. It was on a peninsula almost entirely surrounded by the Black Sea and the smaller Sea of Azov to the northeast.

This was going to be different from anything she had ever been through, and she was unsure what it would be like that close to the front. In her gut was the distinct feeling of being here before in this same situation. Fleeing from something in one place only to run towards a more volatile thing in another. But this time, she was not going into the unknown alone.

About the author

J.L. Robison is an American author who currently lives in western Pennsylvania with her husband and two daughters. She has recently finished the fourth and final book in the Edelweiss series and is now working on a new story in the world of dark fantasy. Before becoming a writer, J.L. Robison taught English as a second language. She has had the opportunity to live in many states and has been to over fourteen different countries, experiencing their unique cultures. She writes in multiple genres, spanning historical fiction, literary fiction, romance, and fantasy. When she is not sitting on the couch with her laptop, she is outside working in her garden, playing tennis, bowling, ice skating, traveling, or doing things with her kids. She also enjoys going on walks with her husband or drinking a glass of wine to relax in front of the TV. Most of her inspiration comes at night when she can't sleep, is listening to music, or when on a walk alone in nature.

Printed in Great Britain
by Amazon